Central Skagit Sedro-Woolley Library
802 Ball St.
Sedro-Woolley WA 98284
Sept 2019

In *Café Budapest*, sequel to *The Dragontail Buttonhole*, the destitute and brutalized Kohut family lick their wounds in Paris. As they struggle to survive they are befriended by the Hungarian owners of Café Budapest. But when the Allies declare war on Germany they face new challenges as the Nazis invade France threatening to destroy the Kohuts' chance to reach England and safety.

For background information on these books please visit:

www.petercurtisauthor.com

Author's note

Other than my own research, major sources for this work of fiction come from family artifacts and stories dictated by my mother. References to historical events, real people or real places are used fictitiously. The characters in this novel, except for the toddler Pavel, are either fictitious or deceased. Real people, places and events have been depicted as accurately as possible in the novel's time frame of 1938 to 1941—always an imprecise venture. Other names, characters, places and events are products of the author's imagination and any resemblance to actual events, places or person, living or dead is coincidental.

The bulk of my writing is based on true events. I undertook to write this trilogy not only as a legacy but as a reminder that life can, at any moment, become dangerous, especially when signals of civil decay or bigotry in a democracy are ignored, tolerated or dismissed. You live as you can, not as you want.

This is a work of fiction. All of the characters, events, and organizations portrayed in this novel are either products of the author's imagination or used fictitiously.

Dedication

To Carolyn, my best friend and partner of fifty years, who has patiently and lovingly helped me on this writing journey—unafraid to comment, edit, suggest improvements, cheer me on and provide comfort in moments of discouragement. Fingers crossed, we will keep on doing this together until the trilogy is completed.

To my parents and grandparents for leaving me so many tangible memories of their lives, and for making sure I was safe in the early days.

I drew my inspiration to write this story from a desire to give our two sons, Elliot and Matthew and their families a solid connection to their European past. My thanks to them for their loving support..

CAFÉ BUDAPEST

Peter Curtis

All rights reserved. No part of this book may be reproduced in any any form by any electronic or mechanical means including photocopying, recording, or information storage and retrieval without permission in writing from the author.

First Printing : 2018

Cover Design by Marlin Greene / 3hats.com

KURTI
PUBLISHING

ISBN 978-0-9993631-2-6

Published by Kurti Publishing, Seattle
www.petercurtisauthor.com

Life is the passage from one deliverance to the next.
Etty Hilversum. *An Interrupted Life*

We live in history the way fish live in water.
Mark Slouka. *Nobody's Son*

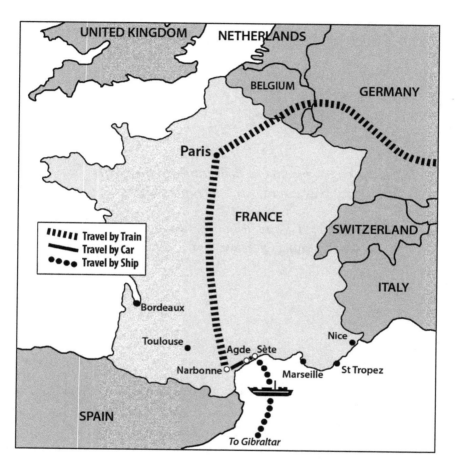

Escape route taken by the Kohut family from Germany to Paris, then to villages in the south of France, and finally aboard ship to Gibraltar.

CHAPTER ONE

Paris
August 1939

On a humid August night in 1939, at the Hôtel de Metz—a flea-bag Parisian hotel near the Gare du Nord—an iron bed stood in the center of a top-floor room. The bed's twisted frame and lumpy mattress barely supported the weight of three people—the Kohut family, Czechoslovak refugees who, three hours earlier, had arrived on a train from Germany. Brutalized and exhausted by their journey but confident that they were at last safe and free, they fell into a deep sleep.

Willy Kohut opened his eyes and reached for his battered spectacles. Early morning light filtered into the hotel room. He moved slowly off the bed, his chest throbbing unmercifully as he tried not to waken Sophie and Pavel who were still tangled together in sleep.

Naked and stiff, he arched his back and stretched his arms. With a grimace, he held his breath and struggled to put on his undershorts—the same pair he had worn for days. He noticed blood-stains on the bed linen where he had been lying. *Damn.* He clenched his teeth. *I'll have to explain this mess to the manager, get him to understand what we've been through.*

Willy tiptoed to the open window and pulled aside the tattered curtain to let in the dawn. He frowned at the stained, peeling wallpaper. *This room is disgusting.* Flies clustered on the window glass buzzed into action, dancing around his head and shoulders, magnetized by his blood and dried sweat. He waved a futile hand.

Willy tugged at the silk encircling his chest—the long blue scarf Madame Panasse had given him on the train. Delicately, he separated the blood-stiffened fabric from where it stuck to his skin. He inspected the cut, maybe three inches long and oozing pink fluid, that curved like a scimitar below his left nipple. He remembered the slicing pressure of Oberführer Heizinger's dagger and the agony that spread hot lava across his chest.

The flies buzzed closer. He took a deep breath and spread the wound's edges with his fingertips. *Thank God, it's not so bad. Just flesh, no muscle.* He re-tied the scarf. This would have to do for the time being.

Willy looked through the window at the landscape of clay and metal roofs touched here and there by the first rays of sunlight. Beyond the expanse of garret windows and ribbons of chimney smoke, he saw the white pediments of Porte St. Denis, one of the great entry gates to Paris and the neighborhood where he had once been a student at L'École International de Commerce. He sighed at the irony of his present circumstances: *Bienvenue à Paris, Willy le refugié.*

He watched the buff-colored clouds slowly alter shape in the dawn light. Just like those clouds, he mused, nothing ever stayed the same. It was just how slow or fast the change occurred. For years, his career in Czechoslovakia had been a steady, comfortable climb into the business world of luxury fabrics, shared with a loving wife and a lively son. Then the Nazis came and his normal life disintegrated.

Now they were safe, thank God.

As for next steps, everything depended on contacting

Sophie's Tante Freda, who lived somewhere in Paris. They needed money and food. This miserable room and the few francs in his pocket would suffice for a few days—hopefully, until they headed for London to reunite with his parents. How and when, who knew?

Willy tried to bend his right little finger. It was stiff and painful. The smallest movement sent shocks into his hand and along his forearm. The tingling was a constant reminder of his interrogation in Prague—torture for information he never had. The vise that Altman's Gestapo thugs had used to *improve* his memory had turned Willy's finger into an unevenly curved digit—almost useless and covered with scar tissue. Later, as it healed, Sophie had fashioned a velvet finger stall to protect it during everyday activities.

Willy forced his finger to bend, wincing as he straightened it. Exercise it hard, five times a day, maybe for months Dr. Pflinz had advised in Prague. "If you ever want to play piano again," the old doctor had said, "stretch that scar and mobilize the joints, whatever the pain."

He glanced at the bed where he and Sophie had slept, with Pavel squeezed between them. It was their first real lying-down sleep in four days of traveling incognito from Budapest across Nazi Germany to Paris. They had arrived at the Gare de L'Est the previous night with a few German marks, counterfeit passports and family papers, a string bag of possessions and no change of clothes. He remembered his shame when, at the end of their train journey, kind old Monsieur Panasse, who shared their compartment, lent him the five hundred francs that bought supper, a room in this dismal hotel and just enough cash for two more days in Paris.

Willy heard a rasping cough outside in the hallway, a footfall and then a loud rap on the door.

"*Monsieur.*"

He gritted his teeth and moved toward the door. "What do

you want? Who are you? "

"The owner of course. *Le patron, nom de dieu.* Open up."

Willy frowned. No point in keeping his voice low with this idiot yelling his head off. "What do you want? My wife and child are asleep. Leave us alone."

Two thundering blows on the door. "Open up, I say."

"For God's sake, wait, can't you."

Awkwardly, Willy pulled on his trousers, afraid that the hotel owner had somehow discovered that their passports were counterfeit. Willy had obtained false Hungarian passports to hide their Jewishness and their Czechoslovak nationality as they fled across Europe. The ruse had worked until they reached the German-French border. There they had been strip-searched, humiliated and traumatized. That was when Oberführer Heizinger forced him to perform fellatio and sliced his chest open; then, miraculously, allowed them back onto the train.

"Hurry up, damn you."

Willy unlatched the door.

A muscular unshaven man in a sweat-stained undershirt stepped into the room. A silver cross hung from his neck. His eyes widened at sight of the blood-stained scarf tied around Willy's naked chest. "*Merde.*" He wiped his nose with the back of a hairy hand and glanced at the rumpled bed. He lurched forward, eyes wide. "What's all this blood? It's fuckin' everywhere." He shook his head in disbelief. "Whatever's goin' on it'll cost you a bundle."

Willy raised both hands in surrender. This fellow was obnoxious, but he was right to be angry. "Many apologies, *Monsieur.* Yesterday at the German border, the guards were brutal. They hurt us ... I'm sorry ... I ... We ..."

The *patron* sneered. "Refugees, hunh? From Germany you say?" He stepped close to Willy and thrust two passports under his nose. "Well, these are not German. What damned country are you from?"

4

Willy shrugged. "Hungary. *Nous sommes Hongrois*. What of it?" In his peripheral vision he was aware of movement on the bed. Sophie was sitting up.

"The only Hungarians arriving in Paris are Jews," the man said, spitting the words out like melon pips as he moved forward. "Let's be clear about one thing, little squirt. I'll have no Jews in this hotel." His face was inches away from Willy's. "So get the fuck out."

Stale garlic swamped Willy's nostrils as he took a deep, stabbing breath. A wave of resentment swept through him. Here, in the safety of tolerant, democratic Paris, a French racist was cursing him … and on their first day of freedom. He heard the bed clothes rustle behind him and glanced back at Sophie.

Her face was taut and pale. She had pulled the sheet up to her neck. "*Miláčku*," she whispered in Czech, her eyes flickering around the room as if searching for a way out. "Who is this man? He looks so mean. I don't understand him. I'm embarrassed he sees us like this. Why did you let him in?"

Willy signaled her to be quiet. He squared his shoulders, thinking through the options, wondering how to get through this without violence. "What makes you think we're Jews?" he said to the *patron* in French. He boiled inside, wanting to lash out. The *patron* was tall and heavy, but Willy was stocky and muscular. And though he might appear to be somewhat of a weakling, being small and wearing spectacles, he was strong and had learned hand-to-hand fighting in the Czechoslovak militia.

The hotel owner pointed triumphantly at Pavel, wide-eyed, sitting cross-legged and naked on the bed. "There, arsehole, look at your kid. The runt's been circumcised."

Pavel stared at the stranger and began to whimper. Tears trickled down his cheeks. He scuttled behind Sophie's back.

"What does he want?" Sophie asked again, her voice quivering. She ran one hand through her uncombed hair. "Don't be afraid, darling," she whispered to Pavel.

Willy raised a calming hand. He spoke in Czech. "This bastard is the owner. Seems we chose the wrong hotel. He hates Jews." He guessed that Sophie, who spoke only schoolgirl French, might not know exactly what was happening. He knew she could sense danger. She had learned a lot on their journey through Germany.

The tall man leered at her over Willy's shoulder. "Get your Israelite whore out of here."

Clenching his fists in silent fury, Willy shot what he hoped was a reassuring look at Sophie. He wanted to smash the Frenchman's face into pulp. "Keep calm, sweetheart," he said between his teeth.

"Oh, God, *miláčku*," Sophie muttered her hands cupped to her face. Her elbows anchored the bed-sheet against her chest. "This is madness. How can France be as bad as Germany? Last night I was willing to stay in this awful room just to get settled. What will happen to us now?"

Ignoring her question, Willy stepped between the bed and the invader, ready to drive his knee into the man's balls. "*Monsieur*," he said, trying hard to appear polite and reasonable. "We will leave … but it's too early. Check-out at ten, your receptionist said. We paid for the room."

The big man sucked in a heavy breath and narrowed his eyes. He shoved Willy aside and rattled the iron bed frame. "Get out, slut," he growled.

Sophie held the sheet under her chin and shook her head. Her lips trembled. "What does he say, Willy?"

Pavel clung to her. "*Maminko*," he whimpered from behind her back.

Willy again inserted himself between the bed and the Frenchman. "Get the hell out of our room. I paid full price," he hissed as he tried to push the man away from the bed.

For a few moments the two men locked arms, swaying back and forth, Willy grunting as excruciating pain shot through his chest and across his left shoulder blade. The hotel owner wrestled Willy away. "Get out of my hotel, you bald-headed piece of shit," he yelled.

Supporting his chest with his left hand, Willy took a step forward and grabbed the passports out of the man's hand. "Bastard."

The *patron* raised a massive fist … and then froze, immobile, his mouth opening and closing as if he were gasping for air. His eyes bulged. "*Merde, alors.*"

Willy realized the man was staring at Sophie. He spun around, forgetting his pain.

Sophie had dropped the sheet on to her lap, exposing her breasts. Her eyes were on fire, lips tight together, defiance in her face. "*Vypadni,*" she screamed pointing to the door. "*Vypadni.*"

Willy grabbed a heavy glass ashtray from the bedside table. "I'll smash your head in," he screamed.

Pavel was sobbing.

The *patron* backed toward the door, his face contorted. "Your bitch has no fucking morals." He turned on his heel and grabbed the door handle. "You won't get away with this. I'll be back—with reinforcements." The door slammed shut.

Willy, suddenly aware of a sharp pain in his hand dropped the ashtray. There was blood on his palm. He looked up saw Sophie shudder, then tremble. He went to her and kissed her damp forehead. "What made you … show yourself like that?"

As she attempted to calm Pavel with kisses and hugs, Sophie glanced up at him and shrugged. "I was afraid he would hurt you. It … was the only thing I could think of to make him stop." She gave him a weak smile. "Besides, *milačku*, isn't Paris the home of striptease?"

Willy stared, and then burst out laughing. "Well, you saved

us. What an inspired idea." He grabbed at the left side of his chest. "Aagh, God … damn it. I shouldn't have laughed. Feels like something ripped inside. I hope to God tussling with that bastard didn't start me bleeding again." He licked blood off his palm and gave her wry look. "Soon I will need a transfusion."

Sophie didn't laugh. She watched Willy untie the scarf from around his chest then frowned when she saw the beads of blood forming along the wound. She turned Pavel's head against her chest so he could not see. "It looks bad. You need a doctor. You can't walk around like this."

He gave her a grim smile. "Maybe I do, but I have no idea where to go and we have no money. We can't waste time on that. First things first—let's get out of here, find a decent place to stay and get some breakfast. I'll manage. Maybe see a doctor later, after you've found your Tante Freda."

Willy re-bandaged his wound, dressed and scoured the room for a weapon he could use in case the hotel owner returned. He spotted a foot-long brass stay attached to the partly rotted window frame and twisted it off. With the stay at the ready, he escorted Sophie and Pavel to the downstairs bathroom where they washed. He discarded the scarf and with Sophie's help, tied two of the hotel's towels together to make a new dressing.

"I'm ashamed, Willy," Sophie said as they dressed in their dirty clothes. "I'm ashamed of how we look, of what we've done and who we are. That's our blood on the bed-sheets. Yours and mine. We're like animals."

"There's nothing we can do, sweetheart. That bastard is coming back to do us harm. We have to leave. No-one is going to help us."

"I'm hungry." Pavel looked at his mother hopefully.

They packed their things, readying to leave. Sophie took Willy's elbow, holding him back. She shook her head despondently.

"Even though that disgusting man behaved so badly, I would have wanted to pay for cleaning up the mess we made—in the room and the bathroom."

"You are too honorable, my dear." Willy said as they started down the stairs. "We couldn't afford it even if we wanted to. Forget about the room. Just be happy we slept well."

They slunk out of the hotel carrying everything they owned in the string bag. Luckily, the reception desk was deserted. "That bastard was bluffing about coming back." Willy forced a smile to reassure Sophie though he was afraid *le patron* and his anti-Semitic friends would return. They might even search the neighborhood. "We paid him. We owe nothing."

He pulled a couple of French banknotes and some coins from the side pocket of his jacket and showed them to Pavel. "Are you hungry, my little frog? This is French money, enough for a nice breakfast. After that we'll go find Tante Freda and cousin Feri."

Pavel grinned waving his toy lion's paws in the air. "Furry Lion say he wants a pastry. Me too."

"A quick breakfast, then," said Sophie with a faint smile.

CHAPTER TWO

Gossip at Café Vietto
August 1939

It was almost seven o'clock and shafts of sunlight on the facades of houses and stores promised a stifling day. The Kohuts found themselves in a narrow street busy with pedestrians. Horse-drawn delivery vehicles rattled along the cobbles, scattering hay and torn newspapers and leaving mounds of manure. Street cleaners with cigarettes stuck to their lips cleaned up after them, grumbling to each other as they swept the gutters.

Worried that someone might notice their disheveled clothes, Willy discreetly led his family around a street corner and farther on, about three hundred meters from the Hôtel de Metz, they found Bistro Vietto. Hidden by a row of tall potted shrubs, they sat at the handkerchief-sized terrace under the shade of a striped awning.

A portly man wearing an apron approached their table. "Vous desirez, M'sieu?"

Keeping his jacket buttoned to cover up the bloodstains on his shirt, Willy, still fuming at being ejected from the hotel, ordered breakfast and a hot milk for Pavel. They ate hungrily, dipping honey-smeared croissants into the coffee.

A sparrow fluttered close to Pavel's plate and hopped about, feasting on crumbs. The boy's face lit up. "Birdie is my friend," he said in Czech. "He likes me."

Pavel's obvious pleasure and the strong coffee softened

10

Willy's mood, even though he was still in pain and not sure what to do next. During their escape through Germany, Willy and Sophie had been forced to discard three suitcases. They had lost nearly everything, but now, Willy reasoned, they were light on their toes, adaptable, ready for anything. His pianist's soul saw their future like a blank sheet of music waiting for a new melody to be written.

"That little birdie likes your pastry," said Sophie, wiping Pavel's chin with a rumpled handkerchief. "People at home would think we were very naughty, dipping a pastry in our coffee. Here in Paris I expect things are different. Sometimes it's fine to be naughty."

Willy leaned over with an affectionate smile and removed a smear of honey from Sophie's cheek. He sensed that she was trying hard to appear relaxed. "So, what do you think, sweetheart?" he said, stretching an arm round the back of her chair. "Isn't this better than the hellish train journey from Aachen?"

Sophie gave him a reproachful look. "We are no longer in Germany and we are still alive if that's what you mean. And yes, it's nice here but please, let's not stay near that hotel. That horrible man and his friends might come looking." She looked down at her stained, wrinkled dress and scuffed shoes. "Look at these things, I've never felt so disgusting. We *have* to find Feri and Tante Freda, and soon. I'm sure Tante has a nice bathroom and spare clothes."

Willy gave her a wry smile, not wanting to agree that his once-glamorous wife looked like a tramp. He scratched the thick stubble on his chin. "And I need cleaning up too. Five days without a shave and a bath is a record I want to forget."

Sophie's distant relatives had lived in Paris for twenty years and he felt certain the Lihçets would extricate them from their dire predicament. Family was family and Jews helped each other—except that Tante Freda from Rumania had married Özgür Lihçet, a tight-fisted Turkish carpet importer. God willing, Freda would persuade her Muslim husband to lend Sophie some money. A two-week supply should be buffer enough.

If the Lihçets refused, Willy had a final arrow in his survival quiver: gold coins he had acquired in Budapest and hidden in the heels of his shoes. Selling them could be difficult but might buy him enough time to organize a way to get to London.

"I have her address but no telephone number," said Sophie, despondently.

Willy frowned with pain as he pushed back his chair and signaled for the bill. "We'll get it."

The café owner re-appeared, wiping hands on his blue apron. He glanced at the croissant flakes carpeting the table and winked at Pavel. "The little one was hungry, *hein*? Blue eyes and gold curls to charm the ladies. How old is he?"

Willy smiled at Sophie. "Three years. *Il a trois ans.*"

"Do you desire another café, *M'sieu, Madame*? Perhaps, a chocolate croissant for the little one?"

"*Non, merci*," said Willy. "How much do I owe?"

"Thirty-five francs."

The man slid the money into a leather pouch attached to his low-slung belt. His gaze traveled from Willy's face to the blood stains on his shirt and jacket. His face was impassive. "If I were you I would keep to the back streets. The police are arresting tramps and homeless refugees. Blood-stains suggest criminality, *M'sieu*."

Willy eked out a smile. This was not reassuring. "Thanks for the advice. Is there a post office near here? I need a telephone."

"*La Poste*?" said the bar owner. "*Certainement. Place de La République*, a twenty-minute walk. But I have a public telephone inside. You buy *jetons* for the slot." He crooked a finger. "*Venez*."

The noise inside the café made Willy's ears buzz. Men in berets and caps stood shoulder to shoulder at the zinc bar, drinking coffee with their morning cognacs and *eau de vie*, talking in loud tones and listening to what sounded like a harangue on the radio. A cracked mirror in a gilt frame hung behind the bar; the papered walls were decorated with battered advertisements of Dubonnet, Lillet and Pastis. Cigarette smoke hung like fog in the air. Sawdust had been spread on the ceramic-tiled floor. Spittoons were stationed at each end of the bar.

Willy walked to the telephone niche at the far end of the bar while Sophie and Pavel waited inside the swing doors, looking around the café. Sophie pointed to an orange cat dozing in sunshine on the ledge of a dirty window. Tentatively, glancing back at her for approval, Pavel made his way past chairs and a spiky plant in a brass pot and timidly began to caress the cat. With each stroke the cat arched its back, its pink tongue emerging and retreating, like a mechanical toy.

Willy opened the chained telephone book and gestured for Sophie to leave Pavel with the cat and join him. With a hopeful smile, she threaded her way back through a group of men who had just come in. With a nod, she acknowledged their collective "*bonjour Madame.*"

"Success, sweetheart." Willy showed her the page, a gleam of triumph in his eyes. "Two numbers for Lihçet. One is a store, Treasures of Turkey—on the Boulevard de Sébastopol—and the other has an expensive address in the Bois de Boulogne."

Sophie clapped her hands. "That's it. Good work, my darling. But *you* make the call in case it's someone French and I can't understand them." Sophie glanced over her shoulder and smiled. Pavel was still cuddling the cat. "But if it's Tante Freda who answers, I'm the one to speak to her. She doesn't know you."

He listened to the ringing for a long time and shook his head. "Damn, no one home. We'll try the store. Read me the number."

Willy dialed again. A woman answered. "*Bonjour, Trésors de Turquie.*"

His eyes widened with satisfaction. He nodded at Sophie. "I wish to speak with Monsieur or Madame Lihçet, please. My wife, Madame Sophie Kohut, is a close relative."

"They are not available, *M'sieu*."

"It's urgent. We arrived in Paris last night from Germany. An escape, from Prague."

Willy heard the intake of breath.

"An escape? *Mon Dieu*. You must forgive me *M'sieu*, but so many strangers call these days. I have instructions to be very careful about giving out information. Please, may I ask your wife's relationship to Madame Lihçet?"

"Madame Lihçet is my wife's aunt." said Willy, drumming the fingers of his left hand on the bar surface.

There was a pause. "I regret to inform you, *M'sieu*, that Madame Lihčet and her husband left two days ago from Marseille, on a boat for Turkey."

Damn. Willy tightened his grip on the edge of the bar counter. He looked glumly at Sophie. "They've gone to Turkey," he said in a low voice, his hand over the speaker. He spoke again into the receiver. "What about Feri, their son? He's a student at the Sorbonne medical school. He must still be in Paris. Can we leave him a message?"

"He has not come home for several days. I have no telephone number for him."

"Oh, well, thank you." Willy grunted in disappointment as he put down the telephone. "I'm hoping Feri did not leave with his parents. Unless we find him we're completely on our own and in a mess."

Pavel pulled at Sophie's skirt. "Come see pussycat, *Maminko*. He kissed me."

"Please, we must find Feri," said Sophie She pointed at the barman who was replenishing the beers and cognacs of a group of men close by. "Find out from that man how to get to the Sorbonne Medical School. I have to see to Pavel."

As Willy asked for directions, he noticed how the customers' and barman's eyes tracked the motion of Sophie's hips as she followed Pavel. He sighed; nothing much had changed in France since his student days.

"Easy," said the barman. "Take the Metro from around the corner to the Odéon station. Odéon is right by the medical school. A taxi would be quicker but—from the look of you—you won't be able to afford one." He scooped a pile of coins off the counter into the pocket of his leather apron and wiped the surface. "Have a *petit blanc* before you go? A glass of wine on the house for a new customer."

Willy declined with a smile and a wave of fingers. "Thank you for your help, but no."

"You may be wasting your time at the Sorbonne."

Willy turned sharply. "What do you mean?"

"Last night's *Paris-Soir* reported that the government is closing all the medical schools. Most of the students have been recruited as soldiers or military doctors." He sniffed his disapproval. "No need for medical students to take qualifying exams anymore. They'll learn their trade on our wounded boys."

"I don't understand."

One of the nearby customers, an old man with a mass of wiry gray hair and a pince-nez, better dressed than the others, turned to face Willy. He held a tumbler full of milky Pernod in a knobbly hand. "Georges here is talking about President Daladier's general mobilization order. *La France* prepares for war." He frowned and stepped back, mouth open. "There is blood on your shirt, *M'sieu*. Do you need assistance?"

Willy's shoulders drooped. He had no wish to launch into complicated explanations or tell more lies. "It's nothing bad. Tell me, what is going on in Paris?"

"If you do not know of these important events, you must be strangers, *hein*?"

"We are refugees," said Willy, turning to him. "Just arrived from Czechoslovakia."

"Let me guess, *M'sieu*. You must have come through Holland or Germany. You are what—Jewish? We have so many here now."

Willy felt his heart jump. This man was asking too many questions. He shrugged, splaying his hands out defensively. He was not going to admit to being Jewish in public. One bad experience was enough to fill the day's quota. "As I said, we're Czechoslovaks." He had denied being Jewish in Germany and then again last night at the hotel, to get a room, rest and sleep. He didn't want to hide who he was anymore but he didn't want to advertise the fact either. France was not the same as Germany, but the warning signs were there, and he was wary.

The small man proffered his hand, eyes twinkling as if he clearly understood Willy's reticence. "*Moi aussi*, I am a Jew. Claude Semmel, delighted to meet you." He sighed. "Yes indeed, sad times. You and more than a hundred thousand other *refugiés* have swamped Paris in the past few weeks. Minister Béranger says our country is at saturation point."

"Can they all move around freely?"

"Yes—but only if they have legal French documents. Periodically, the police round up the illegal refugees. Pull them off the street, put them in custody. So keep to the back streets, away from the trafficked areas."

"Paris always welcomed strangers. I was here as a student."

"Not any more. The French are fed up. They don't even like the Jewish *citoyens* who grew up, lived, and worked here for years, like me." The men at the bar sniggered and laughed.

Willy looked away, too upset to respond to this old man's

sardonic humor. It fit with his experience at the hotel and made him fearful of what was to come. "I still don't understand the reason for this mobilization."

"A defense treaty. If the Germans attack Poland, we promised to fight with the Poles. Honorable solidarity, *mon vieux.*"

Willy remembered his father's bitter dictum about how the Poles hated Jews: *Polish babies get their anti-Semitism from the mother's breast.* So now, the Poles needed help. He sighed and looked over at Sophie crouching down with Pavel, talking to him as he kept stroking the cat. Willy was fed up with politics, war games and betrayal. It was amazing how people and nations demonized each other, and for what? To gain power and land, or just to blame someone else, like the Jews, for their misfortunes. Right now, the only things on his mind were safety, enough to live on and finding a way to England.

"I am sorry for you and yours," said Monsieur Semmel, looking Willy up and down with a pitying look. "You both need cleaning up. I would invite you to my home but I am a widower living in a simple room. Are you and your pretty wife alone in Paris? If you need assistance, I think there is a Jewish refugee center in the Marais district. They might give you a bath, decent clothes and temporary lodging. At least you're better off than most; you speak good French."

Willy frowned. Monsieur Semmel was very direct. Refugee centers were for the desperate ones, and their staff collected a great deal of personal information. Lists and addresses of refugees could be passed on to the police, for example—used for good or evil. He remembered that when they escaped from Prague, Adolf Eichmann had recently arrived from Berlin to set up a Central Jewish Emigration Office that would document the details and possessions of every Jew. Such an office already existed in Austria and Willy knew that its records were being used for plunder, dispossession and transporting people to camps. No, he and Sophie would find cousin Feri and stay away from officials. "Thank you," he muttered. "We'll manage."

Sophie returned after ungluing Pavel from the cat. Willy noticed that she was limping. She gave him an anxious smile. "So, did you find out, *miláčku*? How do we get to Feri's medical school? I want so much to see him."

Willy put his arm around her shoulders, turning her towards the Frenchman. "I asked this gentleman, Monsieur Semmel, about the Sorbonne. He thinks that medical courses have been suspended, the students dispersed. Who knows where Feri is?"

Sophie's face crumpled. She ran anxious fingers through her thick hair. "We must find him" she said in a low, choking voice. "Without Feri we have nothing."

Willy gave her a reassuring squeeze. "Monsieur Semmel said there was a Jewish refugee center not far away. We could go and ask for help, though I'm wary of their staff knowing too much about us and passing it on to French officials. Let's take a chance—go to the Sorbonne, find out about Feri. Do you think you can walk to the Metro? I noticed you limping. What is it?"

She nodded. "I have some pain low down in my stomach. Don't worry, I'll manage."

As they turned to leave, Monsieur Semmel pulled on Willy's arm. "One more item for you, *M'sieu*. If you want to stay in Paris, you must have an official residence permit and proof of enough money for three months' lodging. Without such things they might send you to one of the internment camps in the southwest, near the Pyrenees—bad places. They were built for the Spanish refugees from Franco: hot, terrible conditions, mosquitoes, infections and rotten food. Many died there, from typhus."

Willy carried Pavel as they walked along the street toward the Metro station. How the hell would he get a residence permit?

Perhaps through the official Czechoslovak Consulate that was somewhere in the Sixteenth Arrondissement. And to stay in Paris he needed money for food and clothes. Meanwhile the police could easily spot them as newly arrived refugees. They looked shabby and miserable enough.

Tears ran down Sophie's cheeks. She was limping again and Willy slowed his pace. "I'm not sure why I have this pain. It is worse than usual."

Willy stopped and stared at her. "Is this anything to do with what happened to us at the frontier?" He prayed that her pain was temporary, that it would get better with some rest. Their plight was serious enough. He cringed at the thought of trying to find a doctor for her. How would he pay? More shame. No—no doctor, unless she got worse. Food and lodging came first.

She shook her head. "I'm not so bad. Let's find Feri."

CHAPTER THREE

Heels of Gold
Paris. August 1939

Sophie admired the art nouveau ironwork at the Odéon Metro Station, but she was puzzled by the strange method of opening the train doors.

"Your job next time," laughed Willy as he flipped the door latch and gently propelled Pavel inside.

As the train rattled along, Sophie couldn't shake off a feeling of lassitude that had started soon after their unpleasant awakening. Luckily the pain in her belly was easing and she absent-mindedly watched Pavel on Willy's lap. He clung to his father's arm, inspecting the other passengers with what she guessed was curiosity and anxiety; the underground Metro was just one more new experience for a child who had already been through more than his share of unusual situations. For months now, nothing had been regular and familiar. Children need a routine and a stable home; that's what Judit, Willy's mother, always said.

She thought about cousin Feri, imagining how he looked now. It would be lovely to see him. They truly needed his help. But with his parents on the way to Turkey, she was afraid he might not be able to loan them more than a few francs. After all, he was only a medical student.

Her father had always made a point of keeping in touch

with Tante Freda—but Sophie only knew Feri from photographs: a serious-looking, thin-armed boy with shiny black hair, dark skin and huge eyes. She guessed he was twenty-two now, about to become a French doctor. Tante Freda, of course, was Jewish and kept the holidays, but Feri's father was a Turk. A Muslim, probably. Sophie wondered how they meshed as a family. They probably felt at home in the melting pot of Paris.

Entering the Faculté de Médecine from the street, they walked through a cobbled interior colonnade and followed the signs to the main office. Two sweaty-faced men in double-breasted suits passed by, carrying briefcases. A workman wheeling a cart of shiny metal boxes crossed their path. He nodded a greeting. After that, the hallway was empty and their footsteps echoed on the flagstones. The building seemed deserted and Sophie's heart sank. How would they ever find Feri?

They followed the signs and found the medical-school office on the ground floor. The ornate glass doors were not locked and the room was cooled by blue-green ceramic floor tiles. Blinds, half-drawn on the tall windows, blocked out the sun.

A middle-aged woman with plucked eyebrows and braided hair sat behind the counter. She inspected the shabby Kohuts, her mouth pouting in what Sophie interpreted as disapproval or resentment. "You have blood all over your shirt and jacket, M'sieu. This is the medical-school office, not an emergency clinic. Please leave."

When Willy enquired about Feri, the woman rolled her eyes and spent the next five minutes scanning lists clipped to wooden boards, sighing irritably as she turned the pages.

"Not here," she said with an almost triumphant shrug. "All our students over a specified age have been sent to military camps in the north; the rest have gone home. This is the summer vacation, you know." She sniffed into a lace handkerchief and dabbed her cheeks. "I do not understand why our administrators assume these half-trained boys can give adequate medical attention to our soldiers. If you want to find your relative, contact the authorities."

Willy translated for Sophie, frustration suffusing his cheeks. He leaned over the counter. "We are strangers in Paris. Do you have an address or a telephone number for these authorities?"

"Your search is not my affair." The receptionist fanned herself with a sheaf of papers and frowned at Pavel, who circled the waiting area following the pattern of the floor tiles, singing. He sang the same words over and over as his hand skipped along the wall. "*Paci, paci, pacičky, táta koupí botičky.* Clap, clap, clap hands, Daddy will buy the shoes."

"Tell that child to stop. This is not a nursery. Good day."

Sophie clutched at Willy's arm. "What did she say?"

"Complained about Pavel making a noise, that's all."

Sophie sagged against the counter and buried her face in her hands. Her knees felt ready to give way. "*Miláčku*, I can't bear this. Why does our life have to be such a struggle? I was counting on Feri. I wanted something good to happen to us."

The receptionist gave them a cold stare and turned away.

In the hallway, Willy put his arm around her. "Cheer up. We are struggling now, but remember, something good *has* happened. We escaped from Germany and Monsieur Panasse lent us money. We had a good sleep and a nice breakfast. The sun is shining. With Feri it would have been much easier, but we will manage."

Sophie lifted her tear-stained face. "How will we manage?"

"A better hotel for a start," said Willy as he led them back across the colonnade to the entry gate. "We can still afford that ... for a day or two ... until Monsieur Panasse's money runs out. Coming from the Metro, I noticed the Hôtel St. Pierre at the end of the street. It looks nice. We'll try there." He laughed. "At least we don't have any luggage to worry about."

At the Hôtel St. Pierre, the family crammed into the brass-and-steel elevator operated by a gap-toothed, green-aproned concierge. On the fifth floor he showed them a room with large windows, patterned wallpaper, floral curtains, a tilted wardrobe, a wash basin in one corner and a large double bed—a definite improvement on the Hôtel de Metz. Only the oppressive heat was unchanging.

"There is a communal bathtub," said the concierge, opening the windows inward. "One floor below—thirty francs, water no more than fifteen centimeters deep." He pointed to the windows. "It's August. Keep the outside shutters closed unless you want to be roasted alive."

Sophie's question, translated by Willy, about cooking facilities at the hotel, generated hand-waving and amused astonishment. "No kitchen and no cooking allowed, Madame. Eating is what cafés are for."

While Pavel bounced on the mattress, throwing Furry Lion in the air, Sophie and Willy sat on flimsy bentwood chairs taking stock of their worldly goods. Aside from their Hungarian passports and documents proving he owned a business in Prague, Willy wore underpants, socks, one of two blood-stained shirts, shoes and socks, and his rumpled suit. He had his glasses and no watch.

Sophie wore a beige silk blouse with a rip in the collar, a slip, skirt and shoes. She had an extra pair of panties, her fur-collared overcoat and her beloved Hermès scarf. For toiletries, she had a powder puff, an ivory-backed hairbrush, a lipstick and two toothbrushes. They had no change of clothes for Pavel and nothing to use for his underpants except for a small towel stolen from the Hôtel de Metz.

Pavel ignored the review of their worldly goods. He was happy to have his favorite toys: a red truck and the Furry Lion that his *babička* had given him for his first birthday. He had clung to them tenaciously all through the tortuous journey from Prague.

Sophie sat slumped in her chair, sadly observing Willy as he unlatched the outside shutters to let in some air. "I'm unhappy, *miláčku*. I so much wanted to see Feri, and then we wasted all that time in the medical school—dealing with that awful woman. Ugh! I'm worn out. I feel like going back to bed. "

Willy nodded. "You look pale. Worn out. Not surprising. It'll take time to heal and recover from what we've been through. Perhaps, you should take a nap."

Sophie studied her fingernails so he couldn't see her face. Willy did not know the half of why she felt so hollowed out. In spite of her utter exhaustion from the train journey, she had woken several times during the night, her heart thumping from nightmarish dreams that replayed what she had been subjected to in her cell at the frontier—the female guard's merciless eyes, the pain and shock of rubber-gloved hands probing and jabbing into every part of her body—and poor Pavel watching the blood run down her thighs, his round blue eyes as big as bird eggs. She would never tell Willy everything that happened to her at the German border.

"We need cloth diapers," she said brightly, trying to revive her energy and not betray her thoughts. "I must have new underwear and something like small hand towels for my bleeding. And I would love a bath."

Willy came over to Sophie, kissed her, and took her hands in his as he knelt down by her chair. "I will ask the concierge where we can get our clothes washed. And we all deserve a bath," he said briskly. "Unfortunately, they charge thirty francs per person and we would be using those pathetic little towels from the armoire. At the moment, we can't afford a bath. A good hand wash will have to do. Anyway, I'll go out and get what you mentioned. What about a fresh dress? Socks? Underthings? We probably have enough cash left over from Monsieur Panasse's donation. What do you say?"

With a wry smile, Sophie touched Willy's thick stubble. "Definitely, you need shaving soap and a razor. But I wonder how you, the esteemed fabric merchant, will manage to swallow your pride and buy all those woman's things for me—and not be embarrassed?"

Willy smiled. "No one knows me in Paris, so what's the harm."

Sophie clapped her hands together, shoulders shaking with silent laughter. "What a critical moment in our relationship; here you are, offering to buy intimate clothes for your wife—and by yourself. I can see the newspaper headline: *Prague businessman goes underwear shopping for his wife!*"

She was surprised how ebullient Willy had been all morning in spite of the heat, the wound on his chest and the horrible argument in the hotel. It was as if arriving in Paris had given him an extra blast of energy. He seemed ready to draw curtains on the past and concentrate on the future.

"In desperate times," said Willy as he rose to his feet, "we need desperate measures, like buying you underclothes. Now, I must hurry. The shops close at noon for lunch. If I pass a post office, I'll send a telegram to my parents in London saying we're safe. And I'll bring back a *casse-croute*. That's French for a lunch snack."

Sophie nodded, twisting fingers in her lap, her eyes blinking back tears. "*Miláčku*, I was so counting on a loan from Tante Freda. If you buy everything on your list we'll have nothing left to live on."

Even though his chest hurt, Willy drew himself up to his full height, half closed his eyes and curved an arm above his head. With the other hand on his hip he drummed his heels on the floor staccato, flamenco-style, and shouted, "*Olé.*"

Sophie stared at him, astonished. "What is this, *miláčku*? Are you mad?"

"Do you not recognize the rhythm, *mi amor*," he said attempting a Spanish accent on top of a grin. "Can't you hear the chink of gold ducats on the floor."

She shrugged, for a moment uncomprehending. "Nonsense. You *are* mad."

"In my heels. At the frontier, sweetheart. The idiot guards missed our treasure."

"Treasure?" She gasped, clutching at her cheeks. "*Ó pane.* Now I remember—the gold coins you bought in Budapest."

Willy laughed. "Good thing you forgot about them. You might have given the game away when we were searched. When I called the Lihčet store from the café, I looked in the telephone directory ... for a coin dealer. I found a place called Florange near the Bourse. I'll go there later, after we're back from shopping and have eaten something. If I can sell those coins, we'll have plenty of cash." He put on his jacket.

Pavel stopped bouncing on the bed. "We go walk, Táta?"

"Leave him here with me, *miláčku.* This is his first day in Paris."

"Exactly" said Willy bluntly. "You need to rest and he will help me choose the food and the clothes. The sooner he gets used to hearing French, the better."

It was twelve-thirty by the time Willy and Pavel got back to the hotel room. Sophie was sitting by the window in her slip, watching pigeons jostling each other on the sill. Willy had bought cotton diapers, dressings and a long bandage for his wound, all wrapped in brown paper. With a conspiratorial grin at Pavel, Willy laid out the underwear and a blue cotton dress covered with sunflowers. He threw another parcel on the bed. "*Et voilà, Madame. Serviettes hygiéniques* ... hygienic pads. Also a cotton belt and safety pins for you and for the boy's diaper. I never realized that life was so complicated for women. Luckily Pavel was not as embarrassed as I was."

Sophie bit her lip and looked away. "You astonish me," she murmured.

"We found a *mercerie* that sells almost everything." He lifted a string bag full of food and fruit onto the bedside table. I think we did well. Pavel chose your dress—and we bought grapes and two ham-and-cheese baguettes for lunch. He already ate half the grapes."

Sophie laughed out loud and slipped her arms around her husband's neck. "I had a nice short sleep. It seems you are a gifted shopper." She kissed him lightly on the lips. "But when I awoke and you weren't there, I couldn't stop worrying. Whenever you leave me, I am afraid you won't come back." She unwrapped one of the baguette sandwiches and sniffed it. "This smells heavenly. Some sort of cheese? I'm ravenous."

Willy smoothed her hair with his hand as she popped grapes into her mouth. "The cheese is Brie. Heavenly smelling cheese is France's gift to the world." He tore a section off the other baguette and handed it to Pavel. "Let's eat."

"*Mmm, c'est bon.*" Sophie closed her eyes as she chewed.

Willy nodded approvingly. "After we've eaten, you should go out with Pavel and explore the *quartier*. Go to the Jardins de Luxembourg, only two or three streets away. It's a lovely park with a pond for model boats." He opened a small booklet and unfolded a map from the back page. "I got this from the hotel concierge and marked our hotel's name and the street: Rue de l'École de Médecine. It's for you."

"You are not coming with us?"

Willy shook his head. Sending her alone with Pavel into the neighborhood was a little harsh but the quicker she learned French and acclimated herself to the *quartier* the better. She needed French survival skills. "No, we need money. I have to sell the coins as soon as possible. Besides, you don't need me hovering over you."

Sophie, her mouth still full, gave him a nod of acquiescence. "Very well. We'll do our best to have fun in the park, won't we, Pavel?"

It took Willy three quarters of an hour by foot and bus to find the numismatic house of Florange, at 17 Rue de la Banque in the Deuxième Arrondissement. On the way, he was surprised to see the columns of troops marching along the streets and the barricades of sandbags stacked around important buildings, with police and soldiers everywhere. Pill boxes guarded the main boulevards. *Paris has dressed for war,* he thought. His pulse quickened as he walked. Perhaps France would do what the Czechoslovak army hadn't been able to—defeat the Germans.

Florange occupied the ground floor of an imposing stone building adorned with elaborate iron balconies. Willy peered through the steel-meshed store window at an array of velvet boxes filled with coins. The shop was empty except for a stout figure in a cutaway jacket and striped waistcoat standing behind a glass display cabinet. As Willy entered, a bell sounded and he noticed the man frown. Almost immediately a tall, heavily-built assistant burst from a side room and grabbed Willy's collar. "You want me to throw this tramp out, *patron.*"

Willy twisted this way and that, trying to slip from the bouncer's hand. "I have a gold rooster to sell," he yelled, wincing at the searing pain in his chest. Using all the force he could muster he struggled toward the counter, dragging the bouncer with him.

"*Ça va,* Joseph." The salesman waved the bouncer away. He turned back to Willy, eyebrows arched over above his half-moon glasses. "*Incroyable*—a tramp shouting about gold roosters. I expect you stole them. The truth now, or I call the police."

Willy straightened up and adjusted his rumpled jacket. "I

have two coins to sell. A twenty-franc 1911 Napoleon Rooster and a 1915 Emperor Franz Joseph ducat—fine condition, *très beau*." Willy did not mention the twenty-franc Swiss gold piece sewn into his jacket lapel, just behind the dragontail buttonhole.

The salesman narrowed his eyes, sucking in a breath of astonishment. "*Ça alors*, you seem know your coins. Your accent—you are a foreigner, yes?"

"I'm a Czechoslovak, *un refugié*," said Willy, bracing his shoulders, trying to assume dignity in spite of his dirty clothes. "I smuggled the coins through Germany."

The man pulled a jeweler's loupe from a drawer and nestled it into one eye. "*Eh, bien*, I am Monsieur Jaccoud, the owner. Let's see what you have."

"They're in my shoes," said Willy bending down to untie his shoelaces.

Jaccoud nodded calmly as if he found this procedure quite normal. He signaled to the bouncer. "*Allez Joseph*, fetch the hammer and chisel." He turned back to Willy. "With men, the coins are always in the heels, sometimes inside the backside." He winked. "As you can imagine, *mon ami*, it is different with women who have other hiding places. *Certainement*, the smuggling of gold and valuables out of Central Europe is booming. Refugees in Paris trade their gold for francs, and we French do exactly the opposite, burying our gold in the garden or under the floorboards."

Ten minutes later, Willy walked out, heel-less, with directions on where to get his shoes repaired. He had just fifteen hundred French francs in his pocket—disappointing. He had obtained just one third of the amount he had paid for the coins in Budapest. The astute Monsieur Jaccoud had taken full advantage of his vulnerability and desperation. On the other hand, fifteen hundred francs was probably enough for two weeks of food and a hotel room—a breathing space for Sophie to recover and for them to get used to Parisian ways. And that would give him time to wrangle something at the Czechoslovak Consulate. Getting to England was still his absolute priority.

Over the next three days, Paris sweltered in temperatures over thirty degrees Celsius. The hotel room with its small window was uninhabitable until late evening, so Sophie and Willy, carrying Pavel much of the time, explored the Left Bank, bought provisions and scrounged second-hand clothes at nearby Marché Mouffetard. In the afternoons, they lingered on shady café terraces or strolled along the quays of the Seine, watching the boats and barges. They established one routine: taking Pavel to play in the Jardins de Luxembourg. While they kept an eye on him, Willy taught Sophie practical French words and phrases which she wrote down in an exercise book. There was nothing much else to do except walk, eat, sleep and apply to the Czechoslovak Consulate for help and stay away from the gendarmes.

When Willy visited the Czechoslovak Consulate, hoping for a quick way to get identity cards and residency permits, he found it overwhelmed with people seeking assistance. He was turned away but given an appointment in two days when he would have the opportunity to perhaps talk to an official.

The Kohuts slowly came to terms with their predicament. Their initial relief at finally being safe faded, leaving them with two existential challenges: how would they survive when the fifteen hundred francs were spent, and how to get to England. If the Czechoslovak Consulate could not help them, then perhaps the Jewish Relief office would.

"We'll not use that place if we can help it," Willy said to Sophie during one of their favorite walks along the Boulevard St. Michel to Notre Dame and the Isle St. Louis. "At the Jewish Relief Center you have to register and complete application forms. We could be forced to report to the police every week. Remember what we learned at the café? If the police stop us in the street and we have no French documents, they'll send us to an internment camp. I'll keep my appointment at the Czechoslovak Consulate. They might be able to help us get the documents we need; they might even know the best way to get to England."

CHAPTER FOUR

The Czechoslovak Army in France
Paris. August 1939

Two days later, on a fresh sunny morning, Willy headed for the Czechoslovak Consulate. He kept a firm grip on the paper bag that held their old passports and documents proving ownership of Anglotex, his Prague fabric store. He told Sophie not to expect him back until mid-afternoon; bureaucrats were the same everywhere, and those at the Consulate would surely take their time.

He took Metro Line Six from the Bir Hakim stop to Avenue Kléber and after a short walk, arrived at the Rue Dumont d'Urville. A long line of glum men and women, a few with children attached, snaked along the street up to the Consulate's front entrance. The office had already been open an hour, so this was a bad sign. Willy took off his jacket and knotted the corners of a handkerchief to protect his head from the sun—resigned to looking silly as he waited on the hot pavement. He realized that he needed patience and probably a pile of luck to get what he needed: new passports, food vouchers and identity cards.

By ten-thirty he was inside. The Czechoslovak Consulate occupied the lower three floors of a nineteenth-century *hôtel*. People filled the dusty corridors and waiting areas: sitting, standing, some camped out on the floor. A plump-faced secretary in a brown cotton dress gave Willy a waiting number, 145, typed on a small card. He leaned against the wall. As soon as someone got up to leave or go to the toilet there was a rush for their empty chair.

Two hours later, another employee, seated at a small desk in an alcove, called Willy's number. "Passports," she said abruptly. He sat down and with a polite smile passed them across the table. "*Madam*, I know these are Hungarian documents but we are *really* from Czechoslovakia."

Putting on thick lens glasses, she skimmed the passports and glared at him. "Why should I believe you? These look genuine to me." With a look of disgust, she pushed the documents across the desk. "Hungarians are in bed with the Nazis. They invaded Slovakia. You have no right to come here." She looked past him. "You had better leave."

Weathering her tirade, Willy posted his most winning smile. "Dear *Madam*, we are genuine Czechoslovak citizens—from Prague and Slovakia. I have documents to prove it." He pushed the passports back at her. "These are counterfeit. We used them to escape across Germany. We are Jews."

He watched her lean back with a skeptical frown, tapping her teeth with a pencil as if she was reconsidering her outburst. "Czechs and also Jews, eh? So… how did you get to Paris?"

"From Prague, we traveled to Budapest and then by car and train through Germany. At the Dutch border the Nazi frontier guards strip-searched us and confiscated the Czechoslovak passports they found sewn into my suitcase."

Willy opened his paper bag. "Here are copies of birth certificates, my Czechoslovak business papers, bank statements and a letter from the British textile company I did business with. In Prague, I owned a store called Anglotex on Masná Street. Please, take a moment to study them. I have a wife and little boy and we have almost no money. We need help." He lied about having no money but it was close enough to the truth.

For several minutes, *Paní* Vicková, Irena—Willy had noticed the name tag pinned to her cotton blouse—examined everything with a magnifying glass. She adjusted the perch of her glasses and then looked at him, her frown softening. "Very well," she said. "Here is a form to fill out. When you have finished, I will review it. If I'm satisfied, you can take it to the Red Cross Office in Room Twelve to receive the family assistance vouchers we provide to refugees."

"Is there a telephone somewhere?" By now, Willy knew that this process would take far longer than even he had estimated.

Paní Vicková sniffed. "There's no telephone for applicants. Go to the post office on the next street."

"I suppose I'd lose my place if I went there?"

She nodded.

Willy borrowed a pencil and, leaning against the wall, completed the form. When he handed it back, *Paní* Vicková told him to wait in the Red Cross Office, a much smaller room, also packed with people.

Eventually, he was called to the desk of another, younger woman, neatly dressed with fair hair pinned up in a bun. She handed him a booklet of vouchers, riffling them like a deck of cards. "Listen carefully, *Pane* Kohut. These vouchers are gold dust. The Paris City Council has decreed that all stores and hotels must accept them as legal tender. You only get a month's supply. But—if you can persuade the administration there to issue you a residency permit, your family will also be eligible for vouchers on a regular basis. Most importantly, the residency permit will protect you from arrest by the police." She held out slim manicured fingers. "Good-bye now."

Willy hand-kissed her fingertips, inhaling their floral scent. It had been a long time since he had enjoyed that sensation. "Thank you for your kindness," he said, but he did not let go of her hand. "Listen to me, *Madam*," he said. "It's vital I talk to one of the diplomatic staff about visas for my family. I have to get to England—as soon as possible. My elderly mother there is dying of tuberculosis. Please, I beg you."

He emphasized his blatant lie about tuberculosis by gently squeezing her hand and putting on a tragic face. Ever since his incarceration in Pankrác prison, Willy had developed armor against shame and guilt. Deception was an essential skill for refugees on the run.

She nodded sympathetically. "I am sorry about your mother, *Pan* Kohut. If you are willing to wait, I'll ask if the Consulate Secretary will see you."

Willy smiled and released her hand. First hurdle overcome. The office pendulum clock striking three reminded him that he was hungry—and uneasy that he had left Sophie and Pavel for so long. He had food vouchers now, but reliable information about getting to England would be invaluable.

Again, he waited in the corridor, this time facing a wall graced by a canvas map of 1920 Europe, showing the redrawn frontiers agreed on by the powers attending the Versailles Treaty at the end of the Great War—the treaty that created Czechoslovakia.

Hitler, Willy mused, was well on the way to redrawing this map: he'd already swallowed up Austria and Czechoslovakia. What would be next? Gazing at the route they took in their escape from Prague, he reviewed his family's balance sheet. On the positive side, his parents were safe in London. Sophie's father and brother had escaped Berlin for Australia, and he, Sophie and Pavel were now in Paris. Cousins Janko and Laci, who had worked under him at Anglotex, were somewhere in Turkey or the Middle East having escaped by barge down the Danube.

On the down side, he and Sophie, dispossessed by Hungarian fascists and Nazis, were here in Paris, almost penniless. The future looked grim. What Willy wanted now was to join his parents in

England and, if he was allowed, fight with the British.

Sophie, he knew, yearned for a happy home life of safety and stability. For the foreseeable future that was an impossible dream. What they needed at this moment were the basics: food and shelter.

When Willy was finally called into the Czechoslovak diplomat's office, he took a chair opposite a chubby, balding official seated behind files and dossiers stacked like castle ramparts. He noted the name, Vlásek, L. Consular Officer, on a wooden plaque set against an ashtray of crushed Gitanes stubs.

Vlásek nodded a weary welcome. Willy watched him take a mouthful of coffee from a tin mug and felt the growling emptiness in his own stomach; he had been without food for close to six hours.

"So, you are *Pan* Kohut, Vilém—a Jewish merchant from Prague," Vlásek said in Czech, looking at his notes. "When did you arrive in France?"

Willy adjusted the second-hand wire-frame glasses he had bought at a market stall. They dug into his nose and distracted him. "Two days ago. Me, my wife and son. My parents are in London."

"How did you get here?"

"Train, car and feet. Budapest, Munich, Wiesbaden, Aachen, Gangelt, Liège and—here."

Vlásek scribbled something in his ledger, his face twitching as he wrote. "Quite a zigzag route with those false passports, my friend. Have you been in touch with any Jewish groups?"

Willy readied himself to take notes with a pencil and pad filched from the first receptionist's desk. "No, I prefer not to. We are secular. But I do need Czechoslovak passports. Ours were confiscated at the frontier. How can we travel here without some form of identity?"

Vlásek raised an eyebrow over his coffee cup. "Speaking of identity, did you know that the Nazi Jewish Registration office opened for business in Prague last week? Since then Jews have had their possessions and financial assets recorded. Same thing happened in Germany and Austria. You got away in time."

Willy shrugged. He was here for only one purpose. "Are the British still giving out immigration visas? I need three."

Vlásek had sorrowful brown eyes that Willy interpreted as sympathetic. "Sadly no. The quotas are full and the international situation is tense. The Channel Ferries are closed to the public."

Willy wiped the sweat off his forehead and jotted down his first notes. "What can we do?"

Vlásek seemed unaffected by the humidity of the room. "To get a ship to England, you'll have to go south, cross the Pyrenees and then on to Gibraltar. Anything else I can help you with?" He took a sip from his mug.

Willy's right knee started to jiggle as he tried to control his frustration at the wreckage of his hopes. "That would take a lot of money, *Pane* Vlásek," he said with a bitter smile. "It seems that with no funds, my family is stuck in Paris. Nothing more to say, is there?"

Vlásek shifted a pile of files sideways and looked at his watch. "Listen, my friend. You're in the same pickle as thousands of other refugees."

"What do we live on then?"

Vlásek sighed. "As I said, try the Jewish Czechoslovak Association in the Rue du Faubourg, Montmartre. They might keep you afloat for a while."

"Any other options?"

Vlásek rubbed his chin. "The ideal ... would be to get your family registered as official refugees at the Mayor's office—official refugees get ration books, and identity cards. The golden egg is the residency permit. If you have that the gendarmes leave you alone." He gave Willy a cynical smile. "Some say getting a residency permit is harder than digging a hole with your bare hands. But—if you know who to bribe and if you have the money, most things are possible."

As he made another note, Willy felt a wave of lassitude and gloom sweep over him. The barriers kept stacking up. "I don't know anyone important and I don't have any money," he said with a bitter smile. He rose to leave.

"That curly-shaped buttonhole on your jacket," Vlásek said as he pulled a flattened pack of Gitanes from his breast pocket and selected one. He pointed with the unlit cigarette. "Unusual. I've seen one before."

Willy stood stock still, fingering his lapel. "It's the trademark of a famous Prague tailor I once worked with," he said. "I sold top quality British fabrics, he made the suits. The most expensive ones had what he called his dragontail buttonhole."

"Ah, yes. Now I remember where I saw it," the official said. "About two weeks ago, I signed a man up for the Czechoslovak army-in-exile. He wore a suit with the same buttonhole design as yours. I suppose you might have sold him the fabric, even know him—a tall sort of fellow with an unusual face: blinking eyes, glasses and floppy yellow hair; probably in his late twenties. "

Vlásek opened a ledger and ran his finger down what Willy saw was a list. "Here we are. Lussik. Hans Lussik—said he was a Communist, an anti-Nazi extremist. Ring a bell?"

Willy shook his head and sat down abruptly, hunger forgotten. His heart hammered against his ribs. His mouth was dry. *Hans. The bastard's in Paris.* He gripped the seat of his chair. Vlásek's description fitted Hans Lessig, the pigshit who had betrayed him to the Gestapo in Prague. Thanks to Hans, Willy had been arrested, tortured and lost his business. *When I find that pigshit…*

Willy tightened his fists. Out of the blue, he was close to catching up with the only human being he truly hated. But he meant to keep this knowledge to himself—not even tell Sophie. He had vowed to kill Lessig if he ever found him, and the less anyone knew about this the better. So … Lessig was now a soldier in this mysterious Czechoslovak army. "I don't understand. Why is there is a Czechoslovak Army in France? How? "

Vlásek grinned. "*Fait accompli,* my friend. We've been putting posters up all over Paris, encouraging Czechoslovak volunteers to fight with the French troops. Lots of Czechs live here. They settled and got married to French girls after the Great War. The others who've signed on escaped the Nazi invasion last March. As I said, we call it the Czechoslovak Army-in-Exile or sometimes the Czechoslovak Army-in-France. This Consulate is a recruiting center."

"I still don't understand. How can you have a foreign army operating in France? It doesn't make sense."

Vlásek leaned back, resting his chin on splayed fingertips. A smile played on his lips. "After last March when the Nazis occupied our country, many men from our army made their way to France through Austria and Switzerland. Now we plan to reconstitute at least three regiments that will also include volunteers: men like you and Lussik, as well as Czechoslovak civilians living in France and other European countries." He tapped the desk with a pencil, clicking off the statistics. "So far we have mostly Slovaks, about a quarter are Czech, and around fifteen percent Jewish. The bulk of the officers are Czechs. Your friend, Lussik, is already getting paid, even though the whole operation is still in its formative stages."

Willy sat forward, his mind clicking like abacus beads. If he signed up he would be earning money they needed for rent and food, and at the same time he might find Lessig. "Well, I was mobilized twice in Czechoslovakia, before the Munich charade. What kind of men are you looking for?"

The sound of banging and angry voices percolated from the

corridor.

Vlásek put aside his lists and glanced at the door. "Ignore the noise, Kohut. These days we have to deal with many unhappy people." He paused. "Ah, yes, you wanted to know what kind of men we're looking for. Well, anyone who can march twenty kilometers with a rifle and a forty-pound pack. The rest comes with training. You seem interested." He glanced at the brown velvet fingerstall covering the fourth and fifth digits of Willy's right hand. "What's that thing on your hand?"

"Oh, a small mishap in Prague. It's getting better."

Vlásek raised his eyebrows, one higher than the other "Show me."

Reluctantly, Willy untied the string round his right wrist and exposed the crooked little finger covered with puckered skin. "It works," Willy said in an optimistic tone as he tried to move the finger up and down. He studied Vlásek's face, hoping for a friendly reaction but expecting the worst. Who would take on a soldier with a fucked-up hand?

Vlásek frowned. "Looks a mess to me. We need fighting men, not cripples. I suppose you could apply, but because of your hand our doctor would need to check your fitness and eligibility very carefully. So—we can't take you without medical approval."

The words battered Willy's hopes; he gulped and squared his shoulders. He wasn't ready to give up. He needed the money. "Come on, Vlásek. There's more to an army than marching and rifles. What about organization? I ran an international business in Prague, I know how to plan, maintain inventories and negotiate— and I speak six languages: Slovak, Czech, German, Hungarian, English and French. In this army of yours, is there anyone like me who can deal with a slew of ethnic groups *and* speak fluent French?"

Vlásek raised his eyebrows. "Good point, Kohut. I admit

our troops and volunteers are a ragtag lot: professional soldiers and officers, and a bunch of civilians. I expect we'll also take on a few Czechoslovak Communists from the ashes of the Spanish Civil War—and, of course, Jewish refugees like you. I suppose you could be assigned to administrative duties."

"So where is this army—in Paris?" Willy wondered if he would be able to serve in the army and still live with Sophie and Pavel. "Can I …"

Vlásek raised his hand, blocking the question. "No, Kohut. Our army is being assembled at a camp on the Mediterranean coast. This is no fly-by-night operation, my friend. The army will fight under the direct command of our own General Ingr, with oversight by General Faucher who once headed the French Military Commission in Prague."

"Look. I want to fight those Nazi bastards, but I also have to think of my family. I can't leave them on their own in Paris."

Vlásek used his blotting roller to soak up the coffee he had just spilled and smiled reassuringly at Willy. "Look, having your family together is unusual. Eighty to ninety percent of our enlisted men are here on their own—families left behind, dispersed or dead. Our proposed agreement with the French military states that in the event of an emergency, the Daladier government will ship our troops *and their families* to North Africa."

"Oh! That's interesting."

"Of course, this is an unlikely scenario. No-one believes France can lose this war. Britain controls the seas and should have no trouble blockading German ports to cut off her fuel imports. The pundits expect that within three months the Nazi cupboard will be bare. Hitler will fall to his knees."

Willy wanted confirmation. "You mean, the French would really guarantee my family's safe passage?"

Vlásek nodded sagely. "As I said, if there were to be an

evacuation from France, your family would have priority over other civilian refugees—it's stipulated in the contract you sign with us."

"And what do I get if I sign up?"

"One hundred francs on signing, good food at the camp, a monthly paycheck plus nearby lodging for your family." Vlásek paused and looked down at what Willy guessed was his dossier. "And also ... new Czechoslovak passports."

Willy took a deep breath. A wave of relief and enthusiasm washed over him. "So I and my family will be living at this camp?"

Vlásek spoke hesitantly, studying his fingernails. "Can't say yet, my friend. The camp at Agde has to be spruced up, made ready. If you enlist now it will be a month to six weeks before you leave Paris. Then, it's basic training for four to six weeks. After that, your family can travel south to join you."

"You mean my wife and boy have to stay in Paris while I'm gone?"

Vlásek nodded, his brown eyes apologetic. "We expect to have about five thousand soldiers stationed there. Soldiers with attached families will probably be billeted in nearby villages and hamlets, none of them far from the coast." He smiled and tapped the side of his nose with a forefinger. "Think of it, Kohut: wonderful sunshine, sandy beaches, delicious oysters, cheap wine, even flamingos." Vlásek grinned affably. "Your family will love the South of France."

Willy laughed. "Sounds like paradise. You should be a travel agent." He could think of only one serious drawback to being a soldier in paradise; being captured or killed. He wiped the thought from his mind. "So if there's war, we Czechoslovaks fight for the French," he said. "What if we're pushed back, defeated? No one has stood up to the Germans so far."

With a stern look, Vlásek picked up the France-Soir

newspaper lying on his desk, and jabbed at the headline: ONE MILLION AND A HALF FRENCHMEN IN UNIFORM. OUR COUNTRY IS READY FOR ANYTHING. "My dear Kohut" he said. "France is not *no-one*. The Nazis are outnumbered and the French have the magnificent Maginot defense system all along the northeast border." He let the newspaper slide to the floor. "If I sign you up now, you will immediately receive pay slips in the mail. You must bring them here to be cashed. That is, once our doctor has approved your fitness. What do you say, eh?"

With the prospect of some regular income, Willy was tempted to sign up right away. "What do I get paid?"

Vlásek's face transmitted regret. "Not much. This is a shoestring army we're putting together: a signing bonus of two hundred francs, sixty francs a week in Paris, and a few francs less when you are at the camp. There you get a uniform, good food, plenty of exercise, a bed and cigarettes."

Willy bit his lip. Not much. Still, every franc would help. "What if we're evacuated from France? Where do we go?"

"I can see you're a man who considers the possibilities," Vlásek said. "Obviously, you would head west. Maybe contact the Jewish and Czechoslovak Agencies in England or America. They've been renting steamships to move refugees from Europe to places like Latin America, the USA and Palestine."

Willy was tempted to sign immediately but he expected that Sophie would react badly to a *fait accompli*. She wouldn't want him to leave her. All the same, the opportunity to enlist in the Czechoslovak army-in-exile was his only viable option.

"I'll consider volunteering but I have to discuss it with my wife."

"Of course," said Vlásek crushing his cigarette and hastily pushing papers aside. "Here's the conscription form. Fill it out and sign your name at the bottom. Come back tomorrow and a secretary in the recruitment room will start the process." Vlásek looked intently at Willy. "You look pale. Eaten anything today?"

"No, not yet."

The official opened the capacious briefcase at his feet and retrieved a paper bag. "Here, friend, take this. I've already eaten two." Willy hesitated, took the bag and peeked inside: a large croissant. An enticing aroma of buttery flakes flooded his nose. He rose from his chair, swallowing the rush of saliva. "Thank you for this, sir. Most thoughtful."

"Wait a sec!" said Vlásek, scribbling some words on an official sheet of paper. He opened an ink pad, stamped the document and passed it across the desk. "I'm presuming you will enlist. This is an official request form for a residence permit and temporary identity cards for your family. As soon as you've passed your medical, take this to the Paris Police Commissioner's office at the Hôtel de Ville and hope for the best."

"Thank you." Willy paused. "There *is* one more thing." He opened his jacket, unbuttoned his shirt and pulled up the dressing. He watched the shock dawn on the official's face.

"My God." Vlásek's jaw dropped. He shuddered, averting his eyes. "Cover that awful thing up."

"The Nazis did this to me at the French frontier. You mentioned you had a doctor? Is he here? I need stitches."

Vlásek mopped his face, blinking rapidly. "*Pane bože,* goodness me, yes." He picked up the telephone.

Willy spent the next hour with Dr. Otmar Bartoš, in his mouse-hole office on the top floor of the Consulate building. The old general practitioner, whose work was confined to screening recruits, resurrected his old forceps, catgut, needle–holders and scissors from a black bag, and boiled them in a steel dish. "I was never much of seamstress," he grumbled as he closed the skin edges on

Willy's chest wound. He applied a fresh dressing and taped it. "Six mattress sutures, each one with an uncertain life-span. Don't blame me if they fall out and it doesn't heal properly."

"Thanks, doctor," Willy said as he picked up his shirt and jacket. "It might save time if you gave me the once-over now. I'm a new recruit. They want me for an administrative position and I need a medical approval of fitness."

Dr. Bartoš raised luxuriant eyebrows. "We only do fitness assessment on certain days of the week, in groups. You will have to come back when your wound is healed."

Willy hesitated, his mind racing. "Be a mensch, doctor. I've traveled all the way from Chartres to get here. I heal quickly … and the army needs me now. Let's get the intake exam over with. Anyway I don't have the money to travel more than this one time."

Pensively, the doctor massaged his chin with a cluster of fingers. "Hmm, all right then. You are a persuasive fellow, even though I'm not sure I believe you." The doctor picked up his stethoscope and pointed to an upright scale set against the wall. "Take everything off. Your weight first."

As Willy left the front doors of the Consulate, he started on Vlásek's croissant. He remembered that in France, eating on the street was frowned on as a lack of respect for food, but he didn't care. With the conscription form and residency application tucked in with his documents, he walked through the Trocadero Park, past the Tour Eiffel and along the Champs de Mars. His head buzzed with all the new information and the big decision almost taken. His chest throbbed like hell, but then Dr. Bartoš did not use any local anesthetic.

It was past eight in the evening when Willy got back to the hotel room. Sophie stared at him reproachfully. Pavel was asleep in a cot by the window. "Where have you been all this time?" she whispered fiercely. "I thought you had been arrested or robbed. Pavel threw a tantrum and I spanked him. You know how I detest doing that."

Her reaction, Willy thought, was perfectly justified. He wanted to make it up to her and defuse the anger so he could give her the good news. He put his arm around her but she shrugged him off. He tried again and managed a kiss on her forehead before she pushed him away. "Please, Sophie. Don't do this to me. I'm truly sorry. It was just as hard for me, you know. I was at the Consulate for over *nine* hours."

She slid off the bed and went to look out of the window. "You could have telephoned the hotel front desk," she said bitterly, "asked them to give me a message. I was worried to death."

"Look, there were hundreds of people there and they refused to let me use the telephone. I was moved from one office to another. I had nothing to eat the whole time—except that one of the Consulate officials was kind enough to give me one of his croissants." He paused, sensing her anger softening.

"When you hear about what happened, I'm sure you'll be pleased." He pulled out the voucher booklet and waved it in the air.

She looked away, as if determined to resist his wheedling. He spread a fan of documents on the bed coverlet. "Look, sweetheart: vouchers. This means we can eat one good meal a day for at least a month. And we have forms to request identity cards and a city residency permit from the mayor's office: documents to protect us from the police detention."

He wandered around the room hands clasped behind him, and came to a halt in front of her. He held out his hand as a peace offering. "You should be happy. My long wait was worth every minute—and deserving of a kiss from an annoyed spouse. How about forgiving me?"

Sophie sat down on the bed, silently twirling her black curls with a forefinger. She appeared mollified but her tight lips showed she was still annoyed. "Was that all you got for the nine-hour wait?"

"All? Come on, my dear. Don't be so snarky. I accomplished a lot more than getting vouchers. Their doctor sewed me up and then I was offered an opportunity that will benefit all of us."

A smile broke out on Sophie's face. "That's wonderful about your wound, *miláčku*. I've been worrying it won't heal properly. I hope it looks better."

"It's fine now. Now, please listen to me. Our worries are over,"

Willy described his meeting with Vlásek and catalogued the advantages and rewards of enlisting in the as-yet-unformed Czechoslovak Army-in-Exile. "I'll be paid a steady wage, get food and lodging, and there's something else ..." His eyes gleamed. "We get new Czech passports."

Sophie slowly shook her head, though a smile hovered on her lips. "Sounds too good to be true. Where's the fly in the ointment?" Willy took off his spectacles and studiously polished them. He looked at her with a winsome smile, reached for her hand and stroked it. "In the grand scheme of things," he said, kissing the tips of her fingers, "it's only one *little* fly. They want to send me south for military training while you and Pavel stay in Paris—until there's a place for you to live near the camp."

Sophie stiffened. "You mean you'll be surrounded by comrades-in-arms at the camp while Pavel and I struggle here on our own. That's horrible. I hardly speak French. It's not fair. How long do we have to stay here on our own?"

"A month, possibly six weeks."

She shuddered. "*Já se bojím.* I'm afraid to be alone."

She watched Willy's face turn stormy red.

"For God's sake, don't make it seem worse than it is. This is Paris, not Prague. Things happen, we take them in our stride, and then we adapt. I'll send you money and you'll have the food vouchers. Before I leave, I'll do my best to get you a Paris residency permit. Being a Czechoslovak soldier fighting with the French should help me cut through red tape at the mayor's office. Anyway, I didn't actually sign anything at the Consulate. I wanted to discuss it with you."

She sat cross-legged on the bed in her newly washed, second-hand slip, hands on her knees, pouting. "Talking is fine, Willy. But what happens if your arrangements don't work? What if they reject you because of your ruined finger?" She began to tremble, pulling at the bed cover. "How can you trust what those Consulate bureaucrats say after what we've been through? It sounds so strange, a Czechoslovak army in France."

Willy bit his lip. "Look, sweetheart, they can't reject me, because the doctor I saw today signed the medical approval form. Besides, we're in almost the same situation as when I was mobilized in Prague, before the Sudeten crisis. You handled the danger then, so why not now? I'm doing this to provide for you and Pavel. I'm proud to be able to fight for my country and France. I think you should do your part and support my decision without hesitation."

Sophie walked to the window and looked out at the dusk over Paris. Above the rooftops, purple and gold streaks scissored the sky. What more was there to discuss? She could tell from Willy's glowing eyes and his determined mouth that she couldn't change his mind. The memory of her day of aloneness in the hotel room lingered and a wave of self-pity threatened to spill from her chest in a flood of tears. They had only just reached Paris and Willy was planning to split their family apart.

She turned to look at him, admitting to herself that he had made a sensible, logical choice. What if he hadn't gone to the Consulate? They would have no food vouchers and he would never have heard about enlisting. Their only alternative would have been to stick together and beg for assistance from the Jewish refugee center in the Marais.

She put her arms around his neck. "I could not help being angry and my stomach was hurting," she breathed as she put her cheek against his. "I should not have been so tetchy."

Willy smiled at her. "All right then. Let's forgive each other."

She smiled and kissed his ear. "Agreed."

Willy frowned. "Are you still bleeding?"

She shook her head and gave him a hopeful look. "The pain is better than it was."

Willy lowered his gaze. "There's something else I learned, my dear. I wasn't going to tell you but …"

"Something bad, I can tell."

"Hans Lessig…"

Sophie's head jerked back.

"Yes, that bastard. He's here. He signed up with the Czechoslovak army a couple of weeks ago."

Sophie turned away so he could not see her face—could not see her expression of alarm. The memory of Lessig's blackmail and fumbling assault in their apartment blanketed her mind. What if Willy found Lessig and they talked?

CHAPTER FIVE

Waiting
Paris. August & September 1939

Through the early days of August, the Kohuts remained at the Hôtel St. Pierre, subsisting on what cash was left from the sale of Willy's gold coins. He returned to the Czechoslovak Consulate to have his stitches removed and find out if Vlásek had any news. As usual, the place teemed with refugees and officials were too busy to see him without another long wait. Willy decided to give up; the consulate was too exhausting and depressing.

By the fifteenth of the month, still waiting for news of his army call-up, Willy calculated they had only enough money for ten more days. The room cost seventy-five francs a night, breakfast was thirty. Only the two course lunch *menu du jour* they shared at the Café du Soleil was covered by vouchers. For dinner, they ate half-price day-old baguettes, cheap pâté and damaged fruit culled from the market stalls.

Waiting patiently for the first pay slip to arrive from the Czechoslovak Consulate, the Kohuts filled their days with walks through the *quartier* where hundreds of refugees lived on the streets, camping on doorsteps, occupying park benches or sleeping under the giant plane trees that lined the nearby boulevards. The family walked the quays of the Seine, observing the barges and *bateaux mouches* while Pavel chased pigeons, scavenged for dropped coins and admired the fishermen. They did their best to stay far from gendarmes on patrol and turned it into a game with Pavel. Willy would give him a ten-centime reward for spotting the uniforms.

On Sundays, they visited the flower and bird market on the Quai de la Corse. It seemed as though every conceivable avian species from France and her colonies was available for purchase: parrots, canaries, pigeons, ducks and geese. A donkey ride for Pavel on the Champs Elysées cost a precious five francs; the carousel in the Tuileries was only two francs. The free Punch and Judy outdoor show in the Jardins de Luxembourg was Pavel's favorite. When the show ended, more often than not, he demanded a repeat performance. When the curtain stayed closed Sophie never knew what might follow, sullen acceptance or a tantrum.

On several occasions, still hoping to get the vital residency permit, Willy took his certificate of military enlistment to the Paris mayor's office. On the two occasions when he had waited long enough to reach an official's desk, he was met with a request for a 'donation' of five hundred francs. "To smooth the way," the official said with a wink and a twirl of his mustache. "It guarantees your next step in the application."

Willy gave up. He had no bribe money—so why bother?

On the way home he noticed posters near the Metro stations showing the crossed flags of France and Czechoslovakia, encouraging citizens of Czechoslovak origin to enlist in the Army-in-Exile. He was reassured; what Vlasék had offered him was endorsed by the Parisian authorities.

The Kohuts could see that, all over the city, defense preparations were in full swing. Walls of sandbags protected statues and government buildings. One morning they were lucky enough to watch a crane installing an anti-aircraft battery on top of the Arc de Triomphe; an hour of thrilling entertainment for Pavel.

They saw soldiers everywhere, standing guard, marching, climbing into open trucks and, of course, relaxing at café terraces. In addition to the usual traffic, convoys of military trucks and horse-drawn artillery pieces often wound their way along the boulevards. At Pavel's insistence, the Kohuts could not leave until each convoy was out of sight.

"Why do you like those big guns on wheels so much?" Willy asked.

Eyes sparkling, Pavel held his nose with two fingers. "I like to see the horses pull and do pooh."

At the end of August, Willy's anxieties piled up. Why hadn't the Czechoslovak passports and his pay slip arrived? Was the plan for a Czechoslovak army to train in the south really going to happen? And the big question. Was France going to fight Germany?

Sophie tried to distract him. "Come with us to the Marché Mouffetard, *miláčku*," she would often beg. "Just before it closes at noon everything is much cheaper; charcuterie and cheese go for half price. Pavel loves to find damaged fruit and tomatoes behind the stalls even though the vendors scold him. It sounds silly but I enjoy it too; it's like a treasure hunt."

"I'm not going to spend my time poking around the market," Willy said. "Do you see any other men picking over boxes of rotten fruit? No. Well, maybe a few beggars, but not me. I'm humiliated enough trying to make ends meet and dealing with Pavel's public tantrums. I prefer the Café du Soleil—I can get a drink, listen to the gossip and pick up useful tips. In fact, I have a regular rendezvous there with a couple of Czechoslovak refugees and a Parisian, Monsieur Amédée Dupuis. He has connections and I'm hoping he can help with the residency permits."

Sophie's face brightened. "Really? How can he help?"

"He's a parliamentary *deputé* from Amiens: about my

father's age, a dapper widower. He insists his information about France's intentions is more reliable than the dross put out by the newspapers. He told me he had friends at the Hotel de Ville. I'm waiting for the right moment to ask him. To get a favor from a Frenchman, you need either money or a solid friendship."

Sophie smiled at him. Her tone was sardonic. "I suppose that's why you spend so much time at the café talking and drinking."

Willy raised defensive hands. "Come now, sweetheart. One cognac per hour isn't much … and I'm getting an education." He remembered Dupuis's conversation with his cronies the previous day.

"I suspect, *mon ami*," Monsieur Dupuis said, downing yet another *petit blanc*, "that the Germans will waltz into Poland as they please."

Willy stared, his cognac halfway to his lips. This was not what the newspapers reported. They crowed that the Western Alliance with over one hundred divisions would easily smash the Germans if they were arrogant enough to attack Poland. And he wondered why this silver-haired *deputé* believed the newspapers were wrong? "Why do you say this, Monsieur?"

"Because *mon ami*," said Dupuis, breaking off a piece of baguette and spreading it with jam, "our French generals are toothless lions trapped in the old strategies of the Great War. They embrace defense and a war of attrition. The Germans have superb up-to-date equipment. For example, they use the tanks and guns that your country Czechoslovakia built and handed over—without a fight, I might add. *Les Boches* want to avenge the beating they got from us in 1918."

* * *

On August 23rd, the French Government announced a new *alerte* and called up 360,000 army reservists. Britain did the same, instituted rationing and announced a plan to move children out of London in case of bombing.

That same day, in the afternoon, Mademoiselle Houlot, the nosy concierge of the St. Pierre Hotel, handed Willy a thick brown envelope. "It's from your Czechoslovak Consulate," she said, studying the print in the left upper corner. She gave him an accusing look as she felt the package with thin fingers. "It feels important. Passports, hunh? Are you *refugiés* about to disappear? If so, I need a week's notice or you lose your deposit."

"Disappear, Madame?" said Willy contemptuously. "Of course not. I will be fighting with the Czechoslovak army to help defend your precious France. We are Allies."

"I expect yours is only a little army," she said curling her lip as she walked off.

Up in their room, he opened the packet and with a broad smile gave Sophie a new booklet of food vouchers. "At last, another month's worth of food and my first pay slip to be cashed at the Consulate. And look, we're genuine Czechoslovaks again. Everything is fine." He pulled out two new passports and then handed her a sheet of paper bearing the Czechoslovak coat of arms. "Orders. I've been assigned to the Third Infantry Regiment. I leave from the Gare de Lyon on October fifteenth."

She scanned the text. "My God, six in the morning! We'll have to be up by five."

He hugged her. "You and Pavel don't have to see me off at the station. I'll get the pay slip cashed tomorrow. A soldier's pay—just saying that feels good after all this waiting."

She slipped her arms around Willy's waist and rested her head on his shoulder. "I would love for our life to be predictable, *miláčku*, if only for a little while. Soon you'll leave and we'll be on our own."

He stroked her hair. "I know you are sad, sweetheart, but I don't expect it will be for long."

A small embroidered badge had slipped out of the envelope on to the chair seat. Willy handed the badge to Pavel. "Look at this, Pavelko. It means I'm going to be a *voják*, a Czechoslovak private. I'll put this on to my uniform—when I get one." He winked at Sophie. "Pity I don't know how to sew."

Pavel put the badge into his shirt pocket. "Pavel want be soldier with *Táta*," he said, shaking the envelope to see if there was anything more inside. With a clunk, a metal chain fell to the floor. He picked it up, eyes gleaming. "For me?"

Sophie examined it and handed it to Willy. "A bracelet … with your name on it. What's it for?"

Willy held out his hand. "Identification—in case I get lost or end up in the wrong place. See, on the back, my number is A1508." He guessed she didn't know the bracelet's main purpose was to identify a dead soldier.

Everything changed on September 1. Without warning or any declaration of hostilities, Heinkel 111 fighters and Stuka dive-bombers entered Polish airspace and indiscriminately bombed villages. Panzer divisions swarmed into western Poland, followed by the SS who set about massacring peaceful civilians—"cleansing and control operations against trouble-makers" was the expression used by Nazi propaganda in their radio and newspaper reports.

In France, the government ordered a general mobilization and posted bulletins on all the public buildings. Belgium mobilized 650,000 men. Britain passed a law of compulsory military service and evacuated 650,000 adults and children from London to the countryside. French newspapers *France-Soir* and *Le Matin* carried rumors that wealthy Belgians and Parisians were emptying their bank accounts and making plans to move to the South of France or abroad.

Willy and Sophie could hardly bring themselves to talk about the brutal invasion of Poland. A war between the Allies and Germany was now almost inevitable and they were, once again, trapped by circumstances, made all the more unreal by the beautiful, hot days of Paris in summer.

Two days later, Willy, Sophie and Pavel took coffee and were sharing a pear tart in the Café du Soleil when *le patron* turned on the radio to hear the Minister of the Interior speak. France and Britain, he said in somber, measured tones had a duty to intervene on Poland's behalf. If the Germans did not immediately cease their invasion, war was inevitable. The café exploded with noise, discussion and expletives.

When Willy translated the ultimatum, Sophie burst into tears. "What will happen now? What can we do?"

"I'm not sure, my darling," he said patting her hand, though he felt his stomach turning over as he tried to keep fear out of his voice. "Unless the Germans withdraw from Poland, I expect France will go to war." He transferred Pavel onto his lap and gave him an extra piece of tart. He couldn't bear to look at Sophie's face. "If the war comes and, God forbid, the Germans prevail, they'll surely occupy Paris and plunder the industrial north. There's nothing much to grab in the south except wheat, cows and vineyards. So you see, if we go to the South of France with the Free Czechoslovak Army we will be out of danger—with a good chance of getting to England."

Sophie gave him a withering stare. "*Miláčku*, you said you would leave me and Pavel in Paris, while you're down there, training? With a war on! What if the Luftwaffe start bombing here? What if Pavel gets sick? Better we come with you straightaway and stay in the camp, or close by, anywhere will do. I don't care how rough it is."

Willy flashed a conciliatory smile and drew her close. "I

understand how you feel, sweetheart. Let's wait and see how things develop over the next few days."

When the Kohuts returned to the hotel, their sharp-tongued concierge announced that France had just declared war on Germany and that the *Athenia*, an unarmed cruise ship, carrying thirteen hundred passengers from Glasgow to Canada had been torpedoed by a U-boat. Many had drowned. "*Une tragédie*," she said sorrowfully. "The *Boches* are savages. No respect for human life." She gave Willy an apologetic look. "Maybe your little Czech army will be needed after all."

* * *

"What I find strange," Monsieur Dupuis told Willy a few days later at the Café du Soleil, "is that, now that war has been declared, the Germans do not want to fight us." They were standing at the bar, surrounded by a lunchtime crowd. "Poland is being destroyed, but the German Panzers on *our* frontier sit on their backsides, oiling their guns. Only in the Atlantic is there war. U-boats are attacking the supply convoys sent from America."

"What do your political contacts say? What is France's strategy?"

Dupuis's eyes narrowed. He shrugged as if surprised by Willy's naivety. "*Mais bien sûr, mon ami*, we have a huge mobilization of resources. All factories switch to war production. The government has taken control of the railways and gasoline supplies. It is organizing mass evacuations from the north. As for fighting—we make small forays across into Germany to satisfy public opinion. Our soldiers man the Maginot defenses, our air-force has intercepted a few Luftwaffe airplanes and a French tank division crossed the eastern border. It's frankly pathetic. To me everything feels defensive and short-sighted."

"Why is this?"

Monsieur Dupuis tapped his forehead with a derisive finger. "We declared war, but France's stomach is not to fight—only to swallow food and wine. We are afraid. The memory of the Great War's slaughter haunts us." He banged his glass on the table and waved at *le patron* for a refill.

This was not what Willy had wanted to hear. "Surely your leaders can whip up France's patriotism. The legacy of Napoleon's great campaigns, you know…"

"*Ah, mon ami,* we have no single philosophy of governing in this country. Some groups believe in fascism, others believe in communism, and the rest have little respect for our leaders." M. Dupuis, watching his glass being replenished, took a pipe from his breast pocket and began to stuff the bowl with tobacco.

A craggy-faced man wearing a stained beret turned to face them, beer in hand. "Communism is what this country needs, comrade," he said in a hoarse voice. "This war is the result of Jewish bankers looking for profits. I can tell you this. French workers will refuse to fight a capitalist-fascist war driven by the elites."

The *deputé* grabbed the man's arm. Willy could tell they knew each other well. "*Alors,* Roland. You're a blind idiot. If we don't fight the Germans, Stalin will team up with Hitler and they will both suck France dry. Who do you love more, Stalin or France? Now, please, stick your nose back into your own beer, not someone else's."

As the patron served Monsieur Dupuis his third Pernod, Willy shook his head. "So why isn't there more fighting? What is going on?"

"Because, *mon ami,* the French and British are ill-prepared. They need time to modernize and build up their armaments. For the moment, it is a war of talk and posturing. *Une drôle de guerre.* The phoney war, the Americans call it."

* * *

With Willy's army pay in hand, the Kohuts moved to a cleaner hotel, La Florida, on Rue Thenard near the Jardins de Luxembourg. The family abandoned the Café du Soleil—which was now too far away—and ate their daily lunch on Café Montfort's seedy terrace, next to the Florida's main entrance. The café was a simple, grubby place, undecorated except for an oversized sepia photograph of the owner, Marcel Fontaine, one arm clamped on his bicycle handlebars, the other hung around the shoulders of a *stage* winner at the 1930 Tour de France. There was the usual café *zinc* bar, above which wooden shelves displayed dust-covered bottles containing unusual liquors and mysterious herbal aperitifs collected from distant corners of France.

Madame Fontaine, the proprietor's wife, cooked a different *plat du jour* for each day of the week. As was the case for many Parisians and foreigners renting cramped rooms, the Café Montfort acted as the Kohuts' living and dining room—and their communication center. It offered a telephone, newspapers, radio broadcasts, and gossip.

Didine, the proprietor's eight-year-old daughter, included Pavel in her make-believe games and stories in the unused back *salon* which housed crates of potatoes and carrots, dried goods and restaurant supplies—and an old upright piano. Often, other children ate at the café with their parents and joined Didine and Pavel in their games.

While Pavel played in the adjacent *salon*, Willy fell into the habit of taking a leisurely cup of coffee, studying the roller newspapers and listening to workmen arguing over their beers. And, of course, there was always *le patron* Marcel reminiscing about his one and only ride in the Tour.

Periodically, Willy checked on the children and even though it was badly out of tune, he would tinker with the piano, running arpeggios with his left hand, picking out tunes with four fingers of the right.

As the days passed, he cast aside the fear that he would never play well again. Sophie and Pavel both loved to hear him on the piano, and for their sake—and for his own spirit—he was determined to recoup at least some competence. For nearly an hour each day, Willy exercised his damaged little finger, bending and stretching its stiff joints with his other hand. For half an hour he would hit a key with his damaged finger in an attempt to harden the skin and strengthen the muscles. It was painful and frustrating, but soaking in hot water helped the stretching—and he toughened the skin afterward by dipping it in a glass of cognac.

He made progress. His ultimate goal was to use both hands without the shame of frequent mistakes and false notes. *Le patron* not only allowed Willy open access to the *salon* in the daytime hours, he encouraged him to learn some popular songs from the radio. He even brought in sheet music for the current patriotic hit, "Ça Fait d'Excellents Français" sung by Maurice Chevalier: a ditty designed to boost public morale after the mobilization.

Willy worked on scales, chords and timing in the salon while he waited for the weekly scheduled telephone call from his parents in London, or he would pore over old magazines and newspapers that Marcel never bothered to throw away. Some were over ten years old and reading them brought back memories of Willy's student days in Paris: days of independence, wildness and lust.

*   *   *

September in Paris started out dry and dusty, and the Phoney

War dragged on. The city was full of uncertainty about what the Germans would do after crushing Poland. On September 17, the British aircraft carrier *Courageous* was sunk by a U-boat and over five hundred sailors drowned. From then on, U-boats continued to sink British shipping at an alarming rate. Finally, a British Expeditionary Force of 186,000 men crossed the Channel and was defensively deployed along the French-Belgian border. The phoney war had turned into a real one.

Willy's parents wrote from London that there were now 70,000 Jewish refugees in the city and the government had set up internment camps for the 80,000 enemy aliens, mostly Austrian and German residents in Britain, before shipping them to Canada and Australia.

The Kohuts watched Paris wake up from her summer torpor as *la bourgeoisie* straggled back from their vacations at the Atlantic and Mediterranean beaches. Theaters, cabarets, cinema, concert halls and the Opera Garnier opened their doors. Even if they had wanted to attend a concert they could not afford the tickets— besides, what would they do with Pavel? They made limited forays to different *quartiers,* browsing the open markets and book stalls on the banks of the Seine, hungrily watching other people buy food, books and knick-knacks. Willy did his best to show Sophie the city while spending as little money as possible. It was eight francs to travel on the metro or the bus. Even the *taxis-bicyclettes* that carried two passengers charged the equivalent of ten fresh eggs. They walked everywhere.

The Hôtel Florida had no refrigerator so Sophie took Pavel to the Marché Mouffetard or the Rue Monge market for fresh milk and bread—and if they could afford it, a couple of slices of charcuterie. The noisy bustle and vivid colors of the stalls piled high with summer vegetables was an antidote to her anticipation of Willy leaving. Thanks to her willingness to ask the names and the meanings of words, she soon learned simple French phrases from the vendors. The market women insisted on correcting her stumbling words and passed on recipes for the food she was buying. She never understood, but nodded as if she did, feeling embarrassed but excited. The human contact softened her feeling of isolation.

In the ensuing weeks, Sophie resurrected some of her high school French and grew confident enough to attempt conversations with other mothers she met while walking Pavel in the parks. More often than not she was rebuffed or ignored.

"Refugees are not welcome in France," she often said to Willy. "If only I had another woman to talk to, a friend. It would help so much."

He would hug her. "I'm your friend and I love you, but I understand what you mean. There are too many refugees here, all looking for food and help. Don't despair. Something good will turn up for us."

CHAPTER SIX

Café Budapest
Paris. September/October 1939

At Café Montfort, sheltering from the mid-day heat in front of a brass fan, Willy showed Sophie the heading of a small column on the third page of *France-Soir*:

CLASSES AT THE SORBONNE MEDICAL SCHOOL RECOMMENCE

"Cousin Feri might be back in Paris," He smiled at her hopefully. "Shall we…?"

Two hours later they were at the same *bureau* where they had been rebuffed. This time a different receptionist told them that Feri was now a medical assistant in an army medical unit at the Ouvrage Hackenberg, a huge Maginot defense complex in the Moselle *département*. There was no way to contact him. He wouldn't be back for a long time. In low spirits and with the sun burning their faces, they trudged along the Rue de Carmes, back towards the Metro.

It was then that Sophie noticed a vivid and intricately painted sign set above a glass-fronted door: two dancers in traditional Hungarian dress—above them, a sign: PATISSERIE. On either side of the partly opened door, store windows displayed baguettes and special breads stacked on the right, and on the left, cakes and pastries set on shelves.

She looked at Willy in delight. "What a lovely sign, *miláčku*.

63

They're dancing the *czárdás*."

Willy shrugged. "It's just a bakery, sweetheart. Come on, let's get home. I've had enough of this heat."

Sophie's eyes gleamed. "No … I smell something … something special … something we love."

Willy went to the open door. He sniffed and his face broke into a smile. "Sophie, you're right, definitely. That aroma… it has to be … I know… it's goulash. Here in Paris." He took Pavel's hand and drew him closer to the window display. "Look at those, delicious-looking cakes. What a discovery!"

Pavel pulled on Willy's hand. "Come on *Táta*, I want some."

Willy chuckled as he stepped aside, motioning Sophie and Pavel to go inside. "We lose Feri and we're sad and miserable. We see cakes and smell goulash and, *voilà*, we're happy."

A brass bell jingled as they entered, sniffing at the aromas of freshly baked bread, cinnamon, and coffee. Old photographs of Vienna and Budapest hung on faded pink walls. A customer, tall and well-dressed, stood at the counter opposite a diminutive, older woman in a pinafore and lace cap who was sliding a glazed plum tart into a pastry box.

Sophie nudged Willy. "Look at the picture on the lid. The same dancers … and the name—CAFÉ BUDAPEST."

After the customer had left, Willy ordered two coffees and a glass of warm milk for Pavel. He spoke to the old woman in Hungarian.

Her eyes glistened with pleasure. "*Jó napot*, good day," she said rubbing her hands together in delight. "I am always happy to meet Hungarians from the old country. Are you refugees? There are more and more of them in Paris." She sighed, wiping the counter with a cloth. "It is sad. Most of them are too poor to buy our pastries. Please … take a seat and I'll bring your order to the table. I am Madame Szigeti. My husband is the baker."

Sophie gave her a radiant smile. "I was born in Hungary but my husband is a Czechoslovak. We just arrived in Paris."

"In fact, we are both Czechoslovak citizens, from Prague," said Willy quickly, frowning at Sophie. Hungary supported Hitler's policies. The last thing he wanted was to be mistaken for a Nazi sympathizer.

Madame Szigeti waved a finger at him. "But you speak perfect Hungarian."

Sophie looked around the café, took a deep breath and let go of Pavel's hand. "Please, we would like to look at everything your husband has baked. It smells and looks so good."

The baker's wife patted the colorful kerchief that imprisoned a mass of gray curly hair. "Take your time. You will see that we also sell cooked food … here in the heated cabinet. Eat here or take it home. Today I have chicken goulash, piroshky, stuffed cabbage, noodles and sauerkraut."

"Wonderful. But I really want to look at your pastries." Sophie inspected the contents of the glass case beneath the counter. She laughed exultantly. "Look, Willy. Everything we love is here: strudels, croissants, hazelnut and chocolate cakes, fruit tarts and spiced cookies. Now we know where to come for home baking and cooking. What a marvelous change from the Café Montfort."

"Hunh, if only we had the spare francs to eat here," he said, reaching down to prevent Pavel from grabbing a cookie through a gap in the display case.

"I want that," Pavel said, pointing a grubby finger, "and that."

Madame Szigeti chuckled. "Your boy reminds me of my grandson Stefan," she said, trying to control the twisting curtain of hair over her forehead and eyes. She placed a cake with a dark topping on the counter. "How about this one? My husband baked it this morning. *Dobos torte*. Five layers of filling, ground hazel nut paste on the sides and caramelized, crunchy icing on the top." She crinkled her eyes at Pavel. "I'm sure you could eat a slice. Do you know Hungarian, little boy?"

"No, he doesn't," said Sophie, noticing that both of the woman's hands were swollen and distorted. Some kind of arthritis, she thought. "He only speaks Czech. Of course, now we've arrived in Paris, we'll have to learn French—my husband is already fluent."

"Poor boy. He must be getting confused." Mme. Szigeti straightened her apron which had slipped below her plump midriff. "Now, about the *Dobos*. Nowhere else in Paris can you get anything like this. Please, try some."

Sophie looked hopefully at Willy. Cake was a luxury.

"Just this once," he said, with a frown, taking out his wallet. "It's twelve francs a slice, so we'll share it. Three forks, please."

Madame Szigeti sighed as she cut three separate slices and slid them on to plates.

"Oh, no," said Sophie quickly. "My husband said only one slice."

Mme. Szigeti looked at them with twinkling eyes. "As you are from the old country you get a slice each and there's no charge … this time. But, I know you will return. They come from all over Paris to buy my husband's *Dobos*..."

A tall stooped man in a white apron, Sophie guessed he was in his fifties, appeared behind her. "*Bonjour*," he said with a sideways twitch of his head and a flash of gold teeth.

"This is my husband, Andreas," said Mme. Szigeti with a flourish of her fingers. "When you come back next time, you can call me Rózsi."

Andreas Szigeti wiped his fingers on a towel, leaned across the counter and offered a large hand to Willy. "*Üdvözlöm*," he said in a low thrumming tone that sounded as if it had originated in a beehive. "How do you do. I'm the baker." His head jerked again. He laughed and tapped his temple with a finger. "I see concern on your face, sir. Be reassured. This twitch of mine is not a disease—simply a permanent gift of war: a French grenade on the Siegfried Line."

"I too have an injury," said Willy, just before they shook hands. "So please squeeze gently. I damaged my little finger in Prague. I'm trying to get it strong and moving so I can play piano again. I exercise it on an old piano in a bistro … almost every day."

Andreas gave him a thoughtful look. "That's frustrating. You do exercises, or what?"

Willy shrugged. "I just move it as far as it will go, stretch it, hot-water soaks, that kind of thing."

The baker rubbed at his mustache, flecked white with grains of flour. "Not enough, my friend. You should be working it against resistance." He paused, rummaged in a drawer and pulled out a handful of flat brass discs of different sizes and laid them on the counter. "Baking weights—ten to one hundred grams. I don't use 'em any more. Have your pretty wife make a little bag, put the weights in and suspend it from your finger. Lift it up and down for half an hour, three times a day, minimum. Take as many as you want."

Sophie clapped her hands. "That's a wonderful idea. I'll sew the bag for you."

Smiling, Willy selected three weights and pocketed them. "Two hundred and fifty grams should do it. Thanks. You are a very thoughtful baker."

One hour later, after many cups of coffee, another round of pastries and occasional interruptions to serve new customers, the two women had forged a friendship. Sophie could not stop talking, explaining how they escaped from Prague, traveled to Budapest and were driven by a smuggler from there across Germany. At last, she had someone she could respect and confide in: a woman, a benevolent mother figure really.

The Kohuts patronized Café Budapest almost daily, relying on Café Montfort for local telephone calls, Pavel's playmates, Willy's piano practice and city gossip. Café Budapest was different, catering to a variety of Central European customers who dropped in for pastries or hot food. The café was a hub of news from Czechoslovakia, Hungary, even Germany. It was not long before Sophie began to help Rózsi Szigeti with some of the tasks that often made her arthritic hands worse, particularly in the mornings when they were stiff and painful.

"It's so sweet of you to help me, Sophie," Rózsi said one morning as Sophie set out the pastries while Pavel accompanied Willy to the Czechoslovak Consulate to sign his volunteer's loyalty pledge to France. "I've had this arthritis fifteen years. My mother had the same thing."

"I love helping you. It's like being with family."

"Andreas and I were talking about how we could thank you for helping here. The least we can do is to feed you and give you and Willy some time to yourselves. You can explore Paris, and—be a man and wife together." Rózsi winked. "You know… without having the boy in the same room…or the same bed for that matter. We can keep an eye on him here."

Sophie shook her head. "I don't think you will want Pavel to be in your way, Rózsi. He can be a handful. I don't think your customers will enjoy a three year-old running about."

Rózsi chuckled. "He does no harm. After so many years separated from our family, I will be happy with a little boy to cuddle and spoil: a replacement for my grandson." She blinked away tears.

"Pavel loves you already," said Sophie. "I'm so happy we found you. Now he and I won't feel so alone when Willy goes off to join the army."

"And don't you worry about your husband," shouted Andreas, eavesdropping from the bakery ovens. "Hitler's craziness will be over soon enough. The French will smack him down. Then you can all go home to Prague."

Pavel loved Café Budapest. The Szigetis said he never cried or threw a fit when Willy and Sophie left him there—probably because he was absorbed by the constant stream of customers, mostly women who commented effusively, in French, on his blond curls and the innocent look in his sky blue eyes. He spent three afternoons a week at the café without his parents. He made the rounds of the coffee tables, engaging the customers in Czech and learning a few French words as time went by. He clambered on and off a high stool that Andreas had placed next to the cash register and watched people give their orders. Pavel learned bakery French, mimicking the words and phrases Rózsi used when they bought bread or *pâtisseries*. He would say, *"Bonjour M'sieu, Madame,"* when they entered the café and *"Merci à vous, Madame,"* when they left. Rózsi, who spoke some Czech, reinforced his learning with translations, explanations and by drawing pictures. Willy insisted that the Szigetis spoke French with Sophie and Pavel. "The faster my family learns, the easier they'll manage when I'm gone."

With Willy's and Sophie's amused approval, Andreas offered Pavel the job of bakery detective. The baker thought it might give the boy something else to do other than play with his old toys, get in the way or watch the flow of customers from his observation post on the stool. The idea was to spot the occasional Sorbonne student who tried to filch cookies when the café was crowded at lunch-time.

"When you sit on your stool," Andreas said to Pavel, "and you see someone taking a pastry without paying, you tell Auntie Rózsi. Shout *voleur*—robber! Understand? You will be our gendarme. Would you like this job?"

Pavel nodded as he turned to his father. "What is...? Gendarme, *Táta*?"

After listening to his father's explanation, Pavel nodded gravely and accepted the position—and when he was not *on duty*, as Sophie called it, the boy played in an under-stair alcove partially filled with cardboard boxes, watching Andreas prepare and mix the dough. The boxes contained a treasure trove of old games: playing cards, dominoes, puzzles and small blocks of wood.

One day Pavel actually caught a cookie thief, a student nurse from a nearby clinic—a noisy incident that turned out to be very embarrassing for everyone. That was the end of Pavel's role as pastry gendarme. Andreas held a formal ceremony of thanks and awarded Pavel an old brass baker's weight with instructions to polish till it glowed.

"The Szigetis have been so kind and generous to us," Sophie said as they climbed on to the 24 autobus headed for Montparnasse. "What if I worked behind the counter at the café—with Rózsi—regularly, I mean? I see in her eyes how much pain she is in. A few hours here and there would give her a rest. I can keep an eye on Pavel at the same time."

"And you'll learn a bit of French from the customers and the radio that Andreas keeps on all the time," Willy said with an approving laugh as he hugged and kissed her. "Immersion ... a splendid way to learn. The Szigetis will keep you busy. All this makes me feel less worried about leaving you in Paris."

"About you leaving ... there is something at the café that is making me nervous," Sophie said as they all sat together near the front of the bus. "There's a young policeman who often comes to the café. He's nice, always joking. Rózsi calls him François. The other day he came in with an older gendarme, his supervisor. No smiles, just poker faces. I stayed in the bakery helping Andreas form the dough. When the supervisor found out that Pavel, who was on his stool, didn't speak French he asked Rózsi questions.

Where were the parents ... did they have identity cards and a residency permit?"

"Damn. What did she say?"

"She said was minding Pavel for a friend visiting from outside Paris."

With a gloomy look, Willy took her hand. "I'll try the mayor's office again."

"But, *miláčku*, you are leaving soon. What happens when that gendarme comes back? He said he would. He sounded very suspicious. *Agent* François looked embarrassed, Rózsi said."

"You'll just have to keep out of sight. Rószi must persuade that friendly *flic* to keep his supervisor away."

"You can't expect us to play hide and seek with the police for six weeks. And it's not fair on the Szigetis."

"What else is there?"

* * *

"Tell me about the bread you bake," Sophie said to Andreas one day as she helped him stack the bread shelves behind the counter and in the window. As usual, she was breaking Willy's rules, talking in Hungarian instead of French. "We always bought the same style loaves in Prague. But here, bakers like you make bread with different grains and in different shapes. Why?"

He hoisted a long apron over his undershirt, tightened the frayed cord round his cotton pants and slipped on wooden clogs. "Let's go into the bakery and I'll explain."

A smile crossed his lined face. "I started as an apprentice at the age of thirteen so there's not much I don't know about baking. So ... what shall I say about bread? Well ... the shape of each loaf is a message, like a mariner's flag. The shape signals taste and grain and must be easily recognizable by the customer. You must understand my dear, that in France bread is regulated: Napoléon's doing. All the long breads are raised in cloth-lined baskets before baking. This *baguette*, for example, must be sixty centimeters long and a standard diameter, six centimeters. No preservatives like vinegar or sugar are permitted, which is why it goes stale after a day."

"What about these other sizes?"

He told her about the *flûte,* half the length of a baguette, the *bâtard* and the ultra-thin *ficelle.*"

"And those big round ones with the deep cuts on the top?"

"Hunh! Feel the weight of it. We call that a *Boule Miche,* a pan loaf. A family can live on this for several days. I also bake pumpernickel, rye, sourdough, and *challah* loaves to go with the Hungarian and German dishes Rózsi cooks."

"More complicated than I thought," said Sophie watching Pavel chew on the end of a *ficelle.* "How many different kinds of bread are there?"

Andreas roared with laughter. "You mean in the world? Who knows? There are three hundred different kinds of bread baked in Europe. Wouldn't it be wonderful if the Nazis baked bread instead of making guns, eh?"

Sophie didn't respond. A thought circled in her head: here was an opportunity to learn how to bake. She was a novice in the kitchen, After Willy's arrest in Prague and the departure of their domestics, she had been forced for the first time in their marriage, to cook in their apartment—also for his two cousins who helped in the store. Their kind but unjustified flattery lasted less than a week. With her head full of worries about how they could leave Prague, with Willy being injured and still weak, she threw ingredients together, not bothering to follow her mother-in-law's recipes. It was too much like school homework. Her more vital and time-consuming task was to run Willy's store.

Another possibility was to ask Rózsi to teach her how to cook. That would be daunting, for the baker's wife was just as precise as her husband in following her recipes—and Sophie preferred the idea of flair and experimentation.

By spending more time at the café, Sophie learned that Andreas's right leg had been shattered by shrapnel in the Great War. He walked with a permanent sway. That and the jerking of his head always attracted strange looks on the street. He preferred to stay inside the café, tending to the breads and confectionary while he listened to the powerful short-wave Philips radio that brought news from different European stations. Even though he cocooned himself in the bakery, Andreas, fluent in Hungarian, German and French, was as well-informed as any Parisian newspaperman.

One day, late in the afternoon, Sophie was in the bakery kitchen, scrubbing the giant ceramic mixing bowls and iron baking pans, listening to the radio and chatting with Andreas. Willy had taken Pavel to the quays along the Seine, near Notre Dame, to watch the barges and fishermen.

"I have been listening to two new radio stations from Germany," Andreas remarked as he levered baguettes out of their pans. "Propaganda—both in French, both full of lies. The one from Stuttgart says our industries are decrepit and that we mustn't trust our neighbors because they might be spies. The other one calls itself *L'Humanité*, the same name as the banned Communist newspaper. They want French factory workers to go on strike."

"Why do you listen to such rubbish?"

He shrugged. "We are deluged with propaganda … from both sides. But, y'know, those Nazi broadcasts sometimes reveal a few nuggets of truth. Now, hand me those baking pans. I have to start on the Black Forests. Have you prepared the fillings?"

Sophie nodded and was glad to change the subject. She didn't want to listen to any nuggets of truth. "It's interesting. Some very elegant customers come to Café Budapest," she said. "But, I have to say that the Budapest is not elegant. It's nice and homey … bourgeois. Is it because you are famous that the rich people come to you from all over Paris?"

Andreas, whose glum face hid a genial disposition, gave her a crooked smile. He had started on cutting warm apple and nut strudel rolls into angled slices. "I'm not really famous, my dear." He gave her shy smile. "But I do have a reputation for the best and most expensive Hungarian pastries in France. Let's see now," he said, running floury fingers through the sparse hair on his scalp. "My most important regulars include Monsieur Faucheron, assistant chief of police, Madame Jaujard, wife of the director of the *Musées de France* and Monsieur Loiret, a senior official at the Paris Gas Company."

"Don't forget Monsieur Citroën's widow," Rózsi called out from behind the counter, "and Charles Trenet."

On her way back to the hotel, it dawned on Sophie that with such important customers, Café Budapest might offer a way to obtain their desperately needed residency permit. What if she asked the Szigetis to get one of their wealthy customers to put in a good word at the Hôtel de Ville? Influence-peddling and who you knew—this was how it worked in Prague. It would surely work in Paris. She talked it over with Willy as they sat on the bed in their room with Pavel asleep under the covers. The weather had cooled and they had been layering their clothes over the thin bedspread to keep warm at night.

Willy gave her a hug and kissed her ear. "Worth a try, my darling, even though I doubt a Hungarian cake will help us break through the impenetrable wall of French bureaucracy."

"More than worth a try. That gendarme will be back soon."

He put his arms around her. "Let's celebrate your idea with more than just a little cuddle."

She pushed him away gently. "Not now, *miláčku*. We'll wake Pavel. Making love is for the afternoons when we are free and Pavel is 'on duty' at the café. Tomorrow I'll talk to Rózsi and ask her if she can persuade one of her customers to help us. She'll know the right one."

The Szigetis thought about the plan for a day or two and then agreed. Rózsi said that at first Andreas had voiced concerns that some customer might report them to the police for illegally obtaining a permit for aliens. But then he relented when she explained who her chosen customer would be.

"I first thought of asking Monsieur Faucheron who is at the Prefecture de Police," she said with a shudder. "But then, I had a feeling he might be too important to be bribable and we might lose his custom if he was offended."

Sophie gave Rószi a horrified look. "Please, I do not want you to bribe anyone. I was hoping you would just ask for a favor."

"There will be no bribing with money, my dear. We have someone in mind."

Andreas rubbed his hands together, almost gleefully. "Monsieur Jean-Jacques Loiret. An accountant in the Gas Company. A friend of the mayor. Comes every week. A very gentle man. Sometimes he brings his grand-daughter. He will help."

"He does his wife's bidding," interjected Rószi. "They give a formal dinner every Saturday and always get their dessert from us. Madame telephones the order, and Monsieur comes to collect it. Just make sure Pavel is here this Saturday morning around ten. Make him look a little tattered. You know what I mean: like a sweet refugee boy."

"You mean to show how needy we are?"

Rózsi laughed. "Of course, and you should wear something that shows off your figure nicely. Monsieur Loiret has a roving eye."

Sophie's shoulders sagged. "I don't have anything like that."

"Well, do the best you can and … smile."

At ten the following Saturday, a rainy day with gusts of wind funneling along the boulevards, Rózsi and Sophie were busy working behind the counter at the Café Budapest watched by Pavel. Willy was at the Café Montfort, talking war strategy and escape routes with his refugee acquaintances, skimming newspapers and practicing piano.

As Rózsi and Sophie simultaneously served three customers, the doorbell rang and a well-dressed, rotund man holding an ivory-topped cane entered. He took off his fedora and, leaning on his cane, waited calmly until the others had left.

"*Bonjour, Monsieur Loiret*," said Rózsi as she nudged Sophie. "This is Loiret, the one we want," she murmured in Hungarian.

"I have your order almost ready, Monsieur." Rózsi lifted two cakes from the display case and put them on the counter. "As Madame ordered," said Rózsi, "our weekend special: raspberry-filled, chocolate-covered hazelnut. My assistant will box them up for you. "

At Rózsi's nod, Sophie lifted the cakes into white cardboard boxes embossed with the Hungarian dancer design from above the café entrance, and tied them with gold ribbon.

Rózsi whispered, "Smile at him." Then, in French, "That will be fifty-five francs, Monsieur."

With a sigh, Monsieur Loiret unbuttoned his fur-collared overcoat and pulled out his wallet. He placed a one-hundred-franc note on the counter. "This damned *drôle de guerre* keeps pushing up prices, but … my wife insists we serve only the finest *patisseries* to our guests."

"I understand completely, Monsieur." Rózsi opened the cash register then paused as if she could not find the correct change.

Monsieur Loiret looked up, caught Sophie's smile and made a little bow. "*Charmant*, your new assistant," he said with a bold stare.

Sophie kept smiling. She was used to Frenchmen's admiring eyes, even when she was out walking arm-in-arm with Willy.

Rózsi pointed to Pavel sitting on the high stool—a ragamuffin in an old red cardigan, wrinkled brown shorts, socks and sandals. Blue eyes below a halo of blond ringlets stared at the portly man.

"Monsieur le Directeur," said Rózsi. "This lovely boy belongs to my assistant, Madame Kohut. She and her husband are Hungarians like us. They just arrived in Paris with only the clothes on their backs. Fugitives from the *Boches*—and no money."

"Eh, bien," said M. Loiret, a smile playing around his mouth. "It seems they have landed well at your café. It's very good of you to give your charming assistant employment. I trust you have the correct work permit for her. " He pulled off his leather gloves.

"You are right to point this out, Monsieur. Unfortunately, Sophie also has no residence permit. As you know such things are very difficult to come by."

M. Loiret frowned.

"So I give her food instead of money. Poor thing, she hardly speaks French. With a residence permit I could pay her and help her out of her miserable situation."

With a sorrowful shake of the head, Monsieur Loiret patted Pavel's springy blond hair. "Ah, Madame Szigeti, this is a sad situation. Where is this woman's husband? Is he not looking for work? There are also refugee centers that provide temporary support." He put his hand out for the change, unable to tear his gaze away from Sophie.

"He's leaving Paris to join the Czechoslovak army in the south," said Rózsi, holding on to the cake boxes. "They will be fighting under French command."

"Excellent."

Rózsi smiled at him. "My husband and I were wondering if you could find time to help this delightful young woman and her boy acquire official refugee status in Paris. You know so many important people."

M. Loiret's eyebrows climbed up his forehead. "An unusually assertive request, I must say. I am not in the habit of bypassing official channels … and I'm a busy man."

Sophie watched Rózsi push the hundred franc note back to him. "Please, Monsieur, as one of our most favored customers there is no charge for the cakes today. And I was wondering if your wife would like to receive two similar cakes for your next two dinner parties … *gratuit*."

Monsieur Loiret rested his hands on the counter and stared. His eyes flicked from Rózsi's face to the cake box and back again. "You mean a gift of *four* cakes?" With a hint of a smile he, glanced at Pavel.

Sophie saw that he was tempted—probably he was thinking that his wife would be extremely pleased with Rózsi's offer.

Pavel, still on his stool, began leafing through Le Journal de Mickey, a well-used French nursery comic that Willy had found on a Metro train seat.

With a sigh, Monsieur Loiret tucked the money back in his wallet. "*Pas de problème, Madame Szigeti*. We accept your generous gift." He glanced at Pavel. "This little fellow and his mother are clearly deserving cases. I will arrange things with the *Préfecture de Police*— discreetly—and, as you know, she needs a *carte de travail*. I will arrange that also."

M. Loiret looked anxiously at the cake boxes still resting out of his reach and pulled a small black notebook from his waistcoat. "Please give me the name of each family member and the address."

Sophie carefully wrote the Kohut names and address on a

square of wrapping paper and put it on the counter. Rózsi smiled as she pushed the paper and cake boxes toward him. "You are a kind man—and please do this quickly because the police visited here last week. I can't afford to lose my beautiful assistant to an internment camp. We need her too much."

"You have persuaded me, Madame Szigeti." M. Loiret said with an admiring smile as he tucked the paper slip in a waistcoat pocket. "If I had someone like you working in my office, we would certainly accomplish many more things than we do."

Rózsi inclined her head and kissed the crucifix that hung from her neck. "May the Good Lord remember what you are about to do for these poor people. France should be proud of your great heart."

As soon as the doorbell announced Monsieur Loiret's departure, Sophie threw her arms round Rózsi, laughing and crying at the same time. "Thank you, thank you, you wonderful friend. I believe you saved us. I would be happy to work off the one hundred and sixty-five francs you just gave away on my behalf."

Leaning against the doorway to the kitchen, absent-mindedly rubbing his cheek, Andreas watched them embrace. Sophie enveloped him with smiles.

"I did not realize that my wife was such a good negotiator. In any case, I pray you *do* get the residence permit, not just the promise of one," he said gravely. "Now I have to tell you what I just heard on the radio. Warsaw surrendered. Poland is finished."

In the silence that followed, Sophie glanced at Rózsi and knew they were thinking the same thing. With Poland gone where and when would the next attack come?

Within two days, late in the afternoon, a city official knocked on the door of the Kohuts' hotel room and sat down with them to complete and counter-sign an official refugee assistance application. He gave them a receipt, which saved them the next day when the two gendarmes returned to the café looking to interrogate Pavel's parents. A week before Willy was due to leave for the south, the residence certificates, Sophie's carte de travail and permanent food ration books arrived directly from the *Conseil Général*.

"You have a good base now, working with Andreas and Rózsi," said Willy as he watched Sophie laying all the administrative documents out on the small table in their room. He reached over and with a smile, stroked her arm. "I'm relieved and happy. For a few terrible days I thought we would have to leave Paris and run for it."

Sophie raised her eyebrows. "Run? Where to?"

Willy laughed. "No idea. So, don't think about it anymore." He gave her a wistful look, kissing the hand that still held one of the ration books. "Sophie, my darling, I will miss you and Pavel. But it has to be this way, and I know you will manage here without me."

"In spite of all the bad news," said Sophie, wiping her eyes as they clung to each other, "the prospect of getting a residence permit makes me feel very happy. It will be hard for both of us. I will do my best."

CHAPTER SEVEN

Time to Leave
October 1939

At the Café Montfort, Willy waited in the telephone alcove watching slant-lines of rain spatter the dirty windows. For what seemed endless minutes, with the receiver clamped to his ear, he endured the old-fashioned accordion waltzes blaring from the radio behind the bar. As far as he was concerned, Radio Paris was overdoing this form of patriotism.

At last, a switchboard operator at the Czechoslovak Consulate came on the line. "What do you want?" A shrill French voice. Willy grimaced thinking that the usual courtesies had been abandoned in wartime—but then these women had a lot to deal with.

"Mr. Vlásek, please. I'm one of the newly signed soldiers."

"*Un moment.*"

In the alcove by the bar, Willy waited impatiently, submerged by cigarette smoke and conversation. He drummed an arpeggio against the wall, testing the nimbleness of his right little finger. Not bad; in fact, much stronger. Andreas Szigeti's weights were definitely working. A group of habitués argued about why the government had dissolved the French Communist party. He waited resignedly, looking through the windows at hunched figures hurrying under umbrellas in the street. It was the wettest October in a hundred years, floods everywhere.

The radio switched to Tino Rossi's reedy tenor and then to a *reportage*. Willy half-listened to a contentious discussion about government-controlled food prices … followed by an announcement that 80,000 German-speaking aliens had been interned in British camps.

"Vlásek?" A sharp overburdened voice at the end of the line.

Willy straightened up. "Kohut here. You signed me up for the army four weeks ago. Look, I don't want to be a nuisance, but what's happening about me going south? There's really a war on now."

"Not to worry, dear fellow. Your travel orders will arrive any day. With the other volunteers you'll take a special train to Béziers in the southwest, then a convoy of trucks to the port of Agde. Be patient."

Willy thought he would try again. "My wife and child—I suppose they can come with me on the train."

A moment of silence was followed by Vlásek's cough. "I told you before, my friend. That's impossible."

"Well then, what if I decide to back out?" Willy heard what he thought was a disapproving grunt.

"You signed a loyalty oath, remember. If you quit, you get a dishonorable discharge, Kohut. No pay and the police will confiscate your Paris residence permits, identity cards and vouchers. Do you really want your wife and child to live in a filthy camp with a few thousand other refugees?"

Willy smothered an exclamation. "My God, if you put it like that, I'll be there on the day. Thanks." He put the phone back on the hook, frustrated, but also relieved at Vlásek's assurances that the journey south was on. "Give me an anise, Marcel," he said. "Two shots." The skinny owner poured the anise and then water into the tumbler.

"*Eh, bien, M'sieu,* by the look of things you've had some

good news?"

"Good one way, bad another," said Willy. "I've been called up to join the re-formed Czechoslovak Army. We go to a town called Béziers."

Marcel Fontaine shook his head in astonishment. He called out to his regulars clustered along the bar. "Listen up, my friends. This *mec* is joining what he calls the Czechoslovak Army in Béziers."

"This is incredible," someone said. "Seems like we've got foreign armies bouncing all over the French countryside. *Les Anglais* face the Boches in the north—and Slavs defend us in the south? Weird, illogical and cowardly. I expect these foreign *mecs* are busy, right now, eating our best food and chasing women. Why the hell do we need foreigners when we have a million and a half French soldiers sitting on their whats-its behind the Maginot Line?"

A regular, known as 'the goat' because of his bulging eyes and odd jaw motion when he swallowed, came up to Willy and patted him on the back. "I know Béziers, *M'sieu*. A sleepy place inhabited by uneducated peasants—no toilets, no culture. They wash once a month, not once a week like here in Paris. Even their wine is garbage. They mix it with the piss they get from the colonials in Algeria, and sell it cheap to the coal miners in Mons. And what they speak isn't even decent French; it's some dialect from ancient times."

The customers laughed.

Marcel paused to take another swallow of cognac he had poured for himself. "I have to tell you, *mon ami*, it's a damned different world down there ... and putrid hot in the summer. I should know. I cycled through there when I was in the Tour de France." He pointed proudly at a large photograph of a thin-legged man in singlet and shorts, leather helmet and goggles, holding onto a bicycle's handlebars. *"Cela, c'est moi."*

"God forgive me for boasting. Every detail of that Mont Ventoux climb is burned into my brain. When we began the ascent I was up there at the front of the *peloton,* tucked in behind Antonin Magne for a while, and then…"

"Shut it, you boring old fart," someone yelled. Marcel shrugged helplessly and leaned over to shake Willy by the hand. "Anyway, *bonne chance,* Monsieur Kohut. Come back to see us. Before or after the war is over."

* * *

"What is this place, Béziers?" In their room, Sophie was getting Pavel dressed for the family's afternoon walk in the Luxembourg Gardens. Afterward, they would drop Pavel off at Café Budapest which re-opened at four. "Do you know anything about it?"

"Almost nothing," said Willy "While Pavel is at the Szigetis we could go to the public library; take a look."

But at the café, Andreas had a better idea. "I have everything you need, a good map of France, a Guide Michelin and a Larousse Encyclopedia, among other reference books. Sit down, have a coffee and pretend you've turned into Sorbonne students. I'll keep Pavel with me in the bakery." He smiled, sat Pavel on the counter and presented him with a battered wooden box.

Pavel opened the lid and peered inside. "Soldiers," he crowed, eyes glowing with joy. He pulled one out and showed it to Sophie: a flat metal Zouave infantryman with a swinging arm and shouldered rifle.

With a low chuckle, Andreas slung Pavel over his shoulder and grabbed the box. "Before I start preparing dough, I'll show him how to build a fort and set up the soldiers. Come on, *Pavlíček.*"

From the moment they met, Willy had recognized that Andreas excelled at his craft; a kind, intelligent, but uneducated man. So, he was surprised that the older man owned what turned out to be a small reference library: books on baking and *haute cuisine*, magazines, political history, and classic French authors.

Willy and Sophie huddled around the map and made notes from the Larousse Dictionary. Béziers, once a Roman city, was in the lower southwest corner of the country, on the river Orb, about thirty-five kilometers from the Mediterranean. The famous Canal du Midi, a seventeenth-century engineering wonder, ran through the town and connected the Mediterranean with the Atlantic.

"Peasant country," said Willy, running a finger down the page. "They told me at the café. They live off peaches, fish, goat cheese and cheap wine."

Sophie squeezed Willy's arm encouragingly. "The geographical description fits in with what you told me—lovely sand beaches and warm water to swim in. That will be wonderful. Pavel has never seen the sea and my parents only ever took Geza and me to the coast north of Berlin—the water was terribly cold." She shivered a little at the memory.

Willy sipped his coffee, "Traveling with Pavel from Paris will be a big step for you. But once we're together down there, we'll be that much closer to getting out of France."

A few minutes later, Willy took the opportunity to tap Andreas on the shoulder. The baker was chiseling out tart shapes from a wide flat expanse of dough. "A favor, Andreas." His voice was low and urgent.

The baker nodded, concentrating on his task.

Willy took the baker's arm. "If Sophie wants your opinion," he said, "about my going south with the army I want you to back me up. Say it's the best thing for us."

"It probably is."

"There's a man I have to find there."

Andreas nodded, waiting.

"He had been a good friend in Prague—then he betrayed me to the Gestapo. Said I was a British spy. Imagine, just a couple of weeks ago, I found out he had enlisted here in Paris—same damned army as me. He's either still here or at the camp near Béziers. I have to settle accounts—if I can find him. Understand?"

"Does Sophie know?" said Andreas with a frown.

Willy rubbed his cheek. "When I told her, she just gave me a strange look … sort of embarrassed. I didn't pursue it."

"I don't like your 'settle accounts' words. Don't do anything stupid, Willy. Grudges eat at your soul."

*　*　*

Willy opened the official-looking letter and nodded. "At last." He handed it to Sophie.

Czechoslovak Military Administration
52 Avenue de la Bourdonnais. Paris.
October 7th, 1939
Private Willy Kohut. Orders:
You will undergo basic training at the Czechoslovak Army Camp in Agde, Département Hérault. Check in at Gare de Lyon.
October 16.Quai 4. 06.30 hrs. Follow the signs to CZECHOSLOVAK ARMY EMBARKATION. One small suitcase is permitted. Uniforms and equipment will be issued on arrival at final destination.

Signed: Captain Janíček for General Rudolph Zientek, Commandant, Béziers, General Ingr, Paris.

Three days later, the Szigetis held a noisy farewell dinner in the closed café—a mixture of joy and sadness, friendship and love, served to the accompaniment of rich *pörkölt* stew and dumplings, Bordeaux wine and a chocolate hazelnut cake. Later, Willy and Sophie would remember it as an emblematic moment.

Long after Pavel's usual bedtime, Andreas opened a bottle of Rivesaltes dessert wine he had been keeping for a special occasion. Sophie cuddled her drowsy boy on her lap, wondering what life in Paris would be like without her husband. Willy, eyes moist with emotion, stood up and raised his glass. "Friends, I don't know what the next few months will bring. Whatever happens, we thank you for your generosity of spirit and your love for Pavel. A stroke of fortune brought us to you and we will always remember you with great affection. You have been our family's guardian angels."

Tears flowed down Sophie's cheeks. Pavel looked up at her, alarmed, as if he couldn't understand why she was crying. Andreas applauded and embraced Willy and Sophie with his long arms. "You have been like a son to us," he said to Willy, "and Sophie is our well-loved daughter. It is sad that Willy has to leave Paris without his beautiful wife and child."

Willy stayed silent, shocked by Andreas' warm embrace. Willy's own father, a man of steely determination and business acumen, had never done what Andreas had done. Willy clawed the memories back: a disciplined childhood, long hours at the piano and being shouted at when he helped at the fabric store. Had there ever been a time that his father hugged or kissed him—praised him? Not that he could recall. There had been pats on the back, the occasional kindly word spoken with a fleeting smile, but the physicality of affection and intimacy had been absent. Willy felt an urge to cry, a lump in his throat, as if he were losing control. He would miss Andreas.

"It will be a long time before you eat as well as this again," said Rózsi, kissing Willy on both cheeks and squeezing him tight against her plump frame as the Kohuts took their leave.

"I will come back. I'm sure leave will be granted every so often."

That night at the hotel, Sophie and Willy, both a little tipsy, made love in the cold hotel room. Between the trembling kisses and the passionate uniting of their bodies, neither dared speak of the fear that this love-making might even be their last if their luck ran out—if they fell afoul of the authorities, if Germany defeated France. Nor were they aware that Pavel was watching them from his mattress on the floor. Still naked, they fell asleep in each other's arms.

CHAPTER EIGHT

The Camp at Agde
South of France. October 1939

At five in the morning on October 16 Paris was still dark. In the bitter cold, Willy walked three and a half kilometers north to the Gare de Lyon. From time to time he touched his face, remembering the places where Sophie, still in her nightdress, had placed so many kisses and tears in their lingering, whispered goodbye. Pavel had been asleep. Willy had stroked his cheek and gently hooked a finger through a couple of his boy's blond curls before he pulled on an overcoat over his suit.

Willy carried a small cardboard suitcase containing a change of clothes, shaving kit, spare spectacles, a photo of Sophie and Pavel, two apples and several sandwiches. In spite of the damp cold, he sweated inside his layers of clothes. It was hard to drag himself away from Sophie's embraces and now he was afraid of being late.

No one else was on the streets except for a few street cleaners in baggy clothes, peak caps and red kerchiefs on their shoulders who were sweeping trash with twig brooms.

At the Gare de Lyon, he followed the French hand-painted signs—ARMÉE TCHÉCOSLOVAQUE—to platform four, and found noisy chaos. He guessed there were more than five hundred men milling about, carrying bundles or suitcases. Most wore civilian clothes but some were in rumpled Czechoslovak army uniforms. He noticed large, shield-shaped plaques affixed to the sides of the train's railcars showing the crossed flags of France and Czechoslovakia. Men were laughing, and chalking patriotic and ironic slogans on the compartment doors. He felt his throat constrict and blinked tears. This was splendid. Two countries united against a common foe.

By one of the massive iron pillars, supporting the station's glass canopy, an immaculately dressed French officer and his armed platoon stood at ease, watching the jostling crowd. Willy remembered that Vlásek had said their journey was officially sponsored and financed by the French High Command.

Further along the platform, he saw two soldiers at attention, holding rifles on either side of a Czechoslovak officer seated at a table. When he came close he read the name tag: Captain Zdeněk Kordina. The captain was checking names in a ledger as one recruit after another stood before him and saluted. The men waited in a long wavy line, shrouded by clouds of cigarette smoke. *Registrace Dobrovolník* was scrawled on a placard that hung from the desk.

"Wagon number six," Kordina said when it was Willy's turn. "Be quick about it. We have to squeeze several hundred men into seven railcars—and we leave in forty minutes. No seats for latecomers. They'll have to stand in the corridors."

For the next six hours, Willy's train traveled south through central France. Each compartment held eight army recruits. Most shared their seats with those standing outside in the corridor, each seat rotating every half hour or so. This created a sense of camaraderie as strangers introduced themselves, joking and offering each other cigarettes and sometimes a swig of wine or cognac. Willy felt he had re-joined a gregarious men's club or the Sokol gymnastics society.

He shared the sandwiches Sophie had made and tried to find out what the Agde camp was like. No one knew much, except that it was run down, almost uninhabitable. Willy wondered whether his life in Paris had, perhaps, not been so bad. Even though he and Sophie had scraped along on very little, at least they had been safe and together.

As he forced himself to drink the tepid chicory coffee provided in an otherwise non-functioning dining car, he began to question his decision to enlist. He had stepped from a relatively stable situation in Paris to an ill-defined endeavor over which he had no control and which might get him wounded or killed. And there was no guarantee that Sophie and Pavel would be able to come from Paris. Moreover, tracking down Lessig, the man who betrayed him might turn out to be a waste of time.

Whether sitting in the compartment or pacing the corridors of the railcars, Willy was astonished at the stories of journeys, misfortune, escapes, and good luck recounted in different languages. The men on this train had traveled to France from Nazi-occupied Czechoslovakia, Poland, Palestine, the French Foreign Legion in Africa and Russia, a river of recruits winding south to become the Czechoslovak army-in-exile.

No one paid much attention to the passing countryside other than the few who gazed blankly at the rainclouds and brown fields as if they were the backdrop to an empty stage; they were patiently waiting for the show to begin.

Standing in the packed corridor, eating his last sandwich, Willy recognized someone he remembered from his home town of Lučenec: the unmistakable arrow-head nose and jutting chin of Josef Svoboda. Squeezing past other men, Willy introduced himself. They shook hands. Svoboda, like the majority of Czechoslovak military men, had secretly made his way, after the German occupation, to France through Austria and Switzerland. They chatted, reviving old memories and discussing the complexities of the Phoney War.

Svoboda, a career captain in the Czechoslovak infantry, was skeptical about the fighting abilities of the French army and apprehensive about the proposed formation of the Czechoslovak Army-in-Exile. "Y'know, Kohut, this train carries a fucking witch's brew of recruits—Gypsies, Hungarians, Ruthenes, Poles, but mostly Slovaks, and Czechs. Too many Yids, if you ask me." He lifted a sardonic eyebrow. He shrugged. "How the hell are people like me supposed to turn this rabble into fighting men," he said, lurching to the rhythm of the train.

"Trouble is, Kohut, that even when they do understand each other, their willingness to fight as a unit depends on religion and politics. Think of it—Jews, Christians, Fascists, independence fanatics, democrats—and worst of all Communists."

Willy gave him a glum look, remembering why he had never liked Svoboda. The man was a dedicated racist. "Looks like we're on an impossible mission. Not much cause for optimism."

Svoboda glared into space. "Fucking Communists! Everywhere they go they proselytize their evil cause and make trouble. Our leadership is taking a lot of risks with this lot."

Willy had not given much thought to this problem. Svoboda was right. Assembling a fighting force was a major undertaking. As they shook hands and parted, Willy was glad to get away from him, but hoped that his acquaintanceship with Svoboda might come in useful.

When Willy wasn't half asleep in a seat, or talking to someone, he passed the time walking the length of the train keeping an eye out for Lessig. He didn't catch even a glimpse of yellow hair. Probably, Lessig had left for Agde on some earlier train.

He bumped into an old schoolmate from the Lučenec Gymnasium: Jiří Madrun, a corporal in the Czechoslovak tank corps. They stood in the corridor and reminisced. Every so often, Jiří pulled a bottle of schnapps from his jacket pocket and took a swig. He did not offer any to Willy.

"At the Gymnasium you were a weedy kid with twisted wire glasses," Madrun said with an unfocused smile just before he tilted the bottle against his lips.

The bile rose in Willy's throat. At high school, he remembered Jiří as an overweight shit who picked on the Jewish boys. Physically the man was just as hefty; Willy studied the jowly face. Maybe a few years had improved his attitude?

Madrun shrugged at Willy's silence. "You've changed, Kohut—gone bald early. How is it you never joined in all the fun on the playground or played football? Too busy studying, I suppose. My papa used to say that just a handful of Jews in Lučenec owned most of the stores. Tell me how that happened, eh? He said they made their money from sneaky deals, lying and stealing. Then they had the gall to demand forgiveness from their God by chanting over their rolls of paper. If I remember right, your papa owned one of those stores, didn't he?"

Willy played along, careful to keep his temper. There were probably plenty more Madruns on the train and the prospect of dealing with them at Camp Agde was disheartening. He shook his head. "Wrong impression, Jiří. Actually, I was desperate to play football, cycle and climb trees. I wanted to do all the rough, risky things you bullies were up to. I couldn't. My parents wanted me to be a pianist. They didn't want me to hurt my hands punching you in the nose."

"Ha!" Madrun's eyes dilated in astonishment and he took another swig. He looked away and noticed Willy's injured hand. "Looks like one of your hands got fucked up. How did you manage to get past the medical inspection, for Christ's sake? That finger won't last long in basic training." He grinned.

It was mid-afternoon when the train reached Béziers, thirty kilometers from Agde. The air was cold and misty: puddles everywhere. A drizzle started. The men—Willy overheard someone say there were about six hundred—were assembled in the forecourt of the station, stamping their feet and rubbing their arms to keep out the chill. Willy was assigned to the First Artillery Regiment, 3rd Command Group and told to wait. Two hours later, several tarpaulin-covered Renault trucks and a handful of dilapidated buses drew up outside the station. The chilled, exhausted recruits climbed in.

After an hour's travel through hilly countryside the convoy passed through the village of Vias and reached the outskirts of the Agde. The trucks and buses turned off the road where barbed-wire fencing channeled them under a metal sign painted with the words: CAMP 2. Dépôt Tchéco-Slovaque. By the time the trucks and buses finished unloading in the parade ground, it was close to five o'clock and still drizzling.

Willy's heart sank. From the faces of the men standing around him he knew he was not the only gloomy, disappointed recruit. The camp was sealed off from the surrounding landscape by a high mesh fence and rusty razor wire. Beyond the fence were waist-high, dry stone walls encircling leafless vineyards. In the distance, Willy made out the outline of low hills and guessed that was where he and Sophie might find a village where the family could stay.

Men in rumpled uniforms—previous arrivals—straggled out of long wooden huts to watch the new recruits unload. They shouted greetings, but without much enthusiasm. In the parade ground opposite the entrance, the new men lined up in blocks of thirty. Facing them, on a low podium, Captain Svoboda conferred with several non-commissioned officers.

A few minutes later, the NCOs spread out among the blocks

of recruits, giving orders. One approached Willy's group. "I'm Plaček, quartermaster corps. You lot are dismissed. Go to Hut BS 24—half-way down the main alley. That way, you idiots. Take your stuff and find a bunk. Then clean the place up. Pails, mops and carbolic are in the hut."

"Isn't someone going to show us what's to be done?"

"Don't we get uniforms? Instructions?"

Plaček frowned. "These *are* instructions, idiot. One of you has to take charge." He looked at Willy. "You, the one with the headlamps. Name?"

"Kohut."

"Okay, report back to me after you're done."

Willy saluted, cursing under his breath that he now had to manage a bunch of untrained cleaners just like him. He set off with his group. BS 24 was a long wooden building containing stacks of jerry-built bunks. Inside it reeked of creosote, tobacco and urine. Several windows were broken and daylight peeped through cracks in the siding. Along the hut's central corridor, dirt and animal scat were scattered over the floor. Willy shivered and rubbed his hands to keep them warm. His heart sank. *We're supposed to clean up this filth? We're fucking maids for the Czechoslovak army!*

First things first. He picked up a straw mattress and a blanket from a stack inside the door and chose an upper bunk near the stove, calculating that most of the spiders, fleas and lice would stop to dine on the man underneath him and not bother to climb higher. He put his suitcase on the mattress to stake his claim.

A crooked tin pipe ran from the pot-belly stove up through the roof but there was no fuel. The small washroom had no running water, and only brown liquid dribbled on to the dirt when he turned the tap on the wall outside the entrance door. This was far worse than camping.

Willy thought back to his hiking trips in the Tatra Mountains:

primitive, yes, but tempered by youth, beautiful surroundings and fun. Now was the time to use his connection with Svoboda and press for resources to make this hut livable. He left his platoon to fend for themselves and headed back to the parade ground. On the way past the outhouses the stench was overwhelming. He looked down a long row of open stalls, each showing a soldier's hands and knees and a head bent forward. Everyone was smoking.

Captain Svoboda stood on a raised platform at the center of the parade ground. He listened to Willy's complaints, his eyes half-closed in resignation. "So, *vojín*, your little hut is full of vermin and holes—and it stinks?" he said mockingly. "Ventilation. That's why the holes are there. Every hut has them."

Willy saw no sign that they had chatted amicably on the train.

"We have an army to put together, Kohut, and fast. Every day, after basic training is over, all the men in camp are expected to fix up their own huts. You'll be given tools and supplies."

"Are we supposed to organize this on our own? Without supervision?"

"See over there, the building with intact windows?"

Willy followed Svoboda's gaze to a two-story wooden structure.

"That's the officer's billet, half empty. Some of those fellows were so disgusted by the state of the camp when they arrived that they now sleep at the local hostelries in Agde. So, each day, when the basic training schedule is over, they leave. They certainly don't stay to supervise hut repairs. Any more comments, *vojín*?"

Willy saluted, trying to process the absurd information. "Can't say, sir." On the train he had been told that claiming ignorance or showing total obedience were the only ways to react to a senior officer's order or question.

"By the way," Svoboda smiled, lowering his voice as if he

had decided to share an important secret. "This camp has been nicknamed *Camp Průjem*, Camp Diarrhea—a quite appropriate name given the state of the outhouses. Now for Christ's sake, piss off."

Willy tried to keep his anger under control. This was not the friendly Svoboda he had talked to on the train. "What do I do next, sir?"

"Get your uniform and equipment over by those trucks— beyond the officer's quarters. Where all those men are lined up. The Frenchies just dumped everything and took off. Didn't even give us an inventory. Sergeant Stulpa is in charge."

Willy joined a line of grumbling soldiers behind two supply trucks with their tailgates open. Sergeant Stulpa, squat and powerful-looking with a face as flat as a dinner plate, stood on an upturned wooden box between the trucks, directing the issuance of uniforms and equipment. Between curses and cigarettes, he handed each man the same sermon, with minor variations. "Come on, you spineless cretins, you're getting vintage French shit. Any arguing or punch-ups earn extra night duty."

From a pile of clothes, Willy selected a patched French uniform consisting of baggy blue pants, gaiters and a cotton brass-buttoned *blouson*: it had one redeeming feature, a Czechoslovak private's badge and his country's insignia sewn on the left breast pocket. A soldier handed him a dented tin helmet dating from the Great War and Willy retrieved matted woolen socks, gloves and a pair of oiled boots from a series of wooden boxes. Another bored-looking soldier standing behind a table handed him a backpack, a metal mess box and spoon, and a leather cartridge belt.

One fellow had heard that newly minted fatigues and helmets would be shipped sometime before they went into action.

"Thank God," Willy heard his companion say. "At least the Nazi bastards will find out which nationality is killing them."

"Don't be so optimistic, friend," said a tall soldier, standing close by. "If they capture you wearing a Czechoslovak uniform, they'll shoot you. To them we're deserters from the Protectorate of Bohemia and Moravia." He gave Willy a sardonic smile and drew a finger across his neck.

"Hold everything," Sergeant Stulpa shouted interrupting the conversation. With his thumbs thrust into his belt he grinned as if he was enjoying the discomfiture of the new arrivals. "Looks like we've run out of boots. French clogs is all we have left. Take those or use your own shoes."

Everyone was given a pack of cigarettes, a gas mask, and a used *capote,* the heavy felt greatcoat the French military used for winter. They moved on to where Sergeant Kukulka and his team were handing out weapons. Kukulka was a huge man, with gimlet eyes in a scarred, expressionless face. His details handed each recruit a primitive-looking rifle, a long spike bayonet and two empty grenade canisters—until the supply ran out. The remaining recruits were given wooden poles.

"What do we do for ammo, Sarge?" shouted a tough-looking soldier. Everyone looked round. "I mean for those of us who've been given something with a trigger."

"If you're lucky enough to hold a fucking rifle, you get four rounds of pensioned-off ammo."

"Four? They say it takes a thousand rounds to kill an enemy soldier—so with a four-shot limit, well ... that's a fucking waste of time."

Kukulka growled. "Four rounds is what you get for target practice. We're using these old Lebels because the French still have ammo stocks. In any case—we start tomorrow."

"Wonder of wonders, Sarge," was the sarcastic response from somewhere in the line. "I suppose we better start sharpening the rusty bayonets, unless the Frenchies need 'em back to slice their onions."

Kukulka glared at the laughing men around him. "Shut up. As of right now, I've assigned you, Soldier Sharp Bayonet, to midnight sentry duty. Report to me at the NCO hut at twenty-two hundred hours." He spat a large gob of saliva into a bucket ten feet away. After a moment of shocked silence, the men applauded his feat. If he was as accurate with a rifle as he was with his spit, Kukulka was to be feared.

At about seven that evening, a large, gray truck pulled up between the ruined dining hall and outside wash rooms. Hôtel Donjon-Agde was picked out in white letters on the side doors. The smell of meat and onions filtered into the air. Dinner had arrived. A heavy-shouldered man in a canvas coat climbed down from the driver's side, followed by three women in headscarves. A noisy crowd quickly formed as the team from the truck opened up long tables and set up alcohol burners beneath metal stands. An overweight French officer strolled up to one of the Czechoslovak lieutenants and tapped him on the shoulder with a cane. "I am Captain Prud'homme," he said in French. His voice was clipped and self-important. "Camp Administrator. For God's sake, get your men organized and tell them to stop arguing. We must have discipline here."

"Anyone speak the native lingo," yelled the lieutenant in Czech. "I need a hand with this Frenchie."

Willy immediately raised his hand, hoping that his volunteering would be noted and prove to be a good investment.

Other hands had risen above the sea of heads, some hesitantly. The lieutenant pointed at Willy. "You, the one with the glasses—yes, you. Come here and find out what this fat Frenchman wants."

Willy approached the French captain. "My lieutenant wishes to know how to proceed with the food service, sir."

Captain Prud'homme gave a haughty sniff. "At last, I find

someone who speaks decent French. Tell your officer he's the one who must deal with the food-van people. For only this week, Monsieur Jean Felix, the mayor of Agde has graciously ordered the Hôtel Donjon to provide food for the Czechoslovak army, under contract from your Commandant in Béziers—after that you Czechs are responsible for setting up a field kitchen and purchasing supplies."

Willy translated as several soldiers helped the driver and the women unload and set out food on the tables. Sitting on rocks, boxes and hut steps, the men ate a beef stew dinner accompanied by plenty of wine. Willy swallowed a couple of mouthfuls of stew but he was too busy translating and helping organize the service to satisfy his hunger.

As a team of soldiers started to wash their mess tins and forks in tanks of soapy water, the fat-bellied man, Alphonse, from the Hôtel Donjon invited Willy to join him in the back of the truck where the three women were eating. There was not only plenty of beef stew and vegetables, but pâté and salad.

When he had finished and was climbing out of the hotel truck, the Czechoslovak lieutenant was there, waiting. "Good work, Kohut," he said with a gold-toothed smile. "You are to do this every day until our kitchen is functional."

Trying to suppress a grin, Willy saluted. His stomach full, he felt more at home already. Although he had no idea how he would manage life in the camp, he had been noticed by the officers and demonstrated his potential. That was a start.

Before lights out at ten, Willy led a search party for fuel and soon the pot-bellied stove was burning rotted planks, torn from derelict outhouses. Hut BS 24 was warm, though the heat quickly leaked out through the broken windows. Some men in the lower bunks, attacked by fleas and bedbugs, slept outside in blankets. Once the stove died down, Willy was cold and he couldn't sleep. His thoughts turned to how much he wanted to hear Sophie's voice, feel her warm body and kisses and enjoy the pleasures they shared in Paris; he missed Pavel's liveliness, the Szigetis' friendship and the Café Budapest. He was homesick.

Next day, the units started basic training: reveille at five, a half-hour run, washing in the communal bathrooms, a cup of unsweetened chicory coffee and a piece of bread. At seven a.m. the soldiers drilled in their hand-me-down uniforms, responding to commands. Perhaps a third of the men had Lebel weapons, the rest used wooden poles. Afterward, Sergeant Kukulka supervised the demonstration of how to run an obstacle course over ropes, barbed wire, walls, and rocky terrain. After lunch, Sergeant Stulpa led the men, backpacks filled with rocks, on a three-hour march into the hills.

Late that afternoon, the units started weather-proofing their own huts, putting tarpaper on the roof, replacing glass windows, spraying disinfectant and putting arsenic poison under the floors.

Each day had the same routine: the morning run, rifle and squad drills, obstacle courses, mock warfare in the rough countryside, a distance march and working on the camp infrastructure. Willy hardly found the will, the energy or the resources to write to Sophie—but he managed to send a couple of terse military-form postcards from the camp post office. The first said he had arrived safely and the second reported that he was well and settled. Most evenings, after walking through the camp checking the huts for old acquaintances from Slovakia, he sat by the stove chatting with his comrades. When he climbed into his bunk his thoughts always turned to Sophie and Pavel. At least his family had shelter in Paris, and enough money so they would not starve. Then there was the matter of Lessig. That bastard had enlisted—he had to be somewhere close by.

* * *

The weather turned warmer in the second week. If there wasn't a night exercise, non-commissioned officers and recruits gathered round a fire built in a steel drum, just talking and drinking; there was plenty of local wine. Willy was happy to join in.

On one occasion, Sergeant Kukulka nodded a greeting and plopped himself down on an upturned fruit box next to Willy. He took out his pipe and puffed away in silence. Willy stared at the fire, wary of this intimacy from a superior.

"Listen, Kohut," Kukulka said after a while. His voice was unusually quiet. "I heard you did well with the French food people. You seem like somebody who sees the angles and gets stuff done. How's the basic training going?"

Willy looked down at the blisters and scratches on what had once been the hands of a classical pianist. He shrugged.

Kukulka cleared his throat with a low rumble and a spit. "Regrets, eh? *vojín*. Regret rots the brain. You have to think of the present … which brings me to why I sat down here. I was impressed by the way you volunteered and handled that puffed-up French ass—very smooth."

Willy looked up at the sergeant. What was this hulk after? He hadn't figured Kukulka out. The sergeant was tough and harsh but seemed without guile or malice. He had not even shown any particular animosity toward the Jewish reserve officers or enlisted men—and there were eight hundred of them. Willy kept his face still, waiting to find out which way the wind was blowing. "No one's been this friendly to me since I arrived," he said carefully. "Why you?"

The Sergeant gripped Willy's shoulder with a broad hand. "Listen, private. You're small, short-sighted and you don't even shoulder arms proper. As for hand-to-hand fighting, well—you'd be useless, what with your messed-up finger. This army don't need your body—what it needs is what's in your upper story."

Willy looked up at the giant. He had the impression that some kind of offer—maybe good, maybe bad—was imminent.

Drifting pipe smoke swirled around Kukulka's face, hiding the wide, puckered scar that distorted his left eye and cheek. "I think you and me, we can help each other."

Willy shrugged again, still feeling his way. "Help? How?"

"This camp is a mess, *vojín*. For a start, we've a pile of enlistees who speak different languages, even Yiddish, for God's sake. Somehow, we've got to make them work together." He sucked a breath in through his teeth and Willy felt the man's chest against his arm swell like a vast balloon. "Hungarian or Slovak-speaking recruits 'ave to follow orders from officers who know only Czech. And in a week or so we expect a bunch more. How the hell are we gonna manage?"

Willy nodded. "Obviously, a major organizational task. So far, I think our leaders have been quite effective."

Kukulka grunted and spat on the ground. "You know nothing, *vojín*. Stulpa told me that our inventory people up at HQ can't cope with the French military. Bureaucratic barbed wire. I've been up there. They don't understand or like each other."

Willy nodded, flattered that Kukulka seemed to be confiding in him. The sergeant scratched his chin. "I looked at your file in the CO's office. You ran a business in Prague, you drive, you know accounts, and you're damned good at French. HQ needs somebody like you. "

Kukulka pulled a bottle of wine out of his side pocket and uncorked it. "Here's what I think, Kohut. You should get a job at Division HQ … in Béziers." The sergeant took a swig and offered the bottle to Willy.

Willy pushed it away. "I've already got two back-breaking jobs, Sarge. One is repairing our damned hut. The other is marching around the countryside carrying a pack and a ten-pound blunderbuss that doesn't work. Anyway, a private in the Czechoslovak army can't *get* a job. He gets an order. Is this a joke?"

Kukulka's shoulders shook with silent laughter. "You have a suspicious nose, my friend. But, really, what if I fixed you up at HQ … part-time there and part-time here? Working for Colonel Zientek. A soft job with regular purchasing trips into the countryside."

Willy laughed. "You're having me on, Sergeant."

Kukulka tapped the side of his nose. "Inside grease, *vojín*. Alexi, an old comrade—works for Colonel Z. He asked me to keep an eye open for someone who can really *parlez Français* and keep the regimental accounts straight. Alexi told me their French suppliers are overcharging us for equipment and food supplies, and the man we've got there can't understand a word. You're just what they need. What do you prefer, *voj*? Slogging through the mud with an antique Lebel or sitting in a cozy office reporting directly to a captain?"

Willy shook his head slowly. "Why are you offering me this deal. Why don't they get one of our officers who speaks some French? Why the hell would the CO accept me?"

Kukulka tipped his bottle and took several swallows. "Colonel Zientek and me go back a long way. He trusts me. Besides, we don't have any officers with your library of languages. If I get you the job, we'll set up a nice arrangement regarding the *re-distribution* of supplies. You get my drift?"

Willy stole a glance at Kukulka but his face was impassive. The implication was clear. Comfort in exchange for a pilfering arrangement. Dangerous.

Willy gazed silently at the crackling blaze; thinking about

how much he hated basic training. The job at HQ might help him to find accommodation for Sophie and Pavel—bring them from Paris. There would be a telephone and he could call Café Budapest—far better than a letter. But there was something else he had to know. "I'm Jewish, Sergeant. A bunch of us have been insulted and abused. Is this going to happen at HQ?"

Kukulka pulled on his nose. He seemed to be thinking. "Quite possible, *vojín* … it's the same everywhere." With a grin, he punched Willy's shoulder. "Just put up with it. You're clever enough to avoid trouble."

Willy stared at the flames. *Out of the frying pan into the...?* "Okay, I'll consider the job, especially if you'll help me get my wife and child moved down here."

The big sergeant sucked at his pipe and tapped out the ashes on his boot. He shook his head. "A wife and child, eh? That's too difficult for me. Colonel Zientek would do it, if you got into his good books. You and he would be in the same building."

"What exactly are *you* after, Sarge? No one gives for free these days."

Kukulka's smile split his face. "That's true. Up at HQ I'll want you to put aside certain items for me—small luxuries, you might say, that I offer to the officers here. It's, you know, business."

"Isn't that stealing, Sarge?"

Kukulka put a finger to his lips. His eyes gleamed. "In war, my friend, it is wise to invest in one's own future, in case things turn out badly. And you would get ten per cent of the take … extra money."

Willy nodded. A tempting offer. He needed money to send to Sophie. "The war, Sarge, seems pretty one-sided at the moment. If we lose, extra cash will come in useful."

"Hmm." The sergeant shifted on the fruit box and glowered. "Don't fucking let me hear you talk about losing." He cleared his throat as if about to say something, then spat into the dark. "Holy Jesus, Joseph and Mary, did you see that?"

Willy started back in alarm. "What, for God's sake?"

"I hit some critter at five feet. Did you see how it took off?"

Willy smiled and stood up, stretching his back, pleased that he was about to tread an easier path than basic training. "Probably a rat, Sarge." He paused. "I was wondering. Do you happen to know a soldier called Lussik or Lessig? He's an old acquaintance and he owes me. I heard he joined our army in Paris."

Kukulka emptied the rest of the bottle down his throat. "No idea, but it would be child's play to locate him if you worked at HQ. All the files are there. A good reason to take the job, eh?"

Willy's heart lurched. The scales of his decision on Kukulka's offer had tilted to yes. "All right, Sergeant, I'm tempted, but I need a lot more detail before I agree. I suppose they would pay me more?"

Kukulka shook his pityingly. "Details be damned! This is no fucking employment bureau. I've told you what the work is. I want a yes or a no. You've got thirty seconds." He held up his wrist to catch the light from the fire.

The only downside Willy thought of in those few seconds had to do with being a Jew. "I'll do it."

They shook hands. "Good man."

At that moment, Willy dared to ask Kukulka a question that the other men in his hut had also been speculating on. "Excuse me for asking, but where did you get that scar on your face? We're all curious. Hand-to-hand fighting? A mortar shell? On the eastern front?"

Kukulka fingered the side of his face and with a deep sigh tossed the empty wine bottle on to the fire. The other men turned their heads at the sound of sizzle and crackle of the glass. The sergeant laughed. "Much worse than trench warfare, *vojín*. Years ago, my wife and I had a flaming row over another woman.

Hanka bashed my face with a rolling pin and then poured a pot of boiling water over my head." *Kukulka wasn't such a bad fellow after all.*

CHAPTER NINE

Hard Times
Paris. November/December 1939

Sophie was almost trapped in a new bureaucratic complication one week after Willy left for the camp. As a precaution against spying and sabotage, the French government began rounding up undocumented Austrian, German, and Hungarian nationals. She was Hungarian by birth but had been a Czechoslovak citizen since marrying Willy. That saved her from being swept into a collection center or work camp by her new *Carnet d'Identité pour Personnes Deplacées.*

At the end of the second week without Willy, Sophie received two pre-printed military post-cards—just a few handwritten lines—saying that he was coping. Reading the smooth, angled script conjured up his face and brilliant smile. She wrote a reply, but she wasn't sure whether *Poste aux Armées SP. #2197* on the military card was an address or not. It lacked a number, street or town—or even a *département.* She sent it anyway.

Because of the cold, Sophie visited the second-hand markets and acquired a ragged overcoat and a moth-eaten fur hat for herself, and corduroy pants, two shirts, a thick pullover and a scarf for Pavel. She would huddle up in bed with him, write to Willy and send airmail letters to Australia where her father and brother, being Hungarian citizens, had been sent to an internment camp.

She wrote to Aunt Margit in Hungary and to Willy's parents in London and lied about how well she and Willy were doing—that she had found a job in a café, Pavel was learning French and they would soon be joining Willy on the Mediterranean coast. For reasons she could not explain, Sophie was ashamed to admit how lonely and miserable she felt. After all, she was safe, Paris was a beautiful city and she had the Szigetis for friends. But, being fed and housed were no longer enough if you were starved of a sense of safety.

She worked mornings at Café Budapest. Pavel was happiest in the café, sitting on his stool by the cash register or playing in his 'cave' as Andreas called the alcove in the bakery. Rózsi had created animals and small human figures cut from stiff brown paper, and Andreas showed the boy how to use cardboard boxes to build a farm or a castle and make up stories about them.

One morning, in early November, before the café opened, Sophie was lifting loaves out of the baking pans when Andreas slammed his rolling pin on the marble slab. He pointed at the radio. "Stop," he bellowed. "Everyone. Listen."

Sophie froze, a loaf in each hand. Pavel looked up, half puzzled, half frightened and Rózsi peered in from the doorway, her eyes fluttering, mouth working.

"What is it?"

"A British Government statement," said a bland-voiced announcer, "confirms the eyewitness accounts of executions of detainees at the Dachau and Buchenwald camps."

The café was silent as the announcer went on to report that thousands of Jewish refugees were trying to leave Germany. Many had slipped across the borders. Others avoided arrest by committing suicide. Some had even paid doctors to cut the skin on their bellies, simulating abdominal surgery—hoping that the subterfuge would persuade the authorities to let them stay at home.

Sophie choked back her tears. Everything was going badly in the country she had left behind. She had read about the university demonstrations in Prague with the nine student leaders executed at Ruzyně, and twelve hundred others sent to concentration camps. Uncle Fritz, Pišta, Štefanka, Aunt Margit's family and her grandparent's closest friends still lived in Czechoslovakia and Hungary. What was happening to them? She and Willy had written several times. They received only two troubling replies, full of stories of restrictions, violence and fear.

Andreas heaved a sigh and let go of his rolling pin. He checked the oven temperature gauges, glancing at Sophie with sympathetic eyes. "I can't believe such things are being done to good Catholics and Jews." His voice shook. "And what is more disturbing is France's reluctance to fight. They should throw everything at the Germans. Immediately. A crusade, no less."

Rózsi poked her head around the door. "That's enough, husband. What's the use of ranting? There's nothing we can do to change things and grumbling affects your work. For us life is as busy as ever. No one has stopped buying bread and the cafés, theaters and music halls are packed."

Sophie could not stop thinking there might be relatives and people she knew being killed in those camps. Why all this hatred? What was the point of it all? Why did the women and children have to suffer when it was the fault of stupid, ruthless men who played the game of war? Terrible news like this, Willy's absence, Pavel's whining and tantrums, and even the daily round of minor disagreements between the baker and his wife made her life seem dark and sad.

"A French politician Willy met at the café," she said, trying to cover up her reaction to Andreas's unusually bitter tone, "said that countries like Britain and France have plenty of soldiers but out-of-date equipment. So, until they build enough tanks and guns, they won't fight the Nazis."

A sudden yell came from the alcove and a cloud of white flour settled slowly on to the baskets of newly baked bread. Andreas, hands on hips, watched dumbfounded as Pavel, covered in ghostly white, lay on the floor, shrieking and kicking.

Sophie began to shake, her heart raced. How dare he shame her in front of her benefactors? "You horrible brat," she shouted. "What did you do?" She grabbed Pavel by the arm and slapped his legs. Pavel rolled away, pounding his arms and legs on the floor, spreading flour everywhere. His eyes, two red circles, glared at her. His screams of "bad Mama, bad Mama" thudded in her ears.

Sophie held his ankles tight as he twisted and turned like a fish on a hook. "Stop this you wicked … horrible little…" she hissed. She shook him again and again, her heart racing, her mouth lemon-dry. *He's doing this to me on purpose.*

Rózsi stood in the doorway and slammed her metal dustpan against the jamb. Pavel stopped, his eyes wide with fear.

"Sophie." Rózsi's voice thundered, her face blazing red. "Take him home—right *now*. And don't bother about the mess, we'll clean it up."

Andreas nodded. He was frowning.

Rózsi pointed toward the café's front door. "Home, I said. When you get there look in the mirror. Think about what you did, and why. Leave."

Sophie hurried to dress Pavel, unwilling to give Rózsi or Andreas more than a quick glance. She had never felt so ashamed, but her anger was still there simmering. *If Pavel does this again on the Metro on the way home, I'll…*

The next morning Sophie rose early and while Pavel slept, stripped off her nightdress and washed herself in the washbasin instead of the freezing communal bathroom. After she dressed, Sophie examined her face closely in the faded mirror, unable to explain or justify why she had lost control with Pavel. Was it something to do with what she went through at the German frontier—or because, for three weeks, she had been here on her own? "Admit it." she said aloud, "you're angry with Willy for leaving … and you're lonely and sad."

"Look at yourself," Rózsi had said at the café. The inspection was disheartening. It wasn't only that Sophie felt miserable. Her face was haggard: dry flaky hair, spots on her nose, red eyes, thin cheeks and chipped fingernails. She squeezed her eyes shut but when she opened them nothing had changed. *I'm pitiable and ugly.*

She moved closer to the glass, remembering how much time and care she used to take in Prague to make herself elegant and attractive. She noticed wrinkles at the corners of her eyes. *Oh, God, I'm not even thirty.* She picked at her plucked eyebrows, applied lipstick and patted powder on her rough cheeks. *If only I had some time for myself, away from Pavel—an hour or two on my own.*

While she stood at the mirror, miserable and self-pitying, she saw that, behind her, Pavel was awake, sitting on their bed. For once there was no morning fuss. He was flipping through the well-thumbed picture cards of animals Willy had given him.

Pavel's moods were like light switches: light and dark, charming and clever one minute, obstinate and angry the next. Why had she disintegrated at the café? Why in front of the Szigetis? What will they think? *My God, I must remember to apologize. Pavel doesn't need me to be like this—a miserable bad-tempered mother. He needs stability, playmates, and a home. He needs his father.*

As the days passed, Sophie grew to hate the cheap room with its slanted ceiling laced with spider webs. It had a one-burner spirit stove and a cracked wash basin. The grimy communal toilet was two floors down. She dreaded the stairs that repeatedly plunged her and Pavel into darkness when the timed lights went out.   It was only early in the mornings, before they set off for the café, that she was able to savor a few moments of pleasure. Marcel, the concierge's son, kept carrier pigeons on the roof, and his returning birds, ruffling their feathers, liked to congregate on Sophie's window sill to peck at the bread Pavel brought home from the café. Sophie would watch him stand on a chair at the open window, smiling and talking to the strutting birds. She could not stop shivering in the cold air, but it was worth it to see him happy.

After leaving work at the café, Sophie's afternoons were burdensome. She tried to keep Pavel amused without venturing out in the bad weather. They often stayed in bed, where she told or read him stories. Sometimes, a terrible feeling of hopelessness came over her, and all she wanted was to curl up and sleep. She could hardly bring herself to heat up simple meals—boiled or scrambled eggs, soup or mashed potatoes. Sometimes, as a treat, she reheated a pan of soup or vegetables that Rózsi offered if there were café leftovers.

Sophie's other worry was money ... or rather, the lack of it. Rent was one hundred and thirty francs a week. What with the city's social-security vouchers and sixty francs from Willy's fortnightly pay packet, she barely scraped by. She still hunted for blemished vegetables and fruit in the nearby markets mainly because Pavel enjoyed the treasure hunt.

When Sophie worked at the café, Rózsi usually gave them lunch as well as paying her forty francs at the end of the week. In addition to the morning set-up, mopping and cleaning, Sophie helped run the cash register. She also helped Andreas in the bakery, washing and drying pans and mopping the café floor.

Aside from her own misery, she noticed that the café's atmosphere was changing. Customers were less cheerful, complaining about shortages and government restrictions. Andreas stopped his usual tune-humming and mulled over the constant news flashes. Sometimes he listened to broadcasts in French from Nazi stations. The news was depressing—food was in short supply, citizens was required to work sixty hours a week, and homeless refugees from Central Europe swamped the city. Russia attacked Finland, and the worst news of all for Andreas, Hungary—his motherland—had formally joined the fascist Axis powers.

Even the popular songs Sophie heard on Radio France were bittersweet. Whenever Jean Sablon sang about waiting day and night for his loved one, she would think of Willy and weep.

All the same, Sophie felt she was useful to the Szigetis and she practiced her French with the customers. Often, when she stumbled through a difficult sentence, Rózsi would clap her hands and smile, nodding her head back and forth. "Keep at it, Sophie, my dear. Your French gets better and better."

Despite the loneliness and the daily scrabble of living in Paris, Sophie understood she was extracting a pearl from her unhappy situation: cooking skills. Her socialite mother had never taught her sixteen-year-old daughter how to run a household. In her marriage to Willy, Sophie believed she fulfilled most of his expectations. She provided him a healthy son, was an affectionate bed-companion, and at the cafés and concerts they attended, presented herself at his side as a well-dressed, attractive wife. Her life with him and his circle of friends had once been easy, enjoyable and fun. She loved it when he played the piano and relished his tales of travel to business schools in Vienna, London and Paris.

In their marriage, Sophie did not have the burden of keeping *kosher* or attending Temple. Willy's parents, Emil and Judit, had turned away from Judaic tradition, as did many middle class families living in the Austro-Hungarian culture; enlightened Jews who admired everything German and did their best to assimilate. Their households, with the help of servants, ran like clockwork.

But when Willy realized Sophie could not cook or even manage her home properly, he didn't criticize or show his disappointment. He hired and supervised the servants himself.

Sophie's heart sang when Willy's first letter arrived from the south. She kept it in her apron pocket at the café and re-read it often.

> Agde. November 17ᵗʰ, 1939
> My dearest Sophie.
>
> I miss you both very much. I hope you got my cards from Agde and Béziers. Thank you for the letters. They come with a few days delay. I'm glad you have enough money to get by and sorry to hear Pavel is being difficult. I expect he misses his Táta. Tell him I miss him too. You must wait in Paris until I can arrange better lodging for you near my posting.
> The weather here has been bad: nothing like the sunny paradise promised by Vlásek at the Consulate. We have rain, cold, and even snow. We heard the Loire River is beginning to freeze over. I share a long wooden hut with forty other men. Sanitary conditions are terrible. But the food is better than I hoped for. We have a mobile cooking team with a chef from Hôtel Alcron in Prague. We even had horsemeat stew when one of the officer's mounts broke a leg!
> Basic training is hard. Up at five every morning. I've managed the long marches and drills, but each night I'm exhausted. It should be over in two to three weeks. My battalion is to be transferred to a village south of Narbonne where we will be training with field guns. There's a big sergeant who orders

us around. Not a bad sort. According to him our top brass are fed up with having too many civilian volunteers in the ranks. Another problem is that we have a surplus of officers and not enough soldiers.

Guess what? That Sgt. offered me a job at army headquarters. Something administrative. I talked about you and Pavel joining me down here. He said that soldiers with families can rent rooms in the villages. I could start looking right now but with this terrible weather, I know you would hate it here. Even if I found you a room, I would still be living in camp about five km. away.

Give Pavel a big hug and a kiss from his Táta.

A thousand kisses, Willy

P.S. We heard the Russians have attacked Finland. Things go from bad to worse. P.P.S. I think I may soon get leave to come to Paris

Sophie read the letter to Pavel, imagining Willy in fatigues, thirsty and marching with a heavy pack along winding muddy roads. She longed to see him, put her arms round him.

"Is *Táta* coming?" Pavel asked, clinging to his mother's knee. He took the letter from her and studied it from different angles as if he wanted to find a way to understand the writing.

"No, Pavel, darling, not yet." Sophie turned away, not wanting him to see her tears. She did not know how much longer she could bear to be on her own with Pavel. She rarely had a good night's sleep: tossing and turning sometimes with recurring nightmares or waking in the early hours. She had lost her appetite, lost weight, and cried for no reason. Even simple tasks seemed insurmountable. The sooner Willy arrived, the better.

CHAPTER TEN

The Battalion *Macher*
South of France. November/December, 1939

It was raining in Béziers as Willy walked along Allée Paul Riquet to the Municipal Theater that housed General Ingr's headquarters. With his capote dripping water on to the tiled floor of the foyer, he clicked his heels in front of a sergeant sitting behind a fine desk with brass inlays. "Private Kohut, reporting." Through the adjacent open auditorium doors he noticed that most of public seating had been removed; replaced by a warren of wooden cubicles, some occupied by uniformed men. "Is this where I'm supposed to work?"

The sergeant studied a ledger, shook his head and picked up his telephone. Five minutes later, he said, "You are to go to Colonel Zientek's office at Fifteen, Rue Auguste Fabrégat." He handed Willy a mimeographed map. "A mansion. You can't miss it. Nice door frame. Eighteenth century." He offered an explanatory smile. "I was a wood-carver in Prague."

Half an hour later, Willy, still cold and damp, stood at attention in the Colonel's office, glancing furtively at the beamed ceilings, heavy damask curtains and walnut-paneled walls. A requisitioned *palais*, he guessed. The room reeked of cigar smoke. Colonel Zientek, tall and heavy-shouldered stood at the window, his back to the room. He seemed to be reading a document.

Willy noticed the elaborate pastoral landscapes painted on the stucco ceiling. Voluptuous nymphs disrobed themselves in front of appreciative gallants while deer and other small creatures peered at them from behind shrubs and trees. The naked bodies made him think of Sophie and how much he missed her, holding her close, her smooth skin and the soft give of her breasts. The Colonel's gruff voice snapped him back to reality.

"You're late, Kohut."

"Very sorry, sir. The truck dropped me off at the station and I walked to headquarters. They sent me here."

"I insist on punctuality." Zientek clipped the end of a cigar and put a flame to it as he studied Willy from under heavy gray eyebrows. "You get a two-week tryout. If you don't come up to requirements, you're back at training camp."

"Yes sir."

"You'll work from eight-thirty till three when there's a transport run back to Agde—in the office next to mine. We call it the powder room." The colonel puffed out smoke like a laboring locomotive. "A damned short day by regimental standard, so I expect top rate performance, y'hear me?"

Willy thought Zientek, with his close-cropped hair, rugged features and the cigar jammed in his mouth, looked every inch a career soldier. "The powder room, as in storing gunpowder, sir?"

The colonel winced. "Face powder, *vojín*: it is the room where Marquise de Soulet's lady friends once gossiped and preened. This mansion serves as our headquarters and we must exercise extreme care of the furniture and décor. At the moment, the 'powder room' contains all our personnel, reference and supply files, a typewriter and the regimental safe. You will, of course, familiarize yourself with everything. I presume you can type?"

"Yes sir." Willy locked his hands behind his back, hiding his damaged finger. Stupidly, he had not foreseen using a typewriter, but he would manage.

Zientek paced the floor, flexing his neck to ease out

some stiffness. The man was tense and full of energy, and Willy understood that he would need to impress this officer right away if he wanted to keep this job.

"You're just a private, Kohut, but apparently you ran a successful fabric business in Prague. That means you understand accounting and inventory problems and—you're fluent in French, I hear."

"Yes sir."

The commander pulled up a gilt armchair and sat. "Good. In that case, I expect you can handle the local dialect. We rely heavily on town's people and the French military. They're often difficult to deal with. In my experience they're inadequate at initiating tasks, or even completing them for that matter."

He rested his cigar on the desk ashtray and cleared his throat. "Nothing in the Béziers municipal administration is ever quite what it seems—hidden motives, unexplained actions, and endless discussions. These French are a complicated lot." Zientek stared at Willy, absently tapping his blotting pad with a long finger. "I'm counting on you to learn our operation like the back of your hand, and soon."

Zientek leaned back, steepling his hands. "You are here to enable me to get the best out of our French allies with the least effort and cost. That will be easier now that the French have recognized President Beneš and our National Council in Paris as the *de facto* Czechoslovak government. We can now mobilize and train at full speed."

"Excellent news, sir."

Zientek picked up an ivory letter opener and rotated it between his fingers like a conjurer.

"I'm not unfamiliar with Yiddish, Kohut ... a form of German, I believe? There's a word I like in Yiddish, *macher*. It describes someone who gets things done—a person who lubricates life's creaky wheels and solves difficult problems. Am I right?"

Willy nodded. There were other not-so-complimentary definitions of a *macher*.

Zientek smiled. "You will be our *macher* in the 'powder room'. However, I must warn you. We have a number of young career officers here who were educated at the Hranice military academy—fervent nationalists, of course. They are unhappy with our recruits, especially Jews like you." He hesitated. "Most of these officers speak only Czech. When they hear their men speaking German, Hungarian, or Yiddish—even Slovak—they get irritated."

Willy stayed calm but he was aware of tension in his stomach. An army of grumpy officers supervising inexperienced but independent-minded recruits was a recipe for trouble. "I'll do my best, sir. Are there other Jewish men here at headquarters?"

"One or two. And we have Alex Schwarz—a Jewish chaplain ordained by the Paris *Grand Rabbin*. We brought him in to improve morale after the problem with the three hundred Jewish volunteers who arrived from Palestine."

"Problem, sir?"

Zietenk drummed fingers on the desk and looked away. "An anti-Jewish incident. Unpleasant. Schwarz is arranging a religious celebration at the camp. What d'you call it? Annoka, or something like that. Should settle things down."

Willy had heard rumors about the demonstration and wondered if there had been any injuries. He was getting more nervous about this so-called "easy" job at headquarters but there was no backing out. "Sir, if I may comment on the definition of *macher*. That term is also used to disparage an individual who thinks he is a big shot, but isn't."

Zientek laughed. "I hope you are not alluding to me. In any case, I appreciate your candor, which suggests that I can rely on your reliability and loyalty, yes?"

"Thank you, sir. Are there specific orders for me to follow?"

"Captain Rudček, my aide, is your supervisor. He will show you the lay of the land and specify your daily tasks. Report to him in the staff room upstairs. Dismissed."

Willy saluted and went up the grand staircase to find the staff room. It was almost empty except for four desks, each with a chair, gooseneck lamp and a telephone—a stout, dark-haired woman sat in a corner, frowning and banging away on a typewriter.

"Captain Rudček is *out*," she said in French, when Willy asked his whereabouts. "He has gone to get the Renault van and have lunch, I suppose." She sniffed disapproval. "Captain Rudček takes long lunches."

"In that case, where can I get something to eat?"

"We only have coffee and tea here. When you leave the building turn left. Three hundred meters along the street there is Chez François. Acceptable food, but avoid the *fricassé*."

An hour later, when Willy returned Captain Rudček was still not there. The "powder room" was three meters square with a tall window and pink satin wallpaper. A bank of black filing cabinets stood against two walls. Willy sat in the only chair: green velvet and button-backed, and checked that the telephone on the inlaid rococo desk worked. He smiled. Comfortable working conditions, thanks to the Marquise. He would have time to write letters—maybe even use this telephone to call Sophie at Café Budapest.

Ensconced in the comfortable office chair with a cup of coffee on the scarred desk, Willy considered his new career. He expected it would be similar to civilian business settings, no doubt modified by the strict hierarchy of military tradition—of which he knew nothing except that he would be subservient to officers. He guessed his greatest challenge would be to obey orders and at the same time to offer suggestions. He had no wish to be slapped down or made to look a fool.

The filing cabinets contained commissary and personnel files that encompassed all Czechoslovak units in the Hérault region. A poorly assembled instruction manual on his desk directed the user to check and sort account slips, enter transactions into a large black ledger, and summarize expense totals for each day.

Willy explored his domain, starting at the top drawer of the nearest cabinet and then sifting through the others. Eventually, he found his own dossier among the personnel records. What did they know about him? Not much: owner of a textile importing business in Prague, a wife and one child. Jewish religion. Fluent in Slovak, Hungarian, German, French, and English, with passable Polish. He soon found, on a dusty shelf, a card index naming all the files in the cabinets. He methodically checked whether the folders in every drawer were in order and in the correct location. They were not.

As Willy started on the task of organizing the files, the door swung open and a tall, fair-haired officer stood at the threshold, a white silk scarf knotted at his throat. Willy sprang to his feet and saluted. Unusual, he thought. He hadn't seen any other officers dressed this way.

The officer flicked a speck off his crisp uniform. "I'm Captain Rudček. I expect you're the replacement from Agde assigned to this office? I hope to God you speak acceptable French."

Willy noticed Rudček's white cotton gloves and glanced at the officer's angular face wondering what wearing all these white accessories meant. "Yes sir. I'm Private Kohut—fluent in French and other languages as well."

The captain stared. "So," he said, curling his lip as he studied Willy from top to toe. "Finally we have a linguist. But it's a pity our colonel has seen fit to hang a Jewish private around my neck. Have you met our eminent leader?"

"A fine man, Captain."

"Well said and cunningly circumspect of you. To my mind,

Zientek is too honest to ever make general, but he's a reasonable fellow, all told." He paused to flick another speck of dirt off his lapel. "I will be blunt, Kohut. I don't like Jews. However, I suppose, like many of your race, you are educated and resourceful. In which case, I'll expect you to engage in intelligent conversation and keep me entertained as we undertake our foraging expeditions for regimental supplies. By the way, *vojín*, you look a mess."

"What do you mean, Captain?"

"Go next door and look in the mirror, and then come back and tell me."

In the bathroom Willy studied his appearance. He was still the same person, broad-shouldered with a roundish face and oval wire-rim glasses unevenly lodged on his nose. He was well-shaven. There was no dirt on his *blouson* shirt and his tie was neat. His hands were clean.

Back in the powder room, Willy saluted. "My trousers have two or three tears in the material, sir. They're quite old—what I was issued on the first day. Otherwise, I didn't notice anything wrong."

Rudček curled his lip. "I refuse to work with an unkempt-looking soldier. Take a hundred francs out of the safe, get yourself a haircut and buy a decent set of trousers somewhere in town."

Willy ground his teeth and saluted. He had taken an instant dislike to his boss.

Later, Rudček explained that he was responsible for battalion records, finances, and arranging food supplies for the camps. For Willy, this meant boring paperwork and driving out in the freezing cold to inspect farms, meet wholesale suppliers and make buying trips to town markets. As the afternoon advanced, he realized that his officer had little experience in maintaining inventories.

Rudček talked disparagingly about the working class, Communists and the Roma and Jews in particular. Willy found him to be articulate, sarcastic, and blunt. The bluntness was good. Rudček was unrestrained in his thoughts or opinions, so at least Willy knew where he stood.

Over the next few mornings, Willy found it difficult to restrain his temper and keep a calm face as he listened to Rudček's diatribes—he was an ordinary soldier and vulnerable. Nevertheless, he often wondered what events or beliefs had caused this man to spout so many misconceptions about Jews. Rudček claimed they manipulated the justice system to line their pockets, spread lies that undermined national morale, and used music and doctoring to infiltrate the upper classes. Worst of all, they paid others to do their fighting.

As instructed, Willy studied the battalion files, preparing to assume responsibility and control over the mass of stored information in the cabinets. Guessing that the command structure at HQ was likely to be a jungle through which he had to maneuver, he decided to concentrate on assessing the character and motives of the people with whom he came into contact. Willy understood that he served two customers, Colonel Zientek and Sergeant Kukulka. He would have to act like a *macher*—a soldier who could cross the line of military rectitude; a patriot who wasn't quite a crook.

In late November, Willy's job expanded. Instead of leaving Béziers in the mid-afternoon, he spent each day at Colonel Zientek's offices, hitching a ride back to Agde late in the evening.

He and Rudček took the clattering Renault van on trips to town stores, markets, and farms, buying food and other supplies. Rudček, a Mauser pistol at his belt, paid suppliers out of a suitcase full of French banknotes and left the negotiations to Willy. Depending on the circumstances, purchases were either loaded into the truck or delivered by the farmer. Willy kept his bargain with Kukulka, storing illicit cognac, cigars and candied fruits in a padlocked wooden box kept in the back of the Renault, covered by an old blanket. Rudček never bothered to look there.

Captain Rudček always wore his white scarf and gloves. Willy ignored his superior's eccentricity but as the days passed he became more and more curious.

One day, while driving to the market at Narbonne, Willy discovered from his chatty superior that Colonel Zientek had come up with a solution to the heavy cost of paying wages to the Czechoslovak Army's surplus of officers. "He'll start on the Yids," Rudček gloated. "Demote them to line soldiers. In fact, it wouldn't be a bad idea to make them wear a yellow star on their uniforms."

"A yellow star, sir. What's that?" Willy said between his teeth, as he negotiated around a horse and cart on the road. He feigned ignorance, but fury wound him so tight that his arms and shoulders ached as he tried to control the wobbly steering. The van veered toward one of the tall lime trees along the country road.

Rudček clutched at the dashboard as Willy corrected the van's direction. "For Christ's sake, Kohut, keep to the road. You must have heard the news about the embroidered Star of David. Polish Jews have to wear them on their outer clothes; that way everyone knows who they are and how to treat them. I think it's a brilliant idea."

Willy bit his lip and pressed hard on the accelerator.

* * *

As he had hoped, Willy found time, after Rudček had left for one of his habitually long lunches, to make a short telephone call to Café Budapest. Sophie, Pavel, and the Szigetis usually ate lunch together at twelve-thirty and Willy got in the habit of calling once a week, hoping that his sparse calls would not be noticed by the regimental auditor when the monthly telephone bill arrived.

Even though he could tell Sophie controlled her emotions in front of the Szigetis, it was a wonderful feeling to talk to her and hear Pavel say a few words. The calls seemed almost dreamlike, unconnected to his everyday duties; afterward his imagination would roam, thinking about their time together in Paris. Sometimes, an immense sense of loneliness came over him, and he would get up and walk the mansion, studying the Marquise's paintings and nineteenth- century furniture as a way to overcome his sadness.

This was how he found the music room, open only because an elderly woman was inside, cleaning and dusting. Like the other rooms, it was richly decorated with gilded stucco on the ceiling and moiré silk on the walls. Standing in the middle of the parquet floor was a grand piano, a Pleyel. Without a moment's hesitation he sat down and began to play a Chopin prelude—still full of errors and fudged notes but better than before. His finger ached but felt stronger and more flexible. When he finished, the cleaning woman, smiling and shaking her head with pleasure, applauded, a duster still in her hands. "You play beautifully, Monsieur."

He came up to her, removed the duster and kissed her fingers. "I need to practice, Madame. Will you permit me to play again?"

She looked at him and smiled shyly. "Our secret, Monsieur. I give you a key but you can play only at *midi* when everyone is at lunch." She tapped her nose and winked.

Willy bent forward and again kissed her fingers.

* * *

Strangely enough Willy found his office job intriguing, gaining an insight into military organization and culture. He discovered that a good number of the 11,000 soldiers Kukulka had feared would swamp the camp had been assigned to units in several towns and villages across the South of France: Avignon (Engineers), Montpellier (Signals Unit), Roquefort-des-Corbières (Motorcycle Squadron), Le Lac (Antitank Battery), Lapalme (Cavalry), Sigean (2nd Battalion), Portel (3rd Battalion), and Béziers (Divisional Headquarters).

The dossiers also revealed that about thirty Czechoslovak women and children were lodged with the inhabitants of five nearby villages: Sillat, Sigean, Le Lac, Portel, and Lapalme. Willy assumed Sophie and Pavel would also live in one of these villages if he could get them out of Paris.

One day, in the powder room, he came across a dossier labeled Discharged Personnel. Flipping through the contents, he found lists of soldiers and the occasional officer who, for various reasons, had left the army in recent weeks.

One name caught his eye, *Hans Lussik, Private*. His mouth went dry and his stomach turned over; the same spelling Vlásek had shown him in Paris. He was almost sure now that this was Hans Lessig, the man he wanted to kill—the man who had stolen his correspondence from their apartment in Prague; the man who told the Germans that Willy was a British spy, the bastard responsible for his six weeks of prison beatings and the near destruction of his little finger.

In the dossier, Willy found brief details about Lussik/Lessig, and they matched what he knew: Age: 34. Born: Pressburg. Occupation: Prague journalist. Unmarried. Appearance: height: 1.85 meters, thin, stooped, fair-haired, spectacles. Claims to be part of Czechoslovak resistance group. SUDETENLANDER … UNRELIABLE, was printed in pencil beside his name.

According to the dossier, in mid-September Lussik had made his way across the Sudeten border to Switzerland and on to Paris. He enlisted through Vlásek at the Czechoslovak Consulate.

Lussik had been assigned to a signals unit in Montpellier and was caught stealing money and valuables from officers' lockers. He escaped from detention only hours before a court martial was to be held. The French police had been informed.

If Lussik, or Lessig was at large in the Béziers area, Willy guessed he would be short of cash and not get far. So if they happened to meet, well, Willy would kill him—if he could get hold of a suitable weapon. In his mind, he practiced explanations for shooting Lessig. *An unfortunate accident, sir. He was threatening me. He stole money from our military. The man was a deserter and dangerous.*

Two days later, just before a trip to buy food from a supplier in Narbonne, Willy asked Rudček for permission to get a sidearm from the armory.

Rudček raised his eyebrows. "I don't see the need, Kohut. I have a gun and I'm an expert marksman. I can protect myself."

"I've been thinking, sir … about our mission. Everyone around here knows we carry a lot of cash in the truck. What if we were attacked and robbed? Imagine Colonel Zientek's reaction? Two guns would be better than one."

Rudček laughed. "I don't think so, *vojín*. The locals haven't got the nerve to do something like that. They're simple farmers, not gangsters."

Willy slowed the truck and stopped on the verge by a field of cabbages. He looked earnestly at Rudcek. "I'm serious, sir. If you were able to read the French newspapers, you would know that the south of France is full of desperate people: Spanish refugees from Franco, and thousands from Central Europe. French farmers have shotguns and they set their farm dogs on anyone they don't know. How about it, sir? I cover you, you cover me."

"I'll think about it, Kohut."

Two days later, as they got into the Renault truck, Rudček

pulled the front page of the previous day's Marseille-Matin newspaper from his attaché case and laid it on Willy's knees. "You were right, *vojín*. Sabine, our secretary in the staff room, handed me this. Two men robbed a bank in Montpellier. Refugee Serbs. They shot a policeman in the stomach."

He pulled a pistol from his briefcase and laid it on the floor by Willy's feet. "This is for you, Kohut. To be used only for protecting ourselves."

CHAPTER ELEVEN

The Malakoff Torte
Paris. December 17th, 1939

A cold, dense fog shrouded the upper stories of the houses on the Rue de Carmes. Holding Pavel's hand, Sophie stood shivering on the threshold of the Café Budapest, puzzled at the hand-written sign hanging inside the glass pane: *Fermé*. She tried the handle and banged on the door.

After a minute or so, Rózsi opened it, a frown on her plump, wrinkled face. "It's already past nine. You're late, dear."

Sophie frowned back. Why the reprimand if the café was closed? "So, why aren't you open?"

Inside, in the warmth, Sophie stared at Rózsi, ashamed that she felt so hostile. Why did she feel like this? "I'm sorry. We had trouble getting ready." This had become her regular excuse for the lassitude and procrastination that enveloped her every day and made her late. What she had wanted most of all on this freezing morning was to stay in bed and sleep.

"Why are you still closed?" she asked as she hung up her coat, unwound Pavel's scarf and took off his dirty shoes. Sophie wondered if she would ever get rid of the waves of unease and discontent that swamped her when she opened her eyes each morning.

Rózsi locked the door again. "I don't suppose you remember, my dear. Once a month, Andreas goes to buy supplies at Les Halles market. He takes his cart. No baker, so no bread."

Sophie hung her beret on a peg by the counter. "You mean he pushes it all that way ... and back?"

Rózsi nodded. "He comes back after lunch, but only after a few cognacs with a Hungarian acquaintance. He likes to sober up before getting here. The poor man doesn't get much fun, so I don't complain."

"So there's no work for me today?" Sophie put on her apron, irritated that the Szigetis had not warned her about closing the café, but relieved that she wouldn't have to make the effort to be nice to customers. She found it hard to smile at anyone, even poor Pavel. His whimperings woke her up at night and she often lay awake in bed thinking about Willy's imminent arrival. He had sent her a printed card announcing *un répit militaire*. Three days' leave in Paris.

Of course she was desperate to see him but at the same time her stomach churned when she thought about facing him. In the eight weeks he had been gone, she was no longer the same person. And for God's sake, why was that? She had no idea except that she seemed to be in a constant state of irritability and exhaustion. What was wrong with her?

"With no customers, we have two things to do this morning," Rózsi said briskly, watching Pavel bite into a walnut *kifli*. She handed Sophie a mop and bucket. "We wash the floor, and polish the tables and chairs, and then you can watch me make a birthday cake. I forgot to tell you. Andreas has his sixty-first birthday on Tuesday. I'm making his favorite supper."

Rózsi bent down to wipe Pavel's crumbly mouth but he backed away and gave her a sour look. The fine lines of her eyebrows quivered. "Hmm, this little fellow is rather grumpy today. You too, I think. I'm worried about you, my dear. These days, you always seem sad."

"I can't help it," murmured Sophie, garnering a sympathetic glance from her employer.

"At least the ovens are cool, so Pavel can play anywhere in the bakery." Rózsi caressed the boy's springy curls. Off you go, *Pavlíček*. You can take Andreas' box of wooden animals out of the big drawer but be good and careful with them. They are precious."

He grimaced and then made a face at her. "Don't like *babička*."

"Pavel!" Sophie shook him, black anger swelling in her chest. She resisted a strong urge to smack him. "Pavel—don't be naughty. Go and play."

Pavel stuck out his tongue and threw Furry Lion away, knocking spoons off a rack beside the stove. "I want go park. You said we could, Maman."

Rózsi bent down and whispered in his ear. His eyes widened and then, in a trembly voice, he squeezed out, "Sorry, Maman," before scuttling off through the bakery door to the alcove next to the ovens.

"What did you say to him, Rózsi? He's impossible these days."

Rózsi tapped her ear signaling that Pavel could still hear them talking. "I threatened a week of no pastries. Lead a boy by his stomach. Now let's do the cleaning. Afterwards I will show you how to make a Malakoff."

"What on earth is a Malakoff?"

"A special cake—for Andreas' birthday. Now let's get started on the cleaning."

Sophie shrugged and went to fill a bucket with soapy water. As the two women set about cleaning, her mind returned to Willy and how unfair it would be to tell him how miserable she felt. And what about sleeping together? Willy had slept alone in a bunk bed for eight weeks—he would definitely want her. She wanted him beside her … but not sex. Sex seemed abrupt, like a threat. How would she respond to his desire? Could she even respond?

Later the two women sat on stools at the kitchen counter. "Before we start this confection," said Rózsi, patting Sophie's arm. "I'll tell you the story of how the Malakoff Torte came to be created."

A prickle of enthusiasm punctured Sophie's listlessness. "I need something nice. Tell me."

Rózsi drew in a breath and repositioned her ample buttocks on the stool. "During the Crimean War, long ago, a French Field Marshal called Aimable Jean-Jacques Pélissier defeated the Russian Cossacks at Malakoff Castle. To celebrate the Marshal's victory, his chef invented the torte. The cake is shaped like the round hill where the French Zouaves raised their victorious tricolor flag. Whipped cream spread all over the cake represents deep snow. It was winter."

A memory surfaced for Sophie: her mother's cook putting the finishing touches to a dark layered cake in a warm kitchen. "Similar thing with the Esterházy Torte, I suppose—named after one of the Hungarian princes."

Rózsi smiled, tapping her temple with a knowing finger. "Ah, yes, that one. Chocolate buttercream spiced with cognac and vanilla. You spread it between almond dough layers and a fondant icing. It was the creation of a Budapest confectioner, I think. Anyway, enough history. Let's get on with it. I have all the ingredients ready."

"You have a recipe?"

"No," Rószi laughed. "It floats somewhere in my head."

For the next hour Sophie watched Rózsi make the torte, trying to learn what she did and how she did it. But all the time, Willy's upcoming visit clouded her mind. Finally she said, "Can we stop for a moment, Rózsi? I want to ask you something."

"What is it?"

"Willy arrives tomorrow. He'll see how awful I look. He'll think I've made a mess of everything. I don't know why I feel so worn down."

"You've been through so much, dear."

"But when he was in prison last year, I managed fine. We survived the escape from Prague and got safely to Paris. If we're safe, why do I feel so sad?" Sophie burst into tears and covered her face with her apron.

Rózsi wiped her hands on a dishcloth and soothingly rubbed Sophie's back. "I'm sorry, my dear. I expect Pavel senses you are unhappy."

Sophie nodded, her words muffled as she dried her cheeks. "I feel as if I'm useless … a bad mother. What can I say to Willy?"

"Tell your husband the truth; neither you or Pavel are happy. The way you deal with little Pavel now—it's inconsistent and unfortunate."

Sophie raised her tear-stained face. "What do you mean?"

"One minute you love and spoil him, the next, he gets smacked. He misses his father. You can tell from the way he looks up to Andreas. Tomorrow, you and Willy will be reunited. I hope you will all snuggle up in bed." Rózsi's eyes glinted "Maybe that will help."

Again, Sophie couldn't stop her tears. She and Willy would be together for three or four days, but then he would leave. She felt hot and shaky and suddenly realized why: anger. Willy had left her alone in Paris and made her miserable. "I don't feel that I love Willy any more. Not as I used to."

"Not love him? Ridiculous. Has he changed? What happened?"

"He was everything I had dreamed of. Handsome, even with his glasses. He was charming and knew so much more than me about the world, he spoke several languages, he was a marvelous pianist and he loved to have fun. I was happy then."

"Isn't he still the same, even after your escape?"

Sophie studied her nails, not wanting to look into Rózsi's inquiring eyes. "He brought us from Prague. I'm grateful and I admire him tremendously. But it's different now. *I'm* different."

Rózsi smiled.

"Perhaps, I'm more aware of his faults." Slowly she dried her eyes. "He takes me for granted, doesn't talk things over. He's bitter, you know." Sophie reached out, trying to keep the sadness out of her voice. "You are the only friend I can talk to …"

Pavel walked into the kitchen holding up a small broken giraffe. "Maman, make him better."

Rózsi patted Pavel's cheek and pointed at the mixing bowl. "Monsieur Giraffe must wait a minute, young man. Rózsi is showing your Mama something."

"I broke him, Maman." Tears pooled in the boy's eyes. He pouted and kicked the toy across the floor. Sophie put a finger to her lips and frowned.

With some effort Rózsi picked Pavel up. Breathing heavily, she sat him on the counter by the mixing bowl and winced. "*Szent María*, my joints are bad today. Now *Pavlíček*, take this spoon and scrape up what's left of coffee-nut cream."

Sophie gave her a look of sympathy. "Isn't there anything you can take for the pain?"

Rózsi shook her head. "Only hot wax baths. Now, that's enough about me. Let's talk topping."

Sophie stroked Rózsi's arm. Her friend preferred to keep her pain to herself. "So … what about the Malakoff topping?"

"Just before serving, I put a nice thick layer of whipped cream on top. That's the snow. And to represent the victorious soldiers, I sprinkle the cream with grated chocolate and slivers of caramelized almonds. Pavel can help me do that."

Rózsi turned to Sophie and kissed her on the cheek. "Cooking can be fun."

As Pavel's cheeks acquired streaks of cream, Sophie began to wash utensils and bowls in the sink. This was something she could do to help. "So what else is there for the birthday dinner?"

Rózsi's eyes glowed. "Hot apple soup and dumplings … because it's winter. Then, roasted fish with mushrooms in paprika sauce, stuffed cabbage and egg *spaetzle*."

Sophie tried to generate some enthusiastic words but they wouldn't come. Only, "I'm sure Willy will love it—if he gets here."

* * *

It was mid-afternoon when Andreas manhandled his cart into the bakery. Ignoring Rózsi's disapproving stare he pulled off his wet hat and cape. "Stop muttering, woman," he said as she mopped the wheel tracks and footprints. He and Sophie removed the cart's oilskin cover and began to stack boxes of apples and pears, bags of flour and cans of summer fruits against the walls. Pavel watched.

Rózsi frowned. "Did you get everything on my list?"

Andreas nodded, stretching his back to get the kinks out. He picked up an apple, polished it on his thigh and handed it to Pavel. "I had a good lunch but the prices have gone up. Wartime shortages, I suppose."

"You met Gregor? I suppose you talked war. That's all he thinks about."

Andreas's face crinkled into a smile. "Today, he was in heaven. The British trapped a Nazi cruiser in a South American port. The captain pulled the plug—sank his own ship and committed suicide."

"Ugh, that is horrible. But, for us, South America is a long way from Paris," said Rózsi with a grimace. "All I know is that here … we are losing customers and income. Will this half-baked war go on forever? I hate it."

Andreas poured a cup of coffee from the pot on the stove and took a sip. "Mmm, half-baked you say," he said, giving Rózsi an amused look. "Just the right thing for my wife to say. Anyway, while I was out, did you have time to discuss the excursion?"

Sophie stood stock-still with a crate of apples in her arms. "What excursion? Rózsi hasn't said a word."

Rózsi shrugged. "I was going to tell you. We thought it would make a nice change to take you, Pavel and Willy—when he gets here—to visit our friends who have a farm outside Paris. Their name is Duclet, nice people. They have all kinds of animals. It's only an hour by train. It would make a nice day out—a change for you."

For a brief moment, Sophie pictured Pavel in a farmyard surrounded by chickens and quacking ducks. But then, her heart jumped; what if he threw a tantrum?

"Do you have a *Carte de Renseignements* to travel outside Paris?" said Andreas.

Sophie stared at the baker as if dumbstruck and then the tears started. "I'm sorry. I don't know why I'm crying. It's stupid. I don't think Willy will want to go to a farm. That's what he does as part of his job. Why did you arrange this?"

Andreas leaned back against the door jamb, massaging his stubbly chin. The way he looked at her, Sophie thought, was unusually hesitant.

"No need to cry," he grunted, tightening his apron. "We thought you'd like a change. I sort of thought you might refuse. Willy and me talked on the telephone. He was happy with the idea."

"You talked to Willy? Why, when?"

"Yesterday. You took Pavel home early."

* * *

When Willy telephoned from Béziers HQ, Andreas was quite frank about Sophie's despondency and how ill she looked. He also mentioned Pavel's bad moods.

"That's not what she said in her letters," Willy replied after a silence. "Why would she keep this from me? We will sort it out when I get there."

"Rózsi is very worried about her—two weeks ago, here in the café, Sophie smacked Pavel several times. He was having one of his … outbursts. We've noticed other things … she was always on time for work. Not anymore. She is pale, dark around the eyes and she cries for no reason. It's obvious she doesn't get enough sleep."

"This is difficult to believe, Andreas."

"You have to change the situation."

"I don't see what I can do from here."

"Rózsi thinks Pavel should attend a *maternelle*." Andreas waited through a long pause.

"What is a *maternelle*?" Willy's voice was sharp, uncertain.

"The Germans call it kindergarten."

"Ah, one of those. You have one close by?"

"Yes, but Rózsi says foreigners have to pay—ten to fifteen francs a day."

"We can't afford that. Sophie must cope somehow—until I get there. Thank God, the floods have subsided and the trains are running again."

"I can tell you are upset, Willy. Please be gentle when you get here. How are things at the camp?"

"Could be better." Willy gave a sharp almost bitter laugh. "A different world, Andreas. I learned a few brutal lessons before I managed to find an office job."

"When you come, we want to take all of you to visit a farm in the countryside. It belongs to friends. Are you open to giving Sophie a day out?"

"Of course."

Andreas heard a door bang at the other end of the telephone.

Willy's voice dropped to a whisper. "I shouldn't be using this telephone. Goodbye."

*　*　*

Sophie went up to Andreas and pecked his cheek. She turned to Rózsi, half-smiling, relieved. Willy wouldn't be angry with her; he had agreed to the excursion. "I'm sure we will love the farm."

Andreas sighed. Baking bread was so much easier than dealing with people.

CHAPTER TWELVE

The Soldier's Return
Paris. December 18th, 1939

Willy rapped on the door. Luckily, he had glimpsed the room number just before the automatic hall light clicked off. Silently, he cursed the darkness. It was difficult to stay alert after eight hours on an unheated train and a freezing *taxi-bicyclette* ride from the Gare de Lyon. At Rue Bougainville he had stumbled up five flights of rickety stairs, hoping he was in the right building and not on the wrong floor. "It's me," he called in the dark and banged again on the door. He put his lips to keyhole. "It's me, Willy."

When the door opened, he caught his breath. Even dimly lit by the ceiling bulb, Sophie's once smiling face and pert nose looked pinched. Her cheeks were thin and blotched, eyes a little sunken. Her skin had always been flawless.

Tears glistening, she pulled him into the room. "I thought you would never come."

As they kissed and hugged, Willy stroked her back, running his hands over her buttocks. Her body was warm to his touch. *Gott behüte, why is she so thin?*

She caressed his face, "I'm glad you are back, *miláčku*. You are even more handsome than before. You've lost weight, like me." She touched his lips with her fingers. "You look so healthy. Is everything good? The finger, your chest?"

Willy nodded, forcing a smile to cover his shock. The

140

Szigetis were right to be worried, justified in intervening. "Are you all right?" he said, trying not to appear alarmed.

She half-shrugged as tears trickled down her cheeks. "Not really. I've been miserable … tired, no appetite and I keep forgetting things. Even playing with Pavel seems like a chore." She gave him a hopeful smile. Her eyes wandered over his face. "With you here, my happiness will come back."

With Sophie's head buried against his chest, Willy noticed Pavel sitting on the bed. The boy was in his pajamas, his round face suffused bright pink, his look sullen.

"Go away," the boy shouted, bouncing on the squeaky mattress. "That's my *Maminko*." He came off the bed, flailing punches and kicks at Willy's shins.

Willy couldn't suppress the harsh tone he had acquired in basic training. "NO! stop this Pavel. I'm your *Táta*. STOP fighting me!"

Pavel, his attack momentarily suspended, stared ferociously at Willy, and then collapsed on the floor, face up. His eyes were half-closed, eyeballs squirming under the lids like baby mice. His body jerked and his arms flailed around. "Don't want *Táta*. Don't want *Táta*," he wailed.

Willy gripped Pavel by the shoulder, too hard. He couldn't stop himself. *Sakra, what god-forsaken reason is there for my own son to reject me?* "That's enough, boy. This is your *Táta*. Obey!"

He was vaguely aware of Sophie pulling at his arms, sobbing, "Stop, Willy. Please." He tightened his grip, folding the boy into his chest so that he could hardly move. After a couple of minutes, Pavel stopped quivering and lay quietly in Willy's arms, looking up at his father's face. Suddenly he smiled. "*Táta*'s home."

Willy heaved a sigh, kissed his forehead, and laid him down on the bed. Pavel turned away from his parents to face the wall and began to suck his thumb.

"At first, he missed you terribly," Sophie said drying her eyes on her nightdress. "Then he stopped asking where you were."

Willy sat on the bed and put his face in his hands. "Too many damned separations. I think the army has changed me."

After Pavel went to sleep, Willy did his best to comfort Sophie as she explained how everything had deteriorated after he had left for the camp: her sleep, her appetite and vitality, her mood and her ability to give Pavel the attention he needed. They both undressed and got under the bed covers to keep warm in the freezing room. He held her soft smooth body close, surprised at the boniness of her shoulder blades and hips. His erection swelled against her belly, desire overwhelming his concern for her illness.

"Please, not now *miláčku*," she whispered. "Just hold me. I'm too nervous. Tomorrow we'll have a happy time together in the country and then we'll make love after Andreas's birthday dinner."

For a long time Willy lay with his arms round her, unable to sleep. Maybe Andreas' excursion was a good idea but it would use up time he could spend with Sophie—and there wouldn't be much of that if she was working. As for the condition she was in, well, she had never been like this. He understood why, but what could he do in three days?

* * *

"Regrettably, the nine-thirty is late," the railway conductor said to Willy, stamping his feet on the platform at the Gare St. Lazare. Under his cap he wore ear muffs against the cold and a thick coat over his uniform. With a gloved hand he pointed at the icicles hanging from the interior of the station roof. "Extraordinary, is it not, *Monsieur*? Not in fifty years has this happened." A Gauloise cigarette, glued to his lower lip, danced as he spoke. "Vernon will be your first stop."

The Kohut and Szigeti families, bundled up against the cold, waited with other grumbling passengers on Platform 3B for the delayed Le Havre express. Several morose French soldiers, similarly muffled and waiting, stamped their boots and rubbed their hands to stay warm.

With the typical French gesture of exasperation Willy knew so well the conductor flung his arms into the air. "What do you expect with such weather? Delay is normal. Everywhere trains are cancelled. Floods in the south and freezing here." He looked up and down the track and then at his pocket watch. "Today, you should have an easy run. Most of the rail points in Paris have been defrosted."

Willy exchanged a skeptical glance with Sophie. His own journey from Béziers had been stop and go. It occurred to him that the devastating weather that was freezing Europe was bogging down Britain's and France's war preparations—another reason to explain the *Drôle de Guerre?*

Twenty-five minutes later, Andreas Szigeti led the Kohuts and Rózsi into an unheated Third-class carriage with slatted benches on either side of a central corridor. They sat facing each other. As the train picked up speed, Pavel slid off his seat and ran up and down the corridor, stopping and staring at the other passengers, not saying a word.

"Be a good boy," Sophie called to him, her face red with embarrassment. "Don't bother those people. Sit here with your *Táta* and look out of the window."

Pavel stood between his father's knees and watched the countryside slip by, pointing out the cows standing around mounds of hay in the half-frozen fields. Andreas explained to Pavel that the men who put out the hay feed were farmers. They were the people who grew the summer wheat and grains he used for baking bread.

Sophie, quiet and subdued, leaned against Willy holding

one of his hands in her lap and stroking it.

"Do you think Pavel remembers all those trains we took," she said, "when we escaped through Germany? And what happened on them. We were afraid and desperate—he might still have bad memories and that's why he's become so difficult."

Willy smiled at her. "That was five months ago—summertime. A child easily forgets."

As the train neared Vernon, Rózsi explained that the Duclet farm was three kilometers outside the town divided by the River Seine and connected by a bridge. "Monsieur Duclet will be waiting for us at the station. He has a horse and carriage," she said smiling at Pavel. "The horse has a beautiful red mane and she is called Rosette. He takes her out for exercise on Sundays. Today is Sunday, so I expect Rosette will be there to give us a ride to the farm. Have you been pulled by a horse before?"

Pavel did not reply. He held Furry Lion close to his chest and kept looking out of the carriage window at the silvery ribbon of the Seine River unwinding between the snow-draped woods and fields.

At Vernon, the platform was icy, and soot-stained snow lingered on the station's slate roof. They paused outside the entrance while Andreas knocked icicles off the guttering with his walking stick. "Here," he said offering the least damaged one to Pavel. "Hold it. But don't take your gloves off. This is an ice wizard's sword." Eyes twinkling, he raised a warning finger "Guard it carefully. It's magic for little boys."

Pavel grabbed the icicle and with a sudden swipe shattered it on the station fence. He looked at Willy triumphantly. "See, Pavel makes magic."

Monsieur Duclet was waiting for them outside the station fence, leaning against the haunches of a strawberry roan. He wore a thick wool jacket with leather patches on the elbows, breeches and laced-up hunting boots. He pulled on his black beret and smiled a greeting. The blinkered horse, swishing its tail, stood between the shafts of a canopied carriage. Jets of vapor from its nostrils pierced the crisp air.

Monsieur Duclet introduced his visitors to Rosette, explaining how sweet-tempered she was and then showed Pavel how to feed the horse a carrot from his open palm. Pavel seemed unafraid of the nostril blasts and the beast's large teeth.

Willy watched Sophie smile in relief. "What a brave boy," she said.

Accepting Monsieur Duclet's offer of lap rugs, the visitors squeezed themselves into the carriage, and at a walking pace Rosette pulled them through the medieval streets of Vernon. When they reached the edge of town, Monsieur Duclet clicked his tongue. "*Plus vite, ma petite.*" The mare broke into a trot and for twenty or so minutes they traveled along a country road as far as Saint Marcel, a hamlet surrounded by farmland and woods. Monsieur Duclet turned the carriage onto a long, rutted lane that wound through fields patched with snow. They passed through an open farm gate into an orchard of bare-branched trees, its understory overgrown with shrubs and grasses.

As Rosette slowed to a walking pace along a muddy track, Willy was surprised to see several children running alongside, waving and shouting. In a few moments they reached the old farm where the children crowded around the carriage, calling out "*Bonjour Monsieur et Madame*" in shrill excited voices. They had pink-cold noses, wore coats, wool hats, and gloves and bounced up and down with excitement.

Sophie turned to Rózsi and laughed. "Exuberant little things."

Willy, pleased that she seemed happy, noticed how intently

145

Pavel watched the children's antics. His internal skepticism about wasting a whole day of his leave on this farm waned. So far, it had been exactly as Andreas and Rózsi had predicted, enjoyable and relaxing.

Duclet swung himself down and held Rosette steady by her bridle. "Welcome to our domain." His voice had a deep vibrating quality. "Mind the mud while I put the old girl away." He beamed at Pavel. "Better watch where you tread, *mon petit*. Our animal friends leave their visiting cards all over the place.

Pavel pulled on Sophie's coat. "Can I play with the children, *Maminko*?"

She gave him a warm smile and blew him a kiss.

CHAPTER THIRTEEN

The Duclet Farm, Vernon
December 18th. 1939

"Show us around first, Pascal," Rózsi said adjusting her fur-lined gloves. "I need to stretch and walk a little. Your wagon's springs were unkind to my *derrière*—and I'm sure Pavel wants to see all the animals first. Why not let the children show him?"

While Monsieur Duclet led the mare into a large barn off the courtyard, Willy and Sophie gazed at the farm buildings. The half-timbered farmhouse had a steep tiled roof still holding patches of snow. Brick walls glowed gold and red in the sun. Two gray-muzzled dogs watched from the front step, twitching their tails.

"Completely different from the farms in the south," said Willy. "Much sturdier— and that carved door is lovely. And look at those, mullioned windows. Thick glass, must be very old."

Sophie put her arm through his. "So, you've become an expert on French farms?"

He nodded as the children clustered around them, fidgeting, talking, and peering at Pavel. "Visited about fifteen of them … buying produce and meat for the army."

Sophie wrinkled her nose. "Do you smell something bad, Pavel?" She crouched down beside him and pointed to a dark pile. "That's what smells—manure, made from straw and animal poop. Don't go near it. You might get dirty."

Monsieur Duclet returned with a wheelbarrow holding a tumble of rubber boots. "These are for our visitors. Be warned, my wife, Amélie, insists on stockinged feet inside the house." He parked the wheelbarrow and rapped on the front door. It was opened by a fine-boned woman wearing a black dress; an orange bandana tamed her frizzy gray hair.

"*Ah, mes amis*," she cried, rushing forward to embrace Andreas and Rózsi. Sophie and Willy watched, smiling. Madame Duclet had a kind face and large white teeth that glinted when she spoke. Willy guessed she was in her fifties.

"This is Amélie Duclet," said Rószi. "Pascal's wife. Their son Alphonse is a lieutenant with the *15e Tirailleurs* at Douzy near the Belgian frontier; an engineer before the mobilization."

"Delighted to meet you." Madame Duclet had an effusive manner with busy hands that reminded Willy of fluttering birds. "Come inside. It's an honor to have a Czechoslovak soldier in our home. And do not pay any attention to the children. They will soon stop staring at you." She waved them away.

Rózsi turned up her coat collar. In spite of the sunshine, a cold breeze had sprung up. "No thanks. First, we will take our friends around the property. And please, Amélie, if you could speak more slowly, that will help Sophie understand. Her French is not so good."

"Of course. Go anywhere you like. You know your way around. Afterward, we will have coffee and cake with the children." She looked at Sophie. "What is your boy's name? What golden curls and blue eyes! I wasn't expecting a Jewish child to be so blond."

"Pavel, it's a Czechoslovak name," Willy broke in. He could tell Sophie had not understood Madame Duclet's comment. He hoped her remark about Pavel's appearance was not meant to be unkind. He was more interested, and puzzled, by the presence of so many children about the same age. He pointed at them. "Excuse me for asking but these—surely these are not all yours? Is this a school?"

Madame Duclet laughed. "In a sense they *are* mine, but only for a while," she said. "They come to us from families in Paris, either refugees or unemployed workers. We run a residential maternelle here. My husband owned a factory making shoe soles, but he sold it and I had enough of being a schoolteacher. We bought the farm so that poor city children could come and stay for a while and learn about farming and the countryside."

Willy looked at her admiringly. "That is remarkable. Does your husband run the farm on his own?"

"No," enjoined Andreas. "A couple of local men work for him."

"How do you keep the children busy?

Madame Duclet's eyes glittered with enthusiasm. "We have a play center with picture books, simple construction materials and puzzles. The children help us feed the animals and we take regular walks in the woods to examine nature. Now, off you go. It's cold talking with the door open."

Willy realized now that this was no ordinary farm excursion. In their telephone conversation Andreas had brought up the idea of a maternelle for Pavel. La Ferme Duclet was such a place. What was going on? Was Sophie part of a conspiracy to bring him here? Was this something to do with Pavel? He decided be patient and gather more information. As they walked around the farm, Willy edged close to Andreas. "You owe me an explanation, my friend. On the telephone, you and Rózsi recommended a *maternelle* for Pavel in Paris. I said no because of the expense. Now suddenly, here we are at a *maternelle* in the middle of nowhere. I thought this was a pleasure outing to celebrate your birthday and give Sophie a break. You were not honest with me."

Willy noticed Sophie smiling at a little girl in pigtails who had taken Pavel by the hand to pet one of the old dogs. The girl said something and the dog sat up and gave Pavel his paw. The two children began to giggle.

Andreas gently pried Willy's hand from his arm. "Calm down, my friend. This *is* an excursion and you should damn well be enjoying it. And yes, this place *is* a kind of *maternelle*. We thought Pavel might enjoy staying here with the other children— for a few days while Sophie rested up in Paris. Put yourself in your boy's shoes. See if he enjoys himself. And for your information, Monsieur Duclet's wife is an expert on children's education … and he is a rich man. They charge very little. Make the most of it."

Willy shrugged. "Okay, let's see how it goes."

The tour of La Ferme Duclet included a visit to the walled vegetable garden, empty except for cabbages, and a muddy stroll through the leafless orchard.

A couple of children were playing on the swings and climbing logs that had been set up in a clearing not far from the manure heap. When they visited the horse barn, Rosette was eating hay in her stall and several kittens played hide-and-seek among the hay bales.

The visitors picked their way through the courtyard where chickens, ducks, pigeons and two cats seemed to co-exist harmoniously. Andreas pointed out six white and red cows feeding on hay scattered in a field beyond the farmyard fence. "That's a breed from Normandy. The children drink their milk and the cream makes the finest butter in France."

The farm tour lasted longer than expected because Pavel kept turning up with different children wanting to take Willy or Sophie to see something special—the rope ladder that hung from the lower branch of a huge oak, hutches full of rabbits, two fox pelts hanging from the barn wall, and the stone pigsty that housed an enormous sow called Stephanie.

"Pavel can't stop smiling," said Sophie, slipping her arm through Willy's as they watched him playing hide and seek. "He already loves playing with these children."

Willy thoughts turned back to the traumas of the last year. Pavel had been in the middle of it: Nazis in Prague, his father in prison for six weeks, the persistent atmosphere of fear and uncertainty, and the final desperate escape by train. All that time there had been no children to play with Pavel. Willy squeezed Sophie's hand, drawing her attention away from watching the children chase each other. "You and I are here with him now. But, it might be a different story if he was left here on his own. Did you know beforehand that this was a residential kindergarten?"

Sophie's eyes widened and she shook her head. Willy saw tears forming and looked away. Was she lying? Why did she cry so easily?

Inside the farmhouse, they visited the children's dormitory in the attic and inspected the well-equipped playroom next to the huge kitchen where everyone had their meals at a long table. Willy, noticing a battered upright piano against the wall, opened the lid and tried a few notes. It was out of tune. He rubbed and flexed his little finger and then ran an arpeggio. With a good-humored look at Sophie he started to play chords, standing up. "I'll be seeing you in all the old familiar places," he crooned, "that my heart and mind embraces, all day long..." He stopped, pleased with himself.

Sophie's eyes glistened as she clapped her hands together. "Oh my God! *Miláčku*. One of the American songs you played in Prague! How..."

He closed the lid and waggled his finger. "Andreas's idea, remember? Weight exercises. A few minutes, four times a day. Also, I've been practicing every lunch time at headquarters. It's in a mansion and they have a music room."

At lunch, Sophie and Willy sat together at the long table with everyone else. They enjoyed a simple meal of rabbit stew, potatoes and cabbage, with milk for the children and wine for the adults. Willy was surprised at how the Duclet's allowed the children to talk, laugh and eat any way they wanted. No instruction on manners. He would never tolerate this laxity in his house ... not that he had one anymore.

For dessert, Madame Duclet served golden-crusted apple pies with thick cream from the cows.

"You must learn to bake like this." Rózsi smiled at Sophie, helping herself to second slice of pie.

"Delicious," Sophie admitted with a weak smile. "And now, of course, I know why you invited us here—so we would find out what a nice place this is. I think you wanted to persuade us to let Pavel stay for a while. But I'm not at all sure. Look at him. The poor boy doesn't say anything. He's intimidated."

"Yes, but you can see he's content to watch," Andreas interjected with a laugh. "Look at his smile. He likes the children, he likes it here."

Willy frowned and Sophie grabbed his hand. "Don't get annoyed, miláčku." She spoke Czech so the Szigetis would not understand. "Andreas wants the best for us and I think he may be right about Pavel being happy here. What if I moved here from Paris and lived nearby—I could see him every day."

Willy pushed his plate away, shaking his head. "I don't want to leave him in the care of people we don't know. The boy's only three and a half. Is this how a family stays together?" He steepled his fingers against his lips for a moment, as if reconsidering. "Of course, what you propose would be cheaper than living in Paris, but then you wouldn't be earning any money at the café or eating the Szigetis' good lunches. You would be lonely if you stayed here. At least, in Paris there are parks, people and markets and beautiful buildings."

Sophie looked at him, angry tears in her eyes. "Please, *miláčku*, why can't we join you in the south? I mean, now. The newspapers say the real war will start soon. Paris will be attacked. The Szigetis know they can't rely on me for much longer."

Willy drew in a long breath of frustration. His short visit had become too complicated. Life was easier at army headquarters. Problems were black and white there, instead of the family mess he had come back to. He took a deep breath. "My head is spinning with all these possibilities, Sophie. Let's talk when we get back to Paris, after Andreas's celebration dinner. We might as well make the most of the day and not think ahead for a few hours."

She nodded. "Agreed, but we don't have long. We're catching the sixteen-thirty train back to Paris so Rózsi can start cooking."

After lunch, Amélie Duclet asked the children to sing two *comptines* for the guests, "Alouette" and "Ah, Mon Beau Château," before they went up to the dormitory with Pavel in tow to have an afternoon nap. While Amélie and a village girl cleared the lunch things away, Monsieur Duclet took Willy, Sophie, and the Szigetis in his Citroën to see the medieval town of Vernon. By the time they returned to the farm, the children were up and it was almost time to leave for the train.

Arm in arm at the front door, the Duclets watched the children played tag around the car. "Pavel," Sophie called out holding his coat up while she slipped on hers. "We have to go home now. Say *au revoir* to Monsieur et Madame Duclet, and *merci pour la bonne journée.*" Pavel scowled and shook his head.

Willy went over and took his arm. "You've had a wonderful day, Pavel. Don't spoil it for everyone. Come on, we must catch the train."

Pavel spun away. "No," he shouted, "I want to be here." He raced off into the barn, scattering chickens.

It took the adults and children fifteen minutes to find the

boy, pressed into a crack between two hay bales, eyes squeezed shut. Willy tried to extricate him. Struggling and screaming, Pavel grabbed desperately for a hold.

"That's enough." Madame Duclet stood beside Willy, a frown on her face. "Come out, Pavel. You look like a silly goat with that hay all over you." The children laughed.

There was a moment of silence, and with a downcast face Pavel eased himself out from between the bales. "According to Monsieur Piaget," Madame Duclet whispered to Willy. "It's all about ego. From what I have seen today, your boy behaves much as I would expect at his age."

"I'm relieved you think so," Willy said quietly. "Most of all, I'm worried about my wife. She has been through too much this last year. She gets angry too often with the boy."

With a look of sympathy Madame Duclet patted his arm. "I know, Rózsi told me. But children remember, you know—if you hit them."

As Monsieur Duclet drove to the station, Willy held the boy snug in his arms and smiled at Sophie. He tried to hide how embattled and ashamed he had felt in the barn. "The boy fought me—in front of everyone," he said, trying to keep the hurt out of his voice. "Yesterday, he said he hated me. I wasn't expecting this."

"I'm sorry, *miláčku*," Sophie whispered back, dabbing her eyes with a handkerchief. "This is what I have to deal with almost every day. I'm exhausted from it."

The train journey back to Paris was an anticlimax. Pavel went to sleep with a sullen look on his face.

"We'll give you some privacy," Rózsi with a sad smile as she and Andreas stood. She pointed to an empty bench. "We'll sit there for a while; I'm sure you need to talk."

Willy smiled. "Thank you. Very thoughtful."

She nodded. "I'm sorry today was not a success, but we had to try something. All I know is that if Sophie's situation does not change in Paris, she will be even more unhappy than before."

Willy looked at his son, half-asleep on his military greatcoat … a little angel now. He was embarrassed that he had maligned the Szigetis. Good people. He walked over to Rózsi and embraced her. "Thank you for making such a big effort for us," he said in a low voice. "I must have seemed ungrateful and I admire you for putting up with my bad graces. You have been a wonderful friend to Sophie and I know you have Pavel's welfare in your heart. Without you I have no idea how we would have survived."

Back in his seat, Willy took Sophie's hand and laced his fingers in hers. For a long time, he said nothing and looked out of the window at the grays and browns of the darkening fields. He studied her thin face as she dozed. Even asleep she looked miserable. In his heart, he knew she couldn't go on looking after Pavel, not like this—and he had to go back to Agde.

What harm would there be if Pavel stayed at the Duclet farm for a couple of weeks? He had seen it with his own eyes. The boy fit in well; he almost forgot his parents were there. With children to play with every day, Pavel would learn French quickly. The air and food were good and Madame Duclet understood children. Sophie could visit twice a week and it would not cost much. Andreas and Rózsi were right.

After the train pulled into St. Lazare station, Andreas came up to Willy and held out his hand. He looked contrite. Sophie, holding a sleepy Pavel in her arms, gazed nervously at the two men as if she feared a public argument on the platform. "Not such a good day," Andreas said in his sonorous voice. "I will not interfere like this again. Rózsi and I would be honored if you joined us for my birthday dinner tonight." A smile spread over his face. "Did you know your wife helped make a Malakoff Torte for dessert?"

Willy returned the smile, shaking the baker's hand. He gave Sophie an admiring glance. "You made a cake, darling! And one I never heard of. That's wonderful. Of course, we'll come."

"Good," Andreas exclaimed. "Let's hope Pavel will have forgotten his rampage by the time you come for dinner."

The two men laughed. Willy took a deep breath. "It's best to tell you now, Andreas, because I leave the day after tomorrow. While Sophie slept on the train, I thought about our visit to Vernon. I will be stuck in the Agde camp for quite a while, and I don't know if or when I can come back to Paris. It's better to decide right now about Pavel and the farm."

Willy noticed Sophie's startled look. "I think the Duclet Farm might be good for Pavel, for two to three weeks, perhaps. After that, it's up to Sophie to decide what's best for him."

When he saw the relief on her face, he kissed her. "While you slept on the train, I thought it over. If you don't agree we can talk it out tonight."

Later, after dinner at the café, Willy called the Duclet Farm on the café telephone and asked if Madame would take Pavel for two weeks.

"We would be happy to have him," she said. Willy liked that her voice sounded welcoming and sincere. "Bring him to us soon—he will have fun with the other children at the Christmas holiday. We are atheists, so it's just a decorated tree, games and small presents. No prayers or carols."

"Do you expect other parents to be there?"

Madame Duclet's voice was emphatic. "No. Too complicated."

* * *

After Willy had gone back to Agde, Sophie, at last in possession of a renewable travel permit, accompanied Pavel to the farm two days before Christmas Eve. She had packed a borrowed suitcase with his clothes and toys and explained where they were going.

"I will come to see you twice a week, and then, after your holiday is over, we both will come back to Paris."

Pavel could hardly contain his excitement. "Can I sleep in the children's room?"

"Yes, and you will help feed the animals and have fun all over the farm." She smiled at his happiness but then her stomach tightened. She would miss him. No more cuddles and kisses, no more watching him feed the pigeons on the window sill, no one to walk with, no one depending on her for food and love, and no one to talk to in the evenings. And yet she felt a lightness, a burden had been lifted, she could do what she wanted when she wanted. The tears came, tears of relief and thankfulness.

Pavel stared at her. "Don't cry, Maman." Just like that, he switched to *Maman* from *Maminko*. And his voice had a firmness to it …as if he was surprised by what he had done.

Sophie hurried to dry her eyes, remembering how easy it had been to be a mother in Prague: servants, money, a comfortable life.

A few days later, on their first official day at the farm, Sophie spent several hours helping out and watching Pavel participate in the meals and activities, worried that, when she left, he would pine for her. But when she saw him laughing and playing with the other children, she felt calmer, more reassured. To make sure he was settled, she rented a room in a Vernon inn and after breakfast the next morning, walked the two kilometers to the farm, wondering how Pavel would react when he saw her again.

In the farmhouse hallway, Pavel laughed as he ran to hug her knees. She raised him up and he buried his face in her shoulder. "I like it, Maman," he said. "The children play with me."

"Did you miss me last night, darling?"

Pavel blinked as though he didn't understand what she meant. "We had supper and played with the pussycats. The black pussycat slept on my bed. Are we going home now?"

"Do you want to come home?" As soon as she said that, Sophie regretted it. What would in heaven's name would she do with him over Christmas? She and Willy had only ever celebrated the New Year.

He shook his head. "I want to stay on the farm, Maman."

Sophie felt a rush of relief; her heart beat fast, joyfully. "Of course you can, Pavelkin. You can stay here and enjoy the Christmas party. I will go back to Paris to work at the café and come back again. Is that what you want?"

He smiled. "*Oui, Maman.*"

The afternoon train to Paris was unheated and Sophie had forgotten to bring her gloves. She rubbed her hands to keep them warm. The train's hypnotic rattle marked time in her mind with Pavel's words: *oui, Maman, oui Maman, oui Maman*. It was as if a huge burden had been lifted from her shoulders. She began to cry.

CHAPTER FOURTEEN

We'll Meet Again, Don't Know Where, Don't Know When
South of France. December 27th, 1939

With paperwork spread all over his desk, Willy pushed back his chair and re-read Sophie's letter. Good news. She slept better and her appetite had improved. Pavel was happy at the farm and had been affectionate when she visited. He smiled. Everything was working out.

Sergeant Kukulka was happy as well. Willy had negotiated a "donation" of five cases of wine, olives, salami, cognac, and chocolate from a Montpellier supplier as part of a six-month contract to purchase their food products. The shipment arrived at the Agde camp and the sergeant was planning a Christmas party.

Captain Rudček stuck his head around the door. "I'm off to lunch, Kohut, and I won't be back till three. Don't sneak off though. Something urgent has come up."

"Urgent, sir?" This was the first time such a word had been used in his new job.

"A New Year's Eve party at a local château—the top brass want to have a good time before the Germans decide to launch their Panzers. I've been appointed chief planner."

"Am I involved, sir?"

Rudček glared. "Don't be an asshole, Kohut. You're driving the top brass to the party and then you'll help guard the premises until the generals are ready to be taken home to bed." Rudček gave

Willy a knowing smile as he belted his tunic and put on his military overcoat. "So, cancel plans for anything else on New Year's."

Willy's heart jumped. Did Rudček know about the extras that he smuggled back to Agde? "Is this an *official* party, sir? Our kitty is close to empty."

Rudček's lips formed a thin sarcastic line "Listen to me, *vojín*. Everything I tell you is, by definition, official." He shrugged. "What do you suggest, Kohut? As I heard, you're the *macher*."

Willy rubbed at his jaw, thinking. "We can run up an overdraft with the caterer and then trim our purchases over the next couple of months. As the biggest consumer around here, we have leverage."

"Good idea."

Willy tried to disguise his curiosity by polishing his spectacles. "If I may ask, sir, is there a rental fee for this *château*?"

Rudček wound a white silk scarf round his neck and tugged his cap on. "I don't know. Zientek says the Agde camp is too much of an eyesore for such an event. The *château* is conveniently placed for the region's important guests. He wants to impress the principal guest, Général Jules-Antoine Bührer—from French High Command. He's touring regional French military facilities to assess troop preparedness."

Willy nodded.

"You will be driving Colonel Zientek, General Ingr and myself. I am responsible for supervising guard duties at the château."

"I don't have a clean uniform for this event—sir."

Rudček, exasperated, stepped back into the room. "*Kristus*, you are one presumptuous Jew. Wear what you've got on now. To them you will be invisible. Your task is to drive the limousine and guard the venue with the other men. No mingling with guests. Stay invisible. Got it?"

"Where is this château, sir?"

"Agde, by the Canal du Midi." Rudček dropped a typed sheet on Willy's desk. "Here. Directions and info."

Willy nodded. "Apart from myself, sir, who are the other guards? And what are we supposed to guard?"

Rudček flushed. "You never stop asking stupid questions, Kohut. This is an army, not the chamber of deputies. The guards are to watch for anything suspicious: people who shouldn't be there, people who don't have identification or invitation cards. Got my drift?"

Willy shrugged. He enjoyed provoking Rudček. "I'm still not clear, sir. What's the danger?"

Rudček shook his head in exasperation. "We are hiring Cressant Fils from Narbonne to organize the food and drink. Cressant now employs foreigners and refugees to run its events. Most of their regular staff work in factories or were drafted into the army. Cressant is supposed to check their people's credentials, but they are sloppy. As a precaution, our guards will carry pistols."

* * *

On New Year's Eve, with Captain Rudček beside him, Willy was assigned a rented black Hotchkiss. Colonel Zientek and General Ingr sat in the back with khaki blankets over their knees, briefcases at their feet. Rudček was in the passenger seat.

This was the first time Willy had driven a Hotchkiss and a strong wind buffeted the car. The occasional slip of the tires as he braked made him nervous. A flashlight and Rudček's directions to the party were in his pocket. A Luger nestled in a holster at his waist.

As they crossed the Canal du Midi, the two senior officers were deep in conversation. Willy could only just make out the words. They were discussing where on the Maginot defensive line the Germans might attack and how the Czechoslovak Army-in-Exile might be involved.

"The Germans have been testing assault techniques on the Sudetenland fortifications they captured from us last year," said Colonel Zientek.

Willy tried to listen. General Ingr's voice was quiet but grating. "We modeled our Sudeten defenses on the French system—the Maginot is impregnable."

"I am not so sure about that, sir," said Rudček twisting around to face the back seat. "If I may give an opinion."

"Captain, I fear you presume to know more than I. But go ahead, have your say. I'm interested."

"Well, sir. The Maginot Line is paper-thin through the Ardennes Mountains. If the Germans invade Belgium, they could punch through there and break the Maginot—the Allies would be in trouble."

"Belgium is neutral." That was Zientek's voice. "The Germans can't invade a neutral country."

Willy heard a deep-throated laugh and in the rearview mirror he saw that General Ingr was shaking his head. "Hitler doesn't care a damn about neutrality. If the Germans attack France, it will be a hard fight. And very tough for our small Czechoslovak army; we have too many raw volunteers. By the way, how is the training going?"

Willy strained his ears even as he concentrated on the road ahead. The windshield wipers barely cleared the freezing rain. He was storing every scrap of information. Who could tell when it would come in useful?

"We need another few weeks to knock the volunteers into shape," said Zientek. "These are not uneducated people, General. They're middle-class, unfit, paunchy and argumentative: quite a few of 'em Jews. And they're often used to giving orders, not takin' them. I'm also worried about the Commie volunteers scheduled to arrive from Gurs."

"Worried about what?" The general shifted his bulk. "We need the red bastards. They fought ferociously with the Masaryk and Rákóczi brigades in Barcelona. They're tough as hell."

Zientek laughed. "The problem, General is that Commies don't believe in our kind of discipline. They don't follow orders. The only salute they respect is the Red Fist."

The car skidded on patch of ice and Willy's stomach lurched as he tightened his hands round the steering wheel. He decided to concentrate more on his driving and less on listening. All the same, from what he had heard, the Czechoslovak Army was a long way from being ready.

Willy drove past the château's open gates, wrought in the shape of giant butterflies. Lights blazed across the lawn from tall windows. Several cars and a couple of vans were already parked in the gravel turning circle. He stopped at the wide steps leading up to the entrance. As Willy got out and opened the rear doors for his passengers, he heard the strains of an orchestra and grinned—an unexpected bonus. Even if there might not be much for the guards to eat or drink, listening to the music and observing the elegant guests having fun might offer some compensation for missing Kukulka's party at the camp.

He followed his three passengers under a display of French, British and Czechoslovak flags into the chateau's warm hallway and was met by the strains of We'll Meet Again coming from the Grand Salon. The hall was astonishing: blue and vermilion walls painted with graceful lilies, fruits, and tropical leaves. He joined the other drivers and guards, who waited for orders in an open side-salon off the hallway, most smoking. They hid their cigarettes behind their backs when an officer walked by.

Willy watched his superior officers pass through open double doors into the Grand Salon and merge with the milling throng. A small orchestra in faded evening wear played on a dais.

All this reminded him of Prague—of his days as a prosperous merchant and the parties he and Sophie had attended. The guests here looked much the same, dressed in tuxedos or formal uniform and their women in long satin dresses, bare arms and flashing jewels. Cigarette and cigar smoke wreathed the air. He watched tray-laden waiters move among the guests bearing glasses of champagne and noticed bottles of red and white wine lined up on a long polished sideboard. *Play my cards right*, he mused, *and I might get a few bottles into the trunk of the Hotchkiss.*

Willy glimpsed the cornucopia of food displayed on an enormous dining table in the center of the Grand Salon. Even though he had translated for Captain Rudček when they visited Cressant to order the food and wine, he had not been involved in any follow-up. The food looked magnificent: crusty bread, bowls of salads, plates of *foie gras*, *pâté* and garlic sausage, cold chicken, roasted duck, and dark cured ham. In the center, a boar's head rested on a silver platter surrounded by slices of roast beef and pork. On a separate sideboard, lobsters, oysters and crabs, lay on a mound of cracked ice.

Doing his best to stay hidden from the guests, Willy noticed a tall waiter at the far end of the room. His height, yellow hair and black-framed spectacles seemed familiar. He wanted to take a closer look, but Rudček appeared, a glass of champagne in his hand, and closed the door behind him. He handed out paper slips. "Here are your assignments, men. And check your pistols, six rounds each." He waved the cigarette smoke away. "And no more damned smoking."

"The old laboratory. What's that?" Willy said, looking at his slip.

"The owner's hobby was chemistry, Kohut. Upstairs … the terrace there might be an entry point for a mischief-maker."

"What about a bit of food, sir?" said one of the guards. "We're starving." The others nodded vigorously.

Rudček glanced at his notes, and then his watch. "Very well. Madame Flore, the housekeeper, has something for you in the kitchen. You've got thirty minutes. Then get to your posts and stay there. And no hidden wine bottles."

"How long are we supposed to be on guard?" someone asked.

Rudček drained his glass and checked his watch. "It's on your slip. First shift, three hours. Meet me here at eleven. That's when you will switch posts."

Madame Flore, a tiny, henna-haired woman in a high-necked velvet dress, was waiting for them with plates of *pâté*, *Quiche Lorraine*, *Salade Niçoise*, goat cheese, and marinated olives. Rows of baguettes lay on wooden boards waiting to be sliced.

While the men were serving themselves, she spoke to them in French. "After you have eaten, would anyone like to take a short tour of the château?" Madame Flore's black-currant eyes sparkled behind thick lenses. "It is in the Art Nouveau style. *Très spéciale.*" She looked around hopefully.

The men smiled at her, shrugged and shook their heads.

Willy saw the disappointment on her face. "Madame, my comrades don't speak French and they're hungry. I'll come with you, if it's a quick tour." He wanted to thank her for her hospitality. "I like Art Nouveau. The hallway is superb. I'm surprised to find this place in a small town."

"Monsieur Laurens is rich. An industrialist."

They started from the base of the grand staircase with its carved balustrades. The red and ocher walls were covered with symbolic designs—Egyptian friezes and stylized flowers. They passed through several rooms including an enormous music room where Willy spotted a grand piano. He made a note to come back and try it out—if he could avoid Rudček.

Madame Flore ended the tour in the château's main bathroom. "This is the finest room," she said with a laugh. "You must get down on your knees and inspect the gold mosaics on the floor. The artist was Gian Facchina—the one who restored the mosaics of St. Mark's in Venice," she said proudly. "Now, Monsieur, the tour is over. Go to the kitchen and eat something."

On the way down the stairs, they met a young woman who stopped to kiss the elderly lady on the cheek. She wore a low-cut silk dress and her long hair was braided with silver ribbons. "My niece, Francine," said Madame Flore. "She loves parties, don't you, dear?"

Willy could not stop staring at Francine, who nodded coolly. Desire flowed into his loins as he watched the way her hips moved with each step. *Don't look, don't touch.* Rudček had warned at one of their planning sessions for the party. Willy wondered if there might be a way around that directive.

Shortly before eleven, Willy left the laboratory where Monsieur Laurens had once tinkered with his experiments. Willy had spent most of his time thinking about his family. His short trip to Paris had achieved some benefit. Pavel had settled in at the farm and Sophie seemed happier. But on the down side, she had only allowed him to make love to her once, the night of Andreas's birthday dinner. Even then, she had been stiff and resistant.

"Don't you love me anymore?" he'd asked her after she refused his advances. Tears followed but she refused to explain why. Maybe women reacted like this when they were close to a breakdown? He was sorry for her, and sorry for himself. Next time he hoped things would be better. He needed a woman.

A clock on the upper landing of the château struck eleven. He ran down the stairs. Time to report to the captain. Willy joined the other guards in the downstairs hall. They stood around and waited. After twenty minutes, still no Rudček.

"He's had three hours of boozing. I bet he's tipsy," someone said. "Let's go back to the kitchen and have a good time." The group dispersed.

In the Grand Salon, the orchestra blasted away. Guests were laughing and dancing. At midnight there would be corks popping, hurrahs and kisses. Willy and the other guards would be left out, envious and sad, yearning for their loved ones, or at least some fun.

New Year's Eve without Sophie. Fuck Rudček, wherever he is.

Willy knew where he would find solace—the music room. When he got there, it was empty. He strolled around the perimeter, carrying a glass and a bottle of red wine. Like the main entrance, flowers, birds, and gracefully posed nymphs decorated the walls. An intricate blue and gold frieze edged the doors and windows. Gilt chairs were stacked against the wall close to the piano. Willy sat on the stool and read the inscription: PLEYEL BOUDOIR GRAND. He smiled, sipped some wine and lifted the lid. What an instrument! He remembered the gleam and beautiful tone of the Bechstein in his Prague apartment. Before they escaped, he had shipped it to his parents in England. Except—there had been no mention of its arrival in his father's letters.

He spread his fingers over the keys and glanced at his disfigured right little finger. Against the discolored ivories, the scarred digit looked as if it no longer belonged to him. "Now you behave yourself, little fellow and play the right notes for me," he muttered. *So what if some officer comes in? Too bad.*

This instrument had clearly suffered the fate of so many pianos. It was dusty, a little out of tune and dying of neglect. He sighed, needing the solace of playing, however tinny the strings sounded. He felt his pistol against the inside of his arm, pulled it out and placed it beside his bottle of wine on the piano lid. He tried a few notes. Not too bad. As he ran the scales, his little finger felt strong, almost pain-free. The tension in his shoulders loosened the muscles relaxed. He took another swig. The wine helped. So what if he made mistakes? No one was listening. He wanted to play the composers he loved best: Chopin, Bartók, or Kodály. No, he'd play whatever came into his head.

His fingers ran over the keys and he felt his hands regain stretch and flexibility. His body moved to the cadence of the music. Hammering the *fortissimo* sections, he played in a river of sound that flowed on and on.

Finally, Willy stopped and took a drink. He heard applause and spun around. At the far end of the room, guests stood at the open door. They called out *bravos* and raised their glasses. "Play some more."

He shook his head. He had played for himself.

A handful of officers came up and one clapped him on the shoulder. "Well done, private." A French captain shook his hand. "*Felicitations, mon brave,*"

Beaming with pride Colonel Zientek patted Willy's back. "Splendid, splendid."

"A fine musician," said General Ingr, a fat cigar between two fingers. "You have a sensitive touch. Perhaps we should arrange some future entertainment. What's your name?"

"Kohut, sir." He stayed sitting, knowing that he ought to stand and salute. Too much wine. He was afraid he might stagger and ruin the accolades.

The general wrapped an arm around his colleague. "Fine party, Zientek, you old dog. I wasn't expecting this quality in a little French town. Quite charming."

They turned away, but Willy heard Colonel Zientek's

comment. "This fellow is one of our Jewish volunteers. Talented chap, but I don't suppose he's much good as a fighting man." *Wait and see*, Willy thought, anger mounting in his chest. *Just show me a Nazi.*

Willy closed the piano lid gently. The officers and their female companions slowly filtered out of the music room. "Thank you, piano," he murmured, stroking the Pleyel's smooth wood and reaching for his bottle of wine. "It was a pleasure to listen to both of us." He felt a gentle touch on his shoulder and detected a lemony fragrance.

"Francine Lepichet," said the young woman with the sinuous hips. She stood by the stool gazing at him with jade eyes. With her hand still on his shoulder, she bent down. "We met on the stairs. Do you understand French? My English is primitive and my Czech is ... sadly, *zero.*"

Willy nodded, appreciating the design of her *décolleté* silk dress, too tight to be couture elegant and shaped to fuel desire. A gold crucifix hung between her half-bare breasts. Chestnut hair fell over white shoulders. "You played the most gorgeous music," she said, with a long sigh, running a pink tongue along her lips. *Like a cat whetting its appetite*, Willy thought.

Willy rose from the stool, bumping against her soft body. The touch of her skin jolted him. He apologized clumsily, his pulse racing. After months of camp life and one night of unsatisfactory sex with his wife in Paris, he desired this woman more than anything in the world. He turned away, trying to hide his erection. He was in an impossible situation. Rudček had laid down the rules—no mingling.

Francine took his arm and pulled him down on to the piano stool next to her. She moved her face close to his, and holding his chin with two fingers, gazed into his eyes. "Now, *M. le Pianiste*, I must be frank. While you were playing so wonderfully, I was completely overcome—sensually I mean. It was extraordinary. While you played I felt like an ice maiden melting in the sun. We will make love, yes?" She leaned against Willy and licked his ear.

Willy could not believe this was happening. He also knew that if some French or Czechoslovak officer surprised them, there would be hell to pay. "I'm an ordinary soldier on guard duty," he stuttered. "I'll get into big trouble flirting with such a beautiful guest."

She moved her hand across his thigh and on-to his erection and began to massage it, keeping her face close. "I take and do what I like." She looked at him hungrily and kissed his ear, licking him again with her tongue.

Willy sat still enjoying every second. "Surely a beautiful woman like you has an escort at this party, someone who is wondering where you are."

"No one, *mon chéri*. I am here to entertain. I am in the business of love—*une poule de luxe.*" She smiled at him dreamily and showed him the tip of her pink tongue. "I am *la sous-gérante*, assistant manager, of La Maison de Plaisance in Béziers. "The mayor asked me to arrange female companions for the officers. Please, call me Francine."

"You run a bordello?"

Francine fluttered her eyelashes. "That is a vulgar expression, *chéri*, but, yes, my house is *une maison tolérée* and belongs to the Municipality. Everything is proper, clean and inspected. After all, we have important regular customers." Her hands slowly unbuttoned his pants. "Now, *Monsieur le Pianiste*, for you I offer one visit of *entrée libre*: free entry at our establishment."

Willy suddenly remembered how a knife pressed to his neck forced him to give head to the Nazi officer at the German frontier … and his nausea at the acrid taste of semen. His erection collapsed. Ashamed that she might think him unmanly or impotent, he forced the memory away and gently moved her hand. "Mademoiselle Lepichet, Francine, I'm sure our acrobatics would be sensational, but in Paris I have a faithful wife and a little boy. You are beautiful. You shouldn't tempt me like this."

Francine stroked his cheek. "Come now, we are at a New Year's Eve party, we live in *La Belle France* and there is war about to be fought. Who knows if you and I will be alive in six months?" She tilted her head coquettishly. "Do you know the Boulanger song, '*Avant de Mourir*'?"

"No, why?"

Francine placed two palms against his cheek, her nose touching his. "It's sad and tells us to make the most of what we have now."

She kissed him on the lips and her hand continued its exploration. "In France, you know, everyone expects variety in their sex life, in the marriage and outside. My customers' wives accept that their husbands come to us. *C'est normale.* It adds spice to a marriage."

Willy inhaled deeply. Why not? Sophie would never find out what was about to happen.

He put his arm round Francine and, pulling her hair back, kissed her neck. "Where can we go? My supervising officer will have my balls if we are discovered here."

Francine slid two fingers into her tight décolleté. They reappeared with a key. "*Voilà, mon soldat pianiste*, the key to the main bedroom. It is I who will have your balls, not the Colonel." She giggled again and took his hand as they got up from the piano stool. "Madame Flore is my aunt, and we have a bedroom arrangement whenever I and my girls are invited to a big party here."

She threw her arms round Willy's neck and kissed him, thrusting her tongue deep into his mouth. "*Dieu est avec nous,*" she whispered in his ear, rubbing herself against his groin. "Follow me."

Willy buttoned up his fly and retrieved the pistol from the piano. Everything around him glowed with vivid colors. He admired Francine's tight buttocks as they mounted the main staircase. This was turning into a more-than-interesting party.

For an hour, Willy forgot everything—where he was, that he was a soldier on guard duty and that he had a wife and son. He knew only that he was a man who was being given what he needed. Francine lay naked on the bed, half asleep, arms and legs splayed so languorously that he was tempted to throw himself back on top of her. But it was too risky to stay longer.

He dressed, shoved the pistol into his holster and left the bedroom. Across the hall, the bathroom door was half-open and he saw a Czechoslovak officer sprawled on his knees. Holding the sides of the toilet, he retched again and again.

Kristus. It was Rudček. His white gloves lay on the mosaic floor. Willy gasped at the livid-red and white patches covering the back of the captain's hands. Fragments of skin fell to the floor like miniature snowflakes. Willy noticed that Rudček's fingernails were brown and ugly—pitted as if someone had hammered a hundred needles into them.

He flinched; he had never seen anything like this. It was like some medieval affliction. "You have a serious problem, Captain. Now I understand why you wear a scarf and gloves."

Rudček's eyes rolled and he retched again. "Oh, God, help me." He burped and wiped his face with the silk scarf. Recognition dawned in his eyes. "Kohut … er … I …"

Willy turned on the tap at the nearby sink, pulled a cotton towel off the rack and started to clean the vomit off the front of Rudček's tunic. The rancid smell made his stomach turn over. He felt disgust and pity for the man. "You can't go back to the party looking like this, sir."

As he washed the limp officer's face, he noticed more red patches extending up the back of his neck into his hair. Rudcek made a weak attempt to stop Willy's ministrations, then slumped. "They call it psoriasis," he mumbled. "I have it everywhere, except for my face."

Witnessing this weak spot in Rudček's armor, Willy could not restrain a low whistle of surprise, or his curiosity. "Terrible. Is it infectious? Isn't there treatment?"

Rudček sat on the floor, resting his head against the toilet. Willy saw self-loathing on the man's usually expressionless face as he studied his hands, turning them over and over. He spat on them as though they were vermin, not part of him.

"Started when I was eight. The town quack was useless. We went to Vienna to see a famous skin doctor, a Jew. He gave me special creams and said it might get worse before it got better. We went back, again and again. He took our money—it got much worse, never better. That's why I have to hide it with all this paraphernalia."

He picked up his gloves, starting another cascade of skin flakes. He gave Willy a rapier look. "That's just one reason I hate Jews. They take your money and let you down."

There was a moment of silence. Willy realized then, that they both carried ineradicable curses: one on his skin, the other his circumcision. Rudček looked up. "I expect you to keep this to yourself," he mumbled.

Willy helped his superior to his feet. "Captain, I'll do what I can to respect your secret."

Rudček nodded as he straightened up and re-tied his scarf. "Good. Actually, Kohut, you're not such a bad fellow," he said and retched again. He swayed as he made for the door. "You have a certain intelligence … and you get things done. Just forget what you saw in this bathroom."

Sometime after the Marseillaise had been sung and the New Year feted, Willy, hormones and body drained, rejoined the military drivers, talking and smoking in the kitchen. From the noise level, it was clear the party was still in full swing. In the Grand Salon, a gramophone replaced the orchestra and was set to full volume, blaring the songs of Charles Trenet, Edith Piaf, Jean Sablon and Louis Armstrong.

Hunger surged back into Willy's befuddled consciousness. There was still plenty of food and wine on the kitchen table. While he ate, old Madame Flore brought Willy a large snifter of cognac. He could tell from her bloodshot eyes that she too had imbibed her fair share.

"This is a special gift for *Monsieur le Pianiste*, from Monsieur Laurens' cellar: forty-year-old liquid gold." she said, swaying and holding on the edge of the table. "Courtesy of … Francine."

With an engaging wink, the diminutive caretaker pulled down his head and kissed him on the forehead. "Francine likes you, I also like you," she purred, sliding more cognac, oily rich, into his glass.

Willy nodded. "I like her too," he said, remembering that during the few quiet moments of rest, in between twisting and thrusting with Francine on the lace-covered four-poster, he had agreed to visit her in the Rue des Guyanes. Did he have an excuse? None, except that he would be fighting soon and this was a terrific chance to take pleasure before something terrible happened to him.

It wasn't until two in the morning that the party wound down. Willy, somewhat sober after several cups of coffee, contemplated the winter fog outside and decided to drive his important guests back very carefully. The catering staff were packing silverware, plates and glasses, and sweeping the floor. The orchestra had long been released to feast on the remnants of food and wine.

Willy waited in the hallway where a crowd of guests were putting on their coats. He spotted General Ingr and Colonel Zientek. Rudček, disheveled in his stained uniform but with white gloves and scarf in place, called out. "Get over here, Kohut. Time to go."

Willy paused as two of the catering men, one tall and thin, the other stocky, blocked his way carrying a collapsible trestle table to the main entrance where the catering vans were waiting. The tall man was the waiter with straw-colored hair who, earlier, had triggered a flash of familiarity. Willy trailed the men and as they approached the front door, guests stepped aside to let the table be carried out. The waiter turned sideways to negotiate the main doors and Willy saw his eye-lids flutter; a heart-stopping moment of instant recognition and shock. It was Lessig—the man who had betrayed him to the Gestapo in Prague. Willy managed a hoarse cry. "Lessig—LESSIG!"

The tall man spun round, his eyes wide with surprise. His end of the table crashed to the floor. This *was* Hans Lessig. Everything around Willy blurred—people, voices, lights, the hallway—all distant, blotted out. *Grab the bastard. Kill the bastard.*

Lessig made for the front entrance and started down the steps. Willy went after him. In the reflected light of the *château* windows, he saw Lessig's figure duck between the parked cars

Willy pulled the Luger, aimed and fired three times— metallic sounds echoed from the cluster of parked cars. No cry of pain, or sign of a hit. No Lessig. Only then did Willy realize he was breathing hard and his heart pounded like a blacksmith's hammer.

A gloved hand pulled him round, wresting the gun from his hand. "What the fuck are you doing?" Rudček's face was incredulous; his breath stank of vomit.

Willy, his body twitching and tensing, stared at his senior officer. How was he going to explain this? Would anyone believe Lessig had betrayed him in Prague, was in cahoots with the Nazis, and had been kicked out of the Czechoslovak army in Montpellier for robbery? And that was hardly a justification for trying to kill him—too complicated to explain in a few phrases. Willy needed something immediate, relevant to the party and the guests. "A thief, sir. He was in the coat closet. I saw him open a briefcase and challenged him. He ran."

"Did you recognize him? Was it one of our men?"

Willy looked at the angry faces around him. "No idea, sir."

"You could have killed him." Colonel Zientek spat the words. He jabbed an angry finger in Willy's face. "Or maybe some bystander who happened to be in the way. Inexcusable." The colonel scowled as he drew on his greatcoat. "You are in deep trouble, private."

Willy squared his shoulders. "I acted as a guard should, sir; protecting the guests and their property. Besides, I only intended to wing him." He forced himself to look calm but he seethed inside. Lessig had defeated him. Even worse, he knew that this incident put everything he had worked for in jeopardy.

Zientek snorted contemptuously as if he understood the impossibility of "winging" a fugitive in the dark. "Drive us back to Béziers where you will be detained. Understand one thing, Kohut. You will no longer work in my office."

Willy saluted. He was in trouble, but how hard and how permanent his punishment would be was anyone's guess. He had said enough.

General Ingr, winding a scarf round his neck, looked angry. "What will the French guests, especially the ladies, think of us? That we're trigger-happy foreigners who can't control our own men?"

Rudček raised his hands trying to calm the tension. "There is a possible counter-perspective, General. Our guests will understand and appreciate the prompt response our military has shown during a criminal act. In any case, I will deal with Kohut once you have been returned to your quarters at HQ in Béziers."

Willy nearly smiled. Perhaps their bathroom encounter had shifted Rudček's attitude. Maybe he would get away with a reprimand.

On the drive back to the camp, his passengers were either asleep or semi-conscious. Willy peered at the foggy road ahead, grateful for the French practice of painting large white patches on the tree trunks at the verges. He'd acted impulsively at the *château*, lost his self-control. At worst, he faced a court-martial, or if he was lucky, a month of cleaning latrines.

CHAPTER FIFTEEN

Changed Circumstances
South of France. January 1st, 1940

Willy woke to a bang on the door and the sound of a key grating in the lock. His back ached and his mouth was a dry sponge. He sat up, rubbing sleep from his eyes.

A soldier stepped in, and, without giving him a chance to urinate or wash his face, marched him upstairs to the operations room. The soldier stood guard outside. The wall clock showed eight o'clock. Except for Rudček at his desk, the room was empty.

Rudček didn't waste time. The look on his face mirrored the way Willy felt: hung-over. "We don't shoot people on sight, Kohut, even if they are petty criminals. I told you to use that pistol defensively. Zientek is livid. I recommended a court-martial. You will be kept in the basement until a hearing can be arranged."

Willy's mouth was bone-dry. His bladder cried out for relief. "Court-martial?" He could hardly get the words out.

The shadow of a smile crossed Rudček's face. "Yes, and at the minimum the army will discharge you. As of this moment your pay is docked."

Willy caught his breath. *Damn—kicked out. No pay, nowhere to go.* "I need to urinate, sir. It's urgent."

In the toilet, with the guard pacing outside, strategies on how to extricate himself raced through Willy's mind—most of them unrealistic. If only he could persuade Rudček to rescind the court-martial recommendation. Escorted back to the operations room, he re-visited the image of the officer's disfigured hands clutching the toilet bowl—the skin disease. He had given his word not to tell … but …

Five minutes later, facing his captain once again, Willy took the unethical gamble and broke his promise—to save himself. "If you make me face a court-martial, sir, I'll make sure everyone in the regiment knows what I saw in the castle bathroom."

Rudček's lips clamped together. His face was sheet-white.

"Get Zientek to go soft on me," Willy said as firmly as he could, "and I'll keep my mouth shut. I mean it."

Rudček screwed his eyes tight. His words blew out in a rush. "Jewish bastard." Silence reigned as he gazed at his gloved hands resting on the blotting pad. Shakily he rose from his desk. "Bastard," he repeated softly. "How the hell do I know you won't betray me even if I do what you want?"

Inwardly, Willy exulted. Rudček was going to cooperate. "You don't. You'll have to take the chance. I know Colonel Zientek listens to you."

"Wait on that bench over there." Rudček stalked out of the room.

Willy nodded, mentally crossing his fingers.

Half an hour later, Willy, stiff and tense, stood, in front of Colonel Zientek and Captain Rudček, searching their faces for clues to his fate. The hint of a smile or a curl of the lip could mean hope or despair.

"I'll get straight to the matter." Zientek face was a wall of granite. "You have not only brought shame on the Czechoslovak army but we have to use our limited funds to repair glass and bodywork on two automobiles. I admit there are extenuating circumstances. Your attempt to apprehend a criminal was understandable, but not the means. Understand?"

Willy's fists unclenched. Good for Rudček.

"Yes, sir."

Zientek's chunky face was impassive. "I've decided that a court-martial is not justified." He looked down at some scribbled notes. "I also discussed your case with Colonel Němec, our local military court judge. Our decision is as follows: solitary confinement for seven days followed by three weeks in prison. Then you go back to basic training. Your pay is docked for two months. Lastly, you will not be permitted to send or receive mail until further notice. Captain Rudček will supervise your punishment." The colonel turned to Rudček. "Anything to add, Captain?"

Rudček nodded, glancing at Willy. "I propose a shorter confinement, sir. I received a message while you were consulting with the judge. Kohut is needed for a special assignment, in Agde."

Zientek looked up, surprised. "Why should we give this fool a soft landing?"

"Our ordnance specialist made the request; a priority job; rehabilitating outdated weapons for the First Regiment—artillery, tracked ammunition carriers and various small arms and rifles. A shipment of Châtellerault machine guns arrived—donated by the French Cavalry. They are antiquated but our troops must have functioning weapons."

The colonel glanced scornfully at Willy and switched his gaze back to Rudček. "What the hell does this piano-playing private know about ordnance?"

Rudček gave a wry smile. "Kohut is perfect in French. We need him to translate their instruction manuals. Sergeant Kukulka asked for him specifically."

The colonel shrugged a reluctant assent. "Oh, well, get on with it."

Willy stifled his relief. *Not so bad.* At least, he would be with

Kukulka, a decent fellow under all that bluster. But, for his family's sake, Willy pushed his luck a little further. "Excuse me, Colonel. I would like permission to let my wife know about my changed circumstances. She and my little boy have a difficult financial situation in Paris. They depend on me."

Zientek scowled and threw Willy's dossier into a tray. "A family man, eh? You should have thought of that before you tried to kill that waiter. Very well, then. One letter, but it will be censored."

Willy saluted. Zientek was right about him being foolish. How would Sophie take the news? She had been so low when he left Paris. He had made everything worse.

Zientek picked an unlit cigar from an open box and rolled his lips around it before using a silver table lighter. He puffed out a cloud of smoke. "Dismissed."

Back in the basement room, after another visit to the bathroom, Willy sprawled on the tattered hide couch, ready to make up lost sleep. He lay on his back, hands tucked behind his head and passed the time looking at spider webs on the ceiling. One thing was certain: returning to the supervision of salt-of-the-earth Kukulka would make a pleasant change from Captain Rudček's racist comments.

As for Sophie, Willy decided—in the one censored letter permitted to him—to convey the gist of what happened and why, and express his remorse. He even wrote that he had found Lessig. His sentence meant that she and Pavel had to stay in Paris and there would be no letters or money for at least a month. He apologized for making her life more difficult. He would make it up to her, but when, where and how, he had no idea.

* * *

Ten days later, Willy was back at camp where his old bunk waited.

Other than wearing a bright red armband, a mark of confinement to barracks, he took his meals and paraded with the other men.

Under the supervision of Sergeant Kukulka, Willy joined a detail of other men assigned to construct an ordnance rehabilitation workshop inside one of the disused huts. They removed mouse and rat droppings, cleared the traps of dead vermin and washed the walls and floors with carbolic solution.

They built work benches, shelving and lockable cupboards to store the weapons, which were temporarily housed in a disused Panhard truck, set up on bricks. They installed lathes and vises and placed tools in labeled drawers. Outside the hut they filled two degreasing tanks with solvent and covered them with tarpaulins.

Other soldiers removed the French Hotchkiss and Châtellerault machine guns and rifles from their original WWI boxes: eighty-seven weapons, in all, including one or two models from Belgian manufacturers. The guns, Hotchkiss machine guns, French MAS36 and Lebel rifles wrapped in oil paper, were thick with old grease and had to be soaked in acetone or benzene. After cleaning and drying, the guns were reassembled, oiled and after a while, test-fired. Willy's grease-stained fingers were soon covered in cuts and scratches.

As for the importance of what they were doing, Sgt. Kukulka was skeptical. "I'm pissed off," he said one day as they took a break, sitting on rickety chairs around the tarpaulin on which lay a disassembled Grande Puissance machine gun. He had brought a crate of beer. "I don't know what Zientek hopes for, other than to keep us busy. These fucking guns should be in a museum." He jerked his head toward three metal boxes with leather handles stacked in one corner. "See those," he sneered. "Ammo. Each Châtellerault magazine takes twenty-five cartridges and that pathetic pile is all we've been given."

Jaromír, a fat, sour-faced corporal next to Willy said,

"Pathetic is right, Sarge. Those guns have only one trigger, no exchange barrels and the first one we tested overheated. And out of the six heavy ZB-35s we cobbled together, only three work." He pointed to the soldier who sat opposite. "He tested two yesterday; one jammed straight off and the other one's barrel overheated after only two minutes of firing."

Willy listened, trying to wipe lubricant off his glasses with his shirt sleeve.

"I don't like the idea of machine guns, Sarge," said Hugo Probl, a volunteer like Willy. "Think of all those bullets cutting fellows like us to shreds."

Kukulka got up, arched his back and stretched his arms. "Shut up, Probl. You have too much imagination."

Willy marveled at how the sergeant was built—square as a bank safe. He was not nicknamed "Hulking K" for nothing.

"Holy Jesus, Joseph, and Mary, this is a tedious business," the sergeant growled. "Let's have a beer and take a break. How about one of your stories, Kohut?"

Willy shrugged, embarrassed. He and Kukulka had previously shared some alcohol-fuelled reminiscences and they had established a kind of alliance. But he didn't know Corporal Jaromír or the scrawny Hugo, except that the latter was Jewish and had been a tax official in Slovakia. These days it paid to be careful and not reveal too much to strangers. "I'm not sure about doing that, Sarge."

Kukulka picked a long-necked bottle out of the beer crate and uncapped it. "Come on, *vojín*. That's an order."

Willy opened his hands in apology. "I'm not in the mood, Sarge."

Kukulka shrugged and spat on the ground. "Fuck!" He turned to Hugo. "What about you, then? You're Jewish, like merchant Kohut here. I expect you were rich like him before the

Nazi occupation. They say there are rich Jews in every country on earth. How is that possible? They arrive as penniless refugees, waggling their caps and tassels. And then—zump! They have money and own property."

Hugo ran fingers through his frizzy hair. His thin mouth twisted in a rueful laugh. "I've never been rich, Sarge; I'm just a simple pen-pusher in the town's tax office. As for Jews being in every country, what do you expect? They were kicked out of their own a thousand years ago. Had to go somewhere. We call it the diaspora. You should read about it."

Kukulka's massive head shook a vehement no. "Me, I only listen to stories."

Hugo and Jaromir threw their empty bottles into a cardboard box. "Don't expect no stories from us," said Hugo.

Kukulka half stood up and then sat down again with a lop-sided smile. "Well, it looks like no one has anything interesting to say. So, instead, I'll show you something special."

Willy watched Kukulka unbutton and pull off his battle-dress tunic and under-shirt, revealing thick arms and a hairy chest crowned by paving-stone sized pectorals.

With his hand open as if waiting for a tip, Kukulka straightened out his right arm. "Whadyasee, men?"

Hugo raised his eyebrows and shrugged. "A colorful tattoo, Sarge. A naked woman—her upper body on your biceps, her hips at the elbow and her legs on your forearm. So what's special?"

"Right. Now watch." The sergeant bent his elbow making a tight fist. His biceps turned into a mound, the size of a melon.

Willy leaned forward. "My God, you've made her belly swell. She's pregnant. That's clever."

Kukulka grinned. "A Chinee did this for me in Gdansk, a few years back—but the design was my idea, making her pregnant with my muscle. One of a kind, the Chinee said, on account of the size of my biceps."

Jaromír's eyes gleamed as he watched Kukulka repeat the maneuver and recreate the pregnant belly. "Sarge, have you shown this masterpiece to anyone else?"

"Oh, once or twice." Kukulka crimped his mouth in an embarrassed smile as though he now regretted showing the tattoo. "These days I try to ignore it."

"Why?"

"Me and my wife—we used to joke about the tattoo. Only it turned out to be a fucking mistake because we couldn't have babies. Now she can't bear to look at it. I have to take my shirt off in the dark when I'm home."

There was a moment of silence as the soldiers watched a dark blush of embarrassment cross the sergeant's face as he slowly put on his tunic.

Willy got up. "Well, thanks, Sergeant Kukulka. We are deeply honored that you shared your tattoo with us. Can we get back to work?"

"I'm off to have a piss, Sarge," said Hugo. "Back in five?"

"Permission granted, *vojín*," said Kukulka, getting to his feet rubbing the puckered scar on his left cheek. It often seemed to itch or irritate him. "Yes, Kohut, you get back to work. I've been watching those pinkies of yours assembling the guns. Not bad for a beginner. We'll have a regimental weapon speed contest soon. You should take part."

"Thanks Sarge. I'll try but as you know, one of my hands is messed up. Anyway, I have a question about the only letter I was able to send my wife. Do you happen to know if she sent an answer?"

Kukulka put his hands on his hips and nodded solemnly. "She sent you three letters. But you can't read 'em yet. You've got a couple more weeks to complete the punishment."

Willy, nearly twenty centimeters shorter in height, rested a pleading hand on Kukulka's chest. "Help me out, Sarge. Slip them to me. You don't have to tell anyone. I can't sleep at night thinking about what's going on with her in Paris."

A grin spread across the Sergeant's face. "I'spect you're worried, boy. You once showed me her photo. Lovely woman. As long as she don't meet a handsome Frenchie in the dark, you've nothing to worry about."

"Come on, Sarge. I just want to know how she is."

Kukulka turned serious. "Not possible, soldier. Orders is orders."

CHAPTER SIXTEEN

The Painter's Model
Paris. February 1940

Sophie kept Willy's letter in her purse. The fact that he had confronted Lessig, would get no wages, and could no longer make contact with her pushed her into a tailspin. At the café, she read it to the Szigetis, shedding tears at times. Even Rózsi couldn't calm her. "Now I can only afford to visit Pavel every other week, maybe even less often," Sophie said to Rózsi who was setting out pastries on the glass shelving.

Until the arrival of Willy's letter, Sophie traveled to Vernon late every Saturday afternoon and took a room above the Brasserie de Monet. She rented a bicycle and rode to the Duclet farm the next morning. She could tell that Pavel had been absorbed into the life of the farm. He looked happy, played with the other children and was almost fluent in French. But he often cried when she left, saying, "When are you coming back, Maman?"

Rószi embraced her. "Don't worry, my dear, we will help pay your expenses. I can't bear the thought that Pavel will be expecting you and you don't turn up."

Sophie sighed, put her hands on Rózsi's shoulders and kissed her forehead. Gratitude and obligation. She hated being dependent on the Szigetis for everything. "I can't accept your offer of money. It would make me feel even more useless. Willy is responsible for this. We must manage our own problems. Visiting Pavel every other week will have to do. I know he's happy there. I have the feeling he isn't missing me that much."

She turned to Andreas, who was at the bakery door rubbing flour-coated fingers across his forehead, a nervous habit. "What if they change their mind and Willy gets a court-martial?"

The baker stiffened. His eyes narrowed. "My God, I hope not. That would mean a long period in jail or worse, being thrown out of the army. But…" He reached out and touched her shoulder reassuringly. "Your man is a clever one. He'll find a way out of it."

Sophie turned away, to hide her bitterness. "He didn't think about me and Pavel."

"Don't jump to conclusions." Rózsi was writing labels for the hot buffet dishes. "You don't know everything that happened. He might have had a good reason."

"There is something else that worries me," Sophie said hesitantly, brushing flour residue off her blouse. "I…" She faltered. She wanted to share her burden with someone whom she trusted—and she loved the Szigetis as if they were her own family.

"Go on, girl." Rózsi slid a tureen of veal *paprikás* onto the hot buffet shelf. "Don't be shy."

Sophie polished the counter fiercely, not looking at Rózsi's face. Her face felt hot. "In his letter, Willy mentioned seeing a man he knew from Prague; the one who betrayed us to the Nazis. Willy hates him. When Willy's sentence is over, I'm afraid something terrible will happen." She could not help shuddering as she polished. "Willy wants to kill him. He's said it many times."

Rózsi crossed herself. "My Lord Jesus, that's a terrible thing for him to say. No wonder you are upset. Was this betrayal just between Willy and this man or were *you* involved as well? I don't understand how a friend could do this."

Sophie froze. For ten months she had kept that shameful night with the Sudetenlander to herself—except for Ruth, her confidante, who lived upstairs at Masná Street. Afterwards, Lessig had blackmailed her and threatened to destroy her marriage.

She avoided Rózsi's stare. "Hans was Willy's friend. I disliked him. Turned out he had connections with the Gestapo. I gave him money to bribe officials, and then..." She shrugged helplessly, unwilling to reveal any more.

Andreas put an arm round Sophie's shoulders. "There's nothing much to be done until Willy is released. We have to be patient."

Rózsi took Sophie's hand. "So, this is what we do. We pay the train fare for you to visit the Duclet farm. You pay for the room in Vernon. Pavel should not miss his mother. A compromise, isn't that right, Andreas?"

The baker nodded. "Of course." A buzzer rang in the bakery. "I must go check something. Perhaps we should discuss Willy's threat of revenge later."

Sophie buried her face in her hands. "Oh, God, I shouldn't have told you. Promise you won't mention this again?"

* * *

Alone in her hotel room, Sophie thought about Willy, hoping for a telegram or letter from him. She missed his letters but she also felt angry. She was lonely and had to watch every franc. She was paying for his actions.

But life in Paris wasn't so bad now that Pavel was happy and healthy at the farm. During the week, she was free in the afternoons, though it was dark by half past four. She roamed the local neighborhoods, breathing in the smells and sounds of a beautiful city, something she had never done as a girl or as a bourgeois wife. It was wonderful to be free and not rely on someone else.

Sophie had a routine. When she wasn't working at the

café and the weather was rainy or too cold—which was often—she would stay in her room, snuggled in bed, reading newspapers and second-hand children's books to improve her French. If the weather was half-way decent, she walked to the Champs de Mars to inspect the new air-raid shelters and trenches being built and watched workmen stack sandbags in front of important buildings.

Sometimes, columns of French soldiers marched along the boulevards on their way north to the Maginot line and the Belgian frontier and Sophie joined the crowd to watch and applaud—she thought of herself as an apprentice Parisian. But she could not avoid the heart-breaking sight of sad-faced refugees in loaded cars and horse-drawn carts on the same boulevards, all going south.

To pass the time, and forget her troubles, Sophie nursed a daily coffee and a croissant at Chez Dupont and then explored the *quartiers*, umbrella in hand. She enjoyed the quirky alleyways and interesting shops. Her favorite department store was the art deco La Samaritaine, where she could imagine herself in the beautiful clothes.

Sophie's "home café " on the Left Bank was Les Deux Magots on the Place St. Germain, where she would spend a couple of hours each day, nursing her second cup of coffee, writing letters, and reading newspapers to improve her French. The café was a rendezvous for expatriates and refugees, but it was also populated by shabbily dressed young men and women, many of them students, who argued and lectured each other about art, life, love and whether the French army would prevail over the Germans when the real war started.

Sophie tried to sit close to the packed tables so she could overhear the discussions. "I'm getting a good café education," she explained when Rózsi questioned the purpose and appropriateness of her wanderings. "And when I'm there, I write letters and think about what Willy and Pavel are doing without me."

"You are an attractive young woman," Rózsi warned. "And sometimes impulsive. Does Willy know what you are doing?"

Sophie protested. "Of course, Rózsi. I listen, I read and I speak with people. Nothing more. That's the best way to learn French, listen and speak, you said so yourself. That's my only entertainment. What else should I do?"

* * *

One rainy afternoon, Sophie decided to go to one of the places she had heard of but never seen, Montmartre, the neighborhood of cabarets where the Sacré Coeur Basilica towered over Paris.

It was a one-hour walk north to Montmartre, about four kilometers. Using a map Andreas had lent her she found the Place du Tertre, a cobbled, sloping square surrounded by old, misshapen houses. He told her that a couple of famous artists had studios in the *quartier*. "Don't know their names, so you'll have to find out yourself. Check the bars," he said with a grin when Rózsi was out of earshot.

The square that Andreas had described to her as always being crowded was deserted. Sophie noticed a few inert forms curled up in doorways—she guessed they were refugees and blessed the Szigetis for their kindness to her and Pavel. At least she could afford a room. Andreas had explained that most of the destitute people on the streets were from Belgium and Spain.

A policeman in a rubberized cloak stood at a corner, smoking. He gave her a nod. "You should be carrying a gas mask, Madame. There is a penalty."

"I'm sorry, I forgot it."

"*Eh, bien, prenez garde.* Do not stay late around here."

She raised her umbrella, gave him a timid smile in acknowledgment and hurried on. Even though her papers were

191

in order, she was afraid of being stopped. "Even with your identity card, stay away from the police," Willy had warned. "You'll get caught in the mesh of French bureaucracy. Like a little fish. And then—they will *grill* you!"

The street lights switched on. She looked around the empty square and shivered.

Just beyond the square, Sophie noticed a brightly lit café with a small blue windmill perched above its entry. It was full of people. Peering through the café's steamed-up windows, she decided on a warming drink before going home. She checked her purse … enough for a cheap cognac and a Metro ticket home.

Inside, as she sipped the fiery liquid, she looked around at the customers hoping to see someone who looked like a famous artist, someone bearded perhaps, wearing a beret, with a silk scarf around his neck. Then she would have a story to tell Andreas. But everyone looked ordinary: shabby and bourgeois.

She recognized a hollow-cheeked man with matted hair falling over the collar of his great-coat; one of the regulars from her haunt at Les Deux Magots. He sat at one of the café windows, arms draped around the backs of two other men. A couple of youngish women, both with uncombed hair and wearing overcoats, shared the same table and appeared to be having a serious argument, jabbing fingers at each other to make a point.

He caught Sophie's eye and smiled. She looked away but then when she stole another glance, he rose from his table and came over. *Who is he?*

Sophie studied her cognac, her heart thumping, ready to say: *Laissez moi tranquille, m'sieu.* Leave me alone.

He held out his hand. "I recognize you from somewhere. My name is Rafaël, Rafaël Albert—once upon a time a Barcelona native, but now a tragic *immigré*. It's a miserable evening to be on one's own, especially for one so beautiful. Please join me and my friends."

He had an open face, a nice smile and he was not promoting himself. She hesitated. Be careful with strangers when you are alone, that's what Willy said. Well, Willy was far away.

"I'm not sure I should, *m'sieu*."

He nodded and gently took her elbow. "Don't be afraid. I am not dangerous. Come, join our group. It will be amusing. You look a little lonely."

His words struck home. She hungered for interesting conversation and the company of people other than the Szigetis. "I'll join you for a little while. Thank you. I'm Sophie Kohut."

"From where? You don't look French."

"I'm a refugee like you—but from Czechoslovakia."

Chairs were shifted, hands shaken and Sophie, despite her poor French, was soon drawn into conversation. She had trouble understanding the women's Parisian accents, mixed in with Rafaël's tortured French. The small, balding man sitting next to her, who seemed older than the others, spoke more slowly and with a strange intonation. He was not particularly handsome, but his attentive eyes, stocky frame and well-shaped, nervous hands held her gaze. He wore a battered trilby hat, tilted so far on the back of his head that she was tempted to reach out and adjust it.

She saw the others respected him. They listened raptly as he described his visit to an internment camp in the French Pyrenees where he met Spanish refugees and escaped Republican soldiers. "Their situation," he said, looking around the table, "is deplorable, bestial. Many are dying of disease and starvation—that such a terrible thing happens in France, the country of liberty and fraternity, is an outrage."

"*Je m'appelle Pablo Ruiz*," he said, abruptly turning from his companions to look at Sophie. A brilliant smile split the olive tan of his skin. "From Spain." He grasped her hand and held on to it. "When I saw you walk in all wet and trembling, I said to myself, here is a winter gift." He placed her hand over the center of his chest. "Mademoiselle, you have an interesting face. Hazel eyes, succulent lips, and apricot cheeks—like a tropical plant. As soon as possible, I will paint you. And you have a good body, I think." He slipped off his chair, squatted down and peered at her legs under the table. "Excellent shape," he muttered, touching her skin.

Sophie froze, afraid of what he might do next. This was far worse than harassment at Les Deux Magots. She jumped to her feet, knocking the chair over. With a knowing smile, Rafaël picked it up for her. No one seemed the least disturbed by Monsieur Ruiz's action—not even people at nearby tables.

He looked up and smiled. "You look intelligent. I hope so. I need intelligent women around me, like beautiful planets circling the sun. I will pay you a small fee to model for me, fifty francs for each sitting."

In spite of her shock, Sophie almost smiled back. He was impulsive, attractive and a puzzle. Most interesting of all was his offer. "Some men claiming to be painters have asked me to be their model, but it's just a trick to pick up foreign women." She waved a warning finger. "How do I know that you are a genuine painter?"

Pablo chuckled. "I see you are a skeptic. Very well. I will show you something and you can be the judge. Sit down." He turned to the others, who were arguing about something else.

"Come, my friends, move all these glasses and bottles out of the way so I can draw something for our new friend."

Pablo Ruiz tore off a section of the brown paper that acted as a disposable table covering. He pulled a blue crayon from his breast pocket and everyone fell silent, as if they had seen this before.

In a sinuous motion, Pablo outlined a nude with almond-shaped eyes, a perfect nose and voluptuous lips. The forefinger and thumb of one of her hands pinched the nipple of her perfectly shaped left breast. He drew her hips and thighs enormously out of proportion. The center of the nude's upper thighs was surrounded by a halo of fine, curly hair.

One of the young women giggled. "I wonder if that's me?" She looked round the table expectantly but no one said anything.

Sophie was spellbound by the drawing's eroticism. She could not stop staring, or resist the magnetism the man projected as he worked his crayon.

"So, what do you think?" He drained his cognac and pushed the glass across the table for another refill. "Is this creature's attitude one of pride in her body, or of sexual anticipation?"

Sophie wasn't sure what to say. The drawing pulsed with movement and tension. It made her mind whirl and at the same time she felt unsettled, uncomfortable. Pablo held her eyes.

"The nude? I think she anticipates an orgasm," laughed one of the women at the table.

"No, I think she's afraid of something," said Rafaël. "There is terror in her eyes."

"Yes, my friend," Pablo said with a laugh. "She fears she will be the victim of the Minotaur."

"What is a Minotaur?" Sophie saw the others look at her with amused eyes and she shrank inwardly.

Pablo smiled, a sardonic smile, as if he was playing with her. "The Minotaur is the mythic beast who will perish unless he penetrates and devours at least one woman a day." With a swift and seamless movement of wrist and fingers he began to draw. Within moments, Sophie saw that a powerful male figure, molded on a bull's body, had pressed itself against the blue nude's torso—almost inside it, Sophie thought.

She was astonished at the speed at which the animalistic ravisher had appeared. Pablo's blue crayon hardly ever lost contact with the paper. It was an act of supreme confidence as if he needed no thought to transfer what was in his imagination to the drawing.

Her senses whirled at the savage beauty of the drawing.

"So, am I an artist, or not?" An appealing smile spread across his face.

Sophie felt dizzy. Cognac on an empty stomach was not such a good idea. She nodded. "Yes, monsieur … you *are* an artist … but you did not sign your name." Everyone around the table seemed amused by her words.

"No need," said one of the young women with a mischievous glance at the others. "He's starting to make a name for himself. He…"

Pablo reached across and put a finger on her lips. With a graceful inclination of the head, he handed the drawing to Sophie. "A souvenir of our first meeting."

She folded it carefully and put it in her purse.

"For the second time I ask. Will you sit for me?"

"Maybe," she said hesitantly, thinking that sitting for the man who had drawn this brutish creature would be an intense experience. She remembered Rózsi's warning about impulsiveness. "I've heard about you artists. No clothes off."

The young women nodded at one another other. "Isn't she the respectable one?" one remarked, lapsing into a tinkle of laughter.

"I'm married."

Giving Pablo a rueful look, Rafaël refilled his wine glass from a carafe. "Leave her be, comrade." He turned to Sophie. "Your lucky husband, where is he?"

"In an army camp, at a town called Agde," she said quietly. "In the south."

"I know Agde," said Pablo. "On the Mediterranean—it was a Greek colony two thousand years ago. Listen, Sophie, my painting of you will live forever in some gallery or museum. Maybe for two thousand years." He took hold of Sophie's hands and kissed her fingertips, one by one. "Come—tomorrow at eleven. I promise to paint you only with your clothes on. Fifty francs per sitting, remember?" His friends laughed and clinked glasses. "Do you have the courage to come?"

Sophie felt herself blush. Was this a joke? Was this man well known? If he *was* how could she refuse such a moment of glory even if it meant being a little scandalous? Why not?

Pablo smiled and scribbled his address on another part of the paper table cloth, tore it off and handed it to her wrapped in a banknote. "Here is the fifty-franc fee I promised. You can't refuse me now."

"Go on, take it," said one of the young women—she had said her name was Sylvie. She took Sophie's hands. "I will chaperone you. He won't try anything if I'm there. We'll meet tomorrow at eleven at the Minotaur's studio."

"*Bravo*, Sylvie," Raphaël shouted, slapping the table. "I can't wait to see what he puts on the canvas." He turned to Sophie. "The only person you will recognize in the painting will be your inner self, turned inside out and sideways."

Sophie rose, reassured, her heart fluttering with excitement. "Thank you." She turned to Pablo. "I have to go, *m'sieu*. If you turn out to be famous, I'll expect you to sign the drawing you gave me."

He blew her a kiss and turned to speak to someone else.

Rafaël put on his coat. "I will accompany you to the Metro, Sophie. Outside, the rain has turned to snow." He took her arm and guided her to the Abbesses station, keeping up a stream of conversation. "Please, let me buy your ticket."

"*Non merci*," she laughed. "I have fifty francs now. I can afford it."

CHAPTER SEVENTEEN

The Portrait
Paris, February 1940

When Sophie arrived at the artist's studio on the second floor of an old building on the Rue des Grands-Augustins, the door was slightly ajar. She knocked, and when there was no response she walked into a spacious room with slanted walls, masonry buttresses and heavy cross beams. Along one wall, generous, paned windows let in gray winter light. Metal lamps hung from wires looped across the beams.

She was surrounded by chaos: colored glass fragments, carved picture frames, swatches of Asian carpet, old bronzes, patterned fabrics, African masks, oil lamps and odd lengths of rope—propped up against walls, lying on chairs, or stuffed on to shelves. Paintings and blank canvases were stacked into racks, drawings strewn over tables. A few paintings, vibrant with color, hung on the drab walls. Their scrawled signatures meant nothing to her. Willy was the art enthusiast.

One canvas echoed the brutal eroticism Pablo had sketched for her in the café. On a background of dense green-blue color, a jumbled mass of triangles surrounded a rampaging bull in the act of impregnating a helpless woman. It was unsigned but she knew he had painted it. A few feet away, she found another one; an overweight nude raised her arms against a vivid pink background. The woman's head was divided into two with one eye positioned atop the other.

"I think you paint to shock," she said when the painter appeared from behind a tall armoire and kissed her on both cheeks. He had substituted a wool cap for the trilby he wore at the Café du Moulin.

She pulled the Minotaur sketch from her purse. "Before anything else, I want you to sign this for me."

He put the sketch on a nearby chair seat and, with a pencil he took from his paint-stained smock, signed "Pablo" in one corner. He returned it and led her to a table in front of a roaring pot-bellied stove in one corner of the studio where Sylvie, her volunteer chaperone, was waiting with cups and a pot of coffee. They exchanged cheek kisses and a *Bonjour*.

"Don't mind me," said Sylvie as Sophie sat in one of the rickety chairs. "I'm reading a fascinating novel by Malraux." She showed Sophie the title. "It's about the Spanish Civil War."

"I don't read much French. Only newspapers."

Sylvie lit a cigarette and started reading.

"Remind me, from where is it you escaped," said Pablo, taking her hand.

"Prague, but I'm Hungarian by birth." She trembled a little. Was it cold or nervousness, or both? She was going to show her body, at least part of it, to a stranger. Girl foolishness Rózsi would have called it.

"Ah, you Slavs," he sighed, "such difficult people. Dora, who lives with me now; her father is from Croatia. Before her, I lived with another Slav, my wife Olga—a dancer—beautiful but hard to deal with."

Sophie smiled. "Olga was my mother's name."

Pablo gave an exultant cry and threw his arms in the air. "*Voilà, ma chère*, somehow I knew you and I had a special connection. In fact, we have no time to lose. I want you remove everything from the waist up. In the café, you said wouldn't do it but, in art, a woman's breasts should be as visible as ears and lips."

Sophie burst out laughing. "I don't think so. As we agreed, I will sit for you, fully dressed, wearing my hat." She shivered. "It's cold in here. Even with the stove, your studio is like an icebox."

She watched him add wood to the stove and set up the easel. As he prepared brushes and paints she wondered what Willy would say if he was there, watching. She wasn't sure. He certainly loved art. A few months before the Nazis occupied Prague, he had bought a couple of Czechoslovak impressionists. Sophie decided that he would be pleased that Pablo Ruiz was painting his wife.

After an hour, Sylvie took her leave. "I'm off, Sophie. Don't worry. Everything is normal here and I have errands to run." Pablo, immersed behind his easel, did not say goodbye.

Two hours later, with a break for squeezed lemon juice in hot water, he stopped painting. He stood back to inspect his work, hummed, did a little dance and then crooked a finger. "Come and see. I will call this one 'Bust of Woman in a Striped Hat.' Do you like it?"

"Yes, nice colors, but it doesn't look the least bit like me."

"Of course not. I dismantled your face, discarded the dross and kept the essentials. As you can see I gave you two naked breasts even though you were covered."

"I like the background, mauve with yellow stripes, like expensive wallpaper."

Pablo grunted, as if he did not regard this as a compliment. "Do me a favor, Sophie; let me sketch you naked to the waist. Take your things off behind the screen, or if you prefer, drop them on the chair. I will create something you will find interesting and the world will love. Please?" He bowed beseechingly.

Sophie, reassured by the painter's gentle manner and intrigued by his promise of her immortality, could not control her wish to comply. This was Paris and a genuine artist was painting her. It would never happen again. She slipped behind a patterned screen. When she re-appeared he sat her down and knelt, gazing raptly at her breasts. "Mmm, delightfully shaped, as I had hoped." He took a single stem from a vase of silk sunflowers and made her hold the flower stem against her chest, so that her nipples peeped through the flower-head's upper petals. "That's good. Stay like that, absolutely still."

Sophie watched his head and arms moving behind the canvas, astonished at how she had got herself into this. Even more astounding, she was enjoying it.

He worked quickly and after a while he put down the brushes. "Come *Madame* Sophie. Have a look at what I've done."

She stood behind him, still half naked. He had painted her face, eyes and mouth as a series of colored boxes, each one filled with a circle. Thick curving lines ran down from her hair to the rounded breasts that merged into the head of the sunflower. He had transformed the ends of the petals into delicate human fingers.

He nodded sagely. "It is going well. Another half hour of sitting, then we stop for refreshment and for making love. This is natural, no?"

Sophie stared at him. She admired his work and wanted him to finish it. Now she feared what he might do. He was small but well-muscled, and she remembered from films and the opera that Spaniards and Italians were passionate men. What if Pablo insisted, forced her? She remembered what Hans Lessig had done to her. She would fight back if she had to.

"*Non*, Pablo." She walked toward the screen. "Instead, we finish now."

"*Merde*," he pouted, throwing his brushes to the floor. "You make me hungry for love. If you don't let me make love to you, I will destroy this portrait. It will be a tragedy. Your body will have no legacy." Opening his arms he moved towards her.

Sophie laughed nervously and drew back in alarm. The price of immortality was too high. With a confused feeling that she had let him down, she started to get dressed. As she buttoned her blouse, Sophie heard a key scratch at the studio door. A slim woman, wearing a red hat with peacock feathers sewn into the band, let herself in. She carried a heavy shopping bag, from which protruded two baguettes. She threw her hat on a chair and ran slender fingers through her silky brown hair, seemingly unconcerned at the sight of Sophie.

"Why are you here, Dora?" Pablo exclaimed. Sophie noticed how much older he looked when he frowned. "I told you to stay away till the afternoon. Weren't you supposed to collect Maia from school?"

Dora looked quizzically at the new painting, picked up the sunflower and waved it in Pablo's face. "I like it. I see she undressed for you." She smiled sympathetically at Sophie. "He's always looking for the perfect body—first to paint and then to caress."

Pablo grinned, raising his hands in mock despair. "What can I say? You are both so beautiful."

Dora laughed. "You're a diplomat and charmer, and at the same time also a swine." She grabbed one of the baguettes and broke it over his head. "Punishment delivered." She turned to Sophie. "It's time for you to go home, young lady."

"I have not finished," Pablo called out. "Come back again, I beg you."

On the Metro back to Café Budapest, Sophie was in two minds about what had happened. A little ashamed, perhaps. On the other hand, she had enjoyed the experience and asserted her independence. She even wondered what it would be like to have sex with him. The way Pablo had drawn the Minotaur for her suggested he was wise in the ways of physical love. Would he be as unusual and skilled as a lover as he was a painter? But then, he was much older—almost middle-aged—more like her father-in-law, Emil. Did age make lovers better or worse?

As Sophie turned the corner and walked toward Café Budapest, she remembered how, a month ago when Willy returned to Paris, she had resisted his desire for sex. She regretted it now. She had not been ready then. Now she wanted him back in her arms, melting her with his kisses and caresses.

CHAPTER EIGHTEEN

Willy Resurfaces
Paris. March 1940

Leaving the hotel to renew her work and residency permits from
the Hôtel de Ville, Sophie first made her regular stop at the letter
box in the concierge's office. She treasured the moment she saw an
envelope waiting in her cubbyhole, a golden gift from family or
friends.

Two days earlier, she received a letter from her father and
brother in Australia. The misery of their refugee lives had hardly
changed. After being released from the internment camp, they
now worked for a pittance at a tomato farm. A card had arrived
from Cousin Feri, saying that he was now a qualified doctor and
stationed at La Ferté fortress on the Maginot line. His parents had
decided to wait out the war in Istanbul. He promised to meet her
on his next leave.

"You have a letter, Madame," said the concierge.

A fresh letter post-marked PORTEL 5.3.1940, occupied
Sophie's cubbyhole. Her heart leaped at the sight of Willy's
handwriting. Where was Portel for God's sake? Why wasn't it
from the Agde camp where he was confined? Her hands shook.
A colored strip sealed one side of the envelope and was marked:
VOJENSKA CENSURA. Censored. This letter was Willy's first
sign of life after six weeks of silence. She ripped the flap open and
pulled out a flimsy sheet of paper and a fifty-franc note.

February 18th, Agde.

Dearest Sophie. I was released today!! With great joy I read all your letters. Again, I'm deeply sorry about what happened.

I'm glad Pavel is happy at the farm. I have the impression that you are also more content. I expect the city is very different now: rationing, bomb shelters, shortages and soldiers everywhere. Be careful, especially in the evenings. A beautiful woman like you is vulnerable.

Here is my news. For my punishment, I worked under Sergeant Kukulka repairing out-of-date weapons. That was hard on my hands. In two days, I'm to be transferred to the ███ Hipomobilni Battery at ███ The cart horses we use to pull the field guns have been requisitioned from local farmers who are furious. Frankly, those big animals scare me. They expect us to face German tanks with farm animals and out-of-date artillery? It's ridiculous.

Good news! Lieutenant Vogel, our billet officer, found accommodation for you and Pavel. A village called S███t. As soon as I'm more settled in ███ (another village nearby) I will send for you and Pavel. Unfortunately, there is a chance I will be deployed north in the next few weeks, so you will live in this village with me gone. At least you and Pavel will be a long way from any fighting. If the Germans attack France, it will be in the north, against the Maginot Line, not far from Paris.

I have not yet received any pay. Sergeant K advanced me the 50 francs enclosed in this letter. Read the medieval French motto on the banknote. It says: Un coeur vaillans rien d'impossible. Which translates to 'nothing is impossible for a valiant heart' This is how I feel about us now. Nothing is impossible because, together, we have valiant hearts. We will find a way to get to my parents in England. They sent me a letter. Like us, they have gas masks, rationing and air raid shelters. The Luftwaffe bombed the North of England but lost many planes.

Father got a sad message from Jiri Lask in Prague. Jews cannot go to the cinema, use taxis, or walk in the parks. Most have lost their jobs or been sent to work camps. Jiri works at clearing snow at Ruzn, airport, unpaid of course, if you remember, he was a high-level engineer at Solvay. We live in an upside-down world. Thank God we got away in time.

Cousin Janko is alive! In Istanbul. Their barge trip down the Danube was awful. They were stuck in the ice for a week with only sauerkraut to eat. One of the women got frostbite and a young medical student on the boat had to amputate her arm. God knows what with. Now he plans to marry her. How about that for a love story?

I'm so looking forward to seeing you, my darling, and the little one, only I don't know if I can wrangle a permit to come to Paris. There's a permanent black mark against my name at HQ.

A thousand kisses. Your loving husband, Willy.

P.S. I don't know how they will censor this letter. Kukulka says they just black out a few words, a bureaucratic gesture to keep our French supervisors happy.

Sophie reread Willy's letter many times. She thought about their dilemma. They wanted to get to England, but the Germans had started bombing there. Staying in Paris was even riskier. She was so unsettled that she smoked too much and suffered from morning headaches and stomach pains. There was nothing for her to do except mark time, keep Pavel on the farm and wait for Willy to let her know that everything had been arranged—that it was time to leave Paris.

CHAPTER NINETEEN

A Cascade of Events
Paris. May 1940

Sophie mopped the café tables: a final wipe-down before the café opened. She went to the front door and turned the *ouvert* sign to face the street.

Rózsi stacked the counter shelves with newly baked pastries. "How is little Pavel doing at the farm?" she called out. "Did Madame Duclet say what was wrong with him when she spoke to you yesterday?"

Sophie managed a hopeful smile. "Pavel has a fever. Two or three children at the farm have bad colds. Probably, he has the same thing. The doctor visited and said it was nothing to worry about. Madame Duclet said she would telephone again today. I sent Willy a telegram. I want—"

The bakery door banged open and Andreas stepped out, his face ashen and agitated, his eyes wide. "This time, the war is on, definitely. On the radio…"

"Stop this nonsense, husband." Rózsi shook a finger at him. "The real war started a month ago—when the Germans waltzed their way through Denmark."

Andreas' head was twitching. His eyes flamed. Sophie had never seen him so angry. "That was German bullying, woman, not fighting … they claimed they were 'protecting' Scandinavian people from the 'vicious' behavior of the British and French governments.

The Danes did not fight. It's not a war if only one side fights."

Sophie went up to him. "What did you hear, Andreas?"

"The Germans attacked Luxembourg, Belgium, and Holland—unbelievable. Three neutral countries gobbled up at the same time."

Rózsi pulled at her headscarf. She was blinking tears, her lips trembled. "They must be resisting. They have armies."

Andreas snorted derisively "Yes, but only piddling little ones. Britain and France are sending troops to help the Belgians and Dutch. Too damned late. "The only good news," the baker said as he turned to go back into the bakery, "is that Chamberlain resigned. Our Daladier should do the same."

The café door-bell tinkled and a tall, middle-aged customer walked in. He hooked a silver cane on the counter and nodded at Sophie. "*Bonjour Mesdames.*"

Sophie tried to smile a greeting but her mind was galloping elsewhere. How long before the Germans came to Paris? Sophie's hands shook as she stacked clean cups and saucers on the back shelves. It would be the same here as it had been in Prague. An unbearable memory flashed into her mind—of Willy, thin and unshaven, staggering through the door of their store after weeks of interrogation by the Gestapo. She had to talk to Willy. She had to get out of the city. She decided, there and then, to get Pavel from the Duclet Farm and leave Paris.

"*Vous desirez?*" said Rózsi from the behind the counter.

"*Quatre pains au chocolat et deux mille-feuilles, s'il vous plait.* Packed in one of your gift boxes."

Sophie rushed to the counter as the door closed behind him. "Rózsi, I must talk to Willy as soon as possible. We can't stay in Paris."

Rózsi gave her a sympathetic look. "You can telephone Willy from here. You have his telephone number?"

Sophie shook her head. "Only his address … from the letter he sent. I wrote and asked him to call me here at the café, any morning. All I can do is wait."

Rózsi came around the counter and took both of Sophie's hands. "It's silly to sit here looking glum or endlessly tidying. Run an errand for me and clear your mind for a spell. The news has upset you. If Willy calls, we'll get a number where you can reach him." She pulled money from her purse. "Go to the flower market and buy something colorful for my counter."

It took Sophie twenty-five minutes to walk to the Petit Pont; the side streets were unusually quiet, but the main thoroughfares teemed with soldiers and pedestrians. Convoys of military trucks and horse-drawn wagons clogged the roads. The diesel fumes made her nauseous.

Walking along the Seine toward the flower market calmed her. The cherry trees were in bloom. For a few moments, she sat on a bench watching the barges slide by, clothes drying on lines and flowers and vegetables growing out of rusty buckets on the cabin roofs. It seemed impossible to her that, at this moment, thousands of Belgian and French families were fleeing their homes.

She sighed and lit a cigarette. The question was when, where and how would she and Pavel leave Paris? It would be hard leaving the Szigetis and the *quartiers* she had come to know. In the past weeks, Sophie had even imagined how pleasant it might be to put down roots in Paris—not go to London at all, not join Willy's parents. Their letters from London were full of affection, but she wondered what it would be like living with them in a cramped apartment. Life in London would be strange and new again. Her French would be of no use. She would have to learn English. Start over.

She smoked another cigarette and thought about Willy's

letter … the village he mentioned. He was right. The south of France was the safest place to be—as far from the Germans as possible. Even if Willy was sent off to fight, she and Pavel would have somewhere to live. They would take walks in the countryside and have picnics and go to the beaches.

At the Marché aux Fleurs, Sophie found it difficult to make a choice among the primroses and freesias or the phlox and delphiniums packed into galvanized buckets. Many of the stalls were closed. She overheard a florist say that the Dutch and Belgian glasshouses that grew most of their flowers had been shut down. She remembered how difficult it had been to find flowers in Prague when the Nazis took over.

She resumed her stroll and paused at the Rue Monge market. The competition between housewives at the stalls seemed more intense than usual, with pushing, shoving, exchanging insults and expletives. She knew what they were after—new string beans, snap peas and potatoes, wild asparagus, *mâche* salad, and early cherries from Provence. Did these women understand what might happen soon? Germans in Paris.

"Did Willy telephone?" she asked when she got back to the Café Budapest and handed a bunch of freesias to Rózsi.

The other woman took the flowers and the change, shaking her head as she inhaled their scent. "I'm sorry, no. Not Willy, not even Madame Duclet."

When Sophie went into the back to fetch a bundle of still-warm baguettes to restock the bread shelves behind the counter, the baker was watching the kneading blades turn, hands on his hips. The radio was still playing at high volume and she could tell he was paying closer attention to the commentator than to his work. Sophie listened to the solemn voice on the radio, trying hard to understand the announcer's measured sentences.

"Allied forces have retreated from their positions inside

Belgium. It is reported that Luxembourg and Holland are about to surrender to the Germans."

"Shit in the ocean, what a disaster." Andreas looked at her with tragic eyes. He hardly ever cursed. "The Germans will slice through the Ardennes—a knife through the Allied *brie* you might say," he said with a sad smile.

All through the morning, the café's customers were grim-faced and taciturn. They bought bread and pastries and left without gossiping, sometimes without a word of thanks. No one wanted to talk.

Before their lunch break, Sophie swept the floor in the bakery and helped Andreas shift bags of flour. As he put the finishing touches to icing several cakes, she started to wash and dry his utensils, hoping desperately that Willy would telephone. And there was still the promised call from Madame Duclet, about Pavel's cold.

"Last night Winston Churchill was appointed the new prime minister of Britain," the radio commentator's voice continued above the clatter of the kneading machine. "Churchill made a stirring speech calling for all the subjects of the British Empire to sacrifice and fight the German menace."

In the café, the telephone rang. "Answer that, Rózsi," Andreas yelled, hurriedly washing his hands in the double sink. Sophie's hands were still deep in soapy water. She dried them hoping it was Willy. The bad news whirled around her head. She could not think clearly.

"In the early hours of this morning," said the radio voice, "the Belgian fortress of Eben-Emael, near Liège, fell to a force of German glider troops. In northern France, the trains and roads are swamped by Belgians fleeing south toward Lille and Paris."

"Sophie, it is for you—about Pavel. Madame Duclet."

Sophie hurried to the wall telephone.

"*C'est Amélie Duclet.* You must please come at once. Pavel has some kind of swelling in his neck. Our doctor visited. He thinks Pavel should be in Paris, close to a hospital, as a precaution. The boy asks for you. Please come, Madame."

A precaution … for what! Sophie held her breath. Her heart jumped and pounded. Her knees buckled. She had seen Pavel five days earlier. He had been quieter than usual and not eaten much, but he did not look ill. He played with his friends, ran about and laughed. I should never have left him there. She bit her lip to stop words of self-blame from tumbling out.

"Thank you for letting me know, Madame Duclet. I will come as soon as I can."

Sophie felt angry, guilty and calm, all at the same time. She would try not to panic until she saw Pavel and knew the exact circumstances. It was as if everything was stacking up to test her—Willy's demand that they leave Paris, the Nazis crossing into Belgium and Holland, and now, Pavel. Sophie took a deep breath and put down the receiver.

She scribbled a note and gave it to Rózsi. "Pavel is ill. I have to go to the farm. If Willy doesn't telephone, send a telegram asking him to telephone … send it to his commander's office at the Agde camp. Here is the address. If Willy makes contact while I'm gone, please tell him to telephone the Duclet farm. Make sure to ask him for a number I can call."

Grabbing her raincoat and gas mask, she ran from the café to catch a bus to the station.

The Gare St. Lazare was busy with people carrying heavy suitcases, and children straggling behind them. For nearly an hour, Sophie paced up and down the platform waiting for the train, imagining Pavel pale and shaking with fever. If he needed to be near a hospital, as the doctor said, he must be in danger. What if he was so ill they could not even leave Paris? Would the Czechoslovak army let Willy come to Paris to help her?

The local train stopped at every station. By the time she reached Vernon, she could not stop trembling. As the taxi drove to the farm, she hung on to the strap in the back, biting her lips, looking blankly out of the window. The misty drizzle outside matched her mood.

At the farm one of the attendants took her up to the dormitory. "I'm Suzanne. Madame Duclet is out milking the cows," she said as they climbed the stairs. "Monsieur also is not here."

Pavel lay in his bed smiling weakly. He held his arms out to her. "Maman, Maman, I feel bad."

Sophie was shocked by his appearance: thin and deathly pale except for two bright red patches over the cheekbones. She tried not to show any reaction that might alarm him. As she stroked his arm, she noticed his skin had a moist, yellowish sheen. From time to time, he shivered and his blue eyes were clouded. He moved and whimpered like an injured animal. Sophie folded him in her arms, shivering uncontrollably as fear ate into every fiber of her body.

Pavel clung to her. "Maman, stay, don't go away."

She hugged him. "Of course, I'll stay … until you're better."

He winced and put a hand up to his neck. He pushed her away. "No, stop. My neck hurts."

It was then that Sophie noticed the red swelling, the size of a walnut, below the angle of his jaw. She touched it with the tips of her fingers. It was hot and hard. Pavel shrank back. The tears came instantly from his pleading eyes. "Don't … don't."

Sophie swiveled, frowning at Suzanne who was watching. "Why is he like this? Please, bring Madame here, now."

Suzanne blinked repeatedly and curtseyed. "He became worse during the night. We called the café in the evening but there was no answer. I will find Madame Duclet."

Fifteen minutes later Pavel had dozed off, and Sophie, furious that Madame Duclet had not appeared, went to find her. She was in the kitchen, preparing a large pile of *tartines* on the kitchen table, spreading bread slices with butter and honey. Monsieur Duclet sat at the table drinking tea. The sound of children running in and out of the rooms, talking and laughing was deafening and it stoked Sophie's anger and anxiety. How could these children be so happy when her boy was ill?

As soon as she saw Sophie, Madame Duclet's calm face transformed into worry and concern. She wiped fingers on her apron and held out her hand. "I'm so sorry I didn't meet you, we're very busy. Poor Pavel. This happened quite suddenly."

"For God's sake, when did he get worse?" Sophie blurted out, ignoring the outstretched hand. "Why didn't you telephone earlier?"

"Let me explain, Madame," said Monsieur Duclet rising from his chair. "As you know, Pavel and two other children had headaches and mild fever for a couple of days. When Dr. Grimet checked them yesterday morning he said it might only be a cold or perhaps they were incubating measles. Pavel did not complain of anything special. In fact, he played with the others and listened to stories after suppertime. He woke once before midnight and his temperature was higher than normal. That was when we called the Szigetis' café—but no reply."

Madame Duclet chimed in. "He didn't want to get up this morning and I noticed the red lump on his neck. *Docteur* Grimet came again. He thinks the lump is a swollen gland, probably an infection." She pulled a bottle from her apron pocket and handed it to Sophie. "He brought this medicine. Pavel has taken two doses so far."

"So he will get better with this?" Sophie felt a rush of relief, looking at the label.

She read the word, *Sulphathiazole*, and suddenly felt

ashamed she had spoken so abruptly. These good people had done what was needed.

"Yes, but he said it was better for Pavel to be with you in Paris, close to a hospital, in case he needed further treatment."

"There is no hospital here?"

Madame Duclet shook her head. "The doctor said you must sponge Pavel all over with cool water if he gets too hot, and give him plenty to drink."

Monsieur Duclet took Sophie's arm. "I will drive you to the station. There's a train to Paris at four. Do you have friends or people you can ask for help?"

Sophie stared at the Duclets, her heart pounding. She felt helpless. "Only the Szigetis. What should I do?"

"Telephone them when you get to St. Lazare. They know the Paris hospitals better than us. I can give you some money if you need it."

She nodded, hoping desperately that Willy had called the café. She had to talk to him.

At that moment, several children ran into the kitchen, asking for their *tartines*. Monsieur Duclet took Sophie into the corridor, away from the noise. His usually jovial face was serious. "Some advice, Madame Kohut. If Pavel does not improve with the medicine, avoid the public hospitals in Paris. They have a reputation for poor care and filthy conditions and they don't like refugees. We leave in half an hour."

On the train to Paris, Sophie held Pavel wrapped in a blanket. At her feet was a bag containing his clothes and favorite toys. During the journey some of the travelers in the compartment seemed sympathetic and smiled encouragingly. One or two asked if they could help and offered a piece of chocolate. Everyone else was talking or arguing about the German invasion of the Low

Countries and the exodus from Paris. She nodded politely but turned to look out of the window, wanting to be left alone. Pavel dozed most of the time.

At the Gare St. Lazare, carrying Pavel over her shoulder with one hand and his bag with the other, she wound her way between well-dressed families with children, hurrying for the trains leaving Paris. "Why are all these people leaving Paris?" she asked a porter who was helping her get through the rush. "Is it the war?"

He nodded as he parted a way for her. "War and the *Pentecôte* holiday. The schools are closed." He steered her gently by the elbow. "You, Madame, are one of the few fish swimming into Paris against the current of despair."

She waited in the station for an empty telephone cabin, and then sat Pavel on the floor.

When she had explained everything to Rózsi, she asked, "Should I take him to the hospital now? Do you know of one close by? We are both exhausted." She tried to smile at Pavel. His apathetic look made her want to cry.

"I'm so sorry for you, my dear. We know almost nothing about which hospitals are good. There is a *Salle d'Urgences* at a children's public hospital, the Necker, on the Rue de Sèvres—a long walk from the station with a sick child. Twenty minutes in a taxi."

"I…I'm not sure I have enough money for a taxi, let alone to pay a doctor."

"How does Pavel look?"

Still holding the receiver against her ear, Sophie bent down to inspect his face and neck. "Not so bad. He needs to take his next dose of medicine."

"I want to go home, Maman," he whispered. "I want bed."

"Wait, Sophie. Andreas is saying something. He heard on the radio that because of the holiday, city services had been reduced, including the hospitals. Perhaps it's better you go home and see how the boy is in the morning. If he is no better, come to us by taxi and Andreas can accompany you to a hospital. Didn't you say once that the Czechoslovak Consulate had given you a list of charities in case of trouble?"

"Oh, God, yes," Sophie gasped. Why hadn't she thought of that? "I'll look for it." She paused, gathering her thoughts. "Did Willy call?"

"Yes, he left a number for you to telephone tomorrow. I told him about Pavel and said he had a fever. Nothing more."

"Thank you, Rózsi. You are such a strength to me. We will take a taxi back to my hotel. I don't have quite enough for the taxi ride but, cross-fingers, the driver will take pity on us."

Inside the hotel, at the foot of the stairs, Sophie nearly burst into tears. She didn't know whether she had the strength to climb the five flights up to their room. She took a deep breath, nuzzled Pavel's forehead and picked up his bag. "We will get there, my precious. Slow but sure."

Settled in bed, Pavel took his medicine, drank warm milk, and ate a slice of buttered bread. He smiled at her and fell asleep. She looked at the swelling in his neck and lay down beside him feeling a rush of hope. The lump seemed smaller, less red. Rest, sleep, and the medicine would be good for him. Pray God, he would be better in the morning.

CHAPTER TWENTY

Le Beau Docteur
Paris. May 10th, 1940

The night was exhausting. Sophie was afraid to sleep in case Pavel got worse. On three occasions, she sponged him down. In between, she dozed fitfully, thinking of what she needed to do in the morning—take Pavel to the Szigetis and telephone Willy to let him know what was going on. After that Andreas would help her find a good doctor.

She woke at first light. Pavel was still asleep. As she dressed beside the bed, she stopped to look at his neck, suppressing a sob. The lump in his neck was larger, its color blazing red, tinged with blue streaks. Later, he refused to take anything except warmed milk. His pleading eyes tore at her heart. He raised his hand to his neck. "It hurts, Maman. Why?" Her tears came, her stomach twisted: sadness and panic mixed together. She did not dare touch the lump. What to do now?

Sophie remembered Rózsi's words from the night before—about getting help from a charity. She hauled the suitcase from under the bed and scrambled through the documents and resource materials Mr. Vlásek had given Willy at the Consulate. On the back page of a pamphlet she found the Czechoslovak Red Cross address and telephone number. She was encouraged. She would not have to explain everything in French.

Sophie thought about her promise to call Rózsi at the café.

That would mean carrying Pavel down five flights of stairs to telephone from a nearby café and then climb back up again. Too difficult and exhausting. Impossible. She would take Pavel to the Red Cross on her own.

At nine o'clock, Sophie, with Pavel in her arms, discovered that the main thoroughfares in the *quartier* were thick with traffic and refugees traveling south. All the taxis were taken. She managed to tag a *taxi-bicyclette* and sat Pavel in her lap. The *cycliste-chauffeur* took forty minutes, using side-streets to avoid the throngs and traffic snarls, to ride the four kilometers to the Czechoslovak Red Cross office in Montparnasse.

At the Red Cross office, a shabby room tucked between a *charcuterie* and a laundry on Rue Delandre, Sophie waited with mounting despair as Pavel whimpered on her lap. Eventually, the duty nurse, who said she was from Brno, put him on an old leather couch and took his temperature and pulse. With reassuring words and a kindly manner, she tried to examine the swelling on his neck. He jerked away, his eyes dilated and fearful.

The nurse spoke in Czech. "This is serious, *paní* Kohutová. Your boy has a high fever, and this lump—well, it might be an abscess. I've never seen such a thing before, but something must be done immediately."

Sophie nodded. "Is there a hospital near here?"

"There is a public hospital. We have had complaints from some of the people we sent over. They don't like refugees."

Sophie remembered Monsieur Duclet's warning and shuddered. "Please, I want him to get the best treatment."

"How much money do you have?"

Sophie looked in her purse. "About one hundred and thirty francs."

The nurse gave her a pitying smile. "You would pay many times that sum for good private care. But I know of a place that might help you: La Maison de Santé Chirurgicale on the Rue Villa Marguerite. It is a small private surgical clinic, close to the Porte de Versailles. One of its surgeons has helped our clients, charging very little. Would you like me to telephone and find out if he is available?"

Sophie clutched her purse, praying that luck was on her side. "Yes, please, immediately."

With the nurse gone, Sophie sat by Pavel, who lay half-awake on the couch. She held his hand terrified that he would get worse, perhaps even die if he did not get treatment soon. An idea popped into her mind. She would ask the nurse to telephone army headquarters in Béziers so she could get hold of Willy. She scrabbled through her purse for the slip of paper and caught her breath. Damn it to hell, she had left it on the bedside table.

The red-haired nurse returned with a light step and a satisfied look. She smiled and Sophie's spirits lifted.

"They will see Pavel. We will pay for a taxi to take you to the clinic at Issy-les-Moulineaux near the Porte de Versailles. Quite far from here. Sometimes they take pity and the treatment is almost free. If not, we cover the cost and you arrange to pay us back. For the taxi fare also." She nodded sympathetically. "We are flexible."

Sophie drew a sharp breath and opened her purse again. "How much would it be?"

The nurse gave her a compassionate look. "At least eight hundred francs."

Sophie slumped. That was an impossible sum. Pavel was in terrible danger. She wanted to scream, let out her anger and feeling of inadequacy. She, the mother was helpless. A year ago, in Prague, she wouldn't have thought twice about spending this amount on a party dress.

The nurse handed her a sealed envelope. "Money for the clinic."

"What if they don't accept Pavel?"

"You will have to go the Hôpital Publique Necker in the Rue de Sèvres and return the money to us."

Sophie glanced at Pavel's neck. His lips moved as if he were speaking but there was no sound.

"Open your mouth, little darling," said the nurse. Pavel did as he was told. "*Dobrý Bože!* His tongue is shriveled up like a prune; he is terribly dry. I'll bring you some water." She looked sternly at Sophie. "Make sure he drinks frequent small amounts, every half hour at least. Take this blanket with you to keep him warm if he starts to shiver. We'll get it back later."

Sophie took the nurse's hand and kissed it. Her heart pounded with love for this woman. "I'm so grateful to you. I can't thank you enough."

The nurse smiled sadly. "If you have time, let me know what happens to him. We hardly ever find out. We Czechs must help each other."

The taxi ride took an hour to travel the eight kilometers to Issy-les-Moulineaux with the driver doing his best to get past the horse-drawn vehicles, vans and cars piled with luggage that were on their way out of the city.

When Sophie rang the clinic bell at the Rue Villa Marguerite, two uniformed nurses came to the front door and accompanied Sophie as she carried Pavel to a small room. She laid him, still wrapped in the blanket, on a narrow bed.

The taller nurse took off Pavel's shirt and slipped a gown over his shoulders. He did not resist, glancing at Sophie to see if she approved of what was happening. The nurse inspected the red lump under his jaw. "*Mon Dieu! C'est pas jolie.* As big as a goose egg."

The smaller nurse, older and matter-of-fact, spoke rapid

French, her words tumbling around Sophie's head. "Docteur Mallamet will examine your child in a few minutes. First, I must take your details." She pulled out a form clipped to a wooden board. "I need you and your child's full names, date and town of birth, and current address. I also need your French identity cards and residency permit. If you have a husband, we need the same for him as well. Our policy, in the case of refugees, is payment in cash."

Sophie, bewildered by the speed of what was happening and trying to understand what the nurse was saying, opened her purse and pulled out her identity papers and the envelope from the Czechoslovak Red Cross. "There's a letter and money in the envelope," she said hesitantly. "Here are my permits."

The nurse frowned. "No money, not now." She quickly scanned the letter. "*Ça va*. Now you wait. The doctor will decide what to do with your child. I see from your documents you are from Czechoslovakia: a refugee I suppose."

Sophie detected scorn in her words and lowered her gaze. She hated the word, *refugee*. It meant she was useless and dependent, a pariah. "We escaped from the Germans."

"Hunh." The nurse frowned. "This is a highly esteemed clinic with an elite clientele. But, Docteur Mallamet will sometimes see a few refugees for a reasonable fee. Your French documents are in order but I must tell you, we have a new administrative policy. No Israelites are to be accepted. Are you an Israelite?"

"No," said Sophie quickly. She looked away from the nurse's gimlet eyes, praying that they would not discover Pavel's circumcision until the treatment was over. The problem was with his neck, not his *shmeckel*. As far as Sophie was concerned, these French people with their anti-Israelite attitudes were no better than Nazis! She tried to appear surprised. "What a suggestion! Of course, I'm not Jewish. I'm a Hungarian married to a Czechoslovak soldier fighting with the French army." She was surprised at how easily she denied her origins.

The nurse smiled, her expression instantly changing from suspicious to sweet. "*Ah, oui. C'est bien.* I know the Czechoslovaks and French are allies." She sat on the edge of the bed and patted Pavel's arm. "*Alors mon petit*, we will take you to the doctor now, but you, Madame, will have to be patient and wait in the corridor. If you need the toilette it is at the end of the passage."

Sophie sat on a bench, wondering how long she would have to wait and what would happen next. She picked up a creased *France-Soir* newspaper, looked at the headlines and tried to make sense of the small print. Civilian panic was spreading through the north of France. Parisians were leaving the city. Munitions workers were on twelve-hour shifts in the factories. There was a rumor of a 'secret' meeting between Churchill and General Weygand in an attempt to stem a German invasion. It all seemed distant and irrelevant compared to the danger threatening Pavel.

Forty-five minutes later, Sophie was summoned to a green-walled operating room, its windows obscured by white paint. Pavel rested on the surgical table, naked to the waist, a blanket over his lower body. He was awake and she kissed him, gently massaging his arm. "Don't be afraid, my love. Maminko is here." With terrified eyes he turned his head from side to side, watching the methodical actions of a gloved nurse who handled gleaming instruments on a white-clothed surgical trolley.

"Maman, what are they doing? I'm frightened."

His beseeching look turned her heart over. "Don't be afraid, my darling. The doctor will take your nasty lump away. It's called an operation. But first this nice nurse will help you sleep so it doesn't hurt anymore."

"I'm not sleepy."

She smiled, her eyes caressing his pinched face. "If you don't let us help you sleep, it might hurt a lot. I'll be here with you, all the time." Sophie kissed his forehead.

One of the nurses sat down by Pavel's head. Pavel gazed at her smiling, oval face.

"Be a good boy and listen to her, Pavelko." Sophie said.

"*Bonjour, mon petit*," the nurse said softly, bending over him. "My name is Nurse Perle. I love your beautiful curls. Would you give me one as a present?"

Pavel nodded slightly, his scared eyes, flickering back and forth between Sophie and the nurse.

"*Merci mon petit*. I'll get my curl later, but for now I'm going to hold this little white tent over your nose and drop some medicine on it. It will take away the pain in your neck. Do you understand?"

Pavel looked at Sophie for reassurance and put his hand up to the abscess. "Don't touch me." The nurse gently pulled his fingers out of the way.

Sophie tethered his hands with hers. "Please, Pavelkin, stay still." Earlier, in the corridor, another nurse had told her that mothers were expected to help control their children during an anesthetic.

"You are a very good boy. Don't be frightened." Nurse Perle lowered the mask slowly. "Now you are going to smell something strange. Don't be afraid. Everything will be fine." Slowly she began to drip clear liquid from a small bottle on to the gauze mask. "*C'est de l'éther*," she explained to Sophie. "It will make him sleep after a minute. Hold him tight if he resists."

Letting out a muffled squeal, Pavel arched his back and kicked violently with both feet. Sophie leaned across his chest to hold down his flailing arms. The struggle lasted half a minute. He weakened and lay silently on his back, unconscious.

At almost the same instant, a tall man dressed in a short-sleeved, blue surgical gown swept into the operating room. His white linen cap perched on a mass of chestnut hair. With barely a glance at the operating table and the figures around it, he washed his hands at the sink, humming a tune. He dried his hands, pulled on rubber gloves and approached the operating table. "Please, turn the child on his left side," he said to the nurse tending the surgical trolley.

"*Bonjour, chère Madame,*" he said as he inspected the right side of Pavel's neck, without even looking at Sophie. He shook his head in wonder. "*Ah, Mon Dieu,* this is a big one. The fourth in less than a month. It's become an epidemic." He switched his gaze to Sophie as he straightened up. "I am Docteur Jean-Claude Mallamet. You have a beautiful child, Madame." He gave her a brilliant smile. "Understandable, of course. He takes after you."

Sophie dismissed the compliment as she tried to stand her ground and understand what this was all about. "Please, doctor what is this abscess and how did he get it?"

He shrugged. "Whatever the cause, it must be opened. Now, if you want to stay and watch, Madame, you must remain completely silent." He flashed her another charming smile, quick as the click of a camera.

Sophie nodded. She watched the nurse slowly drip more ether on to the mask.

"How is this little one doing, Perle?"

"Fine, Docteur, he's fine."

Humming what Sophie recognized as a popular tango song, "*Avant de Mourir,*" Mallamet repeatedly swabbed the right side of Pavel's neck with iodine. She watched him anchor the beetroot-colored swelling with index finger and thumb. With a quick motion, he made a three-inch incision in the neck below the angle of the jaw.

Sophie gasped when she saw the flow of blood, and covered her face, trying to hide her reaction. She bit her lip, tamping down the irrational fear that she might not see Pavel alive again. She could not stop trembling. Somehow, she felt the sharp scalpel slicing into her own neck.

Mallamet stopped and glared. "Silence, *Madame* or you leave."

For two long minutes, the doctor sat still, using his fingers to compress the incision's skin edges with a large gauze swab. Again, he hummed the tango's melancholy notes and turned to the nurse dropping ether on to the mask. "Have you ever seen such an ugly mess as this one, *ma chère Perle*?"

She shook her head. "Why did he get this, *Docteur*?"

"His cervical glands have been infected. The bacteria causing this must be completely removed. It is like cleaning out a winemaker's fermentation vat. Smelly, unpleasant, but it must be done—otherwise there is a risk of blood-poisoning."

Sophie shuddered at words she did not quite understand but sounded horrible. How could they talk like this in front of her? And why were they talking? A doctor was supposed to concentrate on operating, not gossip or sing popular songs.

She blinked in astonishment as Mallamet deftly pushed the bleeding wound edges apart and forced angled forceps deep inside the swelling's cavity. A sluggish stream of blood and pus oozed down Pavel's neck. He plunged the forceps in and out.

Acid welled up into her throat. She felt faint.

Pavel moaned but did not open his eyes.

"Hunh, so that's done." Mallamet grunted with a smile. "*Impeccable.*" Using a longer pair of forceps, he inserted a flat strip of corrugated red rubber into the abscess cavity and rapidly stitched the incision together.

Sophie was impressed by the man's swiftness; he was as neat as a seamstress—eight precisely placed stitches with the rubber drain protruding from the lower end.

He pulled his shoulders back, stretched and threw the

instruments on the sterile tray. "Stop the ether now, Perle. I will apply the dressing, and then we're done." He pulled off his gloves and, tossing them into a nearby bin, turned to Sophie. "We will keep him here overnight, maybe even two, to watch how he does. Nurse Perle will take him to the recovery area and later transfer his care to the evening nurse. We will check temperature, pulse and breathing rate every four hours and give him plenty of milk to drink when he wakes. You can stay at the clinic with him. There are mattresses for relatives."

Half an hour later, in the recovery room, Pavel woke and offered his mother a wan smile. His lips moved silently, "Maman." She kissed his forehead. Then he closed his eyes.

Nurse Perle came to the bedside. She stroked the boy's hand and smiled at Sophie. "*Le Beau Docteur* wants to talk to you now. Justine here will keep an eye on Pavel." She nodded to another nurse who sat at a nearby table making notes on a small slate-board.

Nurse Perle escorted Sophie back to the bench outside the doctor's office. "A word of advice, Madame Kohut." She smiled and patted Sophie's shoulder. "The doctor's style with patients is more familiar than most French doctors. Remember how much he has done for your boy and be nice to him."

Sophie understood perfectly. If the doctor wanted to flirt, well and good. He had done so much for her and she had only herself to offer. This was France, there was a war on, he was handsome and she was lonely. She had been there before. She waited on the bench for twenty minutes, replaying the past few hours in her mind. The crisis was over, Pavel would get well. She felt as though she had been pummeled into supreme exhaustion.

Dr. Mallamet approached, puffing on a cigarette. His cap was off and his hair fell in waves on to his shoulders. "Madame Kohut, come to my office please." Sophie followed him and he gracefully indicated a leather armchair by his desk. She sat anxiously on the edge of the seat, disarmed by his dashing appearance. Only actors wore their hair like this.

"How is he, Docteur? Is he all right?"

Mallamet, standing beside the chair, squeezed her shoulder reassuringly. "*Madame*, all is well, for the moment." She sank back into the cushioned chair.

He sat on the corner of the desk, the *Gauloise* hanging from his lip. He spoke slowly, as if he was used to dealing with foreigners. "As you may have learned, I am the chief surgeon here. I'm positive your boy will heal very well. A plucky little fellow." He stubbed his cigarette into a crystal ashtray. "As I said, he should stay here at least one night, possibly two. He had a nasty abscess and is still running a fever. In a few days, his spirits and health will be back to normal. Now, I have some instructions for you on how to look after the wound."

Sophie, anxious to learn and get everything right, shifted forward on her chair.

Dr. Mallamet explained the details of how to trim the drain and dress the wound. As he spoke, Sophie remembered how she had cared for Willy's injuries after he was released from Pankrác in Prague. "How long will it be for him to get better?"

"A few days for the wound to close. There's one more thing. We will examine the material I obtained from the abscess and culture it, to identify the bacteria. It is always good to know your enemy, eh? And please do not concern yourself about the cost. The Czech Red Cross gave us enough to cover everything."

Sophie gazed at him gratefully and was suddenly aware why Nurse Perle had called him *Le Beau Docteur*. He was as dashing as any film star she could think of: Laurence Olivier, Errol Flynn, even Douglas Fairbanks. But in contrast to those stars' Anglo-Saxon features, Dr. Mallamet's olive skin and dark hair suggested a Mediterranean origin. Sophie wondered if his slightly crooked nose was the result of some old injury, but even that was not ugly—just an attractive contrast to gray-green eyes full of concern.

Mallamet flipped the pages of Pavel's file, his hands moving with precise gestures. This was the savior of her son, Sophie thought—confident, full of action. A man to be admired. She thought of Willy, scrambling around the countryside surrounded by horses and artillery, unaware of what she had just been through. She feared he might blame her for letting Pavel get sick at the Duclet farm. Willy was often quick to judge and slow to apologize, but then—they had made the decision about the farm together. How could he blame her for this? If only he was here to hug and kiss her and tell her she had done the right thing. If only she could talk to him. She burst into tears.

Mallamet came around the desk and raised her from the chair. He cupped her chin gently with his hands, looked deep into her eyes and then folded his arms around her. "It is especially good to cry when bad things have turned out well," he murmured into her ear. "Be thankful, *chère Madame*. Pavel will sleep without fear and pain tonight. You do not have to leave him. You can sleep on a mattress at the foot of his bed."

Sophie leaned against him and was comforted: a kind, generous man though this embrace was not how Prague doctors behaved. Perhaps medical practice in France had its own style and standards; not stiff, distant and correct like Dr. Pflinz who had treated Willy's crushed finger in Prague.

"Doctor, I ask a favor. I must contact my husband about the operation. He knows nothing about it. He's a soldier with the Czechoslovak army near Béziers. Can I contact him from here?"

With a reassuring squeeze, Mallamet held both her hands. "Of course. I did not know there was such an army in France. Do you have a telephone number?"

"I will get in touch with my friends, they have it."

"Good. My personal secretary, Mademoiselle Fabrille, will arrange for you to use her telephone. In the meantime you can sit and watch over your boy. He will be in a room with three other patients."

Soon after one o'clock, a middle-aged woman bustled into Pavel's room. "Madame Sophie Kohut?"

Sophie carefully untangled her fingers from Pavel's hand. He was asleep.

"I am Dr. Mallamet's personal secretary, Mademoiselle Fabrille. Please come with me. We contacted your friend, Madame Szigeti, and I have arranged a telephone call to your husband in Portel." She compressed her lips, frowning—then looked at her watch. "The operator will call us in exactly five minutes, and we have two minutes to get to my office. Please make it short. Long-distance calls are expensive."

Willy's voice from Portel crackled, fading in and out. "How is he? Rózsi said he was ill. What happened?" Willy's voice held an edge of irritation that told her he was either close to anger or nervous about something.

From across the office desk, Mademoiselle Fabrille watched her, stony-eyed, tapping a pencil on her blotting pad as if timing every second.

Sophie gripped the receiver with white knuckles. Her pulse raced but she did her best to keep her voice calm. "We are in a clinic in Paris. Pavel has an infection in his neck, no one knows why. The Czechoslovak Red Cross helped me get here—a clean place. One of the doctors operated on what he said was an abscess. He says Pavel will be fine. He must stay here for two or three days." It was hard putting everything that had happened into a few words.

There was a brief moment of silence and Sophie imagined Willy digesting what she had told him. "Thank you, Sophie; I'm sure you did the right thing." His voice had turned firm and gentle. "Do you need me to come? I will have to ask permission. It will be hard, but I can try."

Sophie's heart leaped at the prospect of Willy taking charge of the crisis. "Please come. I'm worn out. I'm to take him home the day after tomorrow. I'm supposed to dress the wound every day. He has a big cut in his neck with a rubber drain in it."

"A rubber drain? In God's name, what's that?" His voice trailed off and then came back strongly, almost shouting. "Wait a moment, Sophie." The line crackled again and she heard male voices talking in the background.

"Sophie, can you wait a minute? My superior is here. I will ask him about coming to Paris."

"Good, good."

Mademoiselle Fabrille pulled off her half-moon glasses, examining Sophie minutely as if she were a biologist studying a bedraggled insect.

Sophie flushed. She knew she looked awful in her shabby cardigan and wrinkled dress, her hair a mess and no make-up. She didn't care what this woman thought. The minute of waiting lengthened into three and from the way Mademoiselle Fabrille fiddled with her spectacles, it was clear she was annoyed that the call was taking so long. She leaned across the desk and rubbed her index finger and thumb together in front of Sophie's face—a clear message that this was costing money. Sophie gave the secretary a what-do-you-expect-me-to-do-about-it shrug.

"Sophie?"

"Yes, darling."

"I'm sorry. My commander—he won't let me leave. The Germans have invaded Holland and Belgium and our regiments are still training on the new equipment. We could be called to the front at any time. All leave, including for compassionate cases, is cancelled. My love, I'm so sorry."

Sophie, still holding the telephone, slumped in her chair, unable to speak, fear and disappointment flooding through her. She wanted to ask whether the Nazis were also attacking France, but she was afraid of his answer. Better to stay ignorant and focus on Pavel getting better.

"At least, the worst is over for Pavel," he said. "You've handled everything wonderfully well. It must have been terribly hard for you. Write me about it."

Sophie took a deep breath. "And what am I supposed to do when we leave the clinic and Pavel improves?"

"As soon as you think the boy can travel, leave Paris. It will be hard, several hours on the train. I will arrange lodging for both of you in a nearby village."

"What if Pavel has a relapse when we get there, and needs a doctor?"

"Don't worry. We have good Prague doctors at the camp. Remember Dr. Brod? He's one of them."

"Why can't we wait until Pavel is really better?"

"Be sensible, Sophie. You have no alternative. If there is the slimmest chance that the Nazis arrive while you are in Paris, they'll arrest you and Pavel. We are Jews and..." Willy coughed and Sophie heard a man's angry voice in the background. "Time's up, Sophie. I have to go. I'm not sure where I'll be in the next few days. Try to keep in touch. Leave messages at this number. A thousand kisses, darling. Goodbye."

Sophie mumbled her thanks to Mademoiselle Fabrille and hurried back to Pavel's room.

Pavel had been moved to a larger room, sharing with four adult patients. Each one offered her a greeting. She sat by Pavel's bed, watching him sleep with his hand curled firmly around two of her fingers. After watching Mallamet operate and then with the strain of talking to Willy, she felt emptied out. But she was also proud of successfully managing a family crisis: as she had done after Willy's arrest in Prague. Mallamet had guaranteed that Pavel would get better. When would that be?

CHAPTER TWENTY-ONE

Gratitude
Paris. May 13th, 1940

The next morning Sophie, stiff and out of sorts, crawled off the lumpy mattress at the foot of Pavel's bed. A disturbed night—she had helped the nurse sponge him several times during the night, and one of the other patients coughed incessantly. Pavel's fever had broken and, after washing him, she fed him breakfast—half a croissant and thick yogurt with honey. Strong coffee for herself. When she asked what gift he would like Papa to bring him for his fourth birthday, he returned her smile. "*Je ne sais pas encore.* I don't know yet." She took it as a sign that her precious boy was recovering.

"*Bonjour, mon petit.*" A cheerful nurse settled Pavel on Sophie's lap while she made the bed. Russet curls peeped out below her cap. "Your little one is smiling. He must be better. It's time to change his dressing, but—I have to watch you do it. Doctor Mallamet's orders. It is easier for the boy if his Maman takes charge right from the start."

Sophie nodded her thanks, her heart racing with hope that she could get Pavel away from Paris in a day or two. "What is the news? About the Germans."

The nurse's smile disintegrated. She looked away, shaking her head. "They crossed the Meuse into France. My family live in Sedan. Like everyone else, they've gone south, leaving everything behind."

"I'm sorry."

With the nurse supervising, Sophie removed the stiff blood-stained dressing and began to clean the neck wound with diluted iodine. Pavel jerked back, putting up his hands to stop her and crying as she dabbed at the stitches and the drain. She remembered her feelings of distaste when, a year earlier, she had dressed Willy's crushed finger. He had been remarkably stoic, put up with her fumbling without a word. But then he was a grown man.

Doctor Mallamet entered Pavel's room at noon and woke the boy with a gentle squeeze of the shoulder. The other patients watched silently from their beds. Unbuttoning his jacket so that he could sit on the edge of the bed, the doctor smiled at Sophie with his gray-green eyes. "I was told you cleaned and repacked the wound effectively. I can see you are a good mother."

Sophie smiled, enchanted by his courtly manner and kind eyes. She could not help comparing his distinguished looks and kindly charm to Willy, whose character and even his face seemed a little distant after their long separation.

Mallamet clicked open a flat gold case and lit a cigarette. He held the case out to her. "Lucky Strike?"

She shook her head knowing that Pavel hated cigarette smoke. She did not complain. This was Mallamet's clinic; the man could do what he wanted.

The doctor sent a stream of smoke into the air. "We stained the bacteria from Pavel's abscess, Madame. He has tuberculosis. We will have to confirm it with cultures. Does he drink raw milk?"

"Ó Istenem!" Sophie blurted in Hungarian, splaying fingers over her despairing face. "Oh, God, docteur. Tuberculosis is dangerous. It means a sanatorium, yes?"

She pictured Pavel on a hospital verandah, getting sun lamp treatment but wasting away all the same. And if she was forced to stay in Paris because he was not well enough to travel, they might never see Willy again. Her equanimity evaporated.

"You did not answer my question, *Madame*. Did he drink any raw milk?"

Sophie frowned. Was he accusing her of doing something wrong? "I don't know. He was living with other children on a farm at Vernon. Every day they drank cow's milk. Will he be confined a long time? My husband is afraid the Germans will attack Paris."

"Very possible. And you are Jewish." Mallamet crushed his cigarette underfoot. "I noticed your boy's circumcision."

Sophie, crestfallen, studied her broken fingernails and nodded.

With a graceful motion, the doctor placed his finely-manicured hand over hers. "*Soyez tranquille, Madame.* Relax. You are afraid of TB of the lung. That is the dangerous kind. Your Pavel has something different. What we call bovine tuberculosis, acquired from cow's milk. It rarely attacks the lungs. With luck, good food and your love, he will recover completely."

"Oh," Sophie gasped. That's wonderful."

"But I agree with your husband." Mallamet's face was somber. "The Jews should leave Paris. If the Nazis overpower the French, you will be in terrible danger."

Sophie clenched her teeth, remembering what the nurse had said about Jews when she arrived at the clinic—Mallamet's clinic. Now this doctor was oozing sympathy for Jews. What a hypocrite. She flinched and pulled her hand away, angry at how she had been treated. "Why did your nurse tell me your clinic did not accept Jews? I had to lie to get treatment for my boy."

Mallamet chuckled and Sophie could not help liking the crinkles at the corners of his mouth. "Aagh, that one, she talks too much." He shrugged. "Like many French people, she does not like Jews—but then that's the way it is here. As for myself, I have no problem with your people, but I have to look to my own future. If the Germans come to Paris, I want to be in their good books right from the start. I want my clinic to survive and prosper. There will be lots of work."

He waved a dismissive hand. "Our new anti-Israelite protocol is simply a preventive measure—political strategy to protect my clinic and staff for when the Germans come. Does this make me a bad person in your eyes? Didn't Jews take similar precautions in your country?"

Sophie looked at him, unable to say anything. She was astonished at his blatant assumption that the Nazis were coming, and shocked at how calculating he was. But then, he was in a way correct. How could she pass judgment on him? Only a year earlier, she and Willy had rented out a room in their Prague apartment to a Nazi officer, by the hour, for a romantic assignation. They were protecting themselves and, at the same time, earning precious Reichsmarks to help pay for their escape. Did that make them bad people, collaborators?

Sophie decided that Docteur Mallamet was a paradox. He helped people, even poor refugees. At the same time, he was brutally frank about toadying to the Nazis and pretending he was a racist. He was pragmatic and amoral, a man who, if it suited him, might easily betray her to the Germans.

The doctor flicked cigarette ash off his well-tailored trousers. "You should know, *Madame*, the Germans have already crossed the Meuse River and broken the Maginot Line at Sedan. Our newspapers blame this on the British refusal to provide air cover, but I believe the French generals are holding back, afraid of repeating the horrendous casualties of the Great War. Instead they retreat—with a show of great bravery." He sighed.

"Why don't you get out? It seems so risky to stay."

He ran long fingers through his thick hair. "I told you. I built this practice from nothing. I don't want to lose it." He walked to the door and turned on his heel. "With regard to your boy, I could have the office of the Santé Publique check the cows at the farm. Confirm the infection." He stuck a cigarette between his lips. "But why should I bother? It will only take time and, by then, you'll be far away.

Sophie stared at him. "Won't the people of Paris fight for their city?"

He shook his head. "*Je ne le crois pas*. If we resist, the *Boches* will destroy the world's most beautiful capital—so, why should Paris fight? She will instead pull the plug and empty like a bathtub." His lip curled with an amused twitch, almost into a sneer. "I seem to remember the Czechoslovak leaders let the Germans occupy Prague with hardly a shot being fired. Prague is nearly as beautiful as Paris—the same reasoning, no doubt?"

Sophie examined her fingernails. He was right, though she did not want to admit it openly.

"If you'll excuse me, Madame, I have work to do. I will check your boy again. He needs another night with us before you take him home. I expect you will stay with him?"

Later, getting permission to use the clinic's telephone again, Sophie had a long talk with Rózsi, telling her what had happened and that Pavel was doing well.

"We will send a telegram. Willy left us the address. Do you want Andreas to come tomorrow and accompany you to your hotel? He doesn't have much to do these days. Business is terrible and food rationing is in full force. We are only allowed to bake standard loaves—no croissants, baguettes or pastries—and we are only open three days a week."

"Yes, having Andreas here would be a great help. Thank you."

Mid-afternoon, under a blue sky clotted with beehive clouds,

Sophie took a break from watching over Pavel. After an hour-long walk around the neighborhood, her stomach reminded her that it had received no sustenance except morning coffee. Entering a small café on the Rue du 4 Septembre, she ordered carrot soup with slices of bread. She picked up a newspaper and as she ate, she haltingly translated the headlines. All bad. Thousands of Belgian refugees were streaming into France. Long-time German and Austrian residents of Paris had been detained in the Buffalo football stadium. Communal air raid shelters were already in place all over the city. She found some solace in a glass of cheap *vin de table.*

By the time she got back to Pavel's room it was six o'clock. She told him stories and read him a Tintin comic book. One of the nurses bustled into the room, preparing to check the other patients' dressings and vital signs. She had a message for Sophie. "Docteur Mallamet visited your son an hour ago, Madame Kohut. He would like to talk to you. Do you remember how to get to his office?"

When Sophie entered Dr. Mallamet's *bureau* he rose from his chair and took her hand.

His grasp was firm and comforting and his eyes conveyed warmth. "Your boy—everything is as it should be, my dear," he said

He flipped open a file, skimmed it and then gave her a satisfied nod. "Tomorrow, you take Pavel home. His temperature is normal. But, you must feed him well—with pasteurized milk, fresh vegetables, and meat. He needs strength to recover."

Sophie protested. "These things will be hard to find in Paris. People are hoarding food, and the farmers don't come to the markets anymore. Pavel is still weak. I don't know if I can manage on my own." Tears spilled down her cheeks.

Dr. Mallamet again took her hand. "I can give you money for food."

She could not resist putting her other hand on his, thankful for his comfort and generosity—here was a real man. He lifted it to his lips and his kiss sent an unexpected thrill through her. "No, no, *Docteur*, I cannot accept money," she said gravely, shaking her head. "You have done more than enough for me already."

He raised his eyebrows. "You could consider it a loan, to a brave mother."

Sophie, overwhelmed by his words and everything that had happened to her in the last two days, began to sob uncontrollably.

Dr. Mallamet folded her in his arms. "Cry as much as you like," he murmured. "You have been through a harrowing time." Very slowly, Mallamet pressed his lips into Sophie's neck. Then, delicately, like a cat, he licked her wet cheeks where the tears had trickled down her face.

At the touch of his lips and warm breath, she stayed absolutely still, paralyzed by the delicious terror of his embrace. She wanted to feel him against her body, kissing her, enfolding her in his arms—at this moment of uncertainty and fear she wanted to snatch comfort and love from wherever she could.

The motion of his erection against her body made her dizzy. She responded, her mind overwhelmed by the pleasure of it as she pressed and rubbed herself against him. Desire and gratitude flowed together into unrestrained hunger. Why not take the pleasure that she was being offered?

"I have a good bed in the next room—I often sleep there after working late. I still have one more operation to perform this evening, so we will make love now. Afterwards, you go back to watch over your boy." He caressed her cheek. "Don't worry. We won't be disturbed. I am the director here. No one will say anything."

Sophie's dizziness returned. She felt like melting into his caresses, drawing his penis deep inside her. Demons whispered in her head. *Go on, do it. No one will know. You deserve some pleasure for a change. Just forget your real life for an hour or two. Let go.*

As he kissed her again she heard another voice: *Don't betray your marriage, Sophie How can you do this with Pavel suffering in another room. If you still love Willy, I beg you don't ...*

Sophie pulled away from Dr. Mallamet. She pressed a resisting palm against his chest. "You are a beautiful and clever man, *Docteur* and I'm flattered you desire me. If I was not married I would not hesitate ... but I am ... so it's not possible. I must go back to see my son."

Mallamet shrugged, his face expressionless. "As you wish, *Madame*. I will not insist." A faint smile crossed his lips. "Indeed, I congratulate you on your admirable fidelity. There are not many women who can resist me."

She breathed a sigh of relief on entering Pavel's room. He was asleep and Nurse Perle was at Pavel's bedside. "*Bonsoir, Madame,*" she said with an understanding look on her face. "I waited for you, in case Pavel woke and needed someone to see to him." She stood, straightened her uniform and gave Sophie a knowing look. "Sometimes Docteur Mallamet's interviews with his female clients take much longer than expected. He is so charming, *n'est-ce pas?* Tomorrow, you leave?"

Sophie narrowed her eyes, keeping her face blank. She understood she was just one of many who had fallen under his spell. Maybe sex was Dr. Mallamet's obsession, or perhaps his behavior was an accepted part of French medical practice. Either way, she did not care. "Thank you for being so good to Pavel. As soon as he is well enough to travel, we go south—before the Germans arrive."

The nurse embraced her, a kiss on each cheek. "*Bonne chance, Madame.*"

CHAPTER TWENTY-TWO

Destination Narbonne
South of France. May 20th, 1940

On the morning of the third day after Pavel's operation, Andreas arrived at the clinic with a basket of pastries and a corked jug of apple juice. He nodded to the patients in the room and beamed at Pavel and Sophie. "Here I am, my dears, ready to escort you back to your hotel." As they left, the nurses kissed Pavel au revoir.

"I would like to say good-bye to the doctor," Sophie said to Nurse Perle.

"He's busy," said Nurse Perle abruptly. "I'll tell him you said *adieu.*"

Two days later, Sophie was back working at the café. Pavel was there as well, resting in the upholstered armchair in Andreas's little office, surrounded by cushions and wrapped in a woolen blanket, a thick bandage around his neck. He watched the comings and goings, and looked at two Tintin comic books that Nurse Perle had given him—a gift from Dr. Mallamet, she said. At intervals, Sophie would let Pavel sit on a rug in his alcove and play with his toys and cut-out soldiers.

Sophie and the Szigetis had agreed that Pavel's convalescence would be helped most if he was surrounded by people in a busy café rather than being holed up in a grubby sixth-floor hotel room. Besides, Sophie needed the wages to help pay for their train journey south. She was anxious; Willy's weekly letter containing the usual banknotes hadn't arrived.

Because Pavel was too weak and getting a taxi was almost impossible, Andreas carried him every morning from Sophie's hotel to Café Budapest. In the afternoon, Andreas brought them back home again, sometimes stopping at the market so that Sophie could buy food or supplies.

Her gratitude toward Andreas and her immense relief at Pavel's improvement was tempered by the anxiety of not knowing what Willy was doing or where he was. At night, she slept badly, dreaming up fearful scenarios of how things might go wrong for both of them: he had been stung by a scorpion or injured handling a weapon; or that he had been crushed when his army truck went off the road; or left to fight at the front, leaving her alone with Pavel.

The flood of Parisians leaving the city and the shortages of flour, butter and sugar severely affected Café Budapest's business. With Sophie's help, Rózsi used the scarcity of customers to spring-clean the premises.

Sophie noticed that Andreas's enforced inactivity made him moody. He often sat in the cold bakery, puffing gloomily on his pipe, listening to the offerings of Radio-Cité: French dance band music, panel discussions that dissected France's politics and moral fiber, and breathless *reportages* about threatening German troop movements.

Early on May 17, braving a morning of low cloud and drizzle, Andreas turned up at the hotel with a miserable face "Bad news, today, children," he said, picking up Pavel and giving him a solemn kiss. Usually he smiled at the boy and ruffled his hair. "General von Richenau has taken Brussels. Soon the Boches will be tearing down our fences."

Andreas looked around the room. "Why aren't you ready to leave the city? Paris is in a frenzy. Radio-Cité says there is a one-kilometer line of people waiting to buy train tickets at the Gare d'Austerlitz. It's high time to leave."

Slipping on her coat, Sophie pointed a finger at Pavel's neck. "We can't go yet. He's not well enough. Besides, how can I buy train tickets if I don't know my exact destination?"

Andreas put an arm around her shoulder. "Fair enough. We have to wait for Willy to tell us. But my young comrade here seems lively enough today. He should be ready to travel soon. "

Sophie forced a smile. "I trimmed the drain. He has less discharge and pain. That means he is healing, I'm sure of it."

Andreas picked up Pavel. "Let's go then. I have to start the ovens. We open today after lunch."

Soon after mid-day, the café telephone rang.

Rózsi answered. "My God," she shrieked. "Willy! Where have you been? Sophie, come quick. It's Willy!"

Sophie grabbed the receiver, rubbing a bruised shin where, in her rush, she had collided with a chair. "Darling Willy, I … I…" Her words tumbled out, ending in a sob and then tears. It took her a few moments to calm herself. "I … I'm sorry. I've been waiting. How are you?" She nodded at Rózsi who was smiling and wringing her hands with excitement.

"Sophie, you have to leave Paris." His words were rushed. "I'm using this telephone without permission. We haven't much time, you understand?"

Her heart pounded at the urgency of his voice. He sounded well, strong, in control. She wanted to tell him about Pavel's operation and how Paris was in turmoil. "Of course, if it's urgent we can travel. I just need to know what to do, where to meet."

"This *is* urgent, my darling. The Germans have surrounded the Allies near Calais. The rest of our forces are retreating south. If Paris falls, you and Pavel will be trapped. Write down what I say."

"Wait a minute." Sophie, lips trembled as she, mimicked

hand-writing at Rózsi, who passed a pencil and a flat pastry box across the counter. "I'm ready."

Pavel, his neck swathed in a thick bandage, sat on his high stool, eyes glued to his mother. "Is it Papa?" he said faintly as if he realized from his mother's face that something serious was happening.

Sophie took no notice, gripping the telephone hard, pencil at the ready. "Go on."

"Tomorrow, take the first train to Narbonne—from the Gare de Lyon."

"*Tomorrow?* How can I? I owe rent and your money hasn't arrived. Besides, I'm afraid that Pavel isn't strong enough for a long journey. How can I stand in line for a ticket for more than an hour—with a suitcase and a sick child in my arms?"

"For God's sake, Sophie," Willy shouted so loudly that she had to distance the earpiece. "Do you want a repeat of what the Nazis did to you at the frontier? Leave on the first train. Damn the rent. Leave the concierge a message saying we'll send it."

Sophie felt shards of fear lacerate her stomach. She knew her hotel concierge only too well ... a sour, leathery Parisienne who would not hesitate to call the police if she suspected her tenants were leaving without notice. "And when we arrive in that town, then what?"

"In Narbonne, go to the Hôtel du Midi on the Avenue Carnot, quite close to the station. Take a room for the night. Got it?"

"Got it. How much will the room cost?" Sophie scrawled the details. "I hardly have any money." The lead point of her pencil snapped. Rózsi grimaced and handed over another one.

"Maybe fifty francs. If you don't have enough, tell them I'll pay for the room when I get there. I can't meet you until the morning after you arrive." His voice was edgy, urgent, grating.

"You sound angry, Willy? I need sympathy and help at the moment, not shouting and orders. Pavel and I have had a terrible time these past few days." Worse than the task Willy had imposed on her was the fear that he might not be there when she arrived in Narbonne, sent off to fight somewhere.

"Listen, Sophie, I *am* helping you—get out of Paris and join me here. The morning after your night at the Hôtel du Midi, wait at the reception desk at nine sharp. I'll pick you up in a taxi, or at least something on four wheels. Understand?"

"Yes. I must tell you about Pavel, how he is."

"I have to go. Listen, if I don't appear at the hotel to meet you, don't worry. Wait another hour and if I haven't appeared have the hotel contact Czechoslovak Army headquarters at Béziers. Ask them for help in finding me. Our orders keep changing. Andreas has the Béziers' number. For God's sake, don't leave it behind."

"Wait, Willy, please. You can't go without saying hello to your son. I'm putting him on—and don't shout." Unwinding the phone's concertina wire, Sophie went to Pavel's chair and held the receiver up against the boy's ear. He looked at Sophie, as if unsure what to make of it.

"Pavel, its Papa. Are you feeling better?" She could just hear Willy's voice.

Pavel's eyes widened and he smiled, tentatively. "Papa, Papa," he whispered.

"Pavel, it's your Papa. Say something."

After a long moment of silence, Sophie took the telephone. "He knows it's you, but he's being shy. We will be there in Narbonne. I can't wait to be with you."

"Me too! I must go. Best wishes to the Szigetis. Goodbye and *bonne chance* on the train. A thousand kisses."

After hanging up, Sophie, tears sliding down her cheeks, told the Szigetis that she and Pavel would be leaving the next morning to join Willy. She hugged Andreas and embraced Rózsi. "It may be for a long time, but we will visit you after the war is over. We will never forget you."

Andreas stroked Pavel's head. His eyes were moist. "I shall miss these curls—and his saucy look."

"Another new adventure for the adventurous Kohuts," Rózsi muttered, dabbing her eyes, trying to smile. "You will come back to Café Budapest, I know it. We will be here; we're your family now."

Andreas put his arm around Sophie, squeezing her close. "You will need some extra money to cover the train and food."

The offer threw Sophie into a dilemma. She definitely needed money, but relying so much on the Szigetis was shaming, unbearable. In Paris, all the generosity, warmth and resources had come from them, and she and Willy could not offer anything in return except friendship and gratitude. "Yes, thank you so much," she said hesitantly.

Andreas looked at her questioningly. "Don't be shy about it. We are family, yes?"

She nodded, her heart fluttering. "I'm not sure. Let me think about it."

On their way back to Rue Thenard, Andreas kept Pavel entertained looking in shop windows while Sophie purchased a battered cardboard suitcase in the market—from the same *brocanteur* stall owner who had sold her the pans she used for cooking in her hotel room. The rheumy-eyed man palmed her thirty-six francs and nodded his approval. "This is a great treasure, *Madame,* and a wise purchase. Everybody wants a suitcase. And this is my last one. What is it they say? Last one gets the most luck."

In the hotel room, Andreas watched Sophie unwrap Pavel's bandage, clean his wound, trim his drain with nail scissors dipped in iodine and apply a new dressing. She looked up at the baker. "I won't have time for this in the morning."

She opened the suitcase on the bed, ready to start packing. She checked her purse: seventy-three francs, almost laughable. As she lifted her folded clothes off the armoire shelf, a folded piece of paper fell to the floor. She picked it up—it was Pablo's sketch of the Minotaur. She sat down on the bed and looked thoughtfully at Andreas.

"At the café, you offered to lend me money for the train? Could you spare me two hundred francs?" She paused and looked down at the sketch. "I would be most grateful."

With a gentle, understanding smile, he pulled out his wallet. "Of course."

She put the sketch, face down on the bed. "I have something for you, in exchange." Giving away the most creative icon of her stay in Paris was wrenching but it was all she had to offer. "Have you heard of a man called Pablo Ruiz—an artist?"

Andreas gave her a quizzical look. "No, my dear. I know nothing about art. Does he have something to do with this piece of paper?"

"Turn it over."

She watched Andreas's eyes widen when he saw the drawing. "*Ó Istenem!*" he spluttered. "Oh, my God! What is this filth?"

"It is modern art, not filth. Pablo Ruiz is an artist who sketched this when I met him and a group of friends in a café. They told me he had a good reputation. He gave it to me. Now it's yours. It's just a sketch on worthless paper, but one day it might be valuable. Please, don't refuse it. It's all I have that's worth anything, except for my silk scarf." She smiled. "And I don't think the scarf's colors suit your complexion."

Andreas grunted and shook his head in disbelief. "You mean this is genuine *art*?"

She laughed at the doubt on the baker's face as he studied

it again. "I know it's obscene, Andreas, and for God's sake keep it away from Rózsi."

Andreas sighed as he slid the paper into an inside pocket. "Maybe I can sell it at the book market. Does Willy know about this—about your café adventure with a painter?"

Sophie put her hand on his and gave him a long look. "There's no need for him to know, is there?"

Andreas scratched at his cheek as if he was nervous about the whole transaction. "I expect this Pablo fellow found you difficult to resist. Did something unusual happen between you and him?"

Sophie flushed and shook her head. "I know what you mean. He didn't even kiss me."

He patted his pocket. "I suppose I have to believe you. I'll regard this arrangement as being purely between *us*."

She put her arms round his waist, resting her head against his barrel chest. "Thank you, dear Andreas. At least now, I feel less of a beggar taking money from you."

At seven the next morning, when the hotel concierge left to buy her usual *pain complet* at the *boulangerie* round the corner, Andreas was already waiting on the pavement, holding a paper bag. With a smile and a kiss, he swept Pavel into his arms. Sophie carried the suitcase and a string bag holding a bottle of milk and some of Pavel's favorite toys. They hurried through streets busy with vendors and shopkeepers rolling up their shutters. On the Boulevard St. Germain, they passed a gang of workmen stacking sandbags around the St. Sulpice church and entered the Odéon métro. They changed at Châtelet for the Gare de Lyon.

The station teemed with passengers and a long line snaked toward the ticket *guichets*. Sophie looked at her benefactor in dismay. Already the hurdle of getting a ticket, with Pavel looking so weak and pale, seemed overwhelming. "We can't wait here long,

Andreas, and you should not have to wait with us. But—if Pavel gets too tired and we have to leave the queue, we'll miss the train." She looked him with pleading eyes. "What can I do?"

With one hand anchoring Pavel over his shoulder, Andreas took her elbow. "I'll fix it. Come." Parallel to the queue, he marched her up to the agent's window and stepped right behind the customer being served. The other travelers protested angrily and one or two tried to push him aside. Andreas pointed to the bandage encircling Pavel's neck. "Be charitable, my friends," he said, raising his voice above the chatter. "This child just had a serious operation at …" He glanced at Sophie for help.

"La Maison de Santé Chirurgicale at the Porte de Versailles," she said loudly after a moment of bewilderment. She put her hands together in prayer and looked pleadingly at the ticket agent. "Please, I need tickets to Narbonne. My boy is very ill."

He nodded sympathetically. "*Ça va, Madame,* you can be next."

The hubbub died down as Sophie put her money on the counter. "Two tickets for the eight-twenty-five train to Narbonne."

"First and second class completely sold out," the agent said with half a sneer. "Our patriotic bourgeois citizens are abandoning Paris to the *Boches.*"

Sophie noticed a red hammer and sickle pin in the man's lapel.

"I can sell you third-class tickets. Still a few seats available. But I warn you, *Madame,* eight hours on wooden seats will be hard on your sick child. "

In the packed carriage, Andreas kissed Sophie and Pavel and handed over the bag he had been carrying. "Sandwiches," he said. "You will need food. *Au revoir.*" He turned and limped away.

* * *

During the long journey south, surrounded by passengers chatting about the war and their personal arrangements on how they would survive in the countryside, Sophie thought about her attraction to the doctor in Paris and what made her resist his offer of sex. Replaying the scene in her mind, she realized that she did not know why; it was not that she was married, or that making love with her sick child nearby was a kind of betrayal, or that she could not bring herself to reward the doctor with her body. So what was it? A subconscious decision to not to do something she desired or just a clue that her marriage was wearing thin?

For long periods, with Pavel asleep on her lap, Sophie watched the countryside pass by and considered her marriage It was clear to her that time, events and separation had altered her relationship with Willy, had eroded their passion and deep affection Now it was more like the traditional arrangement of her parents and in-laws. She wanted an equal partnership; she wanted to make her own decisions. Would he understand that? That's what she would soon find out.

After a while, Sophie moved Pavel off her lap so she could stretch her legs. He opened his eyes and reached up to touch her lips. "Ça va, Maman?"

She smiled down at his innocent face, surrounded by the pastry shell of his bandage. He needed his parents more than ever and she would do her utmost to hold the family together. Whatever situation and conditions existed in this village she was traveling to, she would accept everything, make do—adapt, learn and survive.

*　*　*

Many hours later, after Sophie and Pavel arrived at Narbonne station, the great clock of the nearby St. Just and St. Pasteur Cathedral struck five o'clock. She exited the main entrance, carrying

Pavel hitched on her hip with an arm that also held the string bag. She slowly walked along the street, suitcase in her other hand. Laden as she was, she was glad to be moving instead of sitting, and compared to the rush and panic of Paris, the Narbonne streets were calm.

The late afternoon sun vibrated heat off the pavement, making her feel weak and dizzy, but she summoned enough energy to ask a traffic gendarme the way to the Hôtel du Midi. He pointed with his baton. "*Dix minutes à pied, chère Madame.* That way. Do you need assistance with the little one?"

"*Non, merci.*" The man's musical accent was soft and soothing, nothing like the machine-gun chatter of Parisians. "Come on Pavel, we'll rest at that fountain and then walk on to the hotel." She hoped he could manage a few minutes more on foot.

Pavel smiled. "*Oui, Maman.* I like this place."

The hotel façade was covered in ivy, its windows studded with flower-filled boxes. The terrace, cooled by a faint breeze was decorated with violet bougainvillea and shaded by flowering chestnut trees. A sign on the wall indicated the prices of rooms. Single - 25 francs, Double - 40 francs. She left her suitcase by a table and went in carrying Pavel.

"You are very, very lucky," said the desk clerk as he rang up the cash register. "You get the last room, a single."

"Do you have a cot for my boy?"

"*Je regrette*, no more cots. We have other families here from Paris."

On the terrace, Sophie ordered orange-flavored ice-cream for Pavel and watched children play tag around a stone fountain with water spilling from the mouths of carved lion heads. Pavel seemed to be in a good mood. She could tell he wanted to join the children, but he was too fragile for rough play. She was afraid another child's careless hand might whack the tender wound on his neck.

Sophie studied the hotel menu, hunger gnawing at her belly. Silently, she thanked Andreas, whose sandwiches had saved them from starving on the train. Her only chance on the journey to buy extra food had been when the train stopped at Lyon and then in Valence, but Pavel had been asleep at the time and she had been afraid to leave him.

Sophie ordered a cup of chicory coffee and shared a slice of *Tarte Tatin* with Pavel. To pass the time, she involved him in the task of counting their money and discussing what items they could afford for supper. They had only enough for something cheap—like an omelet, bread, and tomato salad.

* * *

Next morning, Sophie and Pavel sat on the hotel terrace next to tall ceramic pots filled with blue and white alyssum and trailing pink geraniums. The sky was cloudless and the street was a canvas of dappled sunlight and shadows.

They could have waited in the reception area as Willy had said, but it was filled with people, luggage and the smell of early-morning cigars. Besides, some of the hotel guests who were paying their bills had noticed Pavel's pallor and were asking why the poor little boy had a bandage around his neck. Sophie was in no mood to satisfy their curiosity which seemed tainted by an aura of suspicion. Were they afraid of catching something? Or did they think she was the one responsible for Pavel's wound? She didn't care. Her mind was too focused on watching the street for Willy.

A brown canvas-topped truck jerked to a stop at the hotel curb. Sophie recognized the Czechoslovak escutcheon on its side, painted in national colors. Her heart surged with relief. Two soldiers jumped out. One was a giant of a man, carrying a side-arm holstered on his belt. The other one was Willy. Grinning happily, he pushed empty tables aside, pulled Sophie into his arms and covered her with sweaty kisses. "Thank God, you're both here." He dropped to his knees by Pavel's chair, ruffled his hair and gently fingered the thick neck bandage. "What a brave fellow you are," he said in Czech. "How do you feel after the long train journey?"

Pavel smiled shyly. "*Je me sens bien, Papa.*"

Sophie nodded, tears trickling down her cheeks. "He's better."

Willy laughed and took hold of Pavel's shoulders, inspecting his face intently. "You speak French very well. I believe I'm now the father of a real French boy."

"He speaks fluently—from his time at the farm." She touched the military tunic where a crossed Czechoslovak and French flag patch had been sewn over Willy's heart. "You look so handsome, *miláčku*. Tanned and slim."

He hooked an arm round her shoulders and squinted up at the sky. "Today will be a hot one. We must get you sun hats. Welcome to the Languedoc, *ma chérie.*"

Sophie kissed his cheek. "I'm so happy to be here. I don't mind the heat."

The other soldier loomed over Sophie's table, his huge frame blocking out the sun. He looked fierce but then he doffed his cap and bowed awkwardly. His head was shaved and a filigree scar ran down the left side of his sunburned face. She wondered why he had come and felt a quiver of anxiety. Was he a guard?

"This is Sergeant Kukulka," Willy said. "A friend and my supervisor. He arranged our transport this morning. Sergeant, this is my wife, Sophie, and my brave son, Pavel."

Kukulka's grin made his face appear even more threatening. Pavel shrank into his father's arms, his eyes averted. The sergeant reached out to the boy but then hesitated. "That's a big bandage for a little feller." His tone was hoarse, but jovial.

Sophie shaded her eyes against the glare. "I thought only my husband was coming for me."

Kukulka drew a deep breath and winked. "He's not allowed to drive—part of his sentence for disobeying orders. Your husband has a habit of getting into scrapes. You have luggage?"

Sophie pointed to her string bag and the battered suitcase.

Hands on hips, Kukulka glanced around the terrace and shook his head, finally resting his gaze on Sophie's brown suitcase. His face scrunched into an exaggerated frown. "This is all you've got?"

Sophie noticed a sparkle in his eyes.

"I was expecting steamer trunks and hatboxes from the Paris fashion houses. What a disappointment. You must be one of those desperate Czechoslovak refugee women we've heard so much about." He winked again at Pavel as they walked to the truck. He tossed the case into the back and all three adults squeezed onto the front bench seat. Pavel sat on Sophie's lap.

On the outskirts of town they stopped at a *droguerie* to buy wide-brim straw hats for Sophie and Pavel. "So now," Willy explained as they set off again, "we're headed for a small village called Sillat, about half way between the Corbières Mountains and the coast."

"That means nothing to me. Is that where you are stationed?"

"No. Sillat—where you will be living—is five or so kilometers from Portel where our battalion is located." Willy pulled four peaches and a small grubby towel out of his army satchel. "I have a special treat for everyone. These peaches are even better than the ones my father grew in Lučenec." He handed the towel to Pavel who attacked his peach, juice dripping from his chin. "Wipe yourself with this."

"Mmm, that's good," Sophie said, sniffing her peach before taking a bite. "What's Sillat like?"

"Small and dilapidated. White houses, a square and a church set in a wooded valley. Lots of stone walls and shutters to keep out the heat. No windows on the streets. The French don't like nosy neighbors looking in."

"What does your battalion do in Portel?"

"Weapon training," growled Kukulka nudging Willy's knee, it was a signal, Sophie guessed, to keep him from saying too much. "Getting ready to fight in the north, if they let us."

At first, Kukulka drove along a straight road bordered by lines of tall trees. On either side, stone walls enclosed small vineyards. Sophie noticed that the grapes were beginning to set—same time of year as they did in Hungary. They turned off onto smaller unpaved roads, raising dust as they wound through orchards of ripening peaches and almond plantations.

The heat in the truck was almost unbearable. Sophie mopped her face and swatted at the occasional fly and Sergeant Kukulka's acrid sweat stung her nostrils. In Paris, Willy had painted a dazzling picture of wine, sunshine, and beaches. No signs of that! She remembered one of her mother-in-law's favorite proverbs. *Čeho nelze předělati, darmo na to žehrati.* Take the world as you find it. Sophie decided to say nothing.

Willy looked at her. "Did you say something?"

She gave him a quick smile. "I expect our new life will be quiet—not like Paris."

Sergeant Kukulka guffawed. "That's a good one."

Willy nodded. "Sillat is almost too quiet, but it's safe."

"Will there be anyone I can talk to—other refugees, women, Czechs, Hungarians?"

Kukulka sucked on his teeth. "Only soldiers as far as I know, *paní* Kohutová. There's an empty farm on the outskirts. We've got twelve men sleeping there in a barn. A truck picks them up, your husband included, from the town square, at five each morning. You'll have to make do mingling with the local villagers. I suppose you learned French in Paris, but I doubt anyone local will understand you." A rich laugh shook his belly.

Willy smiled. "The local dialect is rather musical—slow and meandering."

The old Renault puffed out clouds of diesel fumes as it labored into the arid foothills of the Corbières Massif. Sophie began to feel nauseous and Pavel coughed so often she wondered if the stitches in his neck would hold. As they rattled through hamlets, the locals standing at the roadside or working in their yards, stared or shook fists as chickens and ducks scattered across the road. Dogs, most of them tied to posts or railings, bared their teeth and barked furiously.

Pavel hid his face. "Don't like those dogs, Maman."

Sophie kissed him and looked at the Sergeant. "Aside from owning vicious dogs, what do these people do here? For work? It seems so barren and primitive."

Kukulka's laugh sounded like an axe splitting wood. "Work! They drink wine, hunt game, pick fruit and make stinky cheese. They're not too bad as peasants go. Of course I don't understand a word they say. One thing for sure, they don't like us foreigners."

Fifteen minutes later, Kukulka brought the truck to a skidding stop in the dusty center of Sillat. He clambered out. On the other side, Willy lifted Pavel down, followed by Sophie.

Pavel resisted her attempt to put the new straw hat on his head. "Where are we, Papa?"

"The village of Sillat." Willy squinted against the sun and pointed to a worn signpost. "And this is La Place de Chamignolles … obviously the village square." He looked down at Pavel and smiled. "This is where we'll live for a while."

Pavel kicked up sand and squinted at the sun, screwing up his nose. "It's too hot."

They stood and looked around, shading their eyes—the glare magnified by white limestone outcroppings that surrounded the village.

Kukulka, nodding his head sagely, set Sophie's suitcase down. "Sillat is definitely picturesque, and it's definitely boring." He pulled an old bicycle out of the back of the truck and leaned it against one of the mudguards. "This is your husband's other transportation. As he will explain to you, *pani,* he spends most of his time training in Portel six kilometers from here. Have you ridden the damn thing yet, Kohut?"

With a wry look Willy took the handlebars. "No, Sarge. In fact, I've never been on a bicycle."

Kukulka blinked in astonishment. "Something to do with being a Jew, maybe?" He opened the driver's door and climbed on to the running board. The truck squeaked and tilted.

Willy let out an exaggerated sigh. "I told you before, Sarge. As a kid, I was supposed to save my hands from injury. No sports, no games, no bicycle—only piano practice."

"Well, I'm off, back to Agde." Kukulka gave Willy a thumbs-up. "Remember, *kamarád,* the truck to Portel is at five sharp—here in the square, by the café. We start training on new artillery that just arrived. And we've got two new recruits, Czechoslovak commies from Spain."

He nodded in Sophie's direction and eased himself into the truck's driving seat. "I'm pleased to have met such a fine-looking countrywoman." He turned on the ignition and leaned out of the window. The white scar on his face danced as he winked at Sophie. "Enjoy your first night together."

CHAPTER TWENTY-THREE

Widow Escobar
South of France. May 19th, 1940

The Kohuts stood looking around at the dilapidated houses: peeling paint, shuttered windows and wrought-iron balconies. The sandy square was shaded at its center by a geometric stand of pollarded trees. A cobblestone road, fronted by two-story houses, ran round the perimeter and at the far end stood a café and two shops. One was a *tabac*. The other was shuttered. It was almost midday and the heat pressed down on the Kohuts like a hot iron.

Willy sniffed, his face crimped in distaste. "I know that barnyard smell," he said. "*Les égouts*—sluggish drains. Typical of these villages." He glanced apologetically at Sophie.

She hitched an eyebrow, wrinkled her nose and said nothing.

He pointed to a stuccoed building on one side of the square. It had tall windows and a tricolore flag drooped from a pole fixed to the portico. Both hands of the clock set in the alcove above the portico were aligned and stationary. "That must be the town hall. As usual in these small places, the clock is stuck at noon … lunchtime." He smiled at her.

Sophie sighed. "At this moment, Willy, I'm hot as hell and not interested in clocks. We need shade and a wash."

"I want to drink … from over there," said Pavel, indicating the moss-decked fountain next to a battered statue of a woman dressed in draperies posed on a pedestal. Water poured enticingly into the fountain's carved basin from the pouty lips of three stone dolphins.

Willy restrained him. "Not from there, *Pavelko*. It may not be clean. Come on. Let's try the *tabac*. We'll buy something to drink and ask the way to the widow's cottage."

Willy pushed the bicycle along as they walked under the trees, passing a well-maintained *boules* court. Close by, an old bearded man rested on a bench, eyes closed. A small white dog lay at his feet. Pavel ran to the dog and stopped a couple of feet away. The panting dog wrinkled its eyebrows but did not move. Pavel ran back to his parents, scuffing the sandy soil with his sandals. "That dog is old, like the man," he said, slipping his hand into Willy's palm.

The *tabac* had a low ceiling full of cobwebs and its wall of shelves was packed with small cardboard boxes and faded merchandise. The proprietor, with close-set eyes in a mahogany face, appeared at the counter. Willy paid for a bottle of warm lemonade for Pavel, uncapped it and asked the way to Madame Escobar's cottage.

"*La vieille Escobar? C'est facile, M'sieu*," he said. "Left at the door. Up the hill on the left, just a few hundred meters. There's a stone St. George and Dragon carved over the door. Bougainvillea on the roof."

"Thank you. Can I leave my bicycle here? I don't want to push it uphill in this heat."

The proprietor nodded, and as they left the *tabac* Willy wondered how Sophie and Madame Escobar would get on together. For two weeks, he had begged the mayor of Sillat by letter and telephone to find a room for his wife and son. The result was a room and board in the cottage of a gypsy widow at thirty francs a week.

Madame Escobar's single-story cottage was built of rough granite stones, the chinks filled with pebbles and weeds. As was the case in many of that region's villages, fragments of medieval stonework—some with holes for bolts and hinges—had been incorporated into the walls. At the front door, above the lintel, an ancient and barely recognizable St. George and the Dragon had been carved inside a sandstone cartouche.

"You do the honors, sweetheart," Willy said pointing to the bell-pull. He wiped sweat off his forehead and cheeks with a handkerchief. "This will be your home now."

Sophie tugged on the brass handle and they heard a distant clang. Two minutes went by. Sophie felt her impatience building. She was thirsty, hot, and tired—and worried about what she might find.

Pavel kicked experimentally at one of the door's iron studs and stared up at the handle. "I want to pull."

As he reached up, they heard the sound of a bolt sliding back and the door swung open. A small bent woman with a wrinkled brown face slowly inspected them from head to toe. She wore a long black skirt and a white blouse with embroidered squares of color round the high neck-line.

Sophie was surprised by the strength of the woman's metallic voice. "*Bonjour, M'sieu et Madame.* You must be the foreigners I'm expecting? *Entrez, entrez.*" She did not smile.

Inside the dark entryway, they shook hands. Madame Escobar peered down at Pavel. "Is this really a boy? With so many curls, it can be difficult to tell. What is this bandage around his neck? An accident? He is sick? Is he infectious? What if he is and I catch it?" After a moment, she shrugged. "*Eh, bien,* I need the rent—and I've had a long life, so I won't mind if the Lord decides my time has come. No, please, no details about his neck. Such things upset me." She stepped back and spread her arms. "Welcome to my home. Shall I show you your room?"

It took Sophie a few moments to adjust and take the measure of the dark cottage. They stood in an untidy room with blackened walls, apparently a combined living and kitchen area. Flies buzzed in hidden places. Sunshine filtered past the edges of two large, shuttered windows. Sophie smiled, relieved by how cool it was. She remembered the villages in Hungary where she had been a little girl—single-story cottages kept the heat out with shuttered windows, thick rush roofs and wooden walls. It was the same here.

Hams, salami, and bundles of dried herbs dangled from a beam over a rough plank table and four straight-backed chairs. Sophie recognized the aromas of thyme and rosemary, and perhaps anise. A granite counter and sink were fitted into a recess beside the open back door. Sophie caught a glimpse of ripening tomatoes and neat rows of green beans—the widow's garden.

"No running water," Willy whispered, raising his eyebrows. "No taps at the sink."

Sophie turned to Madame Escobar.

"Do you have some water, Madame? To drink."

The old lady poured three glasses of water from a metal pitcher covered with muslin cloth. Pavel, drinking greedily, pointed up at a battered shotgun resting on wall hooks above the fireplace. "*Regardez, Papa,*" he said. "Madame is soldier."

Madame Escobar followed the boy's finger as she took off her headscarf. "So you speak some French, *mon petit,*" she said with a chuckle. "My husband's gun." With a proud smile, she waved a knobbly hand at the mantelpiece. "That's where I keep my treasures—a stone axe-head my husband dug up years ago and castanets from when I was young and liked to dance."

"What about that wooden statue in the middle?" Willy said. "It's beautifully carved."

The old lady crossed herself. "*Sara e Kali,* Mary Magdalene's black servant, the patron saint of Gypsies. Every year, we go on a pilgrimage to the Church of Les Saintes Maries de la Mer, in the Camargue. I was there last month. For a few days we eat, dance, play music, and forget our troubles." She sighed. "Good times."

Sophie had trouble understanding the widow whose soft, rumbling sentences ended in drawn-out cadences.

Pavel pointed to a wooden figure hanging on the opposite wall. "*Madame,* why does that man have nails in his arms and legs?"

Madame Escobar looked at the crucifix and then at Pavel, her face scrunched in surprise. "A curious boy, aren't you? Like a woodpecker drilling me with questions. That's Jesus. Your papa will explain." She crossed herself.

Pavel didn't speak. He was studying a green lizard clinging upside down on a roof beam.

"So, I show you to your room." Madame Escobar, limping as she walked, led them into a small white-washed room at the back of the cottage. Pavel copied her, grinning at Sophie as if he thought he was doing something clever. The old woman turned and frowned. A gold tooth glinted. "This is a cheeky one, I think. Better watch out, *mon petit,* Madame Esco isn't as fragile and foolish as she looks."

The rope bed had a straw mattress and embroidered pillows. A mirrored chestnut armoire stood against one wall next to a ceramic washbasin on iron legs. Willy and Sophie stood at the gauze-covered window that looked out on to a sloping vineyard.

Sophie nudged Willy. "Anyone can see us in here. Ask her for curtains."

When he asked, the widow pursed her lips and looked amused. "No one can see in here unless they have a telescope on the other side of the valley—where no one lives. But if you want curtains, fine. You pay for them. There is a sewing woman in the village, her name is Madame Rouspet."

"Let's wait and see," Willy said diplomatically.

Sophie wiped the sweat off her face. She desperately wanted a cool wash. So far the list of amenities was woefully limited—no running water, no bathroom, no curtains, and no stove. What a place! For the moment, she was too embarrassed to ask where she would wash, bathe, or defecate.

Sophie looked out of the window again, shading her eyes from the glare of the white limestone boulders that studded the hills. She noticed a ribbon of sand meandering through a scattering of oak and cypress trees at the bottom of the valley. It was where a stream should have been. She looked hopefully at Madame Escobar. "Is that a river down there? Can we swim in it?" A refreshing stream would answer her desire to get clean and cool.

The old lady's smile creased her face. "You see a stream that thinks she is lost, my dear. In the winter she is tempestuous; in summer she dries out but still flows underground. She comes from caves deep inside the *garrigue*, the hills."

Sophie sighed. She was hot and tired and the bed looked inviting. "I don't understand her. I need to rest…"

"Papa, look." Pavel pulled at Willy's fatigues and pointed at a battered zinc bucket in one corner. A horde of flies buzzed around its rim.

With a laugh, Madame Escobar threw up her hands. "*Eh bien, mon petit*, you have found the soil bucket. Except for the mayor, no one in the village has a ceramic toilet. Every morning, at dawn, a man with his horse and cart collects soil from my house and takes it to the cesspit at the other end of the village." She raised a warning finger. "*Faites attention*—if the bucket becomes full later in the day, you will have to empty it yourself." She eyed Sophie quizzically. "With the three of us living here and your *Monsieur* also staying from time to time, I think you might be walking to the cesspit every day."

Sophie grabbed Willy's arm. "For God's sake, I didn't expect *this*," she hissed in Czech.

He took a deep breath as he massaged his jaw in embarrassment. "We have no choice, sweetheart. There's nowhere else to go."

Madame Escobar led them back to the kitchen. "I prepared a *casse-croute* for lunch. Tonight we have fish soup, sautéed potatoes and my own runner beans. Jo-Jo, the little girl who lives next door, helped me pick them. Your little boy will like her."

"We had better talk about living arrangements and rent," said Willy quickly. "I have to go back to the square and collect the bicycle. Tomorrow, I leave early for Portel-les-Corbières."

"We call it Portel, for convenience," said the widow. "Why not discuss payment and living arrangements after supper—over a glass of wine from Monsieur Robineau's vineyard. That's the one you see from your window. First you unpack and rest. Later you get the bicycle and explore the village. The mayor says we have three things for visitors to see—the stone carvings by the Master of Cabestany at the Sainte Marie church, a stone *lavoir* where some women still wash clothes and the village bread oven—ancient, like me." The tassels of her crocheted shawl quivered as she shook in silent laughter.

Half an hour later, they sat at the kitchen table. Madame Escobar poured wine from a jug into tumblers and gave Pavel squeezed lemon juice laced with sugar. "You cut the bread," she said to Willy, handing him a dark crusty loaf the size of a pillow. "I will get the ham."

The Kohuts watched goggle-eyed as she picked up a knife, raised her long skirt and climbed on a chair and then stepped on to the table, carefully avoiding plates and silverware. She wore clogs and her black woolen stockings were full of holes. She unwrapped the sacking from around a whole ham that hung from a rafter directly above, next to a row of salami sausages. Carving the meat with quick strokes, she dropped the slices on to a plate between her feet. One or two missed their mark and landed on her clogs.

Sophie watched, fascinated and horrified. It reminded her of one of Grimm's fairy tales.

Willy held the loaf against his chest and sawed away, grinning at Sophie. She raised her eyebrows in response. He looked so happy! He had always trumpeted his yen for the simple life and here he was at last, in the middle of it.

"*Pardí*, don't cut bread like that," their hostess grunted as she climbed awkwardly down. "Your slices look like river rocks." Grabbing the loaf from him, she tucked it into the crook of her left arm and chiseled even slices, dumping them on the same plate as the piled-up ham.

Willy and Sophie prepared two slices of bread for Pavel. They copied the way Madame Esco dripped olive oil from a thin-spouted can onto her bread and then rubbed the flesh of ripe tomatoes into its surface. And on top, they laid the slices of smoky ham. After a couple of bites Pavel's chin was covered in tomato juice.

Madame Escobar watched Sophie wipe his face. "If the boy has eaten enough, he doesn't have to stay at the table." She refilled glasses of water from a tall glazed pot that stood in the darkest corner of the kitchen. "Play outside, *mon petit,* until we're ready for the melon."

"*Merci, Madame.*" Pavel slipped gratefully out of the back door.

Afterwards, sated by the food and stunned by the heat, Willy and Sophie took a siesta.

It was hard to adjust to the rope bed and straw mattress that rustled and sank under their weight. Pavel slept on the floor—on a folded-up coverlet.

"What do you think?" Willy murmured. "The old lady seems most hospitable. Will you be all right here?"

Sophie raised herself on an elbow, tapped his nose with a finger and kissed his ear. "I don't have much choice, do I? The cottage is very primitive but we can manage, I suppose. Frankly, I'm not too sure about this old woman. She's a little strange and very bossy."

That evening, before seven, while Madame Escobar worked in her garden vegetable patch, keeping an eye on Pavel, Sophie and Willy went to the village square to collect the bicycle. The locals, mostly men, were out and about, some playing bowls in the park. Others gossiped on the steps of the fountain or occupied the café terrace where a group of Willy's Czechoslovak comrades had commandeered two tables. Willy introduced Sophie.

Later, out in the garden, under an oil lamp, the Kohuts ate supper with the widow.

They sat at a rickety table. Fireflies hovered above the broken picket fence that separated the garden from the vineyard. Pavel ran about whooping in delight, trying to catch the flies in a glass jar.

Willy let him poke around the widow's garden where he found fragments of carved limestone and used them for the foundations of a building that would either be a house or a castle. Pavel spent a long time swinging on the creaking back gate, looking out over the vineyard. Madame Escobar introduced him to Marcel, her friendly, one-eared gray cat, and showed him her rabbit hutch.

"Here, you can hold one," she said, putting a twitchy young buck into Pavel's arms.

"See how soft he is?" The boy nodded, rubbing his face into the rabbit's fur.

Willy smiled at Sophie. "This is a good start for the boy. I think he likes the old lady and it's wonderfully peaceful here," he said. "Who would think France is at war?"

As if in answer, an owl hooted across the valley and the crickets began to chirp. The oil lamp flickered on the faces around the table.

Sophie gave Willy a reproachful look and took his hand. "Please, *miláčku*, don't talk about war and spoil a nice evening." She blew him a quick kiss, not caring what the old lady thought. "I feel so relaxed here. It's as if we were transported to a place where no one is unkind or cruel—and everything is gentle and beautiful."

Madame Escobar poured thimble glasses of the powerful local *marc*, and as they toasted each other, the Kohuts described the turmoil in Paris and admitted they were refugees.

"I know you are," sighed the old lady. "You lost your home somewhere in the east. Monsieur Robineau told me."

Willy polished his glasses and switched the subject. "I hope you don't mind me asking, dear *Madame*. Your name, Escobar, does not sound at all French." During the siesta he and Sophie played a guessing game about the origins of this small dark-faced woman whose only adornments were the cross on her neck and gold circlets in her ears.

Madame Escobar seemed willing to talk. "My husband, God rest his soul, was a wonderful leather craftsman. Of course, the people from around here despised us Gypsies. With him gone to join the Lord, it's many years since I travelled in a *roulotte*. You know, a wagon pulled by a horse. He specialized in making and repairing saddles for the *gardien* horses in the Camargue, and for the bullfights. He was good on the mandolin too—played at all the local weddings."

Willy rested a sympathetic hand on Madame Escobar's arm. "Like you Gypsies, we have the same problem of not being liked, always moving to somewhere new."

She narrowed her eyes. "Are you Jewish then?"

He shrugged resignedly. "Yes, we are."

Madame Escobar pulled her chair closer and pointed a bony finger at him. "I don't care who *you* are, or *where* you are from, but do not tell this to anyone else in the village. Some people here hate Jews—for killing Jesus and drinking baby's blood."

There was a long, uncomfortable silence while Willy and Sophie exchanged glances. The glance that said, *here it comes again.*

Sophie yawned, stretching her arms to hide her confusion and disappointment. Who would believe that ordinary people in a quiet French village still believed these centuries-old lies? "Pavel is worn out. We should all go to bed." She turned in her seat. "May I help you with cleaning up the dishes?"

"Not this first evening, my dear. Tomorrow, after your husband has gone, we can talk about such things."

Willy got up and with a gallant bow kissed Madame Escobar's bony hand. "Thank you for the excellent dinner and hospitality. I think we will be comfortable here."

Madame Escobar snatched her hand back. "A man does not do that here," she said, frowning.

Hearing a discreet cough from outside the fence, everyone turned around. A portly man in knee-high leather boots stood at the vineyard gate, a shotgun slung from his shoulder. "*Bonsoir*," he said in a rich, burbling tone. Three partridges hung from his belt. A fawn-colored Malinois dog crouched obediently behind him, watching the humans with dancing eyebrows.

Mme. Escobar extricated herself slowly from her chair. "This is Monsieur Robineau, our mayor. He owns this vineyard—all the way down to the stream." She pointed to her new guests. "These are Monsieur and Madame Kohut and their son, Pavel. Refugees."

The mayor bowed to Sophie and shook Willy's hand. "We were in correspondence, I believe."

Pavel, wide-eyed, looked at the gun, the dog and the lifeless birds. He opened his mouth to say something but made no sound.

"I visit my vines every evening," the mayor said, "and I often bring something home for the pot."

Monsieur Robineau's dark eyes flickered as he gazed at Sophie. "I wanted to make sure you were settled in with Madame Escobar and aware of everything you needed to be aware of."

"Everything seems to be fine," Willy said, ignoring the mayor ogling his wife. "We were about to get some sleep. But I have a question for you. What if my wife needs to get in touch with me in Portel? Is there a telephone here in the village?"

The major straightened his shoulders. "We are modern here. We have two telephones. One is at my office in the *Mairie*, and one in the café."

His eyes returned to surveying Sophie's figure. "I am always at your service at the *Mairie*. The telephone there is more discreet."

"*Merci*," said Sophie, gathering Pavel into her arms. She felt inept, unable to grasp quite what the mayor was saying. His accent was as thick as treacle, his hungry gaze as well.

The mayor stroked his chin as if hesitating. "Before I go, there is something important you should know that I heard on the radio this evening."

"Is it bad news, Maurice?" Madame Escobar said sharply. She got up and began piling up the dirty dishes. "These nice people are tired. They need to go to bed. Tell them tomorrow."

Sophie had the impression from her tone that the old lady and the mayor were not friends.

The mayor, taking no notice of the old woman, quieted the Malinois that was sniffing enthusiastically at Pavel's crotch. The boy seemed unfazed. "*Une vraie tragédie*," said the mayor breaking the shotgun open, ejecting two shells into the vines. "The whole British Army and forty thousand of our own men are surrounded in the Pas-de-Calais, around Dunkirk. There is no hope. The *Boche* armies will destroy them."

"What did he say?" Sophie whispered in Czech. Her heart pounded. She had seen shock transform Willy's face.

Willy took a deep breath and put a hand on her arm. "He says the Nazis have trapped French and British troops around the port of Dunkirk. Many thousands of men."

Sophie had never seen him so downcast.

"This is devastating. I'll try to learn more in Portel tomorrow."

The mayor unshackled two partridges from his belt and laid them on a rock by the fence. He smiled and bowed to Sophie, with a glance at the widow. "A gift for you and Madame Escobar who is famous for her partridge stew. She uses forest cèpes, black olives and white wine, I believe. *Très bon.*"

The widow walked up to the garden gate and gave the mayor's shoulder a not-so-gentle push. "Enough talk, Maurice. Go home to your Angélique. My tenants are tired and so am I."

Monsieur Robineau saluted. "*Bonne nuit.* In case Madame Escobar forgets, I have a piece of practical advice for you. Check your shoes for scorpions every morning. They grow fat and spicy in Sillat." He chuckled.

Sophie yawned. "What did he say?"

Willy smiled at her. "I'll tell you later."

Sophie lifted Pavel into her arms. "Bedtime, *miláčku.*"

The light of a half-moon created whimsical shapes on the bedroom's uneven walls. Naked and sweaty on the bed, legs entangled, Willy and Sophie stared at the abstract patterns, waiting for Pavel to go to sleep.

Willy talked softly about the news he had received from his parents in London, forwarded from the camp post office. "Father found a little apartment in a Jewish neighborhood called Hampstead. He's happy there, not because of the Jews but because he can get to the delicatessen and buy decent bread when it's available. He has to report his address to the police station every week. The government controls everything now—rationing, travel, work hours, blackouts at night. The Italians and Germans who were living in Britain before the war are all in detention camps."

Sophie raised herself on an elbow. "They were starting to do similar things in Paris before we left. Did they say London was bombed?"

"Nothing about that, but his letter was two weeks old. They're worried about us, of course. Afraid we'll be stuck here and get caught up in the fighting." Willy shrugged and mopped his face. "Father, in his usual pedantic way, described the preparations in London for the bombing—air-raid sirens, taped windows, underground shelters, sandbags stacked up, special police patrols, and a black-out at night."

"Do your parents know you and I are together now?"

"No. We must write tomorrow."

Sophie mopped Willy's damp face with a corner of the sheet. She was glad his family was in London, waiting to welcome them. "I can't believe we're in this little village, *miláčku*. The sun is too hot and the countryside seems harsh and infertile." She wriggled her shoulders and rolled sideways. "Oof, these straw mattresses are so prickly—and the idea of using a bucket instead of the toilet is awful. I never expected this."

"The main thing is that we are safe," Willy murmured, stroking her shoulder. "We can cope."

"Safe? Who knows what's going to happen next? Remember what the mayor said—the Allies are surrounded. I'm afraid." She sighed. "You want to get to England. How are we going to do that from here?"

"For the moment, all we can do is exist and wait," Willy said gently, stroking her shoulder. He caressed her nipples until they

272

hardened, his legs surrounding her firm thighs. His voice was soft, full of desire. "We can't let fear and discomfort ruin what we have now. Being a family together transcends everything else." He licked her shoulder and moved on to her neck. "Why don't we make love? It has been so long. I'm sure Pavel is asleep by now."

Sophie snuggled close and ran her fingers over Willy's chest, tracing the healing scar on his chest. His caresses fanned her desire. "Me too, *miláčku*, but I'm already pouring sweat and this prickly mattress is driving me mad. And Madame Esco might hear us. I thought I heard her moving about. Anyway, do you have a rubber?"

She felt Willy's hand stop moving between her thighs and then slide away. He raised himself on one elbow. "You mean it's no," he said in an angry whisper. "We've been apart for weeks and you don't want to make love? And what's this about a rubber? We're married for God's sake."

"I thought a great deal about this on the train, *miláčku*. It would be a disaster if I got pregnant now. What if you're sent to the front? What if something happens to you? I'm fine with making love if you have a rubber."

Sophie held her breath, expecting an outburst—the aggrieved husband denied his marital rights.

He sat up suddenly, gazing at how the moonlight illuminated her shoulders and breasts and the curve of one hip. "Tomorrow, I'll see if *Le Tabac* has rubbers." He slapped at a whining mosquito and stared out of the window. "I suppose you are right about not getting pregnant. In fact, I'm impressed that you thought about this—the consequences, I mean. What if you were pregnant and we had to hike across the Pyrenees on foot?"

"Aren't you afraid of going off to fight, *miláčku*?" said Sophie, thinking how she was terrified of what might happen to him, but keeping it to herself.

He nodded. "Of course, I'm afraid. So much so, that I thought about deserting and taking you and Pavel off to hide somewhere—to wait things out, hoping the French army would win. Or if the Germans prevailed, we would run for Spain. But I was ashamed at the idea of deserting. I want to do my part—prove that I can fight and be an example to Pavel."

He nestled against her and resumed his caresses. "You're right about being careful, Sophie … but I very much want to make love to you. You are my beautiful wife."

She turned and kissed him, slipping her tongue into his mouth. She slid her hand around his hardened penis. "Tonight, it's best you don't come inside me, that's all."

Later, unable to sleep beside her snoring husband, Sophie got up, walked to the window and gazed at the moon wedged high in a starlit sky, thinking about what she had said about not getting pregnant. Really, it was just an excuse. She had felt desire and then it evaporated. She didn't know why. This on-off feeling was new and confusing. What did it mean?

Back in bed but still wide-awake, she slapped at another whining mosquito. Tomorrow, she would be on her own once again, trying to adapt to new people, a new place and a new way of doing things.

CHAPTER TWENTY-FOUR

Pastoral

South of France. June 1st, 1940

Before dawn the next day, a Renault truck took Willy and the other soldiers billeted in Sillat to Portel. It arrived in time for the battalion to parade and his platoon to go on a seven-kilometer march, carrying heavy packs. After a short roadside snack, the men ran another three kilometers on country lanes without packs. On the march, Willy asked his comrades if they knew anything about Dunkirk. All he got were shrugs and more questions. He decided to keep the mayor's news to himself until he could find Kukulka. He would know.

Back at the camp, Willy found Sergeant Kukulka at the ordnance sheds, surrounded by a small group of soldiers, sitting on empty ammunition boxes. It seemed as if they were waiting for him.

"About time, Kohut. I need you. Special detail."

"Can I speak to you privately first, sergeant?"

Willy walked the sergeant round the corner of the shed. "Tell me straight, sergeant. I heard something about Dunkirk last night ... from the Sillat mayor. Are the Allies really trapped? I need reliable information. I have to think of my family."

As usual, Kukulka's features showed no emotion though Willy thought he saw surprise or perhaps even fear in the sergeant's eyes. "Don't ask questions, *vojín*. What's going on at the front is no concern of yours. Now … see those trucks over there? They just arrived from Toulouse. We have new equipment: weapons and artillery pieces, all French. And about damned time. Our job is to set up and test as fast as we can and I've designated a team that includes you. Come on, let's get back to the others."

Willy nodded. Kukulka's refusal to say anything was confirmation that the Czechoslovak top brass was worried as hell. Bad news, bad morale. Better to clamp down. It was possible that Mayor Robineau had better access to news than the soldiers at Agde camp.

Standing in front of five Renault trucks, two with gun trailers, the sergeant consulted his inventory. "Come on you lot, unload and break open the boxes. I've got to check that everything's here. Apart from the mobile anti-tank guns, we've got grenades, new rifles, mortars and unassembled Hotchkiss machine guns. They all have to be degreased and assembled. Kohut here will translate the specs and instructions. We'll test everything at the firing range."

Over the next three days, trucks ferried weapons and ammunition to an isolated hilly location and stored the equipment under tarpaulins until the team was ready to start degreasing, reassembling, and test-firing. Afterwards, Kukulka ordered the men to dig chest-high trenches— protection for training in the use of live grenades. Willy was spared that task—he translated French military manuals into Czech.

The weather was unchanging. Each day brought a cloudless sky and a red-hot sun that cracked the earth and made the hills shimmer. In the test-firing zone, except for Sergeant Kukulka who remained almost fully dressed, the men stripped to the waist, resigned to sunburn and the torment of mosquitoes and gnats. By the end of the day, red welts covered their bodies. Only later did Willy discover from Madame Escobar that lemon juice and olive oil, mixed together, worked as a preventative and salve against bites and sunburn.

Even though the work was hard, Willy enjoyed it. He delighted in the profusion of butterflies and wildflowers that populated the severe landscape. Madame Escobar called it *"la garrigue,"* a word that reminded Willy of Tomáš Masaryk, the founding father of Czechoslovakia who took Garrigue as his middle name. The rocky terrain battered and scarred the men's boots. Thorny shrubs tore at their battledress and scored their bare arms with blood. Whenever Willy happened to stumble on or fall over the limestone rocks, he would grab at dark green and silver shrubs and inhale the aroma left on his hands.

Sergeant Kukulka, stinking of sweat, grumbled about the heat and told them it would take several days to test all the equipment. An artillery specialist would arrive to check the three rubber-wheeled anti-tank guns.

"This place is hell," the sergeant growled at Willy on one particularly torrid day. "I can't wait to cool off up north and fight the Nazi bastards. Our first and second infantry regiments are still sitting around, ready to go, nearly five thousand men. What the fuck are they waiting for?"

"What's up about the battle around Calais?" someone asked as they were erecting tents to stack ammunition for the weapons. "We can't get any news in camp. Radio's out."

Willy stopped his work and listened. Had anything changed?

Kukulka spat on the ground. "Not a fucking whisper, friend. General Ingr is playing dumb—not like him to do that. Must be serious."

I guessed right, Willy thought. *I've got to start planning our route to Spain.*

"So—Sarge, in a few days, once we've tested the weapons and qualified, are we supposed to move out and fight?"

"Hope to God, boys." Kukulka had climbed to the top of a hinged ladder in the middle of a clearing. This was how he selected sites for positioning the targets; painted cutouts of German soldiers and vehicles. "But now, we've got to fucking wait for the new horses to be trained—with actual field pieces instead of just pulling a hay-wagon around. It'll take 'em at least a week to tolerate artillery fire. *Then* we go."

One day, in the mid-afternoon, Captain Rudček turned up to inspect progress at the firing range. He wore a modified Foreign Legion *képi,* turned around to keep the sun off his neck. Willy, stripped to the waist like the other men, was surprised when the captain laid a white-gloved hand on his sunburned shoulder. They had not spoken since Willy had been released from detention.

"Listen, *vojín,*" said Rudček in a low voice. He jerked his head towards a straggly oak nearby. "Stop what you're doing and come with me—now."

With a skeptical look and a shake of his head Willy saluted and followed the Captain into the tree's partial shade. He was fairly confident that the importance of translating the manuals would protect him from whatever retribution Rudček was cooking up for their past run-ins. He hoped that, whatever this chat was about, the captain might let slip some solid information about what was happening near Calais. Who had the upper hand, the Germans or the Allies? "What's afoot Captain, sir?"

Rudček curled his lip. "Still fucking impertinent, Kohut. Where's your shirt? And what the hell is that scar on your chest?"

Willy looked away. "Too complicated to explain, sir."

"Complicated, shit. Explain, *sakra!* That's an order."

Willy's eyes widened. He preferred to keep his private life private. The truth about his scar would only create fertile territory for more anti-Semitic actions or harangues. But, orders were orders. "A Nazi officer at the German-French border used a knife on me."

Rudček prodded Willy's scar with a gloved finger. "Crazy Jew. I dare say you deserved it. Go get dressed."

As soon as Willy returned wearing his sun-dried shirt, he came to attention and saluted. "You have more orders, sir?"

Rudček nodded. "You will be returning to Sillat with two new recruits in your truck—Czechoslovak Communists, *Španěláci*, who fought against Franco." He flicked a crawling bee off his jacket. "They will billet with the others at the farm. They say they want to fight Nazis and they're tough customers—gold-dust for us. Not soft-bellied recruits like you."

Willy kept a lid on his anger. He was quite proud of his muscled belly. "That's good isn't it, sir? Sergeant Kukulka keeps saying we're short of experienced men."

"Experienced yes, but these commies are also snakes. The big question is: can we trust them not to spread Stalinist claptrap? They're trouble-makers."

"I'm not sure why you are telling me this, sir."

"Leo Povídka, tall, mid-forties—he was a political commissar for the Masaryk Battalion in Barcelona."

Willy nodded, still perplexed. "And the other one?"

"Name's Serbin. Squat, stupid, and ugly, reputedly quick with a knife. Does what Povídka tells him. He already cut a soldier badly at the Agde camp. For cheating at cards, he claims."

"Why are they billeted in Sillat?"

"To keep them away from Agde. So, while they're in Sillat, I want you to keep an eye open for anything suspicious— meetings, arguments, anti-Western statements. Any sign of protest or conspiracy, we kick them out. Use the battalion courier to contact me."

Willy spread his hands, almost a gesture of protest. "I don't like spying on other soldiers, Captain."

Rudček's smile was sardonic. "I'm not interested in your morals, Kohut. But as an inducement to follow orders, I'm willing to offer you some information about that fellow ... what's his name? Lussik, the man you tried to kill at the *château*. I suspect he and you were well acquainted. Am I right?"

Willy stiffened, his pulse accelerating. "What about him?"

"He was spotted a couple of days ago, in Lapalme, laboring for a farmer."

Good, Willy thought. *Lapalme isn't far from Sillat, just a longish cycle ride.* "Was he arrested?"

Rudček gave Willy a malicious smile and rubbed his white-gloved hands together.

"This is not the moment to waste time on pathetic crooks. We have to get battle-ready. I'll let you know what happens to him in due course. Are you prepared to follow my order?"

Willy nodded, wondering if Rudček might now be open to a different question. "According to the mayor of Sillat, the Allies are holed up in Calais. If that's true and the Nazis take France, all of us here have a good chance of ending up prisoners—am I right?"

Rudček frowned. "Not just prisoners, idiot. We *Czechs*," the captain emphasized his last word with a bitter laugh, "could be executed as deserters. You *Slovaks* on the other hand ... well, you'll get off lightly."

Willy grimaced. For once it was better to be a Slovak.

"But for Jews like you ...?" Rudček drew a gloved finger expressively across his throat. "Definitely *kaput*."

"What if our army quit and made for Spain?"

"And accept hospitality from Franco? Not much better than handing us over to the Germans. I prefer to fight."

Willy mopped his face with his shirt tail. "Speaking of fighting, sir. All of us here are itching to see action."

"That is in process, *vojín*. Last night, thirty buses loaded up with our First Infantry regiment. Unfortunately, all they carried were rifles, light machine guns, grenades and ammunition—nothing that will stop tanks. They went north."

"Where to, in the north?"

Rudček sighed. "Can't say, *vojín*. Get back to your duties now."

In the back of the Renault truck, at the end of the day, Willy introduced himself to the *Španěláci* newcomers, Povídka and Serbin. "Do you two speak French?" he asked, offering them a cigarette from an open pack of Gauloises.

The Communists shook their heads. With a grunt, the short one, Serbin, took a cigarette. Povídka helped himself to four. "*Děkujeme*, comrade," he said in thanks, holding them up with yellow-stained fingers, a faint smile on his face. "Excuse that I took more than one—I like to keep a permanent smoke going."

Serbin grabbed Willy's arm. "This village we're going to—any cooperative women there?" he said hoarsely. "I'll take anyone below the age of forty. We had poor pickings in Spain. But then our week in Béziers made up for it."

Povídka nodded. "We were at command headquarters for screening and enlistment. That lasted three days, so we had time for the Béziers fleshpots." He gave his companion a hard look and jabbed him in the ribs. "Until this one screwed up our plans with his knife."

Serbin grinned, ignoring Povídka's remark. "Béziers was terrific fun. We didn't even use a hotel room. Spent every night in bordellos—and everything so damned cheap. Christ, the girls were superb and we guzzled champagne at seven fucking francs a bottle. We were served breakfast every morning—imagine, in a bordello!"

Povídka's gaunt face split into a line of yellow teeth. "B and B," he chuckled. "Bordello and Breakfast. A new style of lodging, you might say. At the classiest place, the salon was all velvet furniture and gold walls. The girls waited for us, sprawled on the couches in their underwear."

"The couches were nothing, Leo." Serbin's heavy eyebrows rose like black fountains. "What about those two giant billiard tables covered in cushions? We watched them fuck each other in the most amazing positions—and then we did it too."

Povídka put his finger against Serbin's lips. "Enough of that, Boho."

Listening to Serbin's vulgar bragging and studying the squat unappetizing figure, Willy suspected that "Boho" was someone who would grab whatever he fancied, whatever the consequences. It would be best that Serbin never caught sight of Sophie.

"What was that bordello called?" one of the other soldiers asked as the truck bucked and rolled. "Sounds like a terrific place."

The truck swayed as they rounded a corner and Povídka put out a hand to stop sliding off the bench. The cigarette plugged between his lips hardly moved. "*La Maison de Plaisance*, the pleasure palace. Everything there was handled by a temptress with a magnificent body. If you go, ask for Francine."

Willy tried not to show his surprise. He was sure it was the same Francine he met at the *château* party—*Maison de Plaisance*, Béziers—same name, same town. He remembered the firmness of her body and her sensuous embraces. So, Povídka and his side-kick had been at *her* bordello. Regret flitted through Willy's mind. If he hadn't taken that potshot at Lessig at the *château*, he too might have had the chance to frequent *La Maison de Plaisance*.

Granted, he was a married man, but all around him, his comrades-in-arms were shedding or forgetting the sanctity of marriage, taking the opportunity of wartime and separation to take pleasure where they could. Life was short. All it took to die was a bullet or a mortar shell.

Thinking this over as the truck rattled through the hills, Willy could not help wondering about Sophie. While he was in prison for six weeks in Prague, she had been alone with Pavel: a beautiful, lonely woman. And later, in Paris, once Pavel was happily tucked away at the Duclet farm, she could have met someone and been tempted. The thought of her in someone else's arms squeezed his heart dry. When a wife deceived her husband—everyone condemned it as a betrayal. But, for a soldier to make love to another woman; well that was part of military life. Take what you can when you can.

"Could you spell that name for me," a soldier said to Povídka, pulling out a pencil stub and licking its blunt point as he held a scrap of paper on his knee. "The name of that bordello."

At five-thirty, the truck unloaded its soldier cargo in Sillat's square. The village vibrated with heat and the men headed to the Café Liberté for cold beer. They preferred the café to their dilapidated farmhouse billet, playing cards, gambling, and telling stories. The café with a radio and a gramophone that only played French records was their only source of entertainment. They could not understand the radio; but the alcohol, snacks and music were welcome.

* * *

Later, in the cottage kitchen, the widow shook her head at Willy's damp, smelly clothes, beery breath, and sunburnt face. "Monsieur, your wife and boy are in the garden. This day is too hot, even for us, and you look exhausted." She pointed toward the vineyard. "Go take a swim. Our supper, *une salade Niçoise,* will wait."

Willy attempted a laugh, but could hardly summon the energy. "A swim! Is this a joke, Madame? Yesterday we walked beside your stream. There was nothing there but sand, gravel and limestone boulders. Not a drop of water."

As Sophie and Pavel came through the back door Madame Escobar smiled, the gash of her mouth revealing gaps and stained teeth. "You are mistaken, Monsieur. That stream—we call it *La Gance*—it is what we call "*un ruisseau caché*", a hidden river in summertime. But you will find beautiful water if you turn left when you reach the bank. Follow the path—nearly a kilometer." She bent down and touched the tip of Pavel's nose with a grimy finger. "The water will appear like magic," she whispered.

Pavel's clogs, borrowed from the next door neighbor, clattered on the flagstones.

"Maman, I want to see magic water."

Sophie gave Pavel a sorrowful look. "I'm sorry, Pavelkin. We have no clothes for swimming."

Mme. Escobar chuckled, idly rubbing Pavel's shoulder as she talked. "*Pas de problème.* On Saturdays sometimes, the locals swim there, *au naturel,* but if you are shy, at this time of day, no one will be there." She shrugged. "So, swim in your underclothes. That way you wash them at the same time. The water is very pure. I will give you towels."

* * *

Blinking in the glare of the sand and rocks, Sophie walked ahead of her "men" who were crouched on their heels inspecting a column of leaf-cutter ants. Even though there was no water in the stream-bed, she noticed clumps of grass and wildflowers on either side of the path. So, there was some water there, probably deep down. The old woman had played them a mean trick with her story of a secret river.

She saw a flash of silver … the glint of water behind tall

rushes. A rush of joy, Sophie cupped her hands to her mouth. "I can see the magic river," she called out. "Madame Esco was right. It looks lovely."

Within a few meters, she was surrounded by willow trees, tall grasses heavy with seed-heads, pink and yellow flowers, and alder bushes through which she glimpsed patches of silvery water. She pushed aside dangling willow branches to reach the bank and waited until Willy and Pavel caught up. They stood in the shade, their eyes adjusting to the dappled light as the stream swirled as clear as glass over smooth stones.

"Not more than a meter deep—perfect." Willy said slowly and reverently.

Butterflies fluttered above the stream's surface where water striders scurried on thin legs and jeweled dragonflies swooped, dipping into the water. A bird with a chunky head looked at them from a branch and disappeared in a flash of black and white. Willy grinned at Sophie. "Amazing."

Pavel didn't wait. He threaded his way in and out of the low-hanging willow fronds talking to himself, pretending he was in a wizard's house.

Sophie smiled and squeezed Willy's hand. "What a place. Paradise."

Smiling broadly, Willy stripped off his clothes and waded into the stream. "Come on, sweetheart, let's be Adam and Eve."

Astonished, Pavel peered through the willow fronds at his naked father with water rippling around his waist. Willy splashed the surface with flat of his hands. "Come on, both of you. Try it out."

Sophie, looking disappointed, pointed to the dressing around Pavel's neck. "He should not get that wet. Dip your feet in the water, darling."

Willy laughed and waded to the river bank, looking up at

them. "For God's sake stop fussing. It's pure water from the hills. Do him good. Here, I'll take the bandage off."

"Oh, my God," Sophie said when she saw Pavel's neck. "It's almost completely healed."

"Told you so." Keeping his glasses on, Willy threw himself backward with a splash, took a deep breath and floated on his back looking up at the trees. A butterfly landed on his forehead, flexing its crimson wings.

Pavel giggled as Sophie undressed him. Soon they were smiling and laughing together. *This is how a family should be*, she thought.

Looking at her naked husband, Sophie experienced a glow of admiration. The army had been good for his body. His belly was flat and he was tanned from the waist up. His chest muscles were sculpted, taut. The pasty plumpness that Sophie had been used to in Prague was gone. Only the curved dragontail scar below his heart blazed white against the tanned skin. Assured that no one else was watching, she stripped and stepped into the cold water, shrieking with shock and delight.

Willy picked Pavel up off the bank and set him down on a sandbank so he could stand in the flowing water. The boy did not object. He was fascinated by the water striders in the eddies and tried to snag one.

Sophie and Willy dipped and floated, gently turning over and over, letting the water carry their body heat away. They listened to the burble of water and birds calling from the surrounding trees. Then, as if scripted, Willy and Sophie locked eyes, stood and reached for each other. Butterflies settled on their wet skin. Willy pulled her to him and they clung, swaying in the current. Sophie felt his erection growing against her. "If only Pavel weren't here," he murmured.

She massaged her slick body against his and they kissed.

Why did she want him now and not last night?

"Perhaps Madame Esco will look after Pavel so you and I can come back here, alone," Willy said with an engaging smile. "We must try harder to be alone—make the most of this paradise before they send me north."

Sophie tightened her arms around him. She wanted to beg him not to leave, but held her tongue. She said it often enough. She was a soldier's wife. "Yes, darling, let's come here again."

When they arrived at Madame Escobar's back gate, Monsieur Robineau was at her garden table, reading a newspaper, a pipe in his mouth. Two bottles of wine stood on the table in front of him. The old lady was nowhere to be seen.

Willy shook his hand. *"Bonjour, Monsieur le Maire."*

The mayor rose quickly, bowed to Sophie whose wet curls clung to her face and neck.

He looked away as if embarrassed. "I brought some of the wine I produce. A Clairette rosé, very light, and a Picpoul de Pinet, crisp and green, a delight to drink with local oysters."

"Most generous, we thank you," Willy said with an edge of irritation. Robineau was a presumptuous nuisance, always turning up at odd times. "Do you have more war news or is this a social visit?"

Monsieur Robineau thoughtfully massaged his nose with two fingers. *"Mais oui, M'sieu.* War news. From the horse's mouth, you could say. My cousin lives in Arras—a town not far from Calais. He telephoned me. The *Boches* have encircled three hundred thousand British and French soldiers in the Pas-de-Calais. It is shaping into a disaster."

Willy understood immediately. If the heart and sinew of the British Army in Calais surrendered to the Germans, Britain would be defenseless. He squeezed the mayor's shoulder. "Thank you for telling me. I hope this does not mean that France will soon be defeated."

The mayor picked his trilby off the table and rose from his seat. "Impossible to predict. But my cousin did say something strange on the telephone. At the very moment when they could have overrun the Allied forces, *les Boches* suddenly stopped their advance. It was inexplicable or a miracle, as if God ordered it."

"Let's hope there's a miracle and the British army is not destroyed."

Monsieur Robineau bowed, admiring eyes once again caressing Sophie's body. "Enjoy the wine. I regret I must leave you with this uncertain news ringing in your ears. Soon, we will know the worst or the best. *Au revoir.*"

CHAPTER TWENTY-FIVE

Village Life
Sillat, South of France. Mid-June 1940

Willy held his bicycle steady and pulled the cottage's bell handle. In addition to an empty metal food container, the satchel on his back held a map of the Pyrénées Orientales. He'd 'borrowed' it from a store-room at the Agde camp and spent two lunch-breaks tracing an escape route to Le Perthus, the village that had the lowest mountain pass into Spain—in case they had to run for their lives.

Sophie opened the door. Her smile changed when she saw his expression.

He leaned the bicycle against the wall, kissed her and slipped off his satchel. "The First Infantry Regiment has gone north," he said somberly. "They are to reinforce the French Army's defense positions, somewhere … I don't know exactly." He put an arm around her shoulders and gave her a reassuring squeeze. "Don't worry; my outfit is nowhere near ready to go."

She nuzzled his cheek. "Pavel wants you to take him to hunt rabbits in the vineyard … and, by coincidence, there's rabbit stew for supper."

"Sweetheart, I have to go back right now. Tomorrow, first light, we start intense training. Night maneuvers, sleeping in ditches, cold rations … all the military comforts I love best." He gave her a regretful grin. "I'm sorry."

"You mean you cycled all this way to tell me you can't stay

tonight? Are you mad?"

He stared at her. "How else can I let you know what's happening? I can't get to a telephone." He dug the map out of his satchel. "Keep this hidden in our room."

"Why, what is it?"

"A map. In case we have to escape to Spain." He paused. "Don't ask me about it, not now."

He smiled briefly. "I suppose Pavel is playing somewhere in the vineyard. Give him a kiss for me. And I want you to stay busy; try to keep your mind off the bad, and the what-ifs. You will see me when you see me."

She watched him freewheel unsteadily down the street and disappear around the corner. May be he was right. She had to keep her hands and mind occupied; busy herself with the daily tasks and routines of village life, even though it had to be under the critical gaze of the old widow.

The next morning, wearing a knotted headscarf and apron borrowed from Madame Escobar, Sophie walked to the fountain in the square with Pavel trotting beside her. She filled two large pitchers of drinking water and carried them home in the widow's shoulder harness. Afterwards, she and Pavel went to gather kindling—vine trimmings—for the cottage stove. Then she shook the straw mattresses and swept their room clean of spiders, grasshoppers and the usual squashed scorpions.

In the afternoon, Sophie and Pavel crossed the dry river-bed below the vineyard to the forest on the other side of the valley. There they filled a large basket with dead branches, carried it back through the vineyard to Madame Escobar's garden, and chopped up the branches, stacking everything, as directed, under the gnarled cherry tree.

When Sophie wanted to be on her own she left Pavel with Madame Escobar. The old lady seemed to be a trusty child-minder and Pavel liked her. The only place to walk and be alone was in the arid *garrigue* where she imagined what Willy might be doing, and thought about their marriage and the uncertainty of their future.

And there was her relationship with Madame Escobar. The old lady did not believe in leaving Sophie and Pavel to their own devices. She inserted herself into the Kohut family's life, treating Willy like a favored son and acting as if she was Pavel's *grandmère*. Once, when Sophie returned from talking to the next-door neighbor, she had found the old lady in her wicker chair benignly watching Pavel perched on the top of a step-ladder picking and eating cherries.

Sophie ran to the ladder and lifted Pavel down.

He glared at her frown and ran off.

"Madame Esco," she said. "Didn't you think what he was doing was dangerous? You had no right. I don't want my boy up on this ladder again."

Madame Escobar waved a dismissive hand. "You asked me to keep an eye on your son? That's what I was doing. He needs to run and play, grow strong and be free. Let the little one do what he wants. He will learn more that way than if you smother him."

Pavel swung on the garden gate looking sullen and Sophie sat down on a wicker chair, gripping her knees till they hurt. This contrary old woman infuriated her—she was also annoyed with herself for over-reacting. But then—what if something happened to him when she wasn't there, an accident or some injury? Nevertheless it was clear to Sophie that Pavel was happy and getting stronger. He spoke fluent French and was well on the way to forgetting his Czech. The other children liked him and he was friendly with everyone, particularly Jo-Jo, the black-haired girl from next door. They played in Madame Escobar's garden or close by in the vineyard.

* * *

Late one day, while Sophie sat in the garden with a bowl between her knees, trimming runner beans for supper, Madame Escobar came out of the kitchen at a fast hobble. Her eyes gleamed with excitement. "Madame Richot from next door says the mayor has called an emergency meeting in the square. It's about the war. Everyone has to go, even refugees. Where is Pavel?"

"In the vineyard with Jo-Jo."

"Get them."

As the church clock struck the hour, Monsieur Robineau, wearing a mayor's *tricolore* sash over his suit, climbed the steps of *La Mairie* to face the sun and a sweltering crowd; perhaps a hundred people was Sophie's guess. A young girl shaded the mayor's head with a beach umbrella.

Sophie, Pavel and Jo-Jo, squeezing close to Madame Escobar, sat on the upper steps of the fountain with some of the older matrons of the village. The same questions lingered on everyone's lips. Has something bad happened? The war or a tragedy in the village?

"*Mes amis.*" The mayor's voice reverberated through the megaphone and he paused to look around and nod, as if to emphasize the importance of his message.

"Citizens, as your mayor, I am forced at this momentous time to make you aware of France's true situation." His words echoed round the square.

"We know there's a war on?" shouted someone in the crowd. "We've plenty of work left to do today. It's too damned hot for one of your bloated speeches. What is the radio for?"

Someone else yelled. "So, what's happening? Make it short."

The mayor mopped his head and put up his hand for silence.

292

He smiled. "Fellow citizens, I have good news. The Allied armies have been evacuated to England from Dunkirk. Hundreds of thousands. A miraculous enterprise. And the *Boches* did little to stop it!" He raised a hand heavenward to still the applause and chatter. "On the other hand, further to the north, the Belgian Army has surrendered. Millions in the Paris region have fled their homes. The *Boches* are coming south, toward us."

Sophie looked at the horrified expressions around her. Except for doves cooing in the trees and the whickers of horses and donkeys, there was a moment of total silence.

"What about Paris?" someone yelled. "Are they putting up the barricades, like in the old days?"

The mayor shrugged. "Unfortunately, I know very little, but I was told the Renault and Citröen factories at Billancourt were bombed … and our army is valiantly fighting the *Boches* on the banks of the Somme. Remember my friends, that fighting is still eight hundred kilometers from Sillat. "

Sophie put her head in her hands. Her heart thumped, almost painfully against her ribs. The Germans were winning. Willy, wherever he was, was surely aware of what was happening. She knew he would be working out a way to get her and Pavel to safety before the Germans arrived. She remembered the map. That was what it was for.

A woman waved her plump sun-burned arms in the air. "I expect, *Monsieur le Maire,* that those thousands of refugees will turn up here. Where in God's name will they stay? What will they eat? They will rob us blind."

"And crap in the mayor's vineyards," someone retorted, to general laughter.

"*Pardí, monsieur le Maire,*" shouted a tall thin man with an empty sleeve pinned to his jacket, "we didn't ask for this war. I say, let the *Boches* come. They know how to run things, keep order. Not like our useless leaders."

The mayor tightened his lips, looking uncomfortable. "Do not be hasty, *citoyens*. The information I receive from our regional office in Béziers is vague. I have no idea what to expect when the refugees arrive. If they do."

"What about the Czechoslovak soldiers billeted here?" someone yelled. "Why aren't they fighting?"

"That's right," someone else yelled back. "Maybe they ran off. They're not here now."

The mayor frowned. "The Free Czechoslovak Army is fighting for France under the *tricolore* flag. We owe them our friendship."

Madame Escobar narrowed her eyes approvingly at Sophie. "He's right."

"*Alors*, what are we supposed to do?" someone called out angrily. "Sit on our *culs*? Do you have real up-to-date information or is this just the usual bureaucratic stew you serve up?"

The mayor winced and spread his arms. "I beg you, *calmez-vous*. Keep to your daily routines, but also prepare for the worst. Fill up your water cisterns, stock up on bread and food. Make preserves of fruit and vegetables. Be sure you have plenty of feed for the animals. Be generous to the refugees if and when they come."

"If we surrender to the *Boches*, the refugees can go back home before they get here," someone shouted in a hoarse voice.

"*Salaud*, bastard," someone else yelled in reply.

Listening to the somber news, Sophie imagined the chaos with hundreds of hungry, desperate Belgian or French people wandering the streets of Sillat. There was bound to be violence, and foreigners like her and Pavel could be in danger.

Her fingers tightened around the flimsy air-mail letters in her pocket. Willy had brought them from Portel. She had read them eagerly—one from her father and brother in Australia describing their release from the internment camp, one from his parents, describing the strict regulations and blackout in London, and one from cousin Janko, written from Jerusalem after his escape down the Danube. And here she was, waiting for the Germans to arrive. Now, everyone in their family was struggling, lonely, and without resources, all caught in the grip of an expanding cataclysm.

As the crowd dispersed, Pavel broke away from Sophie and stood watching some boys play marbles. She did not call him back. He needed all the fun he could get. She recalled how she had balked at Willy's insistence that, in the midst of all their anxiety and unsettling news about the fighting, Pavel, should have a real treat for his fourth birthday—a beach excursion.

"That settles it," Willy said firmly when he got home and heard about the mayor's speech. "We'll fix up some fun at the beach. A swim, games and maybe a picnic. I'll get Kukulka to drive us in his truck. We'll take Jo-Jo … and Madame Esco as well. What's the point of twiddling thumbs and whining about the war when we can't do anything about it?"

After a dinner of rabbit terrine, omelet, and cherry tart, Willy helped to clear the dishes while Sophie took Pavel for a walk through the vineyard to the river to look for a white owl that Madame Escobar said lived in the willows by the stream. In the kitchen, Willy came up to the widow as she washed the dishes. "Let me help dry," he said softly.

She studied him, wide-eyed, as if dumbfounded that a man, especially a soldier, would think to dry dishes for a woman. "This is not like you, Monsieur." Willy did not reply. They worked quietly until she stopped with her hands in the water and looked at him. "What is it?"

Willy paused to wipe his glasses on the dish towel, as if he was not sure he should tell her. "Mussolini declared war on France and Britain. His troops are in France, close to Nice. They may come this way."

The old lady slapped the soapy water as if she were punishing it for being dirty. "*Merde*! Such a filthy war. Why do countries like Germany, Spain, and Italy fight against us? It is beyond belief. We are all Christians and have done nothing to deserve a war. Other than pray to God, what can we do?"

"For the moment, we wait. Somewhere, up north, my Czechoslovak comrades have joined the French rear-guard action. I'll be up there soon and I'm afraid Sophie will be devastated. She has been through so much already. So, please, when I'm gone, be kind to her."

Madame Escobar looked at Willy and lowered her gaze. "It is hard for everyone, *mon pauvre Monsieur*. I'm sure you know your wife—though she does not show it—is terrified of what will happen to you. All over France people pray for deliverance and peace." She shrugged helplessly. "I will pray for your safety."

Willy put an arm round her shoulders. She flinched at first, then turned her head against his chest. Gently, he rubbed her back. "There is something else very sad, Madame—the Germans are in Paris. They draped swastikas over the Arc de Triomphe and the Eiffel Tower."

The widow buried her face in her wet hands.

* * *

Late in the morning of June 18 Sergeant Kukulka reached Sillat in a military van. "You heard the news, perhaps?" he said to Willy, who was waiting for him in the square. "The French are defeated. There will be a surrender. Our own boys are retreating, surrounded by thousands of refugees. Roads clogged with the living and the dead. The Luftwaffe have been merciless."

Willy grabbed his arm. "Listen Sarge, Pavel's birthday was two days ago. If you remember, I promised him a beach outing. Could you to drive us there, after you've checked the men's billet?"

"*Kristus*, fuck!" Kukulka clutched his head. "You've gone mental. I'm your sergeant, not a relative. What the hell am I going to say about this to the motor pool officer? "

Willy smiled. "Come on, Sarge. The Germans are hundreds of kilometers away. We'll have fun and eat a good French lunch. Come, on. What do you say?"

Kukulka hesitated, then patted Willy's head and grinned. "Why not, *vojín*? When I wrote up the motor release slip, I didn't mark any return time." He laughed. "It'll give me a chance to toss you into the sea. We'll take everyone."

Kukulka drove the Kohuts, Madame Escobar and Jo-Jo thirty kilometers to the village of Gruissan, a settlement of fishermen where, the old lady said, Greek traders had culled oysters a thousand years earlier. For two hours, the birthday party relaxed on the sand and lazed in the warm blue water. Pavel and Jo-Jo ran naked through the shallows and played tag and ball with Willy and Kukulka, down to their undershorts, on the long flat beach.

Sophie soon joined in while Madame Escobar sat on a blanket and watched, wearing her headscarf and fanning herself with a newspaper. As they dried themselves, dressed and packed up towels and blankets, the widow—using Willy as interpreter—pleaded with Sergeant Kukulka to take them for a quick but special lunch. "We can eat close to here," she said. "A place by the oyster beds where the fishermen live in cabins on stilts. We might even see flamingoes." She tugged at the Sergeant's arm, staring intently at his tattoo. "We will eat *fruits de mer*—fresh seafood. Then, Monsieur Kohut and you can return to the war."

"I'll see what I can do," Kukulka said, after Willy translated her request. The sergeant's beefy nose twitched at the mention of seafood. "All I know about is mackerel, pike and smoked trout. I wonder what we'll get. Anyway, I'll telephone headquarters from the village center, just to let them know our location—precautions. I'll say we're looking for a missing soldier."

As the van wound through Gruissan, Mme. Escobar issued directions. In a few minutes they reached a handful of shacks built at the edge of a small lagoon. Mounds of oyster shells dotted the shoreline. Apart from the whispering breeze, the calls of the gulls, and a man in dungarees whistling while he painted the gunwale of a boat, the place was serene and still. A fishy smell hit the group as they exited the van.

"Stinks," said Jo-Jo, wrinkling her nose. "Disgusting."

Madame Escobar smiled. "*Non, ma chère*, that is a good smell. Seaweed and oysters, and maybe *les crasses* from the flamingoes. You must learn to like it."

Pavel shook his head and pinched his nose, imitating Jo-Jo. "Disgusting."

"And that, Madame?" Sophie pointed to a dazzling white hill across the lagoon. "What is that?"

Madame Escobar nodded. "A mountain of salt, the best on earth. We call it *fleur-de-sel*." She indicated one of the shacks. "We eat there. Chez Monsieur Cordona, one of the oystermen."

They sat at a bleached table under a tattered canvas awning, overlooking a quiet stretch of blue-green water, criss-crossed with wooden posts and racks that carried the oyster spat. Willy pointed to a flat pink smudge in the distance. "Are those flamingoes?"

At that moment, as if provoked by his words, the smudge expanded into a balloon, changed shape and grew more and more pink as it came toward them, accompanied by a cacophony of noise that sounded like a thousand rusty door hinges. Pavel clapped his hands, laughing. "Red and white birds," he cried.

"I know what to order," Madame Escobar said as the flock banked, flattened and settled on to the lagoon surface. She smiled sweetly at Willy and patted his hand. "Monsieur Kohut or his comrade will pay for all of us. Don't worry, it is very reasonable."

Henri Cordona, the oyster farmer, was a chunky weathered man with speckled gray hair that matched the color of his shack. He said he knew Madame Escobar from the old days when she came with her husband. Even though his kitchen was only open at the weekends for the rich people of Béziers and Narbonne, today he would make an exception. Mathilde, his wife, would cook for them.

Mathilde, skinny in a frayed, sun-bleached frock and just as weathered as Henri, served them freshly shucked oysters, grilled mussels stuffed with spicy sausage meat, pies called *tielles* filled with octopus and tomato sauce. The final dish was *Bourride de Baudroie*, chunks of monkfish slathered with garlic aioli. All of this came with crusty bread and Picpoul de Pinet, the white wine that Monsieur Cordona said smelled of acacia flowers. Although Pavel and Jo-Jo picked at the mussels and fish, they were happiest eating a mound of *pommes frites*. The quick lunch had turned into a feast. No one complained.

They were drinking coffee and sweet wine when the whine of a high-revving engine frightened the flamingos in the lagoon into a scrambled, banking flight. A khaki-painted motorcycle, kicking up sand dust, swerved to a halt at the front of the shack. A young soldier leaped off, took off his goggles and waved. He ran up the steps, shading his eyes against the sun. "Sergeant Kukulka?"

The big man stood up, stained napkin still tied round his neck. "What is it?"

The soldier handed him a buff envelope. "Emergency. Glad I found you. There's heavy fighting in the north. The

French have collapsed."

"That's old news. What's the emergency?"

Madame Esco looked from face to face. "What does he say?"

Willy held up his hand to quiet her. Sophie gasped. She stared at him, mouth open. "What should we do, *miláčku*?"

Kukulka tore open the envelope, scanned the contents and screwed up his face.

"*Sakra*. Our boys are on their way back from the Loire. Brigadier General Miroslav ordered Army headquarters in Béziers to close down."

Willy covered Sophie's hand with his. "Don't worry, sweetheart. There is no immediate danger. The Nazis are a long, long way from here."

"What is it, Papa?"

"I'll tell you on the way home."

Sophie shook her head and looked away—across the dark blue water, toward the pink flamingos and the white crystal mountain.

Kukulka rubbed his sun-burned forehead with one hand and shook his head. "Good God, soldier. You came all the way on that contraption to tell me we're packing up? What's the goddamned rush?"

"I don't know, sir. Just that I have to get this message to all NCOs. At sixteen hundred hours, Colonel Zientek will address all troops at the Agde camp. Mandatory attendance." He glanced longingly at the uneaten food on the table.

Kukulka looked at his watch and took a deep breath. "We go. At least, we had a little fun and a good lunch." He stood up and slapped the motorcyclist on the back. "There's food left on the table. Grab something before you head out."

Willy helped Madame Esco out of her chair and turned to the fisherman. "How much?"

"Soixante francs, m'sieu."

On the way back to Sillat, in the back of the van, Sophie wrapped her arms around Willy—tightly, as if she wanted to keep him a prisoner.

The children sat with Kukulka and Madame Escobar in the front. They were giggling.

Willy stroked Sophie's cheek and kissed her on the lips. "I'm glad we had a good time."

"It *was* beautiful, *milačku*. This meeting at the camp, is it serious?"

"Probably." A frown darkened his face. "We'll soon find out."

In the front seat, Madame Escobar was teaching the children to sing "Alouette, Gentille Alouette."

CHAPTER TWENTY-SIX

Evacuation Plans
South of France. June 18th, 1940

At five o'clock, the army sports field at Agde was packed with sweating soldiers, their bronzed faces eager for news. A hazy sun hung in the sky as if waiting for something to happen.

Willy shifted his weight from foot to foot, listening to the men around him—that the war was over and France had surrendered, that the Czechoslovak army might be forced into a Dunkirk-like quagmire or that General Boromir Miroslav was going to disband the army.

Colonel Zientek, in full dress uniform, stepped on to the wooden dais and looked around at the murmuring crowd. A circular microphone hung from a post in front of him. A few paces behind, officers were chatting and smoking.

The colonel fired his pistol into the air. In the quietness that followed, he saluted, doffed his military cap and stepped close to the microphone. His voice, hoarse and sad, echoed in the loudspeakers. "Men, I regret to inform you that our Allied armies are in full retreat, two of our own regiments included. For those of you not aware of General Pétain's announcement on the radio yesterday, France has capitulated. Pétain will be temporary head of a replacement French government. With France on her knees, only Great Britain stands in Hitler's way."

A collective sigh, almost a groan, rolled across the field.

The colonel mopped his face and sipped from a glass of water proffered by an aide.

There was a long silence, punctuated by the screams of seagulls overhead and the sound of coughing and boots shuffling on sandy soil. A breeze ruffled the men's hair and the Czechoslovak flag on the dais shook and flapped as if in defiance of the Nazi victory. Willy slapped at his cheek and other soldiers started to curse and slap at their arms and faces: the late-afternoon mosquito torture had started. Cigarettes were only a partial help. No one stopped the men lighting up.

The colonel nodded slowly as if reluctant to say what he had to say. "So, what will become of us? The short answer is … I'm not sure … yet." He paused. A sardonic smile crossed his face. "The Germans have ordered all French shipping confined in port so the French Navy cannot evacuate us to North Africa. If our small army stays here we are in danger—the Germans regard us Czechoslovaks to be citizens of Germany's Bohemian and Moravian Protectorate: deserters. If captured, we will face a court martial or summary execution."

Willy's heart sank. He saw alarm, gloom and desperation in the faces around him. The reason he had joined the Czechoslovak army in Paris was to guarantee his family a way out of France. That guarantee was in tatters. What would he say to Sophie when he got back to the cottage? He wiped his wet cheeks and looked around. He wasn't the only one weeping.

Zientek straightened his shoulders. A slight smile crossed his face. "But if we get organized and work hard, there's a way out of this mess. The British Prime Minister, Churchill, has ordered a rescue mission. Exactly how and when the Royal Navy will arrive in the port of Sète to take us to England is not precisely known. But in England, we will continue to fight the Nazis under British command."

There was a prolonged cheer. The crowd vibrated and buzzed with excitement. A number of soldiers launched into the Czechoslovak national anthem, "Where is My Home?" Many joined in. The sound of singing drowned the calls of the seagulls.

Colonel Zientek held up a hand, waiting for the singing and excitement to subside. His face showed no emotion. "Your participation in this evacuation plan is voluntary. Those of you who lived in France before enlisting may want to return to your jobs and families rather than travel to Britain. And the Slovaks among you may want to go back home where you have family and there is less danger." He paused. "Slovakia, as you know, is not occupied and cooperates fully with the Germans. To those making the choice *not* to evacuate to Britain, you are free to leave your units, but only after the evacuation is complete."

There was another cheer and a groundswell of excited voices rolled across the field.

Colonel Zientek mopped his face. "We don't have much time. We will proceed immediately to separate those men who wish to sail to Britain from those who will stay."

Colonel Zientek turned and beckoned to a different officer. He rested the pole he carried on the floor and stepped to the microphone. The Czechoslovak flag attached to his pole lay pooled on the floor. His words were clipped and decisive. "Raising this flag will be the signal for all you men to move to the group they've chosen. Soldiers who *do not* wish to evacuate to Britain are to line up in rows under the banner that says: No Evacuation. Those who want to leave for Britain are to assemble at the other end of the field under the banner: Evacuation. At each location, officers wearing red arm bands will register your names and numbers. Once registered, you must immediately return to your billets. Tomorrow at ten hundred hours, we will distribute orders regarding convoy schedules to the port of Sète and the timing of boarding procedures at the docks."

As the noise in the audience grew louder, he raised his voice. The microphone buzzed and boomed. "Those of you choosing to stay in France will still have duties and must obey orders. Until the evacuation ships have left port, you are required to guard our military equipment, supplies and horses. After that, the French will take over." He raised his standard, the flag flapping in the breeze. "Move," he yelled and jerked the flag into the air.

The men moved quickly and purposefully. Willy joined the rush to the Evacuation banner. Within twenty minutes, the once solid formation of soldiers had separated into two unequal groups—the larger number electing to disband and leave: for wherever home was.

* * *

By six, the parade ground was almost deserted. Sunset glowed between serrated lines of orange-violet clouds. A strong breeze cart-wheeled empty Gauloise cartons and torn newspapers into the air. Cigarette butts littered the ground.

Willy was among the last to leave under the watchful eyes of a handful of officers. Just outside the parade ground, his mind buzzing with what he had just witnessed, he unfastened the twine that tied his bicycle to a post. He felt a hand on his shoulder. Captain Rudček.

"I need you, Kohut. At the camp. Come along, NOW."

Willy hardly noticed the order.

No time to lose. Get yourself home. He stepped astride the bicycle, preparing to leave.

"Did you hear what I said, *vojín*?"

Willy's head cleared as he hopped off the bicycle. He saluted automatically. "Didn't quite catch what you said, sir."

Rudček snorted and struck the bicycle frame with his cane. "As of now, you are on my evacuation team. Leave this lump of iron here and follow me to camp. Official planning meeting."

Willy glowered as he marched behind the captain. *What a bastard.*

In the operations room, crates of beer were stacked on the floor. Wine, beer, bread, bowls of olives and plates of sliced salami were set out on a long collapsible table. Czechoslovak and French officers and a scattering of NCOs and soldiers sat in rows of chairs, eating off their knees. Others helped themselves to the buffet.

Colonel Zientek stood facing the audience next to a blackboard full of chalked numbers and names. He held a notebook in one hand. Two men sat to the right of the blackboard. One was red-faced and sported a bushy mustache. His overweight frame was tightly encased in a uniform laden with gold braid. The other man was small and wiry. He wore baggy pants, rope-soled sandals, a white open-necked shirt and puffed nervously on a cigarette.

Zientek introduced the plump one. "Gentlemen, this is Captain Suter, Divisional Sea Transport Officer, Royal Navy, stationed in Marseille. Our other guest, wearing the beret, is Monsieur Aristide Arnaud, harbormaster of the port of Sète. He speaks English and French, but not Czech. Consequently, we will conduct the meeting in French." He looked in his notebook and nodded to Willy. "*Vojín* Kohut here will translate."

Willy stood and saluted.

"First, the Royal Navy officer will tell us about the ships we'll be using," said Zientek. "Afterwards, I will summarize the overall evacuation plan. These two gentlemen can add comments as needed."

Rising to his feet, Captain Suter spoke in hesitant French. "It will take a few days for the ships to sail from Marseille. We will be using private British and Egyptian freighters with at least one destroyer as escort. From Sète, we expect the freighters will take four days or so to get to Gibraltar. Once there, the troops will be transferred to bigger ships that will convoy into the Atlantic."

As Willy translated his words into Czechoslovak, the Englishman ran fingers through his springy hair. Willy thought he looked weary.

"The transfer in Gibraltar will take time. The harbor is packed with British warships." He turned to face the Czechoslovak leader. "You said you were planning to embark between three and a half to four thousand men? Is that the final approximate number?"

Lieutenant-Colonel Němec, sitting at the other side of the blackboard, flipped through a clipped document and ran a finger down one page. "Not yet. We must wait for our first regiment to return from central France. There will also be some refugees and Czechoslovak families to whom we have guaranteed passage: ninety-eight women and twenty-five children so far. We have set up teams to coordinate convoys from the different villages to the Sète docks."

He stood up and pointed his cane at the blackboard. "In addition, embarkation teams have been assigned for each ship—their tasks include: crowd control, weapon disposal, baggage, passenger registration, food and water supplies, and checkpoint security." He nodded to one of the officers on the dais, who stepped off and handed fat envelopes to several men in the audience including Captain Rudček. "These are your embarkation orders."

Captain Suter took a pipe from his side pocket and sucked a match flame into the bowl. "Evacuating your men is a top priority. Britain needs trained soldiers, not refugees. Of course, I'm aware that there are thousands of civilians trapped in this region. I expect they'll hear of this and want to get on the boats. Your security teams, Czechoslovak and the French, if they are still cooperating with you, should be armed and ready for trouble at the docks."

Zientek nodded at the Englishman. "We can do that. How many ships can we expect—and how big?"

Suter put on half-moon spectacles and flipped pages in a small black notebook he pulled from his pocket. "Three, perhaps four freighters, each one around five to seven thousand tons. With the summer heat, minimal facilities and overloaded with passengers, I expect it to be quite an unpleasant journey. As I said, these small freighters will rendezvous with passenger ships in Gibraltar, form convoys and sail to convenient ports in Britain."

"How soon can we board our troops?"

"In four to six days is my guess," Suter said calmly.

"*Sakra!*" Němec slapped his thigh and sank back into his chair, rubbing his forehead. "That's too damned long."

"What about the German Navy and the Luftwaffe?" asked one of the senior officers sitting near Colonel Němec. "They will bomb us to hell. Merchant vessels are sitting targets."

"Luckily, our reconnaissance boys have seen only spotter planes, Blériots and Bréguets," said Suter. "And what is left of the French air force does not seem to be under German control. I don't think you need to worry." He grimaced. "The Luftwaffe is tied up in the north, bombing England and planning an invasion."

The Englishman surveyed the room and smiled. "So you see, gentlemen, we still control the Med." He flipped another notebook page. "The *SS Darwen* leaves Marseille on June 24 and should be in Sète within two days. The other two ships, the *SS Swithun* and the *SS Northern Fen* are still unloading coal in Marseille. They will arrive here a day or two later. Two destroyers, *HMS Velox* and *HMS Keppel*, will escort the convoys to Gibraltar."

Colonel Zientek sprang to his feet as the other officers scribbled notes. "Thank you, captain. Our senior and divisional personnel, vital documents and what's left of the army treasury will embark on the first boat that arrives at Sète from Marseille."

Lieutenant-Colonel Němec, looking apprehensive, pointed his finger at Captain Suter.

"Those little cargo ships better be here when you say," he growled. "If we are stuck here longer than a few days, we will be disarmed and detained by whatever regime the new French collaborators and the Germans can cobble together."

Harbormaster Arnaud raised his hands in protest. "*Messieurs!* Before any embarkation is possible, I need official authorization from the Regional Marine Administration in Toulon. Sète is a busy port with ships that come and go from many countries." He shook his head violently. "Regulations must be followed."

Eyes afire, Zientek slapped his cane against a chair leg. "Be realistic, Monsieur Arnaud. Surely, it's better to cooperate than witness a pitched battle fought on the docks of Sète." He picked a wine bottle off the table and refilled the harbormaster's glass, placing a friendly hand on the Frenchman's shoulder. "Forget about your phantom, defeated government. We will pay you a nice bonus to make the embarkation go smoothly. *Okay* ?"

Monsieur Arnaud shrugged acquiescence. Willy saw his eyes gleam. "*Eh, bien oui, je suis d'accord.*"

A door jerked open at the back of the room and a young officer ran up to the dais. He handed Zientek a sheet of paper. The colonel read it slowly and looked round the room, frowning. "General Pétain just gave a speech on the radio saying he's about to negotiate an armistice with the Germans. All hostilities will cease."

Everything froze. Silence reigned.

Captain Rudček raised his hand and Zientek nodded his permission to speak. "What does an armistice mean for us, Colonel?"

"It means we have no time to spare." The colonel waved the sheet of paper. "This communiqué also summarizes the German demands." With a grim smile, he looked around the room. "I'm sure it will interest you. France will pay a substantial fee in gold for the privilege of being occupied. French troops will work for the occupiers, here or in German camps and, most significantly— soldiers like us and people of the Jewish race will be shipped to prison camps. The Germans will control the country from Paris. Most importantly, General Pétain is to preside over a new official French administration governing the south of France."

"What is the point of that, Colonel? France is defeated. What's the point of having a French government that has no power?"

Zientek gave a cynical laugh. "International politics, my friend ... and power. If France had no official government, her overseas assets will be frozen. Her colonies will owe allegiance to no one and will keep their resources to themselves. The Germans, of course, want those assets, so Pétain's regime will represent France on the international stage as *the* official French government. Puppetry!"

* * *

Willy cycled home as fast as his wobbling front wheel would allow. In Sillat, grinding up the hill in the dusk, he decided to tell Sophie only the good news about the evacuation—not the bad news that he was assigned to an evacuation team and would be separated from her and Pavel. Rudček had told him at the end of the meeting that he would be on a "completion team", one of the last soldiers to board a ship. It was almost guaranteed that Sophie and Pavel would embark without him. There was nothing he could do about it but he would break it to her gently, later.

Perspiring heavily from the uphill climb, he dropped the bike by the door and rushed into the cottage. He found Sophie and Madame Escobar sitting at the table in the garden. A plate, knife and fork, chunks of dark bread in the basket and a bottle of wine waited on the table.

As the widow disappeared into the kitchen Willy acknowledged Sophie's reproachful look with a shrug, but kissed her all the same. He sat and thankfully drained a glass of wine.

"Pavel is in bed—he was sad you weren't here to watch him blow out the birthday candles. What happened at the meeting?"

"*Můj Bože*, I'm so sorry." Willy poured more wine, leaned his chair back on two legs and exhaled. "I had to stay behind and translate at a top brass meeting." He adjusted his glasses as if playing for time to find a gentle way to say something difficult. "The big meeting at the parade ground was to say our army, or part of it, will be evacuated ... by boat, from the port of Sète. That means you, me and Pavel ... we leave in a few days. The French have surrendered."

Sophie leaned across the table, took his hand and kissed it. "That's wonderful, *milačku*. I mean about leaving, not the French defeat. Where do we go? How?"

"By ship to England. "I am part of several teams responsible for the evacuation. I'm involved."

Sophie nodded. "They need you. That's good."

He shot her a glowing smile; the kind of smile that used to make her quiver, a smile she hadn't seen for months. '*Evacuated*', '*in a few days*' and '*England*' hung like smoke in the air. He leaned forward, excited. "I'm on logistics—managing the convoys and implementing the embarkation at Sète."

He kissed her lips. "You have to be ready, day or night—and there will be chaos when you get to the port. They're expecting thousands of soldiers and refugees." He gave her a contrite look. "I'm sorry, but I have to go back to Agde early tomorrow."

Sophie, eyes glistening with excitement, gave him an encouraging nod. "I understand, *miláčku*. Pavel and I will be ready.

I'll get some food to take with us—cans, sardines, salami, cheese." She laughed. "Not forgetting a can opener."

Madame Escobar arrived at the table with a barely warm beef roulade, salad, bread, and more wine. "Tell me one of your juicy stories, Monsieur Kohut," she said drawing up a chair. "You have so many … from your travels. I can tell you have a new one up your sleeve. It's better than listening to the radio at the café."

Willy studied her over the lip of his glass. *I'll miss the old lady.* "Indeed I have, Madame. We are leaving France—very soon. The French Army has capitulated. There will be an armistice, a new regime. In a day or two, the Kohut family will be on a boat for Britain."

Madame Escobar leaned across the table, eyebrows raised like exclamation marks. She filled her glass and clinked it against Willy's. "*Eh, bien, monsieur le soldat.* I am sad … but I wish you an easy journey." She turned toward Sophie. "*Les Boches* will not stay here forever … come back to see me after the war. If I'm still here." She dabbed her eyes with her kerchief. "I will miss your little one. He has curiosity and inner strength … and I still had much to teach him."

CHAPTER TWENTY-SEVEN

Convoy to Sète
South of France. June 1940

The morning of June 24, Sophie woke to the sound of revving engines and shouted commands. Curious about the noise, she dressed quickly, left Pavel with Madame Escobar and hurried to the square carrying the water buckets. On the way down the hill, she noted the usual blue haze on the distant hills: another torrid day.

In the town square, four motorcycles and nine canvas-covered Citroën trucks spewed black diesel exhaust. Dust hung in the air, stirred up by Czechoslovak soldiers in rough formation, each one carrying a bedroll, rifle, bayonet, pack, and food canister. Sophie guessed there were hundreds of them. She filled the water buckets, tense with excitement. Willy had said it would happen this way, at a minute's notice. Exhilarated, she carried the water back to the cottage. She was ready. There had not been much to pack, anyway. From now on, Madame Escobar would have to gather her own kindling.

Thirty-five minutes later, Willy arrived from Portel on an ancient Peugeot motorcycle. He rested it against a wall by the *Tabac* and ran up the hill to the cottage. Sophie was in the garden, packed and waiting. Pavel and Jo-Jo were at the hutches, opening and shutting the wire doors, cuddling baby rabbits.

"We've only ten minutes to get to the square," he said,

313

grabbing one of Sophie's string bags and Pavel's satchel of toys. "Say goodbye."

Jo-Jo and Pavel looked at him reproachfully, not saying anything.

Willy pumped Madame Escobar's hand and kissed her cheeks. "Thank you, Madame. We won't forget you. You have a good heart. May God bless you."

The widow blinked moist eyes, nodded and crossed herself.

Sophie could tell that Willy wanted to keep everything unemotional and practical with no time for lingering *adieux*.

"Put the rabbits back in their cages, children. *Allons-y*."

Sophie embraced Madame Escobar and lifted Pavel so he could kiss the widow goodbye. Willy led them down the hill to the square. Madame Escobar and Jo-Jo followed slowly. Sophie and Pavel and a handful of other Czechoslovak refugee families who had arrived from surrounding hamlets clustered around the fountain with their meager possessions, waiting for instructions. They watched the soldiers pass rifles, ammunition boxes and packs up to others in the back, shouting, joking, and cursing.

Willy took Sophie and Pavel to the back of the lead truck, pulled a roll of printed sheets from his tunic and handed Sophie a single page. "Instructions about the journey. Wait here. I've got to check names and do a head count. Don't worry, I'll be back."

As Willy walked away, Sophie saw that her truck was nearly full, soldiers mostly with their equipment, talking and smoking. The tailgate was down. She looked around her heart pounding. *How do I get up in the back with Pavel and all my stuff?*

"Need some help, *paní*?" A round-cheeked soldier helped Sophie and Pavel step on to an empty ammunition box and into the back of the vehicle. He handed up the suitcase and bags. Another soldier put them on top of the military packs, rifles, and metal ammunition boxes stacked in the middle of the floor. Sophie kept looking out of the back, hoping to see Willy again. Pavel snuggled in her arms, his eyes darting about at the noise and bustling activity. He held Furry Lion protectively against his chest.

When Willy returned, his khaki shirt drenched with sweat, he stopped at the tailgate to talk. Sophie had to lean down to hear him over the deafening noise.

"I'm sorry, I can't ride with you. I have to stay at the back of the convoy." He stepped up on the ammunition box, put his hands to her cheeks, rose up on his toes and kissed her gently on the mouth.

"How long will it take to get to where we are going?"

He took her hand and pressed it to his lips. "I'm not sure, sweetheart. Three hours, maybe more. The convoy has to move slowly—some trucks are carrying explosives and ammunition. We'll make a stop at Lespignan, a little town about two hours' ride from here, at about eleven. Other regiments will join us there. We'll eat, and then form a long convoy. I suppose it will be mid-afternoon by time we get to Sète."

Sophie stroked his cheek. "But, you'll be there to help us, won't you—when we get to the ship?"

Willy gave her a hesitant nod. He handed her a small cardboard square. "I expect so." He paused. "There are no tickets to get on board the ship, so don't lose this."

She studied the typewritten words: SOPHIE & PAVEL KOHUT. ADMIT TO SS NORTHERN FEN. Below was a scrawled signature: *Captain Novotný*.

She frowned. "SS *Northern Fen*?"

Willy grinned. "It's the name of the British ship. If I'm not there, get on board as soon as you can and find a comfortable place to sleep. They predict about four days' sailing. If I'm not there, ask for help. Kukulka will be around. He's sailing on your ship."

She gripped his hand as if she would never let go. "You too?"

"Don't worry. I'll find you and Pavel. Remember now—the *SS Northern Fen*, it has a British flag. The soldiers in this truck are boarding the same ship. Follow them." He gently pinched her chin. "Now, let me give Pavel a kiss."

Sophie leaned Pavel over the tailgate. Willy kissed his forehead and cheeks. "You are going on a big boat," he said. "Be a good boy and help *Maminko*."

A whistle blasted, the truck's gearbox coughed and screeched, and the vehicle rolled slowly forward. Willy walked behind it, waving goodbye, smiling. The driver of the following truck hit his klaxon, leaned out of the window and gave him the finger.

As the convoy rumbled out of the square, Sophie found some space to sit between the soldiers on a side bench and kept Pavel in her arms. In the dark interior, she saw him look anxiously from soldier to soldier. "Where are we going with the soldiers, Maman?"

"Like Papa said, to a town where we get on a big ship."

Sophie and Pavel were the only civilians sharing the back of the truck. One of the soldiers, squat and ugly, shoved someone else aside and sat down next to her. "I'm Bohumir Serbin," he said with a leering smile, "one of the famous *Španěláci*—soldier comrades from the Spanish war." He grabbed her hand and pulled her close. "A pleasure to ride with you. Was that your husband checking the trucks—a bit bald on top? A Yid?"

Sophie jerked her hand back and shifted away. This man was rude, offensive and he smelled unwashed.

Serbin sneered. "He's just a volunteer private, isn't he? What's he doing runnin' this convoy?"

Sophie tightened her fists. "My husband's useful. He speaks perfect French." She wanted to say, "because he's clever and I love him," but didn't.

How could she make Serbin go away or stop talking to her? She moved Pavel off her lap, handed him his fire engine and Furry

Lion and squeezed him down between her and Serbin. "Perhaps you would like to play with my son?" she said. Pavel looked up, and with an inviting smile showed Serbin his Furry Lion. "You play with me?" he said in Czech. The *Španěláci* grunted, spat on the floor and turned away. The other soldiers grinned.

After a hot and jolting journey, lasting nearly two hours, the convoy reached the village of Lespignan and parked on a soccer field—goal posts, sandy gravel dotted with clumps of dry grass. The soldiers were ordered to unload their equipment, Sophie's suitcase included, and stack everything by one of the goal posts. She wandered about the field holding Pavel's hand, looking for Willy, and ended up at the temporary field kitchen set up underneath an ancient-looking almond tree. The menu was chalked on a board: horse meat stew, *knedlíky* dumplings, and grapes. With another family, they sat on army blankets eating stew. Sophie wondered what their ship would be like. How would they be fed and where would they sleep?

At Pavel's urging, she found a small clearing behind some brambles where he went to the toilet. As helped him, she wondered what the bathrooms would be like on the boat … with so many extra people. One thing was certain, she needed to be prepared and food was a priority. She and Madame Esco had managed to pack some cheese, bread and ham into one of the string bags and, stupidly, she had left the other one on the fountain steps in Sillat. There was still a chance; she had overheard someone saying that the village was just down the road.

Sophie noticed an old man who was gathering some kind of greenery at the bottom of a hedge. Close by, four small goats with clanking bells on their collars nibbled at the hedge's branches. "Excuse me. Is it far into the village? I want to buy some food."

He straightened up slowly and pointed to a church tower above a cluster of tiled roofs. "There is an *épicerie* near the church—better be quick," he quavered, clutching his basket as if he was afraid she would steal it. "It closes for lunch."

Half running, half walking, with Pavel trailing, she reached the grocery with a few minutes to spare and spent her remaining francs on another string bag, food and as many cans of condensed milk as she could carry. They walked slowly back to the convoy while Pavel skipped along, carrying his bag of toys and licking a melting ice-cream. Chocolate drips spattered his shorts and sandals. Sophie didn't care. In Sillat, she had given up on keeping him clean and tidy.

By now, a juggernaut of trucks, motorcycles, mobile artillery and a mass of soldiers and officers filled the soccer field. Sophie was reassured to see there were a few women and children. If the boat journey was hard and long, they would be able help each other. She took Pavel back to where they ate lunch and sat on the blanket waiting for Willy.

"I knew I'd find you," said Willy, turning off the engine of his motorcycle and taking off his leather helmet. He smiled and hugged her. "Everything's going to plan."

He kissed Pavel, who clung to Sophie and was quiet and wide-eyed. "You've been food shopping. That was resourceful. Good thinking. We're leaving in a few minutes." Fifteen minutes later, he helped her and Pavel climb into the back of another truck. This one had upholstered benches. Then he was gone.

Sophie and Pavel dozed, swaying shoulder to shoulder with fourteen soldiers who slept, chatted, or shared wine bottles. Shortly after two o'clock, the convoy rumbled into Sète and proceeded along the Boulevard Camille Blanc. The trucks halted in a small square at the entrance to a long stone jetty.

In staggered succession, the trucks disgorged soldiers who began to unload luggage, equipment, packs, and weapons. Surrounded by noise and activity and holding Pavel's hand tight,

Sophie looked around, hoping, to spot Willy. There were fewer trucks than when they had left Lespignan. "What happened to the rest of the convoy?" she asked the French driver of her truck, wondering if Willy was somewhere else in the port.

"We were split into two sections, Madame. This is the Quai Pierre Paul de Riquet. The other trucks are at the Bassin Orietti."

"Our boat is the *Northern Fen*."

He opened the door, and checked a sheet of paper taped to the dashboard. Looking around with some hesitation, he said, "*Eh, bien, oui. Northern Fen…* I think you go that way, to the end of the quay. You must get there the best you can. I'm supposed to stay here."

Sophie and Pavel mingled with a crowd of civilians, hurrying along the jetty past brightly painted fishing boats, carrying bags and suitcases. She half-carried, half-dragged her suitcase and with the other hand she held her purse and the heavy string bags. It was hot, and when she glimpsed the greasy-gray water of the harbor, full of debris, she remembered with longing the deliciously cold water of the hidden stream at the bottom of Monsieur Robineau's vineyard.

Pavel followed her with his bag of toys. He kept stopping. "I'm tired, Maman. It's too hot. Pick me up. Where are we going? I want Papa."

Sophie's blouse and skirt clung uncomfortably to her skin, adding to her aggravation at Pavel's whiny voice. Get on the boat as soon as you can, Willy had said. *Where was that damned boat?* She looked at the people around her, many unkempt and in worn clothes. Her heart quickened with fear. So many desperate faces. She tried to steel herself, be practical, tough.

CHAPTER TWENTY-EIGHT

Embarkation
June 24th, 1940

Sophie and Pavel were swept in the same direction by a noisy multitude of people—soldiers, men in civvies, and families with battered suitcases and ratty bundles. The smell of diesel and rotten fish assaulted her nostrils and her stomach heaved, making her swallow repeatedly. A young Czechoslovak soldier offered to carry her suitcase. Another one carried her string bags holding the food and cans of condensed milk. She smiled her thanks.

"That's your boat, the SS *Northern Fen*, up ahead," the suitcase-carrier said after he looked at her boarding card. "We're assigned to the SS *Swithun* further along the dock. We'll help you part of the way." He squinted at Pavel as they trudged on. "Have you been on a big ship before, little man?"

Pavel shook his head and stared back, one hand clamped on to his mother's skirt, the other clutching his toys.

"Good-bye, *paní*," the soldiers called out as they veered away. "You might have trouble boarding, even with that card. There must be thousands of people here. If you can't get on, there are two ships further along the quay: the *Swithun* and the *Darwen*. *Hodně štěstí.* Good luck."

Sophie winced as the suitcase and two bags banged against her shins. The discomfort was nothing compared to her fear of being unable to board the ship. As the crowd thickened, she stopped to catch her breath. She lifted Pavel so he could see the stern of the ship above people's heads. "Look at the name. That's our ship, *Northern Fen*. She'll take us to England where *babička* and *dědeček* live."

"What is England, Maman? We live with Esco. I don't want to go on that ship." He paused. "Who is *babička* and *dědeček*?"

"No more questions, *miláčku*. Soon Papa will find us. We have to look out for him." For a moment she and Pavel stood still, a tiny island surrounded by a sea of people. Pavel frowned and dropped his bag on the ground. The corners of his mouth drooped: his bad-temper sign. Maybe a tantrum was brewing. Somewhere, Willy was waiting for them. She needed help.

About a hundred meters from the ship, the crowd slowed to a clumsy, chaotic halt. Sophie watched with alarm as people bumped into each other and either glared, cursed or apologized. Peering between the bodies, Sophie saw that progress forward was blocked by a barrier made of ropes and posts. Beyond it, an enclosure, filled with soldiers waiting to board, stretched across the dock to the side of the ship, forming a secure entry zone.

At the side of the ship, armed French sentries stood impassively on either side of two gangplanks. In front of them three men sat at a collapsible desk. Like a jack-in-the-box, a Czechoslovak officer popped into view above the carpet of military caps and helmets. He lifted a megaphone to his lips but the crowd noise was deafening. Two shots cracked the air—creating instant quiet. She heard him clearly now, first in Czech and then in French.

"Attention, all those boarding the *Northern Fen*. Military personnel get priority. After that, we'll board civilians with special permits. Only then—if there is space, will other civilians be permitted to board, once their identification papers have been checked. This must be done calmly and without disturbance. Anyone causing trouble will be turned away."

Voices were raised. "Can we get on if we pay?" "How much?" "Have pity on us old ones." "My wife needs a doctor." "What will the Boches do to us if we get left behind?"

The complaints swelled around Sophie, a cacophony of fear and frustration, full of panic and anger. She assumed from people's grim faces that most of them had no boarding permits. She tightened her fingers around the card Willy had given her.

The officer fired again. As soon as the noise died down, he addressed the soldiers. "Men, the coal freighter you are about to board has a small crew. Water and food supplies for so many passengers will be limited. Discipline is essential. After you embark, obey the crew and our Czechoslovak officers. By order of the British Navy, except for armed officers, no weapons are permitted on board." He lowered the megaphone and disappeared into the crowd.

With Pavel holding on to her skirt and with baggage in both hands, Sophie slowly pushed and shoved her way close to the rope fence. In one corner of the enclosure, separated from the crowd and guarded by stony-faced gendarmes in *képis* and white gloves, soldiers, under the supervision of officers, were throwing their rifles, bayonets and side-arms onto piles of weapons. They joined a winding line that ended at the desk by the ship's gangplank. Two officials checked each man's identity. Sophie presumed that she and Pavel would go through the same process. She just had to be patient and humor Pavel.

Sophie picked him up and showed him the red marine flag flapping above the *SS Northern Fen's* stern rail. A strong breeze had sprung up and she noticed dark clouds piled up in the sky. She thought it meant rain. In Berlin she had once seen a movie where a sailing ship was caught in rainstorm. People were shipwrecked. It wouldn't be like that on this *SS Northern Fen*. The ship was built of metal and had engines.

At that moment, she felt a firm grip on her upper arm. A hoarse voice vibrated in her ear. "What a wonderful surprise, Sophie."

She swiveled in a pulse of fearful recognition. The words were iron spikes driven into her heart. She went cold. This was not possible. "You! Lessig. How?"

"Yes, my beautiful Sophie. I made it to France—one of the clever ones who fooled the Gestapo in Prague." His eyes darted from side to side, as if he were alert for danger. "I'm the worse for wear, but surviving—in spite of your husband trying to shoot me. Where is the charming Willy? Not too close by, I hope."

To Sophie's eyes, Hans Lessig hadn't changed much. He still looked like a stork, stooped and hunched with a thatch of greasy corn-colored hair and horn-rimmed glasses. In Prague, he had always worn beautiful suits made of fine British wool and tailored with a dragontail buttonhole—gifts from Willy in exchange for mentioning the Kohut store in his newspaper column. In those days, a suede leather briefcase never left Lessig's side. Now he wore a coarse shirt, shapeless trousers and sandals and carried a tattered canvas bag slung over his bony shoulder.

She hardly knew what to say. "Why—are you here?" she stuttered, aware that Pavel was watching with alert eyes, as though he sensed her fear. She could not think clearly, but she knew she had to get rid of Lessig. If he came across Willy what would they say—or do—in the middle of this crowd, with armed guards everywhere? If they created a scene they might be arrested and she and Pavel would not be allowed on the ship.

"Get away from me, you bastard," she exclaimed. Three soldiers passing by paused for a moment, turned their heads towards her shrugged and walked on. She breathed a sigh of relief. *I can't afford to cause any trouble, not now.*

Lessig gripped her arm so tightly she gasped. "I expect you

have a permit to get on this boat," he said, pulling her close again. "I know your husband. He will have made sure there's no trouble for you getting on board."

Sophie dropped her suitcase and bags and tried to pry his fingers off her arm. People looked curiously at her as they passed by. "Leave me alone, Hans, or I'll scream." She prayed her threat would be enough to get rid of him.

He laughed. "Screaming won't help. Everyone is shouting and arguing around here. Look, I'm not asking much. When it's your turn to be checked, tell the guards that I'm a cousin, part of your family—and that I got away from the Nazi occupation of Paris." His voice had a wheedling tone. "Just tell the guards I'm family and you want me with you on the boat. I promise I'll never bother you again."

Sophie felt Pavel release her hand and, horrified, saw him move toward Lessig.

"*Aagh, Kurva*," the man grunted, jack-knifing down to rub his leg where Pavel had just kicked him.

"*Sâle monsieur*," the boy said, glaring at him after retreating behind Sophie's legs.

She grabbed her bag of milk cans and whipped it into Lessig's groin. Not waiting to see its effect, she grabbed her luggage, pushing and elbowing through the throng of people to the checkpoint. "Stay close, *Pavelko*." At the checkpoint, she glanced back to see if Lessig was still there. He had disappeared.

Ten minutes later they were at the narrow entrance to the embarkation gangway, guarded by a Czechoslovak corporal, a French harbor official, and a *milice* policeman. "Is this the *Northern Fen*, please?" Sophie asked, putting on her calmest face. She held out her card.

One of the gendarmes gave her a charming smile as he

glanced at the card and her French identification document. "*Mais oui*. Please proceed, Madame. Take care with the little one on the gangplanks. They are not very firm."

Sophie was about to step forward, documents in hand, when Lessig reappeared beside her and slung an arm around her shoulders. She froze. Every muscle in her body wanted to lash out at him; her fingers yearned to rip at his face.

"Keep your mouth shut," Lessig muttered in her ear, "or your boy gets a beating." He smiled obsequiously at the gendarme. "Please forgive us, Monsieur," he said in stumbling French. "She is my cousin. I just arrived from Paris. We are family." He pointed a bony finger. "See that terrible scar on the child's neck. An emergency operation. He's still very weak. My cousin needs me to help look after him on the boat."

Sophie was speechless. The gendarme nodded sympathetically and as Lessig stepped forward to lead the way, Sophie swung her bag into his groin. Lessig doubled up and she rushed past the guards, with Pavel holding on to the hem of her dress. "That man is no relative of mine," she shouted. "He doesn't have a pass. Don't let him on the boat."

Inside the enclosure, Sophie and Pavel, with several other women and children, all wearing hats or scarves against the sun, lined up at the desk. As they shuffled forward the officials skimmed through their belongings and waved them through. On the quay, held back by the enclosure ropes and guards, people were still shouting, waving their arms, begging and pleading.

Sophie was astonished at the small size of the ship's deck, already packed with soldiers. They stood or sat in rows, leaning against their packs, hands around their knees—most of them smoking. She wondered—in fact, dreaded—how she and they would manage, confined for four days on this little ship.

Making her way to one of the lifeboats, an area that seemed

less crowded, she half-skidded on the greasy deck, grasped a railing, and noticed that the palms of her hands were black. "Don't touch anything," she said to Pavel, who trotted dutifully behind her. "Everything here is dirty."

Two soldiers helped her navigate through a narrow gap between the lifeboat, past coiled ropes and a couple of hatches. "Here's a place, *paní*. There's some shade." They cleared rags and a bucket off a small bench and stuffed her suitcase and bags underneath.

"Thank you, gentlemen." Holding Pavel, she found a rag to wipe off the coal dust and sat on the bench. She fanned herself, trying to gather her wits, wondering what to do next. At least, she and Pavel were on board the ship. The prospect was daunting; her first sea journey—and she would be one of only a handful of women and children, among maybe a thousand men. One thought bothered her more than anything else, the possibility that Lessig might find his way aboard the *Northern Fen*.

She chuckled and turned to look at Pavel sitting beside her on the bench, then laughed outright.

Pavel smiled uncertainly. "Maman, why are you so happy? You were angry before."

"I'm happy because we are on the boat and I saw you kick that nasty man. You were very brave." She smiled, stroking his hair. "I'm happy because we are safe—and now, it's time for us to look for Papa."

CHAPTER TWENTY-NINE

SS Northern Fen
South of France. June 24th, 1940

From time to time, Sophie scanned the quay, at the same time keeping an eye on Pavel. He played at her feet with his toys and scraps of wood he had found under the bench. Whenever a soldier passed by, she asked if he knew her husband and had seen him—Private Kohut, short and wearing glasses. She had a growing premonition that Willy wouldn't show up.

Nearly half an hour passed. The deck grew ever more congested. The shade from the funnel shifted off the bench and Sophie, feeling the sun's heat, gave up. She pulled Pavel to his feet. "Come, *Pavelko*. It's too hot and busy here. Let's find somewhere better, a place to keep our things, where we can stretch out and sleep."

"*Non, Maman.* I made a castle. It's not finished."

She closed her eyes, discomfited by his resistance. "Please, darling, do as you're told."

He glared and took a swipe at his castle which collapsed. "*Non.*"

"Do you want to be left here on your own?"

He blinked tears. "*Non, Maman.*"

"Well then, come on."

Winding her way past soldiers, stacked boxes and storage bins, Sophie walked toward the bow of the ship, carrying their luggage. Twice, she stopped to rest and shake the soreness out of her arms. Her back throbbed from the bumpy ride in the truck. She half-closed her eyes against the suffocating heat and took a deep, exhausted breath. So much had happened. They needed a place to sleep.

*　*　*

At the wheelhouse of the *Northern Fen*, Captain Francis Nesbitt, a briar pipe clenched between his teeth, leaned on the window ledge watching the embarkation. He had been in the merchant navy most of his life, and for the last ten years his small freighter had clawed its way back and forth around the coast of England, carrying coal from Newcastle to London and Southampton.

In the past few weeks, as the war turned against the Allies, he was assigned to transport coal to Marseille. Now the British Admiralty had requisitioned his ship and ordered him to pick up twelve hundred foreign soldiers and refugees, and transport them to Gibraltar.

Nesbitt relit his pipe and ran a jaundiced eye over the deck. He had an extra boss now—in the shape of Captain Colville, master of the destroyer *HMS Velox*, Royal Navy, and, for the first time in his life, he shared the command of his own vessel with an army officer—Lieutenant Novotný, a bloody foreigner.

The *Northern Fen* had been built to carry cargo, not passengers. There was a one-ton derrick, two lifeboats, ten life-jackets, and no safety ropes on the ladders. The railings around the deck consisted of stanchions supporting rusty horizontal bars. The ship had one five-bunk and two two-bunk cabins for the crew, a tiny galley, and a couple of heads next to the captain's cabin. On this journey, Captain Nesbitt mused, his passengers would have to live on deck or suffer in the hold: a toxic, dusty place, as hot as hell, that still held a few inches of coal.

Captain Nesbitt's most immediate concern was whether the ship's toilet facilities would cope with the demand. In addition to two interior heads, two new wooden toilet sheds had been constructed in the Marseille shipyard and bolted onto the deck—one on the port and one on the starboard side. Rubber effluent pipes hung down outside the hull, spilling sewage into the seawater. With a weather forecast of strong northeasterly winds and twelve hundred humans peeing, crapping and vomiting incessantly, Nesbitt expected nothing less than hell at sea.

There was a rap on the wheelhouse door. It was Lieutenant Novotný, commander of the Czechoslovak troops on board. He spoke fractured English. "Excuse, pliss. You have news from the British destroyer? We leave soon, yes?"

Nesbitt sucked on his pipe and blinked assent. "That's right. We leave sharpish. There's a storm coming, headed for somewhere between the Balearics and the Pyrenees." He pointed with his pipe stem. "Ugly sky up there."

Novotný frowned. "Sharpish? I not know word. We get big trouble if we stay here. Refugee people wish to get on ship. They very angry."

Captain Nesbitt nodded. "Can't blame 'em, they're panicked at being left behind." He rang the telegraph bell and called the engine room. Leaving the quay would be a slow and delicate maneuver. The French port's tugs were now forbidden to assist Allied shipping.

* * *

Sophie and Pavel reached the bow where the anchor chain ran down through a hole in the deck and a long-barreled gun surrounded by rusted armored plates was mounted on a square platform. Sophie's heart leaped when she saw an oblong of shade behind the gun's bulk.

A thin-faced man in a torn blue jacket and canvas pants leaned against the gun's platform. He was bare-foot, a pair of boots set beside him. He rolled a cigarette from a small tin box and peered up at her from under a flat cap. Sophie noticed that his bare feet were filthy.

"Ullo, Missis," he said. He patted the platform beside him with an oil-stained hand. "You lookin' for a spot? I'm leavin' in a minit, but before I go—I could fix up a bit more shade for a nice-lookin' lady like you."

It sounded like English to her but was unlike anything she had learned in school or seen in the films at the *Biograf* in Prague. Overcoming her apprehension at the man's appearance, Sophie tried her English. "Pliss, mister. You are sailor? Is good here?" She pointed to where he was sitting.

The sailor's cigarette stuck to his lower lip as he talked. "Could be, missis. Might get cool at night though."

Sophie gave him a thank-you smile and spread out the cotton blanket that Madame Escobar had given her as a parting gift. Pavel lay down on the blanket and she delved into her bag for a bottle of water. She sat cross-legged and watched him drink, water dribbling down his chin. Maybe she would have to look elsewhere. There was shade, but only enough to protect their heads.

The sailor hauled a square of tarpaulin out from behind the anchor winch and lashed its corners between the gun barrel and the rail, creating a larger rectangle of shade a few feet above them. "There y'are missis. All ship-shape and cool. Make yerself comfy before somebody grabs it," he said. He slipped on his boots and bent down to tie the bootlaces. "An' keep an eye on that kid of yours. You're close to the railing an' if the sea gets rough, you and yours might end up sliding into you know what."

"I'd better be off ter check the old tub's innards."

Sophie pointed to the gun and the tarpaulin, her eyebrows raised questioningly. She pointed to herself. "What we do if you want shoot?"

"Bloody useless," he replied. "Bofors … breech-loader, thirty years old. They mounted it a few days ago in Marseels. We don't even know if the bugger works." He waved a farewell hand. "By the bye, I'm Sid Latcher, ship's engineer at yer service. Ship's a bloody zoo, ain't it? I'm orf then. Cheerio."

Two hours slipped by; a stiff, humid breeze sprung up, blowing Sophie and Pavel's hair every which-way. They used food cans to secure the blanket they sat on. The sky was filled with fast-moving, dark clouds, tinted orange at the edges. Sophie kept a hopeful eye out for Willy, but she found it difficult, with so many identical uniforms milling about. The *Northern Fen's* deck was so full of people that the officers—like Sergeant Kukulka, whom she had spotted because of his size—were sending more and more men down iron ladders into the hold. She heard one passing soldier say that the longer they stayed in port the more likely the French authorities would put a stop to the whole operation. She felt agitated, unable to relax wondering what was going to happen, wanting the ship to leave, but not before Willy found them

Pavel and then Sophie eventually drifted off to sleep. They were woken by throbbing engines, raised voices, and the odor of burnt diesel from the smoke stack. Sophie sat up. Nothing had changed. People yelled across the deck, soldiers argued over space and officers barked out orders. She overheard the crew being asked in Czech, Polish and Hungarian for directions and advice. The British seamen shrugged and shook their heads.

A middle-aged refugee, looking for a place to settle, passed by the gun and told Sophie, in Slovak, that a military "Goulash

Kitchen" had been set up in the hold.

"I had some of their goulash," he confided, "canned beef and rice and plenty of onion and paprika. But, it's terribly hot down there," he told Sophie. "Not a good place for your little boy."

"But I have a tip for you, beautiful lady," he said glancing at the food cans in her string bag. "I found a small kitchen close to here. It has a stove. A sailor chased me out. He said it was for the crew, passengers not allowed." He winked and patted her shoulder. "I think sailors will say yes if *you* ask them if you can use it."

Sophie was surprised at Pavel's calmness. He seemed quite unafraid and was intensely absorbed by what was happening around them. From the moment they walked up the *Northern Fen's* gangway, he peppered Sophie with questions. "Maman, can we go down the steps into the bottom of the ship? Why is everyone shouting, saying they want to get on? When will the boat start? Where is Papa?" She tried to answer but she could not summon the energy—even her drive to find Willy had faded into resignation.

As dusk fell, a soldier she recognized from Sillat passed by. She asked him for a favor—to keep an eye on their possessions for a few minutes while she took Pavel to the railings in a last attempt to catch a sight of Willy before dusk fell. It would be difficult; the din on the quay and on the ship was louder: megaphone announcements, shouted commands and engines revving as trucks began to leave. The crowd was still there: men, women, and children pressed against the restraining ropes and gates, reaching out arms, crying, begging the guards to be allowed on board. "Save us, for God's sake. We've lost everything. Have pity."

Pavel put his hands to his ears and looked at his mother, wide-eyed. She couldn't tell if he was fearful, overwhelmed or both. The gangplank area had been cleared and the military police and French gendarmes were active, striding up and down the enclosure ropes with drawn pistols. They shouted at the people straining against the ropes and fences.

Sophie sensed an impending crisis. She feared the crowd's energy and desperation would explode into violence.

"Look hard, *Pavelkin*. Remember, Papa is in uniform."

Dockworkers prepared to release the mooring lines holding the ship against the quay. Sophie felt the ship vibrate more strongly. Willy was nowhere in sight. She and Pavel would have to fend for themselves, for however long the journey took. As she scanned the deck and the quay, near to desperation, she noticed another freighter, moving past the *Northern Fen*, heading out to sea. Its deck swarmed with soldiers, waving and shouting goodbye. *Na shledanou ... Adieu la France.*

At a blast from the ship's horn, the crowd rushed toward the side of the ship, shoving the gendarmes aside. Sophie understood their desperation.

Pavel tugged at her dress. "Pick me up."

Sophie held him in her arms unable to tear her gaze away. "They're trying to get on the ship, darling."

The leading edge of the crowd, mostly men, began to climb the ship's guard rails that stood eight to ten feet above the jetty. Some threw their belongings on to the deck. "Let us get on the ship," they shouted. "See, our luggage is already on board."

Soldiers on the boat threw the refugees' luggage and packages back on to the quay. Suitcases split open, strewing clothes on the cobbles.

Other refugees on the quay, close to the waist of the ship, built a mound of their bags and suitcases, climbed up and reached for the ship's ropes and railings.

Sophie, with Pavel in her arms and surrounded by soldiers, watched from the deck, mesmerized and close to tears. Willy told her before they left Sillat that Churchill had ordered this evacuation to save foreign soldiers who would fight with the British. Rescuing civilians was laudable but discretionary—nothing could endanger the military purpose. She felt helpless, heartbroken for the hundreds, maybe even thousands who would be left behind, especially mothers and children.

Helped by some soldiers, three men scrambled over the railings onto the deck. This encouraged others on the quay to keep trying. Shouts, scuffles and blows were exchanged in an attempt to get a solid handhold.

"Sophie, help me."

The high-pitched man's voice caught Sophie's attention. She knew instantly it was Hans Lessig and searched the faces of those trying to board. She saw him, pale and pitiful—one arm latched around the base of a stanchion, fighting the others off, swinging a foot up to get a hold on the edge of the deck. "Sophie. Help me."

Sophie's mind was in turmoil, unsure whether or not she should do something to save a man she detested and feared. Yes, Lessig was vile but she could not watch and do nothing. "Don't move, *Pavelkin*," she said, and turned to two soldiers close by. She pointed. "Please, help that man. The one with the yellow hair."

Warning shots rang out from the quay. Sophie heard a booming, amplified voice, repeating, "Get away from the boat. Leave the boarding area immediately."

Lessig gave her a despairing look, lost his grip, and cried out. He disappeared just as three men reached for his arms. For a second, she saw two bony hands, fingers outstretched. She pulled her hands tight into her stomach and shut her eyes.

The crowd on the quay and the passengers on the boat fell silent. On the deck, people looked around unsure of what was happening. Sophie, close to the railing, couldn't see Lessig anywhere. She lifted Pavel up again, holding him tight against her chest. He was trembling, wide-eyed.

Passengers leaned over the ship's railings and pointed down between the stone quay and the rusty side of the ship. In a strip of dirty-green water, Sophie saw half submerged bags and bobbing suitcases. Five or six people thrashed about in the oily water, calling for help. What looked like blood covered the chest of a gray-haired woman. Her limbs twitched and jerked. A dinghy with two fishermen at the oars moved toward the flailing refugees.

Still in Sophie's arms, Pavel pulled her chin around to face him. "Why are they swimming, Maman? Why are the suitcases in the water?" His voice was anxious, fearful.

"It was an accident, darling. They fell trying to get on the ship. They'll be allright. The fishermen will get them out." Where was Lessig?

"What a fucking mess," said one of the soldiers she had asked for help. With a jolt, she recognized him—Serbin. He was so close she could smell his tobacco breath and see his dark soulless eyes. He touched her arm. "Come, *pani*. I'll take you and the boy somewhere safe."

She shook her head soundlessly. This man made her afraid and turned her stomach to water. She heard and recognized another voice, deep and hoarse. Sergeant Kukulka—at last, someone she knew. He put a bear paw on her shoulder. "*Servus, pani* Kohutová. I hope the poor buggers who fell in can swim. I can't."

She clasped Kukulka's hand in both of hers. "Thank God you're here. Have you seen Willy? He said he would find us here."

The Sergeant grinned, squeezed Pavel's cheek gently and took him out of Sophie's arms. "No need to worry, *pani*. I'm sure your husband is safe. Last I heard, about an hour or so ago, he was assigned to the *SS Darwen* along with the first regiment who just arrived from Béziers. Willy asked me to look out for you. He said he loved you and he was sorry he couldn't be here. He'll see you at the next port."

Sophie gasped in relief. She *would* see Willy again—in Gibraltar. Earlier, on board, she overheard scraps of conversation. The *Northern Fen* was heading for Gibraltar and the trip might last four days. At least, she knew that they were all going to the same place.

"Look." Kukulka, pointed to the two fishermen in the dinghy. Rowing past bobbing shirts, jackets, trousers and dresses that looked eerily like corpses, they half-dragged the survivors into the boat—four of them, still moving arms and legs.

Sophie let out a gasp. A man's body floated face-down. Tangles of straw-colored hair rippled like seaweed in the blood-tinged water. It was Lessig. Her thoughts scrambled. Horror, pity—and relief.

"That dead fellow," said Kukulka. "He was the one hanging on to the railing—begging for help. He must have bashed his head in on one of those pilings."

A sob caught in Sophie's throat when she saw Pavel's face buried in the crook of Kukulka's shoulder.

"This little one saw a lot of what was going on," the sergeant said, his expression conveying sympathy. "Kids shouldn't see such things."

Shaking, she took Pavel into her arms. She felt her tears run. "I know, I'm sorry—I knew that dead man. He asked me to help him get over the railing … I couldn't do it."

With the shock of Lessig's death, Sophie felt a great weight lifted from her shoulders. The threat to her marriage was over. She was ready now, as best she could, to put up with the discomfort and problems that would surely occur on this overcrowded ship—and Willy would be waiting for them in Gibraltar.

From the wheelhouse, Captain Nesbitt had seen and heard enough. The dead and injured were lying on the quay and the last thing he wanted was to be caught up in the bureaucracy of a French port authority investigating a disaster. He triggered three shrill blasts of the ship's whistle, rang the telegraph handle to 'SLOW AHEAD,' and put his lips to the speaker tube. "Jump to it, lads. We're off."

CHAPTER THIRTY

Storm
Mediterranean. June 25th, 1940

As night fell, the wind strengthened, whipping the sea into white-capped waves illuminated by the ship's deck lights. The *Northern Fen* plowed on clanking and creaking, pounding against the waves. The crew roped tarpaulins over the piles of luggage and military packs. The rain and sea-spray turned the coal dust on deck into a slick slurry.

Most of the passengers retreated into the steamy, cramped hold, although they still had to use the toilets on deck. Some people, like Sophie, stayed on deck, sheltering under tarps against the wind and the rain. Ensconced with Pavel at the base of the Bofors gun, the deck was better than the stinking hold.

She huddled with him on their blanket, retching and groaning. Their once secure spot exacted a stomach-churning penalty as the ship smacked through the waves with an up-and-down, rolling motion. It was too dark, and dangerous to look for someplace else. They were stuck. She did her best to stay awake to make sure Pavel was safe and that he did not get too wet from the rain that forced its way under the edge of the tarpaulin. Eventually, after an hour or so, her lids drooped. In spite of the ship's erratic motion, exhaustion pushed her into sleep.

An overcast dawn revealed endless dirty-green water topped

by whitecaps. The movement of passengers up and down the gangways and the smell of coffee emanating from the Goulash Kitchen signaled breakfast. Sophie fed Pavel crackers, waiting for her stomach to calm and the rush for food to die down.

Venturing into the humidity of the hold, they ate soupy porridge and a slice of bread and jam. A perspiring server handed Sophie two tin mugs. "Water," he said, hardly bothering to look up. "We've only a limited supply. Too many people."

Sophie looked at him, surprised. Was something wrong? They had only been at sea for half a day and a night and water was already rationed? She gave the server her sweetest smile. "If we drink our water straight-away, would you be kind enough to give us a little more? My little one is terribly thirsty. Please, why isn't there enough water?"

He shrugged and without a word refilled the mugs.

After breakfast, with the ship rolling in the wind, she and Pavel struggled across the crowded deck to their home in the bow. Sergeant Kukulka appeared with a green tint to his face and sat down beside them. Sophie noticed that the long white scar on his cheek had turned gray. "I'd prefer hand-to-hand combat with Nazis," he groaned, "than sail in this shitty boat."

Sophie gathered Pavel into her lap, ignoring the Sergeant's curses. She had never been to sea and, so far, the experience was horrible. Her thinking scattered, full of fearful questions. How long will this storm last? What if the ship starts to sink? How good is the captain? Will we have enough food and water? How can Pavel and I bear another night like the last one? When am I going to stop retching?

They had to find a more sheltered place. She looked sideways at Sergeant Kukulka's gloomy face—maybe he would help her even though he looked awful. He was the only friendly person she knew on the ship. "Sergeant, Pavel and I can't spend another night next to this gun, trying sleep and stay warm. Is there a way you could get your commander to find us somewhere sheltered that isn't sleeping on the coal? In Sète, I saw other women and children come on board. Where are they?" She thought of Serbin and the way he looked at her. Safer to be with other women.

Kukulka rose unsteadily to his feet. He gulped. "See what I can do."

As the morning progressed, the wind brought heavier rain and deep swells. In spite of the *Northern Fen's* violent motion, Sophie's nausea lessened and she managed to move about on the deck, holding Pavel's hand. He seemed brighter and asked questions about the ship and the sea: what things were called, how the engines worked, why there was so much wind and what made the waves big and frothy. At lunch-time, they again went down to the coal-scented hold—this time the meal was bean and horsemeat soup accompanied by a thick slice of good bread and a mug of water. That was where Kukulka found them.

"Some idiot passengers are panicking," he grumbled holding his metal canister out to be filled by a kitchen assistant. "They're afraid the ship is not strong enough and will sink in the heavy waves. Others say that they've see U-boat conning towers and want the British sailors to get the gun ready." He laughed sardonically. "Sad to say, some of these tremble-knee folk are soldiers. They're like kids afraid of the dark."

The ship shuddered and shook. Sophie grabbed at one of the safety ropes that had been strung at intervals across the hold. She held on to Pavel's collar with the other hand. "What if it's really true? About the U-boats. What can anyone do?"

Kukulka steadied her. "Nothing, *pani.* I expect these rumor-mongers are like you and me—never been at sea in a storm. Probably, never even been on a boat. Anyway, there's an English destroyer out there escorting our convoy, except we can't see it. They'll deal with the U-boats."

Sophie gave him a wan smile. "And what about somewhere for us to sleep tonight? Did you talk to anyone?"

Kukulka nodded. "That was why I came to find you. Lieutenant Novotný, Sergeant Svoboda and me discussed it with the English captain. The captain says that, to be safe with so many onboard, he must find shelter for the ship until the storm blows over. A delay of a day, maybe two. He offered the engineer's cabin for some of the women and kids—and the use of the indoor toilets. I got you and Pavel included."

"Thank you so much." Sophie smiled her gratitude, squeezing his beefy hand with both of hers and placing it against her cheek.

His face reddened. He withdrew his hand. "Don't overdo the thanks, *paní*. There'll be seven women in the cabin, including a woman with a new baby—her husband is dossed down in the hold. There are five kids as well. Only four bunks. So, some of you will have to sleep on the floor. Best I could do."

Sophie felt sad, guilty and relieved, all at the same time. She was lucky—too bad for the others down in the hold or exposed on deck. Pavel was her priority. His neck scar was still fragile and she was determined to stop him from breathing in coal dust. She had grown up in a Hungarian coal-mining town, Salgotarjan, where her father had been an engineer before he left for Berlin. She knew how coal dust destroyed people's lungs.

Half an hour later, in the assigned cabin, the women introduced themselves and shook hands. It was dirty and hot and reeked of cigarettes. Butt-ends were scattered all over the linoleum floor. There was no porthole to let in the sea air and the cupboards were full of the crew's clothes. The women exchanged names: Irina, Margit, Ana, Marika, Josefa, Ludmila, and Sophie. Ludmila's baby, Alice, wrapped in a towel, was four weeks old and named after the French midwife who had delivered her at Lapalme, where her husband had been billeted.

While the ship rolled and tilted, the children, including Pavel, sat on the floor looking at each other as if they were waiting for something, or a word for permission to play and talk.

Sophie watched Ludmila sit on one of the bunks trying to breastfeed her baby, remembering what it had been like for her with newborn Pavel in Košice—when she had no family to help her. As if called by her thought, Pavel stood up and came to watch the baby, who would not fasten on to the nipple and was making little crying noises. Sophie, seeing that the young mother was embarrassed and frustrated, was tempted to intervene. But she hardly knew the girl and one should not rush such sensitive moments. She smiled encouragingly. "Keep trying, Ludmila. Feeding can often be difficult. Both of you have to learn. How old are you?"

"Ni ... nineteen." The girl was thin and seemed very shy, with frizzy tangled hair and dark rings under her eyes. While the baby fed, she darted nervous glances at everyone in the cabin. "My husband found us a place on the coal but then he heard about this cabin and sent me here. I wanted to stay with him."

"It will be better for you here," said Sophie with an encouraging smile, resting her hand on Ludmila's shoulder. "Alice is too small and delicate to be breathing coal dust."

"We will help you," said Ana, a tall thin woman from Prešov. "Your husband can come and check on you from time to time. But he can't sleep here. No men allowed."

Ludmila shrank back. "Why are we on a German ship? I heard a sailor speak German." She started to tremble, mouthing silent words, nodding and shaking her head.

"German? No, it was English you heard," said Marika, a svelte, fair-haired woman, using a forearm to wipe sweat from her face. "This girl doesn't make sense," she murmured in Sophie's ear. "She's frightened and nervous. We should ask her husband if she is usually like this—or, perhaps it's a reaction to having a new baby in a strange place with only strangers to help her." She pulled Sophie to one side. "Let's hope she gets over it quick—for the baby's sake. Breast milk dries up when a mother is put through too much hardship."

Sophie gently massaged the new mother's shoulder. "We'll take care of you. I can hold your baby if you like."

Looking around anxiously, Ludmila passed the baby to Sophie, who cradled Alice in her arms. Pavel watched as she murmured endearments and kissed Alice's forehead and cheeks. He seemed fascinated and reached out to touch the baby's fingers.

Sophie smiled at him. "Such tiny, pretty hands. You were just like her after you were born."

"Give her back." Ludmila leaned over and jerked the baby out of Sophie's arms. "She's mine." Her eyes seemed glazed, unfocused; her lips quivering even after she fell silent.

The other women, surrounded by a gaggle of children, did not appear to notice. They were busy checking bunk mattresses, inspecting the sheets, pillows and blankets, and trying to work out who would sleep where. It was obvious that some would have to use luggage for pillows and coats for mattresses. What started out as a sensible discussion ended in shouting.

Sophie remembered what her father used to do when she and her brother Geza each wanted the same thing. "How about a coin toss for each bunk," she said. "And another for the cozy spots on the floor."

It took an hour of arguing to work out the solution—one adult per bunk, sleeping with one or two children head to toe. Ludmila and baby Alice would share a bunk with Ana who was the smallest of the adults. Everyone else would sleep on the floor.

"Well, now, at least we have a working agreement," said Marika with a satisfied grunt. "What about daytime arrangements for tomorrow? If the storm goes on, it will be chaos in here. Kids bouncing off the walls and not enough space."

Sophie nodded, marveling at how the children, including Pavel, unconcernedly played on the floor. Oblivious to the ship's pitching and swaying, they were talking and showing each other their toys. She was startled to see that Pavel had so effortlessly switched from French to Czech. "Perhaps," she said, " when morning comes, we should go back to our original places on the boat and reserve the cabin for sleeping at night? Except for Ludmila and baby Alice, they should stay here."

With a murmur of agreement everyone turned to Ludmila, who had put the baby up on her shoulder. She was expressionless, staring straight ahead as if she had not been listening.

"Aren't you pleased you can stay in the cabin tomorrow?" said Ana. "No need to join your husband on the coal or line up at the kitchen. We'll bring you food."

Ludmila blinked and her head jerked a little. "Thank you," she said, weakly.

Josefa, a heavily built blonde, lit a cigarette. "Well that's settled. Unless the storm gets worse or we sink." She laughed nervously.

Marika pointed a furious finger at her. "You, woman … no damned smoking. We have a month-old baby here. Go outside if you want to smoke."

By midnight, the storm had peaked, though at times the freighter climbed a swell and then crashed into a deep trough, decks awash with spray and foam. In the cabin, three of the women and nearly all the children were asleep. The rest of the adults dozed or chatted in low voices.

Sophie sat cross-legged on a folded blanket on the floor, elbows propped up on her knees, hands supporting her head. Exhaustion percolated her whole being and though her eyes were closed, she did not feel sleepy. Rather, there was an incredible tension in her chest; an intense, suffocation that made her want to throw herself on the floor and scream.

Pavel shifted in her lap and she felt his fingers prod her cheek. "I'm thirsty, Maman. I want some milk."

She took a deep breath, dreading the prospect of finding the galley and heating a can of milk while the ship was tossing and bucking. "How about some water, darling? This is not a good time to drink warm milk."

Pavel's mouth turned down and she saw the whites of his eyes. "I want milk." A tantrum was in the offing. She kissed his forehead.

"All right. Be a good boy. I won't be long."

Sophie stood holding her bag of condensed milk cans in the passageway outside the women's cabin. With the other hand, she held the railing trying to keep her balance. The crew's galley was nearby and she wanted to see if it was possible to use the stove.

A lean, stringy man in rain gear and a sou'wester backed out of a doorway, a thermos in either hand. Because of the easy way he rode the ship's motion she guessed he was one of the crew. At least, she knew now where the galley was.

He lifted a thermos in greeting and winked. "Cap'n's cocoa. Ladies' cabin, okay, Missus?"

Sophie caught the 'okay' and nodded. "Okay, yes. We not sleep good. Children sleep." She paused. "You sailor? Where do ship go?"

He grinned. "Right missus, I'm one of the crew. You asking me where we're headed?"

Sophie smiled hopefully, even though she wasn't quite sure

what he said.

"We're headed for shelter, missus. You get me? Soon we'll be safe." He looked at her string bag filled with cans and grinned. "Good luck with the stove." He jerked his curly head in the direction he had come from. "Galley's just behind me. There's a can-opener. Be careful with the matches."

Sophie understood very little—but when he said 'safe' it sounded like *sauf* in French. Did this mean they were going somewhere safe? Her tension eased and she smiled her thanks.

The sailor nodded as he eased his way past her. "Sorry, can't stay, the cap'n needs his cocoa. Bye."

In the galley, Sophie smiled to herself as she lit the small burner ring and heated the saucepan of milk. The ship was still rolling but she no longer struggled to stay upright. What was that phrase in novels about the sea: sea legs? Yes, she was getting her sea legs. And she had some good news for the other women. They were sailing to somewhere safe.

CHAPTER THIRTY-ONE

The Bay of Cadaqués
Coast of Spain. June 25th, 1940

At four in the morning, the SS *Northern Fen* reached the Bay of Cadaqués, dropping its anchor with an almighty clatter that woke everyone still asleep. As the engines fell silent and the ship rode the calm waters, a sharp half-moon revealed dark masses of shoreline and, in the distance, the twinkling lights of a village or small town.

At eight o'clock, Sophie and Pavel emerged from the cabin and ate breakfast on deck with some of the other women, watching the acrobatics of seabirds feeding on a nearby mussel-covered islet that consisted almost entirely of jagged granite. Stained white by seabird droppings, the largest rock was shaped like a giant shark's fin and at least thirty meters high.

Pavel gobbled up the remnants of Madame Escobar's oatmeal cake and drank the condensed milk Sophie had warmed in the crew's galley. Sophie was still queasy from the storm, but managed to swallow the gruel a friendly soldier had brought up from the hold. He said that the ship would be leaving for Gibraltar after the deck was cleaned up and sailors repaired some damage in the hold.

Pavel took Sophie's hand and walked round the deck, asking the usual stream of questions. "Where are we? When will we get off the boat, Maman? What is that big rock? Why do the birds scream?

"Let's just look for now, Pavel darling. It's so beautiful here."

347

Shading her eyes, Sophie recognized the same *garrigue* landscape that she had come to know around Sillat.

At the head of the bay, terraced vineyards and silvery olive groves climbed into the foothills. Even this far from shore, Sophie caught the whiff of wild vegetation, spicy and herbal. Whitewashed houses clustered along the shore, windows glittering in the early morning sun. A simple honey-colored church stood on a cliff-like promontory, dominating the small town.

"See that little town, *Pavelkin*?" She pointed. "So pretty, it's like a painting."

Pavel nodded, looking confused. "Why is our boat stuck by the rock, Maman?"

"Because of the storm, darling. I expect we will leave as soon as all the mess on the boat has been put right."

Sophie and Pavel watched the *Northern Fen's* decks buzz with activity. Soldiers, women, children, and other civilians were out and about, most of them smiling—an optimistic mood that turned to laughter at the sight of a number of half-naked soldiers relaxing in the sun. They had stripped off their sodden uniforms and undershirts and hooked them up to dry on parts of the ship's superstructure.

Crew members and teams of soldiers were busy cleaning up debris, reorganizing stacks of luggage and equipment, scrubbing the vomit-stained deck and hosing down the toilets with seawater. Every hatch and porthole was open, airing the ship

"Beautiful morning, *Paní* Kohutová," said Sergeant Kukulka, appearing at Sophie's bivouac. "That rock out there is incredible, isn't it?" He crouched down beside her.

"*Dobrý den*, Sergeant, nice of you to come and say hello. Why is our ship alone here? I thought we were in a convoy."

For a moment he squeezed his eyes shut, as if trying to remember something. "Something to do with territorial waters.

We should not be this close to Spain. Our destroyer escort is three or so kilometers away, waiting while we clean up. There was damage last night—we lost food and water." He pointed across the bay. "See that village? Our captain hopes they'll give us some supplies—we're short."

"How did all you ladies manage last night?" he said. "I had to use all my powers of persuasion to get you into that cabin."

Sophie took his hand and kissed it, tears coming to her eyes. "You are a good man. Thank you."

"Today will be different," Kukulka said brightly, picking up Pavel, who took the opportunity to study the tattoo on the sergeant's right arm and then check his scarred cheek with a forefinger. "Come on, little frog, let's look over the side and have a look at the bottom of the sea. It's so clear here, you can see everything— seaweed, black spiky things stuck to rocks, and even little fish swimming around."

Pavel smiled. "Yes, please *pane* Kulka."

Kukulka suspended Pavel by his belly over the guard rail so he could look down into the water. Pavel gasped in excitement. "I see everything like a window."

Half-amused, half-terrified, Sophie came to join them.

"Big rocks, Maman, and red stringy stuff like the rag Madame Escobar cleans the floor with—and white stars lying on the bottom." Pavel kicked his legs in delight. "And—there, there— shiny, little fish."

Sophie leaned over the railing. "Oh, my God, I can't believe it. Look, look, *Pavelkin*, over there, where I'm pointing. A creature with twisty legs, it's crawling on the bottom."

Kukulka grinned. "Is that some kind of crab? Shouldn't it have big claws?

Sophie laughed. "Obviously, Sergeant, you didn't go to the fish market in Agde. It's an octopus."

"What's an octopus, Maman?"

Sophie did a little demonstration dance by the railing, twining and twisting her arms through the air. "An octopus is a creature with twisty arms like mine. It has two big eyes and it squirts black ink at its enemies."

Kukulka guffawed. "You're putting me on, *paní* Kohutová. There's no creature that makes ink. Anyway, little frog, how about a ride around the ship—on my shoulders?" He lifted Pavel high in the air.

A hoarse voice sang out behind them. "Attention, we have visitors."

With Pavel on his shoulders, Kukulka accompanied Sophie towards the wheelhouse to get a closer look. Captain Nesbitt was staring through his binoculars. A seaman stood beside him, shading his eyes against the sun.

"Local boats," said the Captain. "Three of 'em. Lamps on the back for night fishing. Slow craft, not more than five or six knots. Front one's got three blokes in uniform—shiny black hats. Pistols, too." He swung his binoculars back to the first boat. "Fuck it—one of 'em has a machine gun. He punched one of his men on the arm. "Go check the Bofors in the bow, Kevin. See if she'll swing round on those boats. Take this key and unlock the ammo bin."

Sophie was close enough to hear his words. "The English captain says they have guns," she said to Kukulka in Czech. "He says to get our gun ready."

"*Kurva.*" Kukulka swore, unbuttoning the holster on his hip holster. He swung Pavel into Sophie's arms. "Here, take him."

"Those men are Spanish police," said one of the older Czechoslovak soldiers, standing nearby. Yellowed fingers anchored a glowing cigarette between his lips.

Sophie recognized the gaunt face from Sillat: Leo Povídka, the Communist commissar.

Povídka turned to Kukulka. "They will want to know why we are in Spanish waters." He flicked his cigarette over the railing. "Franco's men. We fought against them in Catalonia." He nudged the squat man standing next to him as if he needed his endorsement. "Boho and me were with the International Brigades." He looked closely at Sophie. "You are Kohut's woman, yes? I heard you speak English. Tell the ship's captain what I just said."

Stumbling with her words, Sophie tried to convey the essence of his message to Nesbitt. Lieutenant Novotný approached, tunic unbuttoned, a pistol stuck in his belt.

"Police or not, these fellows are a damned welcome sight," said one of the men wearing a cook's apron and hat. Sophie guessed he had come up on deck to watch the approaching flotilla. "We lost half our drinking water in the storm last night."

Lieutenant Novotný tapped Nesbitt on the shoulder. "That's right. We need water … and food. I have money. We can pay in American dollars."

Nesbitt grinned. "That's bloody marvelous. 'Ow much ave you got?"

"Not permitted to say."

When the single-masted boats hove-to within a hundred feet of the coal freighter, Sophie held Pavel up so he could get a better look. "What lovely fishing boats," she said. " Such vivid colors."

Kukulka stood beside her. With a growl, he checked the chamber of his pistol. "Like hell, vivid colors. I smell trouble. Stand behind me—just in case."

They watched the nearest boat, white with rainbow stripes along the gunwales, approach the freighter. Three of the four men in the cockpit wore black and green uniforms, varnished tricorne helmets on their heads, straps under their chins. They stood, one with a submachine gun hanging from his shoulder. The fourth, an old man in ragged clothes, hand on the long tiller at the back, cut

351

the engine. EL PROTECTOR was painted in black on the bow.

"Guardia Civil—so-called police," said Povídka who was standing behind Sophie. "The bastards work in pairs in the villages. One keeps lookout—the other beats and robs the locals." With the authority of a knowledgeable commentator, he pointed a long bony finger. "You see, not one of them looks friendly. They don't want us here."

"That's because Franco is Hitler's arse-licker," someone said with a guttural laugh.

One of the men in the boat took off his helmet and picked up a megaphone. The words boomed over the water: *Somos la Guardia Civil. Identifíquense. Se encuentran en aguas españolas.*

"What's the fucker saying?" Captain Nesbitt exclaimed, frowning. "Anyone here speak Dago? My boys don't. What about your lot, Novotný?"

Shaking his head in irritation, Lieutenant Novotny turned on his heel. "Sergeant Kukulka," he barked. "See if anyone here speaks Spanish. And make sure the other NCOs break out their pistols."

"I can speak a little, captain," said Povídka, stepping forward with a confident smile. "As does my colleague here, Private Serbin. We fought with the Masaryk Brigade in Barcelona. That cop says we are in in Spanish waters."

What followed was an exchange of shouted Spanish, with almost immediate translation into Czech and English for the benefit of the two captains. Sophie put Pavel down, keeping a firm grip on his hand while she turned Povídka's Czech into broken English.

"We are not allowed in Spanish waters without official permission." Povídka said in Czech "They have contacted authorities in Barcelona. If we don't leave now, they will take this ship into custody."

Nesbitt's face darkened as Sophie struggled to translate. "Not bloody likely. Tell 'em we'll leave, but we're low on water. Four water barrels ruptured last night. Can they sell us some water? We could do with extra food as well. " He looked at Novotný. "We can pay for food and water, right?"

The Czech officer nodded. "Pay, yes."

For several minutes, megaphoned Spanish phrases flew back and forth between the police and Povídka. "It is mid-summer. The town wells are almost dry. They can sell us three hundred liters of drinking water. No pesetas, no francs … only dollars or British pounds." There was more shouting. Povídka turned to Novotný. "Two thousand American dollars or two thousand eight hundred pounds."

Ferociously, the Czech lieutenant slapped his thigh. "*Směšný*, ridiculous."

With a sneer, Povídka pulled a cigarette from a crumpled pack in his tunic pocket and lit it. "They're squeezing us, sir. They say that when the wells run dry in town they have to pay for water to be shipped in by tanker. As for food, they have bread, fresh sardines and a few kilos of sweet grapes. Nothing else."

Sophie had the impression that Povídka was enjoying his role as the go-between, seizing on a chance to rise above the ordinariness of being a simple private.

"*Kristus*, they're nothing but crooks," Novotný grunted. "But what can we do? We need the water. I'll have to use the HQ money we're carrying for General Ingr. Go ahead, soldier, tell them we'll pay. It'll be a mix of dollars and pounds."

Povídka nodded, giving his commander the semblance of a salute.

Half an hour later, the fishing boat came alongside. In the well of the boat, one of the policemen took off his hat, handed his weapon to one of the others and climbed the rope ladder to where a gate in the *Northern Fen's* railing had been unlatched.

He was tall and dark-skinned: an athletic type with a trim pencil mustache. He spoke softly and with a slight bow held out his hand. "*Me llamo—el sargento Gonsalves.*"

After some tense haggling—with Povidka and Sophie as translators—the two commanders, Nesbitt and Novotný, finalized the purchase terms with the Spanish sergeant. For two thousand dollars, the Guardia Civil would arrange the delivery of water in barrels as well as one hundred loaves of bread, fifteen kilos of fresh sardines and eighty kilos of grapes.

There were two conditions. First, Novotný would pay Gonsalves a deposit of half the agreed sum, after which the supplies would be loaded on to the *Northern Fen* from small boats. Second, Sergeant Rudolf Lorenc—chosen because he was an NCO and a good swimmer—would be sent to the Guardia Civil boat. He would be held there as a guarantee that the British boat would stay where it was—and only returned after Gonsalves had re-boarded the *Northern Fen* and was paid the rest of the money.

For two hours, a flotilla of fishing boats plied between Cadaqués harbor and the *Northern Fen*. Soldiers and crew, sweating and stripped to the waist, winched the water barrels into the hold using the motorized derrick. Under the gaze of crowds of passengers, the bread and grapes, packed in square straw baskets, were stacked on the deck.

Two hours later, a Union Jack fluttered from the main mast, the signal to the Guardia Civil that it was time for final payment. The fishing boats rocked gently in the whitecaps, about eighty meters away from the *Northern Fen*. Captain Nesbitt, Lieutenant Novotný, Povídka, and Kukulka—with Sophie holding Pavel's hand—had reconvened on the deck, by the wheelhouse, ready to receive Gonsalves.

Nesbitt, his unlit pipe clenched between his teeth, lifted his binoculars. "They're on their way—your hostage bloke, two dagoes and the helmsman in the boat. That machine gunner must be on one of the other boats, thank the Christ."

Sophie stood in front of Kukulka with Pavel between her knees as passengers watched from the railings. She communicated to Novotný and Povídka what the Englishman had said. Novotný nodded, a tight smile on his face.

The *El Protector* came alongside the *Northern* Fen, to where the rope ladder hung down. Moments later, the Spaniard grasped the railing and swung himself on to the deck. Sophie was close enough to observe his dark eyes flit from face to face. She guessed he was nervous at being hemmed in and watched by a mass of passengers, most of them in uniform. He spoke, looking at Povídka, who translated the words into Czech.

"He says he's here for the rest of the money. As soon as he's back in the boat, he says, Sergeant Lorenc will be released back to us."

Captain Novotný saluted and shook hands with the policeman. "*Buén … dia*," he said haltingly and handed the Spaniard an envelope. "Here is your payment."

Sophie watched the Spaniard open the envelope and count the banknotes. He frowned, waved the bundle of notes violently in the air and let loose a barrage of words.

A brief, harsh laugh from Povídka. "I expected something like this, Lieutenant. The fascist pig says we haven't paid enough. He says the town council doubled the price for selling their food. Now he wants an extra thousand. If you don't pay, the Guardia Civil will contact the regional commander in Girona. Don't say I didn't warn you about these crooks."

Novotný snorted. "Tell him we agreed on two thousand. I hope you are being straight with me, Private. I know you Communists like to stir things up with misrepresentation and lies."

"I assure you, sir, everything I said is the truth."

"Here," said Novotný, "the agreement is written on this paper. Show him the agreed amount."

Povídka handed the sheet of paper to the Spaniard who, with a quick glance and snort of derision, tore it into fragments.

Povídka let loose a torrent of invective and turned to the Czechoslovak captain. "I told him he was a thieving bastard and he should stuff a finger up his own and Franco's backside. He said pay three thousand or they will impound the ship."

The policeman glowered. He looked down at the fishing boat and shook his head.

Sophie edged backward. The look on the Spaniard's face frightened her. She picked up Pavel again, bumping up against Kukulka as she straightened up. The sergeant raised the barrel of his pistol and pushed her behind him. "Stay there. I said I smelled trouble," he growled.

Novotný's mouth tightened in fury. "I'm not paying a damned dollar more. *Kristus*, we shook hands on this. Tell him."

Povídka stepped up to the policeman—nose to nose—and, in Spanish, repeated the captain's refusal.

Gonsalves pointed angrily at Povídka and Serbin and let loose a stream of what Sophie took to be insults, in which the words *cabrón*, *mierda* and *coño* were repeated and accentuated. She watched the civil-war veterans exchange meaningful glances and her stomach turned over at the grimness of their faces.

"On top of robbing us, this fucker thinks he can get away with insults," said Serbin, his face seething. He stepped forward and spat in the policeman's face. "He needs a lesson."

Povídka grabbed his arm, easing him away. "Not now, Boho."

Novotný glowered at the Spaniard. "Povídka, tell him to get off the ship. We've loaded the new supplies. He'll have to make do with the cash we already gave him."

"What about Sergeant Lorenc in the boat," said Kukulka? "They could hold on to him, make us pay more."

"If it comes to that, we'll signal Sergeant Lorenc to dive off the fishing boat. Pick him up under covering fire. He knew this was a possibility."

Kukulka shook his head. "Wait, lieutenant. They have a machine gun. We have only pistols—no contest. Lorenc will be killed."

Novotný waved a dismissive hand. "I don't think so. The fellow with the machine gun is at least a hundred meters away. And if he fired on us he would likely kill this Gonsalves fellow and his helmsman at the same time. Go ahead, Povídka, tell the Spaniard I want him off the ship. Now."

Sophie watched Povídka's hand slicing up and down as he shouted in the Spaniard's face. "Our arrogant commie friend is just making things worse," said Kukulka, his face dark as a thundercloud. "It's obvious. Making the pot boil when he doesn't have to."

Gonsalves squared his shoulders and tucked the wad of dollars in a side pocket. "*Cabrón*," he said, turning to the rope ladder. He spat in Povídka's face and pushed Serbin away.

Serbin, his face black with fury, stepped forward.

Sophie saw the knife handle in his fingers, its long blade glinting in the sun. His arm completed a graceful arc and the blade disappeared into the Spaniard's chest. She gasped at the startled look in the Spaniard's eyes and reflexively turned her body away to block Pavel's view.

A drawn-out groan drew her gaze back. Gonsalves had collapsed against the railing, blood streaming down his uniform. His chest heaved. Red foam bubbled on his lips. He swayed and then toppled backward through the gateway in the railing. She heard a cry and a splash.

People rushed to the side to look. The man struggled feebly in the blood-clouded water, calling for help. Looking up, Sophie saw the other fishing boat moving steadily toward the *Northern Fen*. Standing on the engine housing, the policeman raised his machine gun. Her heart jumped against her ribs.

Kukulka's voice roared: "Everyone down." She felt the force of him pulling her and Pavel flat to the deck. "Return fire, men," he yelled, blasting her ear. Like a heavy plank of wood, his arm kept her down, firmly securing her body. "Don't sit up," he hissed.

She heard the popping noise of pistols and something like a bee buzzed in her ear. From the corner of her eye, she saw Novotný on his knees firing from behind a stanchion and heard the whine and clunk of bullets hitting metal on the ship. "Get the one with the machine gun," he yelled. Povídka and Serbin were flat on the deck a few feet away, hands covering their heads.

"We got him," someone yelled. The firing stopped. "Lorenc is okay," someone else shouted. "He jumped into the water. Swimming this way."

Sophie felt Pavel squirm under her chest and babble something. Then, he lay against her, quiet.

Sobs and groans broke the silence on deck. She rolled sideways to release Pavel but her motion was blocked by the inert mass of a body lying next to her.

She turned, terrified. Kukulka lay sprawled on his back, his face slack and lifeless. Thick commas of blood oozed over the white scar on his cheekbone. The scream stayed inside her, running around and around in her head. Her legs wouldn't move. She reached out to touch his arm. "Kukulka?" His arm flopped sideways. She looked away stomach juices flowing out of her mouth. She vomited. This was not possible. Not for a fine man, not in a place like this. Not Willy's friend.

Novotný, white-faced, jaw tensed, stood by the sergeant's

feet. He rubbed at his forehead. "Oh, my God. Jesus, no."

Pavel reached out and touched Kukulka's hand. "Wake up, Kulka." He looked at Sophie. "Is he hurt?" His voice quavered.

Sophie, on her knees, drew Pavel into her arms. Great heaving sobs tore at her chest. "He's hurt, yes."

Novotný looked over the railings. A shot rang out. "Hold your fire," he yelled. "They're leaving."

Sophie watched through her tears as soldiers and civilians scrambled to their feet, yelling and shaking their fists. She stood, brushing dirt off her dress and saw blood on it.

Apart from Kukulka, two other soldiers and a woman lay on the deck. The woman moved, whimpering. Her skirt was torn. Blood ran from her thigh.

"Get the medical aide." Novotný yelled, putting his gun away. His face contorted in fury, jaw and neck muscles rigid. He pointed at Serbin. "Arrest that idiot." Two soldiers pinned Serbin's arms. Others formed a protective ring around the bodies, blocking Sophie's view.

Nesbitt hammered Serbin's chest with his fists. "You fucking turd," he yelled. "What did you do that for? You knew they outgunned us."

Serbin, neither regret nor dismay showing on his face, shrugged. Sophie knew he hadn't understood a word the English captain said, though he must have guessed the meaning. "The Spanish bastard had it coming," said Serbin in a matter-of-fact voice. "He taunted us, and swindled our honored lieutenant. He got what he deserved."

Nesbitt shoved Serbin aside as he walked away. "Bastard. We'll be lucky if they don't come back and bomb the shit out of us."

Someone at the railing shouted in Czech. "They've picked up their man. The boats are headed for the village. Lorenc is coming up the rope ladder."

As Lorenc appeared at the top of the rope ladder, dripping wet, Novotný's face went white with anger. "Captain Nesbitt," he yelled, "come here."

Nesbitt turned to face Novotný. "What's up now, mate? Haven't you fuckers done enough damage?"

"Two soldiers and one sergeant dead—and a woman badly injured," the Czechoslovak officer spluttered. "Telephone your navy ship. It's only five kilometers away. They must come here and fire big guns at town. Do now, before police and Spanish military return."

Sophie shuddered. *Big guns! Kill innocent people in the village?* Horrible.

Nesbitt turned away again. "Piss off, Novotný. What's done is done. I'll radio the destroyer and report what happened. Commander Colvill will decide what to do."

Holding Pavel's hand, Sophie stumbled away, along the deck and then stopped frozen, her face glazed, a far-away look in her eyes.

She could not stop thinking about Kukulka. It had taken only a second to snuff out his genial, boisterous spirit. Three fine men were dead and an innocent woman badly hurt, all because of that revolting man, Serbin. Absentmindedly, she stroked Pavel's head … she couldn't move or think straight.

Pavel inspected his mother for a long minute, a puzzled look on his thin face. He scratched at the scar on his neck, looking around as if he hoped someone might offer to help his mother. When nothing happened, he made a face, pulled on her hand and led his mother away, back through the crowd of passengers on deck to the ship's bow.

As they threaded their way past groups of downcast, murmuring soldiers, Pavel stopped and looked up at her. The questions came in a torrent. "Mama, why did people shoot at us? What happened to Monsieur Kulka? Will the doctor come? The lady with blood on her legs was crying? Will she get better?"

Sophie tried to stave off her tears and the overwhelming questions. "Wait … wait, darling … until we get to our place. I will tell you about Sergeant Kukulka later. We need to lie down and rest."

"I'm hungry, Maman."

"We'll see what there is," Sophie sighed. Her supplies from Sète had run out and she could not muster the will to go to the hold and beg for food. She wanted to close her eyes and forget everything.

Pavel pulled at her sleeve. "I'm hungry, Maman."

Sidney Latcher, the engineer's mate, arrived in the bow carrying a cardboard box. "Ullo missus. I've come to raise the anchor." He put the box down at his feet.

Sophie gave him a questioning frown. "All by you alone?"

He pointed to the heavy chain wound round a metal cylinder fastened to the deck. "I switch on a machine … a windlass wot pulls the anchor up."

"We leave now?" she asked, surprised.

He nodded. "A boat's coming from the destroyer to pick up the injured folk. Our engines will start in a minute." He pulled two large bunches of white grapes and a loaf of bread from the cardboard box by his feet. "There y'are, missus. Nice and fresh from the Spanish town. Eat up. There's more if you need it."

Pavel reached out, grabbed some grapes and began stuffing them into his mouth. "I like grapes," he mumbled, juice dripping down his chin.

"Thank you, mister sailor," Sophie said. She felt the deck vibrate, the throb of the *Northern Fen's* engine. "How far we go to Gibraltar?"

"Gib? Three days sailing, Missus." Latcher shook his head wearily. "Let's 'ope the worst is over." His words were partly drowned by a blast from the ship's horn. A cloud of seabirds rose screaming from the islet. "You'd best take the nipper to the back of the ship. There'll be a terrible clankin' and screechin' when the anchor comes up.

As the ship slid out of the Bay of Cadaqués, Sophie and Pavel shared a bench with Marika at the side of the wheelhouse, watching the monolithic rock grow smaller until, like a whale, it sank into the water. Sophie hugged her knees, reminding herself that there were three more days of sailing. Time enough to erase the shock of the past few hours and pull herself together. In Gibraltar, she would throw her arms around Willy's neck and kiss him a hundred times—and only then would she tell him about his friend, Kukulka.

CHAPTER THIRTY-ONE

Destination Gibraltar
SS Darwen, Mediterranean Sea. June 27th, 1940

Captain Rudček and his three-man embarkation team—which included Willy— boarded the *Darwen* in the pouring rain. It was the last ship to evacuate troops from Sète. They headed south-west, shadowed by the destroyer *HMS Keppel*, to avoid the bad weather. The *Northern Fen*, with Sophie and Pavel on board, had cast off five hours earlier, just as the storm was gathering. Willy was afraid they might have sailed into the thick of it. He would see them in Gibraltar. At least Kukulka would to keep a watchful eye on them.

Exhausted by the intensity of organizing the evacuation under Captain Rudcek's command, Willy found a spot in the hold to stash his pack and rubber poncho. In spite of the noisy conversation around him and the throb of the engines he fell asleep on a folded tarpaulin. He awoke four hours later. A soldier sharing his tarp offered him a chunk of bread spread with olive oil and rubbed with tomato. As he chewed, Willy reflected on the magnitude of what he had experienced in the previous twenty-four hours. The German-French Armistice had been concluded—and thanks to the British Navy, thousands had escaped surrender and imprisonment.

After the *Darwen* departed Sète, Captain Rudček, in command of the troops on board, ordered Willy to accompany him to ask the British captain to join them on an inspection of the ship. They climbed the iron stairway and knocked on the side door of the bridge. Rudček entered without waiting. Willy carried a briefcase packed with the regiment's military documents and inventory lists.

The sailor at the wheel glanced at them. At a small table, a man in a merchant marine uniform looked up from a chart he was studying "Who are you and what do you want?" He looked at Rudček over the top of his wire-rimmed spectacles, staring at the incongruous white gloves and scarf. "Are you the one in charge of the troops?" He had a surprisingly deep voice.

Rudček spoke to Willy out the side of his mouth. "Translate, idiot. Ask if he's the captain." Willy complied.

"I'm Thompson, ship's captain," the man said, staring morosely at the two Czechoslovaks. He sniffed. "What are your white gloves for? Tea with the Queen Mother?"

Willy stood at attention and saluted. "This is Captain Rudček," he said in English, thinking that the Englishman's comment was not a good start to international cooperation "Our military commander on the ship. I translate for him. We are immensely grateful for saving us."

"I was ordered to," said the British captain with a sour nod. "Otherwise, I wouldn't have touched you people with a barge-pole."

After an explanation of why the Czechoslovak army was in the south of France, Willy transmitted Rudček's demand for someone who knew the ship to accompany them to check on how the troops had settled in and assess the adequacy of their supplies. He decided it would not help Anglo-Czechoslovak collaboration if he translated the British captain's exact words and style.

"Can't be me," Captain Thompson replied pushing the chart aside. "My chief officer will go with you, but make it quick. We have work to do." He leaned over to flick on an intercom on the wall. "Lenny."

"What's up, Cap'n?"

"Get Leslie Hill up here. Got a job for him." He turned back to Willy, thoughtfully stroking his chin. "Remind this Cap'n Ridnick, or whatever his name is, we've got a lot to take care of on this trip: a load of unfortunate refugees who've lost their homes and a bunch of soldiers who don't speak English. Likely as not, they don't have much discipline either." He poked a finger into his own chest. "I'm the ultimate authority here—responsible for crew, cargo and the civilians. But there's no way I can handle your soldiers. This Ridnick chap needs to keep a close eye. Trouble is … we don't understand a fuckin' word each of us says. Sticky situation."

"What is he saying, Kohut?"

"That he is the boss on the ship and his chief officer will accompany us on the tour."

Rudček tightened his lips as he smoothed the gloves over his hands. "That was too short a translation, *vojín*. I want to know every damned thing he says. Don't keep anything back. None of your Jew-boy lies and embellishments."

Willy biting his lip, clicked his heels. "So why use me and not someone else who speaks English and is not a Jew, sir?"

"Don't give me that shit. You're the only real linguist we've got."

The door banged open and a tall man in merchant marine uniform strolled in. He glanced at the two Czechoslovaks and gave Thompson a relaxed salute. "What's up, Cap'n?"

"These two blokes want to check on how their men have settled in. Take 'em around and be helpful-like. The one with the glasses speaks English, seems like a nice chap. The other one is their commander, a captain. A bit odd, wearing those white gloves 'n all."

Winding their way through piles of luggage and groups of

soldiers standing, sitting, or laying everywhere, Chief Officer Hill explained that the *SS Darwen* was a small coaster that ferried goods between England, France, and North Africa. "We carry all sorts: cotton from Alexandria, ceramic tiles from the south of France, and machinery from Britain." On each side of the ship he showed them the position of the Lewis guns, mounted on swivel pedestals. "Old 'uns … installed in Marseilles, they were."

"Ammunition? Where is it kept?" said Rudček with a critical frown as he inspected the weapons.

Chief Officer Hill shrugged after Willy translated. "Dunno exactly. Likely to be in the hold somewhere. When we go down, we'll look for it."

Half-way down an iron ladder, Rudček stopped and handed Willy a flashlight. "As we go around the storage areas, use this. We must find the ammunition for the guns. These civilians are sloppy. They have no idea how to organize defense."

"Can we move along, sir?" the chief officer sighed with an air of resignation as they walked across the deck, sometimes stepping over sitting or sleeping men, avoiding stacked bicycles and piles of luggage. "There's the heads and bunkrooms to inspect yet. Then we go down into the hold."

In the dank, dimly lit hold they threaded their way with flashlights across the riveted metal floor, again stepping over and around civilians and soldiers lying on blankets and tarps.

For nearly an hour, they opened and shut lockers and storage spaces and inspected water barrels. "Seems like you've got enough essentials to get by on this trip," Hill said to Willy after they completed the checklists and found the ammunition. He gave Rudček and Willy a piercing look and pointed to empty wine bottles, trash, and cigarette butts scattered over the floor. "If you don't mind me saying so, your blokes are making a god-awful mess down here. Who the fuck's goin' to deal with all this when we get to Gib? Me and my crew? Not bloody likely."

"We'll do our best to clean up," said Willy. Again, he saw no benefit in communicating all of the officer's actual words to Rudček.

Every step they took kicked up a small gray cloud of dust. Under one of the bulkhead lamps, Rudček pointed to his dust-covered shoes. "What is this god-awful stuff on the floor," he said to Willy. "My uniform will be ruined."

"Cotton dust—from the cargo we load in Alexandria," was Hill's answer. "They make the cotton into textiles. On the return journey, we carry machinery: pumps, small engines, and the like."

Willy nodded to the chief officer, a smile on his face "I remember Lancashire very well. I once visited the weaving mills in Lancashire. In my business I used to import British fabric. Now I have a different question. When do you think we'll get to Gibraltar?"

"Four days, all being well. Captain told me you lucky buggers would be transferred in Gib to *The Viceroy of India*."

"That is a ship?"

Hill chuckled. "An ocean liner. Top of the line. Launched in twenty-eight. Twenty thousand tons of fucking luxury, that's what she is—incredible grub and a fancy swimming pool. She sails the Bombay route through the Suez Canal. Fast too—turbo-electric engines."

Willy concluded that such engines were to be much admired. His spirits rose as he looked forward to the prospect of a soft mattress and good food and a quick trip to England.

On their way round the ship, Willy noticed the same mood change among the other soldiers. The gloom of their evacuation had evaporated and was replaced by excitement and optimism. They were busy talking, practicing English expressions in preparation for their arrival in Britain. Some played accordions and harmonicas, others played chess and cards and regular *Sokol* gymnastic routines were organized on deck. Most of the conversations he overheard did not refer to France's ignominious defeat, but to what was going to happen, now that the British army had been saved at Dunkirk. The war was entering a crucial phase and they were on their way to fight with the British. For the moment, everyone agreed, there was nothing to be done on the *SS Darwen* except enjoy the Mediterranean cruise, and learn a few English phrases.

* * *

Three days later, as dusk shrouded Gibraltar's jagged mass, the destroyer *HMS Keppel* and the *Darwen* made their way past the crowded anchorage of naval and merchant ships. On the *Darwen*, happy soldiers lined the railings to catch a glimpse of the battle cruiser *HMS Hood* at anchor, and the *Ark Royal*—the only British aircraft carrier in the Mediterranean.

Later that evening, Commander Heywood-Lonsdale of *HMS Velox*, came aboard the *Darwen* to confer with the ship's captain and Rudček. They crowded into Thompson's cabin and Willy translated. The tall British commander accepted a mug half full of cognac. He raised it in appreciation.

"Well done, gentlemen. I understand your trip from Sète was uncomfortably cramped and somewhat unruly. You are the first to arrive. The *Swithun* and *Northern Fen* are still at sea."

Captain Thompson muttered into his mug. "At least we got here in one piece."

Willy held his breath. Sophie was still at sea. Why? Was it the storm? Were they safe?

"This'll be a quick briefing," the commander said in clipped laconic tones. He drained his mug and stood up, hands in pockets.

"Tomorrow morning, passengers from your ship and the others in the convoy will be transferred to the *Viceroy of India*. She already gained a load of refugees in Marseille. Transfer by naval tenders begins at 0h-nine-hundred hours. Take till noon, I expect."

"How long will it take to sail from here to England?" Rudček lit a cigarette as he watched Willy translate his question.

The commander looked at Rudček, pursing his lips as if irritated by the burden of the translating process. "Normally three days. But there are minefields and now, those damned U-boats. With the armistice, the German Navy now has easy access to all French ports. Things are getting dicey. The *Viceroy of India* will detour into the Atlantic, and then loop back to Plymouth."

"Captain Rudček wants to know how long all this will actually take," said Willy politely. "He means the number of days."

Heywood-Lonsdale shrugged. The look on his face suggested that the Englishman was not fond of foreigners. "Hard to say, four or five days."

Willy translated. What did 'how long' matter? They were in British hands now. Besides, his mind was elsewhere, with Sophie and Pavel. The *Northern Fen* left Sète earlier than the *Darwen*. So, why wasn't she—and the *Swithun* for that matter—already at anchor in Gibraltar? What the hell had happened to them? What if U-boats had got past Gibraltar into the Mediterranean. Attacked Sophie's convoy? It wasn't possible. No, someone would have mentioned it.

He could not help stepping out of his translator role. "Excuse-me, sir," he said in English. "You said the other ships from Sète were still at sea? My wife and boy are on board the *Northern Fen*. Did they come across any trouble?"

Rudček glared. Willy knew he hated being excluded and probably guessed his question was personal.

Heywood-Lonsdale stroked his cheek and gave Willy a tight

smile. "Ah, yes. The *Northern Fen*. Delayed by the weather. Had a spot of bother when they ducked the storm and sheltered on the Spanish coast."

Willy heart jumped. "What spot, sir?" He wasn't sure what a spot of bother was, but the rest was clear.

"A brief clash with the Spanish coast-guard, apparently. Two soldiers killed. The rest of the passengers are fine. Expected to arrive here tonight."

Willy took a deep breath. Sophie and Pavel were safe. He felt a whisper of hope. "Any chance the *Fen's* passengers will be transferred tomorrow, onto the *Viceroy of India*, sir?"

"Absolutely not. They will be put on the *SS Neuralia*, another passenger ship, when she arrives from Marseille."

Willy bunched his fists, turning away to hide his unhappiness. The *Neuralia*! So, he had broken another promise. He wouldn't even see them in Gibraltar. Sophie and Pavel would sail on a different ship to England. He yearned to hold them in his arms.

After a restless night in the hold, Willy grabbed a cup of tea from one of the urns that had replaced the makeshift kitchen. There was nothing to eat, only tea or watery coffee. He climbed the iron gangway to the deck and looked up at the seagulls wheeling overhead. Their piercing cries sounded like recriminations for his broken promises. Around him a crowd of soldiers, stripped to the waist, was clearing the deck of equipment and filling their packs. Even with the sun still only an orange glow partly hidden behind Gibraltar Rock, the air was already stifling.

Willy scanned the harbor. The *Ark Royal* and the *Hood* were gone. New ships had arrived. As he turned away he caught his breath. His arms and legs tensed—with joy or trepidation he wasn't sure. About two hundred meters away, literally under his nose, he saw the outline and single stack of the *Northern Fen*, and the

Swithun moored farther astern. Thank God. He breathed a huge sigh of relief. Sophie and Pavel were close, almost next-door. The question racing round his brain was how to contact them before he transferred to the *Viceroy of India* the next morning He had to think of something.

By seven o'clock in the morning, Captain Rudček, with Willy's translating, had given orders for everyone to assemble with their luggage and possessions at 08:30 hours, ready for transfer by naval tender to the *Viceroy of India*. In the midst of the bustle and noise Willy slipped away and knocked on the wheelhouse door.

Captain Thompson poked his head out. "Come in, feller. You lookin' for something?"

Chief Officer Hill sat at the table by the ship's wheel, tea mug in hand, a pipe stuck in his mouth. A brief, genial wave. "G'mornin' matey. 'Ave you seen the *Northern Fen*? She's 'ere. Good show, eh?"

Willy slapped him on the back. "I have and it's wonderful." It was then that he noticed the binoculars hanging up by the door. He turned to the captain. "My family might be on deck. Could I borrow your glasses? Just one glimpse and I would be the happiest man in Gibraltar."

Thompson shook his head.

"Go on, cap'n, let him," said Hill. "He's been bloody useful to us on this trip."

The captain sighed as he handed the binoculars to Willy. "S'pose so. Take good care, soldier. They're old friends and cost a pretty penny."

Willy stepped out of the cabin and wandered around the deck with the binoculars, scanning the *Northern Fen* from different angles. There were only groups of soldiers on deck, no women or children. He looked at his watch and his heart sank. No time left. In half an hour the transfer preparations would commence. He went back to the captain's cabin. It was empty. He hung the binoculars back on their hook.

The first tender bound for the *Viceroy of India* was to leave at nine-thirty. Willy was assigned to check off soldiers' names as they lined up around the deck, ready to climb down the rope ladders. As the third tender sheered away from the *Darwen*, Hill appeared, tapped Willy on the shoulder and handed him the binoculars. He pointed to the *Northern Fen*. "Captain said I should bring 'em to you. I saw a woman and a kid walking about on the deck. Might be your people."

Willy raised the binoculars and tried to focus the lenses as solders moved past him to line up at the railings. After two sweeps end-to-end, he saw them, in the middle of the vessel. Sophie, haggard but with a determined look, held Pavel up in the air, turning this way and that. Whatever direction she faced, the boy waved his arms. He watched her put him down and swirl the long, crazy-colored scarf she kept through their escape from Prague. He let go the binoculars and started windmilling his arms.

Triumphant, Willy handed the binoculars back to the Chief Officer. He stripped off his tunic and shirt and waved them in the air, jumping up and down, yelling, "Sophie, Sophie, Sophie." He could not remember when he had felt so happy. He didn't care that the soldiers around him looked bewildered and annoyed.

"Good job, soldier" said Captain Thompson, who appeared at the railing with a broad grin on his face. He took the binoculars from the chief officer and chuckled. "I see old Nesbitt's lent her his glasses. She's laughing. Now she's the one jumping up and down."

"What the hell is going on here?" Rudček's nasal voice brought Willy to his senses. The Czechoslovak captain stood in front of Willy, blocking his view. "Holy Virgin, Kohut. You are disgustingly naked. Why aren't you checking these men? What the hell is going on?"

Willy hurriedly put on his shirt and army tunic, trying to

look apologetic despite his excitement. "Sorry, sir. Just saw my wife and child on the *Northern Fen.*" He could not stop smiling. "They're safe."

Rudček was grim. "Fuck your family, *vojín.* Get back to your duties. If you cause a delay, you'll pay dearly." He walked off.

With a grin that split his face, Willy grabbed Thompson's arm and pumped his hand. "I can't thank you enough, sir. That was a wonderful moment."

The captain's grizzled face flushed. "Righty-ho, my friend. Glad you got to see your missus."

CHAPTER THIRTY-THREE

By Sea to England
Gibraltar Harbor. July 2nd 1940

By four o'clock, under a merciless sun, more than a thousand soldiers were massed on the main deck of the *Viceroy of India,* waiting for orders. The men of the Third Artillery Regiment, Willy among them, in full uniform and carrying backpacks, were sweaty, tired and thirsty. But they were patient; Willy felt optimism was in the air.

The luxury liner, a jewel of the Pacific and Orient Shipping Company, had been built in 1925 to carry a thousand passengers comfortably, in three different classes. On this journey, the passenger manifest had tripled and two hundred ship's pursers and stewards—Indian and British—struggled to understand the Czechoslovak soldiers and answer questions, as they offered water, sandwiches, and directions to sleeping quarters and toilets.

After Lieutenant Colonel Němec's instructions had been distributed, the soldiers, moved into action; each man trying to locate his berth.

It took time for Willy to find his sleeping quarters on the lower deck. His ID number was taped to a striped mattress and pillow, one of many lined up on the floor. Willy dumped his pack and headed toward the attendant standing by the door. The dark-skinned man, in a white steward's uniform, had a helpless look on his face as he watched the soldiers find their beds and peel off their uniforms. Sadly, he shook his turbaned head—as if this chaos and rough behavior was beyond the norms of the Pacific and Orient Line ... and he was unable to prevent it.

"How do you do," Willy said in English, extending his hand. "I am Willy Kohut, private, Czechoslovak Army. You look upset. Is there some problem?"

The attendant smiled. "Ah, you speak English, *sahib*. That is good." Frowning, he raised his hands in the air. "But I am not understanding what these soldiers say. I am here to assist, but it is difficult for me."

Willy nodded sympathetically. "Yes, it *is* difficult. Most of the men here speak only German, Hungarian or Czech. I can help, if you like."

The attendant pointed to the embroidered badge on his breast pocket and smiled again. "I am most happy to know you." He bowed. "My name is Samrit, ship steward. No help needed at this moment, sir."

Willy looked around the mattress-strewn library and laughed. "How will you manage, Mr. Samrit? This ship has far too many passengers."

"Not to worry, sir." He swung his arms out as if encompassing the whole ship. "Pacific and Orient Line will perform proper job."

"Excellent." Willy shook hands again with Samrit and wandered off to explore the cruise ship. As he studied a map of the P-&-O shipping routes affixed to a wall opposite the gangway to the third deck, the loudspeaker above his head buzzed ... three times. It was followed by a clipped voice.

"Attention passengers, attention passengers. This is Captain Cummins. For the ladies and gentlemen who have sailed through the Suez Canal, please join me in welcoming a number of refugees who are boarding our ship, as well as more than a thousand Czechoslovak officers and soldiers commanded by Lieutenant

Colonel Němec. I ask you to be tolerant of any discomforts resulting from our crowded conditions, stay calm and make the best of things. *HMS Keppel*, a destroyer, will be escorting us on this last short leg of our journey. We will dock in Plymouth on the south coast of England but, because of wartime measures, the Pacific and Orient Line cannot guarantee a specific time or arrival date."

The loudspeaker clicked off and then clicked on again. "Attention, please. For your information, the Czechoslovak troops will participate in an emergency lifeboat drill as soon as we leave Gibraltar. At this time, you may prefer to stay in your cabins."

Willy lit a cigarette and stood watching people negotiate the crowded stairs. Glancing back at the P & O wall map, Willy suddenly realized that the French side of the Channel was now all German. There would be U-boats stationed in the ports of Calais, Le Havre, Cherbourg and St. Malo—right across the Channel from Plymouth.

Willy wondered if Lieutenant-Colonel Němec had an escape plan in case of a U-boat or Luftwaffe attack. The liner was unarmed and the men had no weapons. What could a commander do except make sure his troops knew how to man the lifeboats in an orderly fashion? The problem with the lifeboats, Willy mused, was that there were not enough of them; not for a thousand extra passengers.

When would Sophie's liner leave Gib? Wouldn't it be wonderful if she arrived in England at about the same time as he did, perhaps even at the same port? Still, finding her would be a needle-in-the-haystack affair. Fingers crossed, Sophie could send a telegram to London from her ship; perhaps he would find a way to do it from the *Viceroy of India*.

The ship's horn gave a single blast, warning of departure within the hour. Smoke rose from the stacks and the engines began to throb. Everyone crowded decks to watch the ship pull away from the pier and follow the wake of her destroyer escort between anchored cargo vessels.

He moved to the stern railings and smoked cigarette after cigarette, his eyes fixed on the *Northern Fen* as it disappeared among the other ships at anchor. The happiness he felt at seeing Sophie and Pavel waving to him was waning. He had wanted to touch them, hold them, kiss them. Outside the harbor, the *Viceroy of India* slowed and the captain announced they would be joined by two cargo ships that would convoy with her to Plymouth.

The lifeboat safety drill was followed by dinner served by white-coated and gloved waiters in the second-class dining rooms. The hungry soldiers ate quickly, joking that finally they had tasted the famous roast beef of England … and it was tough, fatty and over-salted. They drank pints of warm Whitbread Pale Ale, of which there seemed to be an inexhaustible supply.

After dinner Willy discovered the second-class lounge. More luxury: wood-paneled walls, floor lamps, leather armchairs and a billiard table. The cabinets were full of books and puzzles. A few mattresses had been made up as beds in one corner and a couple of soldiers were already asleep.

Relaxing in an armchair by the window, he noticed, on a side-table, the ship's directory of passenger amenities and services. Flipping through it, he saw the heading: RADIO-TELEGRAPH ROOM. He jumped up in excitement. *No time to waste.*

Hastily searching the decks he bumped into a uniformed man with a gold-braided cap. "Excuse me, please," Willy said, using his best English. "I am a Czechoslovak soldier. My wife is on another ship sailing from Gibraltar. I wish to send a telegram. Can you help me?"

The man ran his eyes over Willy's dirty uniform. "I'm one of the pursers," he said after a pause. "I'm not sure about sending telegrams now we've left harbor. But it's worth a try. I'll take you down to the radio room. See if the sparkers can help you out. We're hove-to at the moment."

The young sparkers in the windowless Radio-Telegraph Room had earphones around their necks and sat in front of an array of metal boxes faced with brass dials, knobs and switches. One of them scribbled messages on a pad. The room, not much bigger than a hotel closet, was thick with cigarette smoke. Willy and the purser squeezed themselves in and shut the door.

"This soldier wants to send a wire," said the purser. "Can you blokes oblige?"

"We're supposed to maintain radio silence," one of them said, indicating a notice pinned to the wall. "Captain's orders. The Jerries could pinpoint our convoy's position."

"Radio silence not yet in force," the other operator chipped in with an almost incomprehensible English dialect. "We're s'posed to test and confirm our contact protocol with the other ships—before we gets underway. Flags or Morse code, it'll be one or t'other."

Willy's pulse quickened. There was still a chance to send a message. "You mean this radio silence is not on yet?"

The operator shook his head. "S'right, mate."

Willy stepped forward and waved his right hand in the sparker's face. "See this messed-up finger? Mr. Telegraph Operator. The Nazis did this to me in Prague. My family escaped. We were separated in France. And, now ... my wife and child are either on the *Northern Fen* or the *Neuralia* ... still in Gibraltar, I think. I must let them know I'm safe. Could you send a telegram for me?"

The operator pulled at his lips, then shook his head. "Not if the vessel is at sea."

"Damn ... then what about a wire to London?" Willy wasn't ready to give up. "Let me send a few words, to tell my parents I'm safe. Please."

Frowning, the purser turned to the first operator. "How about it, my friend? Give this foreign bloke a chance."

The telegraph operator shook his head. He seemed to be enjoying his moment of power. "Sorry sir, it's war regs. Only special cases allowed for telegrams before we leave. Cap'n decides."

Willy paused, staring at the young man's pimply face and mocking eyes. He felt around in his pockets and pulled out the antique gold coin he had kept back when he cashed his other smuggled coins in Paris—a last resource in the event of an emergency. He tossed it on to the unclipped telephone jacks on the desk. "Yours, if you send my telegram. Your captain doesn't need to know. That coin is solid gold. Worth many English pounds."

"Crikey … real gold!" The operator grinned at his co-worker, inspected the winged head on the coin and slipped it into his jacket. "Okay, mister—done. Write your text in English. Eight words or less and make it snappy." He pushed a form across his counter towards Willy and added a worn pencil. With a conspiratorial grin, he looked around the room. "This is between us blokes. Three-way split, right?"

Willy wrote down his father's address and the message:

SAFE. DESTINATION ENGLAND.
ARRIVING SOON. WILLY.

He looked at the young man as he handed back the form. "Does all the ship's news comes through here, is that correct?"

The two operators glanced at each other and nodded.

Willy's stomach tightened. He had to ask, even though he feared what the answer might be. "Tell me about the Channel. Is there danger for British ships? Now, I mean, after the French surrender?"

"Go on, you blokes, tell'im," said the purser. "He's paid you well enough."

The operator shrugged and looked down at his log. "Well, there's mine-fields all over the place—and two days ago the Jerries occupied the Channel Islands."

The other operator chimed in. "The *Arandora Star*, mister— sunk yesterday by a U-boat in the Atlantic. Eight hundred dead, most of 'em German and Italian civvies being shipped to camps in Canada. Most of the U-boat attacks are in the Atlantic."

Willy thanked them and left the telegraph room with the purser, his fears confirmed. Every convoy out of Gibraltar was in danger. *Shouldn't have asked,* he muttered to himself, trying to clear an image of a torpedo sinking Sophie's ship.

On deck, Willy said good-bye to the purser and found an unoccupied teak lounger, nodding politely to his neighbors. A strong breeze helped calm his thoughts. He decided to look only to the distant future—no nostalgia or recriminations and no fantasies about what might happen in the next few days at sea. What would it be like to live in England? If the Allies were victorious, he and Sophie would find an apartment in London, close to his parents. Maybe ask one of his British fabric suppliers for a job. Above all, Willy wanted a future in a country where people respected each other, where hard work was rewarded—where Jews could live without hate.

* * *

Late in the evening of July 7th the *Viceroy of India* arrived at Plymouth's Millbay Docks. The five-day journey from Gibraltar had blustery winds, whitecaps and delivered a good dose of seasickness—but no alarms and no Luftwaffe. Disembarkation was scheduled to begin the next morning at eight. None of the Czechoslovak soldiers or NCOs knew what would happen next.

Willy sat on his mattress in the library preparing his pack and equipment for disembarkation the next day. Most of the other men were asleep. Too many beers at dinner he guessed. His mind flitted between Sophie and Pavel and what awaited him on the dock. No orders had been given and Captain Rudček's face went blank when Willy asked what would happen when they landed. If the situation on the Plymouth docks was as chaotic as it had been in the port of Sète, Willy thought he might get a chance to slip away and catch a ride to London; and start looking for Sophie and Pavel. He would feel bad about deserting his post, but his family came first.

By ten o'clock in the morning, the *Viceroy of India* emptied out. In a cold drizzle, Willy and the other soldiers were lined up on Millbay dock, their NCOs and officers at attention.

Lieutenant Colonel Němec climbed on to a small platform facing all the soldiers, standing at attention. A grizzled British officer joined him, tapping his knee boots with a cane. Armed British soldiers, wearing rubber ponchos, stood guard on the periphery looking morose. Behind them, in the distance, columns of smoke issued from the chimneys of the city, forming a low bank of grayness in the sky.

"We are glad to be welcomed to Britain," Němec shouted in Czech. "Our army is now officially at the disposal of His Majesty's Armed Forces. In one hour, we will board a train located at the end of this dock. Officers and NCOs have their orders. We will show our hosts that we are well-behaved and cooperative. Our destination is a camp in the countryside. And there is one more thing: Prime Minister Churchill needs every one of us to fight bravely in step with our British allies. I have personally committed all of you to this aim."

The lieutenant colonel raised his cane. "Finally, I must

emphasize that landing in Britain does not mean you men are suddenly free agents. Any attempt to sneak away will be severely disciplined. Fourteen days confined to barracks, minimum. Pay withheld."

Willy groaned. Getting away, seeing his family, was impossible.

The Captain standing in front of the unit spun around. "Attention, men. We'll move out by platoons when I give the order."

"Any idea what the place we're going to is like, Captain?" Willy asked. "I can't wait to sleep in a decent bed for a change."

"All I know, *vojín*, is that we are going to a great country estate that belongs to an aristocrat." The captain grinned. "Camp beds and tents. Is that decent enough for you?"

CHAPTER THIRTY-FOUR

SS Neuralia
Gibraltar Harbor. July 1940

Perched on the edge of the lower bunk, Pavel nestled against Sophie, his head bent over the book on her lap. Sunlight poured through the single porthole onto the linoleum floor and a warm, rubbery smell permeated the cabin. On the far wall of the cabin, a brass fan whirred erratically.

Sophie was barefoot, and in her brassiere and panties. Pavel was naked. They shared the cabin with Marika and Irina, companions from the *Northern Fen*.

Sophie could scarcely tolerate the stifling heat on the *Neuralia* and, in spite of the liner's luxury, three days of inaction had left her exhausted and irritable. What Sophie missed most was movement. The *Neuralia* lay at anchor waiting for a convoy to form and take the liner—packed with Czechoslovak and Polish soldiers and a gaggle of refugees, two thousand in all—on a six-day journey to Liverpool.

Exploring the ship, she had discovered shelves of books lining a corridor next to the ship's main lounge. Among the few children's books, all in English, she found something written in French that she and Pavel could understand: *The Story of Babar*, filled with colorful illustrations. In their cabin, she read it with Pavel explaining about the dangers of poison mushrooms and how balloons could float in the sky. The incident of King Babar and Queen Celeste's rescue by a cruise ship, after they had been marooned on a tiny island, seemed like an echo of her own transfer with Pavel from the *Northern Fen* to the *Neuralia*.

"Read it again, Maman."

"Again?" Sophie heaved a sigh. This would definitely be the last time. She was beginning to dislike those self-important elephants. This time, Pavel launched into complicated questions about the story. How big is elephant poo? What food did Babar and Celeste eat on the island? Why does a ship go up and down on the water? What is a king?

Sophie enjoyed responding to his questions and the last one was the simplest to answer. "At the end of this journey, *Pavlíčku*, we will get off the ship in a country called Britain, where there *really* is a king. His name is King George. He is much older than your Papa."

"What about his queen? Is she nice?"

"I don't know anything about her."

"Oh," Pavel yawned. "Will you and Papa take me to see the king in his palace?"

"Perhaps." Sophie closed the book, wondering whether she, Pavel and Willy would ever manage to get together again as a family and, one day, catch a glimpse of British royalty. "Are you ready to go to sleep?" He nodded and rubbed his eyes. She helped him lie down, one arm tucked around Furry Lion.

Amazing, she thought, watching his eyes close. A bunk all to himself. What a difference from that awful coal ship. This *Neuralia* had comfortable mattresses, lots of food even though it was bland, games on deck, kind attendants, phonograph records in the lounge and a tea dance every afternoon—Bliss.

The cabin door opened and Sophie grabbed a dressing gown to cover herself, in case it was a steward. When she saw it was Marika in the doorway, she put a finger to her lips and pointed at

Pavel, asleep. A wall of heat thrust its way from the open door into the cabin. "Close the door, for God's sake."

Marika, covered in a film of sweat, her silk dress clinging like wet skin, put down the book she was carrying. She mopped her face and arms at the wash basin. "The tea dance was a Turkish bath. Even the slow waltz was as hot as hell," she said. "But I met a nice English navy man." She glanced at Sophie. "We're meeting for a drink after his work in the Radio Room." She kicked off her sandals and massaged her toes. "He's a terrible dancer, but then…" She sat on her bunk opposite Sophie and crinkled her eyes, obviously pleased with herself.

Sophie raised an admonishing finger. "What would your husband say if he knew you had a date with a British navy man?"

Marika frowned, spoiling the smoothness of her cheeks. "He isn't here, is he? Besides, I'm improving my English. Neville, that's his name, found a book for me to practice on. And he told me something terribly important." She peeled off her dress and sat on the edge of the opposite bunk in her underclothes.

"What's so important?"

Marika jumped up and saluted. "Tatatata-ra! We leave tomorrow. A convoy of five ships and a destroyer. How about that?"

Sophie leaned back, joyfully clapping her hands. "*Báječné.* Wonderful," she crowed.

Pavel sat bolt upright. "Maman?" He scratched his nose, looked round the cabin, then fell back onto his pillow and closed his eyes.

Sophie frowned. "Ssh, we're both making too much noise."

Marika's happy face turned mournful. "Oops, I'm sorry." She sat down beside Sophie and stroked Pavel's leg. "There's a catch to the good news," she said slowly. "Neville said our journey would be longer than expected. Can you imagine, seventeen days at sea?"

Sophie frowned. "I don't—understand. It's only five days

by boat from Gibraltar to England. I was told so by Czechoslovak officers."

Marika shook her head. "British Navy precautions, my dear. *Kličkovat*—zigzag." She lowered her voice to imitate an English masculine tone. "*We have to zigzag out into the Atlantic and back again.*" According to Neville, lots of messages are coming in about ships being attacked by U-boats in the Atlantic. Convoy zigzag is the new avoidance strategy."

Trying to digest the news and suppress a surge of fear, Sophie unconsciously caressed Pavel's blond curls. He did not move.

It was possible, she mused, that Willy's ship might also have to zigzag—but if it did not, he would be in England long ahead of her. Unlike the void that was waiting there for her, everything would be arranged for him by the Czechoslovak army—food, a bed and orders.

Sophie had been told what would happen when she and Pavel arrived at the British port. They would be *processed*. She hardly spoke English and had no money, but maybe people there would help her with advice on how to find her in-laws in London. She would manage on her own, somehow—Willy said the English were kind to strangers.

"But what am I going to do with *you* for seventeen days?" she murmured, kissing Pavel's sleeping cheek. "And what am I going to do with *me*? Walk, eat, play deck games and look out for U-boats."

"Stop worrying about U-boats. We've had the drills and you know how to wear a life-jacket," said Marika. "There's nothing else we can do except—dance." She twisted her arms above her head and with a sly grin gyrated her hips, samba-style. "Find yourself an Englishman to dance with. Mr. Neville has offered to help me with my English. Find a man who will help you learn. Get ready for England."

"I wonder what you will teach Mr. Neville in return."

Marika shot Sophie a disdainful look. "I need him. You and I are about to arrive in Britain, the home of polite and stiff people. We must be prepared, any way we can."

Sophie slipped off the bunk and extracted an exercise book from her string bag. "Marika, you do talk sense even though it is sometimes downright cynical." She flapped the pages at her friend. "For a year, I used this to learn French—I wrote Czechoslovak and Hungarian words on the left and French translations on the right. Willy tested me. Ten words a day. I suppose I could do the same thing now, with English." She was surprised at her sudden surge of enthusiasm. "I—"

"Which means that by the time we get to Liverpool, you will know one hundred and seventy English words. Not bad." Marika picked up the book she had brought from the tea dance and passed it to Sophie. The gilt cover was bent and stained. "Neville chose it for me when we were in the library. He said it was by Charles Dickens, a famous writer. He wants to help me with it. You could select words from it for your exercise book."

"I'm not sure." Sophie frowned. It had been hard enough learning French from the *Le Monde* newspaper. Rózsi at the café helped with word selection and meanings.

Sophie opened the book. On the first page, opposite the title, she recognized the façade of Notre Dame Cathedral—surrounded by flaming houses and people running in all directions. "*A Taale off Tooo... Chities?*" Timidly, she looked at Marika. "What does this mean?"

"*Příběh dvou měst*. A Tale of Two Cities—an adventure story during the French revolution. It's about London and Paris, written more than fifty years ago."

Sophie smiled, suddenly attracted by the thought of reading an English novel and at the same time, preparing herself for a new life. She flipped through some pages. "Why not? We can read it together. That's what I did in Paris, with Willy," she said. Marika was like a slice of blue sky, offering friendship and hope. "That book title, I like it. It has meaning for me. A year ago we arrived in Paris, as refugees. Soon we will be in London, also as refugees. So, I have my own tale of two cities." She laughed excitedly.

Marika eyes glistened. "There you are, my dear, we are already discussing the novel even though you have only read the title. Read me something now? Open up the book—try." She held the book out.

Sophie pushed it away. "No. I'll sound stupid. What use is old-fashioned English anyway?"

"English is English. Go on. The first twelve words Mr. Dickens wrote in this book are famous and perhaps," she raised an eyebrow, "still relevant to us." Marika opened the book and passed it over. "Read. Just the first twelve words."

Sophie cleared her throat. Her eyes flickered anxiously. "Eet vos ze best off tames, eet vos ze wurst off tames." She cocked her head and looked up at her smiling companion. What does all this mean?"

"*To bylo to nejlepší z časů, to byl nejhorší čas.* It was the best of times, it was the worst of times."

Sophie raised her eyebrows. "That is a good line."

Marika closed the book and put her arm round Sophie's shoulders, giving her a squeeze. "You know, my dear, we never talked about what happened on the *Northern Fen*—when your friend was shot, that big sergeant. I would guess that was one of the worst of times for you. You must think about it, often."

A long silence. Sophie rubbed at the rough skin on her arms and inspecting her cracked fingernails, relics from the village of Sillat. She felt a deep ache in her chest. Not physical pain, just an indefinable pressure that caught her breath as if something wanted to burst from her chest.

"The *Northern Fen* is only a small part of what happened to us after we escaped from Prague."

Looking at Marika's calm face, Sophie felt an overwhelming urge to clear what cluttered her mind—to say goodbye to the vivid moments and characters that inhabited her recent past.

"Listen, Marika. I have had enough of memories tapping me on the shoulder. I need to blot them out."

Marika's voice was firm. "What about the happy times— childhood, growing up, school and your marriage? It is wrong to wipe those away."

Sophie shrugged. "That's true. I was a happy chatterbox, full of fun. I had an easy life, a solid marriage, and, of course, this lovely little boy." She laid a hand on Pavel's chest and watched it move with his breathing.

She straightened the strap of her brassiere. "After marriage, Willy was the captain of my life. I kept house and supervised servants. We went out a lot. Everything seemed set and easy." She went to the washbasin and dabbed her face with a wet hand cloth. "I'm a refugee now—poor, confused about what's coming. Whatever happens to us in the future, I want things to be different."

Marika shook her head. "What is your husband going to say to that?"

Sophie shrugged, not liking the pity she saw in her friend's face. "Who knows? In the past two years we've had many separations. I'm not sure that our relationship can take more hardships—I suppose that depends on this journey and what happens in London. But if we survive, I want a more independent life, married or not."

"Oh, my God. Do you truly believe you can cope or succeed on your own without a man supporting and guiding you?" Marika walked to the wash basin and filled a glass of water. She offered it to Sophie, who shook her head. "Are you sure you are thinking straight?"

Sophie took a deep breath. "When the Nazis came to Prague and put Willy in Pankrác prison, I ran his business. I found a way ..." She turned her head away to look at Pavel. "I used my ... wiles to get him out. I know I'm capable—as capable as Willy. If we have to, Pavel and I can manage on our own."

Marika walked over to the porthole and looked out. "My goodness, Sophie. Come see. There are two ships coming towards us from inside the harbor. Perhaps it's part of our convoy." Sophie joined her and they both peered out. Marika slipped an arm around Sophie's shoulders and kissed her cheek. "You have had a hard time. What will you do in London?"

Sophie shrugged. "No idea, except look after Pavel, stay with my in-laws and find Willy. But with all the British men and women making tanks, guns and ammunition in the factories, I expect I can find work. You know, Marika, the one skill I learned in France, apart from learning French and foraging in the markets, was how to cook well. Willy told me the British food was tasteless and the meals on this ship confirm it."

Marika laughed. "Maybe you could work at something that will wake up the English taste-buds? Be a cook?"

Sophie paused. "I just realized. You said your Neville told you there were messages coming in about U-boats attacking ships. Where was it you said he worked?"

"The Radio Room."

"What is that?"

"That's where all the messages between ships and ports come in and go out.

Sophie raised her eyebrows, she felt her heart thump. "Telegrams also?"

Marika nodded. "Come on, you snail, open the exercise book. Let's practice our English."

Sophie stood and pointed a finger at her friend. "I want you to persuade Mr.Neville to send a telegram for me—before the ship leaves. To my in-laws in London."

Marika tossed her hair. "Not me, young lady. It might be illegal. Why should I endanger my friendship with Mr. Neville so that you can get what you want?"

Sophie shrugged. "Don't worry, Marika, I'll go out and find him myself—right now before it's too late. Pavel is asleep. Keep an eye on him. I won't be long."

* * *

On July 19, in the late morning, the *Neuralia* docked in Liverpool. At the dock, the ship's hawsers were attached to bollards. The great engines fell silent and passengers, including Sophie, Pavel and Marika, accompanied by Mr. Neville, gathered on the decks to watch the antics of a large welcoming crowd. Union Jacks, welcome signs and hats waved in the sunshine. A brass band struck up God Save the King. White and green buses were lined up behind the crowd, their drivers leaning against the entry doors, smoking, waiting to ferry another load of foreigners.

As longshoremen rolled gangplanks on wheels towards the open disembarkation doors, the passengers cheered and shouted. The brass band launched into It's a Long Way to Tipperary. Waves of heat shimmered off the dock.

The ship's loudspeakers crackled. "Disembarkation for refugees who do not hold tickets will commence in forty-five minutes' time, at noon. Please be at your collection areas at that time. Our staff will be there to provide assistance. Be sure to have all your luggage in hand. There are no porters to assist you. Once disembarked, you are required to proceed to the refugee reception building in the center of Liverpool—for processing by immigration authorities. Buses are waiting. Be patient and do not rush. The disembarkation process for Czechoslovak troops will begin at two o'clock. Our regular passengers with fully paid tickets may disembark at any time from the rear gangway where our pursers will assist them."

Sophie took Pavel's hand and turned to Lieutenant Neville. "I did not understand very well what the man said."

"We have to take a bus to the refugee center," said Marika in Czech, impatiently tapping the railing with her fingers. "They will give us food, clothes, a medical examination and the gift of a little money—and answer our questions." She looked up questioningly at the tall officer. "Am I right?"

"Absolutely right, ladies."

"That is good news," said Sophie with a smile. "I have many questions and no money." She crouched down to kiss Pavel's cheek. "So, *miláčku*, we will say goodbye to this lovely ship." She spoke in French. "We'll get on a bus to a place where I'm sure they have some nice toys for you to play with." She hoped that this was true.

Pavel looked through the railings at the milling crowd. "Why is everyone so happy? Where are we, Maman? "

She smiled and kissed the top of his head. "Do you remember Papa always saying we had to get to England?"

He looked up at her and shook his head.

"This *is* England, *mon chéri*—our new home."

Dear Reader,

I hope you enjoyed this book. Please show your appreciation by writing a brief, honest review on Amazon books. This will help me get more recognition for my writing and boost my enthusiasm to continue. To submit a review—

Find *CAFÉ BUDAPEST* on Amazon books and click on CUSTOMER REVIEWS. Just a few lines will suffice.

If you haven't read my debut novel, *The Dragontail Buttonhole*, I am sure you would like it. It's the prequel to *Café Budapest* and follows the Kohut family's escape from Nazi-occupied Prague in 1939.

Visit www.petercurtisauthor.com

Many thanks,

Peter Curtis

Acknowledgements

Untold thanks to Marlin Greene of 3Hats for his close collaboration and design of my website and the cover of this book and its predecessor, THE DRAGONTAIL BUTTONHOLE—as well as his help with publishing. I extend my appreciation to Jim Thomsen for prompt and super-efficient line-editing. My thanks also to the unfailing generosity of Jiří Hucek living in Agde, France, for invaluable background information on the evacuation of the Czechoslovak Army from the south of France. I am very grateful to Jaroslav Bouček, former Historian and Archivist of the Military Institute, Prague for reviewing and correcting my manuscript. Thanks also to Tomáš Jakl of the same Institute for permission to use photographs on my website gallery of the Czechoslovak Army-in-Exile in France, courtesy of Státní Oblastní Archiv v Zámsrku-SOkA, Pardubice.

I am indebted to the vociferous comments, steadfast support and energizing encouragement of two writer groups in Seattle. Vios Writers: Lynn Knight, Lauren Basson, Scott Wyatt and particularly Brita Butler-Wall and Gary Bloxham who went beyond the limits of human endeavor to read my final manuscript. Also my gratitude to the friendship and incisive commentaries of Third Place Writers: Teresa Hayden, Elizabeth Gage, Teri Howatt and Brian Schuessler. My thanks to Helen Szablyahj, Sheila Cory, Victoria Farr Brown, Danielle Carr, Larry Smith, Stan Zeitz, Maddy Coelho, Jacqueline Williams, Goldie Silverman, and George Guttman for critical reading and reviews of the manuscript. My special gratitude to Elizabeth Krijgsman for her critique and edits. My thanks to Leann Rayfuse, copy editor and to Kate Cavalerie for offering to review the manuscript for the appropriateness of its French context.

For more information on Peter Curtis, his historical research and his book, see www.petercurtisauthor.com or visit the author's page at Amazon Books, Facebook and Pinterest.

Additional Notes

I have relied heavily on certain published resources: The
Czechoslovak Army in France: 1939-1945. Roy E. Reader.
Czechoslovak Philatelic Society of Great Britain Monograph
#5.1987.
Československá Divize Ve FRancia (1939-1940) Gustav Svoboda.
Ministerestvo obrany České republiky.

Armada druheho odboje. General Oldrich Spaniel. Chicago 1941.
Prague 1945

Master of Spies by General Frantisek Moravec, Sphere Books Ltd.
1975.

Prague in Danger by Peter Demetz, Farrar, Strauss and Giroux
2008.

Prague. My Long Journey Home by Charles Ota Heller. Abbott
Press 2011

On All Fronts: Czechs and Slovaks in World War II. Editor, Lewis
M.White. East European Monographs, Boulder.Co. 1991 (Vols
1,2)

Czechoslovakia in WW2, East European Monographs. Boulder
Co. 2000. Ed, Lewis M White.

Prague in the Shadow of the Swastika, Collum MacDonald and
Jan Kaplan. Facultas Verlags und Buchhandels AG. 2001 Wien.

Prague in the Shadow of the Swastika, Collum MacDonald and
Jan Kaplan. Facultas Verlags und Buchhandels AG. 2001 Wien.

Letters from Prague. 1939-1945. compiled by Raya Czener
Schapiro and Helga Czerner Weinberg. Academy Chicago
Publishers.2006.

The Rescue of the Prague Refugees 1938-1939 by William
Chadwick 2010. Matador Press.

Island Refuge. Britain and Refugees from the Third Reich 1933-1939. AJ Sherman. University of California Press. Berkley. 1973.

The Jews of Czechoslovakia Historical Studies and Surveys, volume 3. Eds. Avigdor Dagan, Gertrude Hirschler and Lewis Weiner 1984. The Jewish Publication Society of America. Philadelphia.

Society for the History of Czechoslovak Jews, Ansonia Station. PO Box 230255. New York, NY 10023

Memoirs of a Volunteer. Henry Baumgarten. The Book Guild Ltd. Lewes. Sussex, UK. 1990.

Escape to England. Karel A.Machachek. The Book Guild Ltd. Lewes, Sussex, UK. 1988.

Praise for Café Budapest

A compelling WWll story with fascinating characters, rich inner and outer dialogue, and boatloads of unanswered questions—fans of the era will be absorbed in this tension-filled story from the very first page.

> *July 2017. Pacific Northwest Writer's Association Literary Award. Finalist Review*

* * * * *

CAFÉ BUDAPEST is an absorbing and powerful account of a Jewish family's struggle to survive in France during the first horrific months of World War ll. The tension between the main protagonists' instincts for self-preservation and their wish to protect the family from fatal fracture is intensely moving and bittersweet. Willy and Sophie Kohut and their young son Pavel are well-drawn and believably flawed characters. The reader is witness to the complexities of their relationships with each other, with the colorful cast of individuals who wish to help or harm them, with the faceless and brutal Nazi war machine that threatens them as they journey, literally and emotionally, towards what they need to believe will be a happy ending.

> *MP Peacock. Author: Murder at the Strike of Five: Russia 1917.*

* * * * *

CAFÉ BUDAPEST is a masterful description of refugee life in Paris under the threat of war, the twists and turns of finding lodging, food and money. When Willy Kohut joins the Free Czech Army being formed in the south, the bonds of their marriage erode. Sophie, left alone with little Pavel, suffers depression but finds friendship and a part-time job with the kindly owners of *CAFÉ BUDAPEST.* Her life unravels when Pavel suffers a serious infection that needs urgent surgery and the Allies declare war on Germany. Millions of French flee south including Sophie and Pavel who wait in a primitive French village close to where Willy is about to be sent north to fight with the French forces. Old enemies reappear, harsh military discipline is used as revenge and the final evacuation of thousands on coal freighters tests the Kohut family's courage, ingenuity and resilience. *CAFÉ BUDAPEST* is a must-read. You will not be able to put down this page-turner.

Helen Szablyah, Honorary Consul General of Hungary. Author: My Only Choice; 1942-1956

* * * * *

CAFÉ BUDAPEST is a clever, interesting and eminently readable follow-up of *THE DRAGONTAIL BUTTONHOLE*: the dramatic escape of a Jewish family from Nazi-occupied Prague to France. This sequel, Café Budapest, starts with their arrival in refugee-drenched Paris and traces their struggle find a way to reach the safety of England. Their year-long sojourn includes the warmth of Café Budapest, the shock of their son's illness, the rigors of enlisting in the newly formed Czechoslovak Army, the demise of an old enemy and the chaotic evacuation by sea of thousands as France surrenders to the Germans. Through his characters and descriptions Curtis vividly evokes the atmosphere and stresses of those times, assisted by his firm grasp and weaving of historical facts.

Jaroslav Bouček. PhDr.CSc, Historian, Former Archivist of the Military History Institute, Prague

CPSIA information can be obtained
at www.ICGtesting.com
Printed in the USA
FSHW01n1459250418
47277FS

9 780999 363126